Through Jennifer's Eyes 2 (Secrets)

J G Perrin

Copyright © 2013 J G Perrin

All rights reserved.

www.jgperrin.co.uk

ISBN-13: 978-1482019766

This novel is a work of fiction. All characters appearing in this book are fictitious. Any resemblance to real persons, living or dead, is purely coincidental

Warning: This story contains writing of an adult nature and is not for any persons aged 18 or younger.

CONTENTS

1	Here we go again
2	Love and marriage, horse and carriage
3	Just one word
4	Outdoor sex
5	Daddy issues
6	Sweet but sharp sixteenth
7	Cherry picker
8	Toyboy thighs and nasty eyes
9	"Ouch" Miss Whitney
10	Doctor Who and the dying wish
11	Dumped and a last fling
12	Choose
13	Cheer me up you miserable sod
14	Three notes and a scare
15	They call me Mister Brit
16	Betrayal
17	48 Hours
18	I didn't say a finger too
19	Hen night and a vodka bottle
20	Eat me
21	Twenty-Four hours, Twenty-Four minutes
22	Explaining with no explanation
23	Oh, but I can
24	Here comes the pride
25	A pink invitation
26	Dam

MEET THE CHARACTERS

Name: Jennifer
Age: 30
Job: Life coach
Appearance: Long blonde highlights, but naturally brunette. Athletic body. Average height. Usually wearing jeans and a casual top.
Personality: Although Jennifer is very talented, she doesn't force her gift onto anyone and would rather wait until someone needs it. She is very loyal, friendly and willing to do anything to improve someone's life.
Relationship: Jennifer is happily married to Bruce and she normally calls on him, if she wants a helping hand with a lesson.
Sex life: Straight Jennifer isn't shy at all when it comes to the bedroom and is a self confessed voyeur.

Name: Amy
Age: 24
Job: Office Worker
Appearance: Bobbed blonde hair. Slim and toned. Average height. Usually wearing something straight from the catwalk.
Personality: Amy is a pink loving princess, that loves to fit in with everyone else. She is so desperate to be accepted, that sometimes it looks as though she is trying too hard. Amy follows the crowd and is often influenced by the older members of the group.
Relationship: Amy has be dating Dean for 5 months. Although she used to be insecure and very jealous behind closed doors, with a little help from Jennifer, she has turned her life around. Thanks to Jennifer, Amy is now a much more confident person and also has an open crush on Jennifer's husband Bruce.
Sex life: Amy is very open minded and willing to experiment all the time. She currently enjoys going out to be naughty and bringing home her stories to boyfriend Dean, then working on her fetish of being turned on by the thought of him sleeping with other people. She has also just had her first threesome with good friend Karen.

Name: Karen
Age: 26
Job: House wife
Appearance: Long brunette hair. Curvaceous slim body. Tall in height. Usually wearing jeans, figure hugging tops and long boots.
Personality: Karen is very opinionated, feisty and often speaks her mind. Although supportive to her good friends, she is also seen as the person to go to if anyone has a problem. Karen has just recently discovered she is pregnant and is trying to make light of it, with her quick witted mouth.
Relationship: After her husband of three years cheated on her, Karen quickly started to enjoy single life again. Although there was a chance of them getting back together, she decided against it. knowing it's nearly time to tell her ex-husband that he is about to become a father, she is having too much single fun to have that grown-up chat just yet, so avoids it.
Sex life: Karen is the woman that will try anything once and most of the time she does. Not scared of a sexual situation, she often jumps in feet first, enjoys herself, then works out after if it was a good idea or not. Karen will have sex with almost anything and she normally improves a partners confidence with her sexual behaviour.

Name: Lucy
Age: 20
Job: Drama student & Part-time supermarket worker.
Appearance: Very long blonde hair. Slim figure. Average height. Usually wearing young fashionable clothes with leggings.
Personality: Lucy is very friendly and will talk to anyone that talks to her. She doesn't go out of her way to stand out in the crowd, but her beautiful smile often catches everyone's eye.
Relationship: She has been dating and engaged to a fellow supermarket worker for the last 6 months and wedding bells are already firmly on the cards.
Sex life: Sexually Lucy hasn't been very adventurous, but has had a number of partners, more than the average twenty year old girl. She usually has good taste in men and good self-control, but when anyone says a really nice thing about her, that self-control goes out the window and becomes her biggest weakness.

Name: Rose
Age: 22
Job: Full-time drama student.
Appearance: Long curly brunette hair. curvy figure. Small in height. Usually wearing flares, jeans or anything from the 70's.
Personality: Rose is the original mood swinger. One minute she is a loving and caring twenty-two year old female and the next she can be moody, aggressive and very touchy. She shares a room on campus with Lucy, but doesn't have to fund her fees due to her silver spoon lifestyle. Rose doesn't consider herself a snob and does live a pretty grounded life, but when she's out with her father, that's when you see her not so attractive side.
Relationship: Rose does have a boyfriend, but it's more a friends with benefits set-up than a proper relationship. Although she does want more attention from her bad boy partner, she doesn't have time to fight for it, focussing all of her attention on her studies.
Sex life: Rose has only had two sexual partners and although she knows what she is doing in the bedroom, her lack of action is usually because boys are terrified of her rich and wealthy father.

Name: Tina
Age: 15 (16 next week)
Job: At school.
Appearance: Long curly black hair. curvy figure. Small in height. Usually wearing flares, jeans or anything from the 70's.
Personality: Tina is Lucy's half sister and lives with her mother and father around the corner from the drama school. Tina is a lovely young girl with a somewhat pink princess attitude and is really looking forward to her big sister's wedding.
Relationship: Tina isn't sexually active and has only just started dating in her first relationship with a nineteen year old, with her parents and sister's disapproval.
Sex life: Although Tina hasn't had sex yet, her boyfriend is putting pressure on her to let him take her virginity. Although she feels ready and enjoys the subject of sex, she is still holding out.

Name: Bruce
Age: 33
Job: Unknown
Appearance: Bald headed. Well built figure. Small in height (For a man). Usually wearing jeans and a button shirt or jacket.
Personality: Bruce is very quick witted, tough and often stands in whenever Jennifer wants to teach her friends something personal about a man. Bruce is everyone's best friend, saviour and sometimes, a woman's guilty pleasure. Bruce is cocky, charming and most of the time can be found wearing a smile or his famous smirk.
Relationship: .He is Jennifer's husband and oblivious to him, is her rock.
Sex life: Bruce is dirty minded, passionate and usually enjoys the sexual perks Jennifer's requests and lessons bring him.

Name: Dave
Age: 19
Job: Unknown
Appearance: Black hair, left parting. Slim figure. Very tall in height. Usually wearing jeans and a shirt with a statement or message on it.
Personality: Dave is Bruce's young prodigy. They met in a nightclub a week ago, where Bruce shared his wisdom of attracting the perfect female. Dave is a typical teenager who likes to drink and party, but has seen a quality in Bruce most people do and has latched onto it.
Relationship: Single but looking.
Sex life: Unknown, but he's male and nineteen.

Name: Dean
Age: 26
Job: Unknown
Appearance: Short shaven brown hair. Medium figure. Average height. Usually wearing black trousers and a white shirt.
Personality: Dean is a happy go lucky kind of person, that enjoys life and lives in the moment. He tries hard not to let things get him down and he always tries to wear a smile.

Relationship: Dean is Amy's boyfriend. After a long and disturbing relationship with Amy's jealousy issues, Dean has stuck by her and it's starting to pay off. He considers himself very lucky to be with someone in Amy's league and tries his hardest to please her in every way he can. Dean is fully aware of Amy's crush on Bruce and doesn't have a problem with it, because he trusts her completely. Also the fact that they have a brilliant sex life helps.

Sex life: Things keep getting better and better for Dean as Amy keeps improving their sex life. Recently, Dean was lucky enough to have a threesome with his girlfriend and her best friend Karen on a train.

QUICK CATCH UP

After being friends with plane and prudish Jane for almost a year, Jennifer was finally introduced to her friends and immediately started teaching them how to lead a more positive life. Over four weeks, Jane, Karen, Amy and Michelle all had their own issues learning Jennifer's new ways. Jennifer eradicated Amy's Jealousy issues, quashed Michelle's drink and self-esteem problems, helped Karen through a break-up with her husband and assisted Jane with her prudish ways and a blackmailer ruining her life. At Michelle's birthday party, after promising to stick around, Jennifer and her husband Bruce moved to the other side of London in search of more women to help, leaving the others behind to walk their paths alone once again.

CHAPTER 1
HERE WE GO AGAIN

The weather late summer in London can be one of the most unpredictable things and today is no different. Where it started off this morning quite humid and sticky, the clouds have opened up and the rain is falling. Jennifer is walking down the high-street in North London where she has just moved to with her husband Bruce. She is picking up a few bits they need for their new home. Jennifer recently spent four weeks changing four of her friends lives for the better across London, before suddenly leaving in search of a fresh start. It's day one of her new start as she puts all her efforts into finishing their new home and settling in. Just then across the street, Jennifer spots a girl involved in an argument with an older man. Jennifer walks across the road to have a better look and continues to watch as the heated debate continues, then the man storm off down the road. Jennifer watches the girl enter a bridal shop and decides to go and find out if she is okay.
Jennifer enters the shop to see the girl running her hand through the wedding dresses on a rail. Jennifer pretends that she is browsing in the shop too and it isn't long before the two girls are standing side by side. Jennifer watches as the young blonde girl carefully checks each price tag on every dress. Jennifer reaches out her arm, as their hands touch on the same dress.

"Sorry" says Jennifer, letting go of the dress and breaking the ice with the girl.

"That's okay, you grabbed it first" responds the blonde girl smiling at her.

Jennifer doesn't want to start a possible new friendship on a lie, so insists that the girl take a look at it first. The girl gratefully accepts, taking the dress down from the rail and holding it against her body.

"That would look really good on you, why don't you go and try it on?" suggests Jennifer.

The girl smiles at Jennifer, looks at herself in the mirror holding the dress up and smiles again, before quickly putting it back on the rail after having a look at the price.

"Expensive isn't it?" sighs Jennifer, understanding the frown on the blonde girls face.

Once again the girl just smiles.

"So when is your big day?" asks the girl, to Jennifer's delight.

Jennifer explains that she is already happily married and is just getting some ideas for a friend, before introducing herself. The young girl holds her hand out to shake Jennifer's hand.

"I'm Lucy, it's nice to meet you Jennifer" says the young blonde, shaking her hand.

They enter into light conversation for another five minutes whilst Lucy tries to find a dress she likes and more importantly, one that she can afford. Again Jennifer watches as Lucy picks up yet another dress that makes her smile, only to return it to the rail after looking at the price tag.

"If you could pick any dress in this shop, which one would it be?" asks Jennifer, before Lucy picks up another dress she is obviously going to reject.

Without even thinking about it, Lucy takes two steps to the left and grabs her dream dress.

"Oh yeah, that's beautiful" says Jennifer.

"Why don't you go and try it on?" she adds, pointing her in the direction of the changing room.

Lucy wants to try it on but knows she will never be able to afford it. She decides nevertheless to humour Jennifer and walks across the shop to the changing room cubicle, as Jennifer takes a seat outside waiting for her to re-emerge. Lucy quickly slips out of her jeans behind the curtain and puts the dream wedding dress on. She stares at herself in the mirror, a complete vision of beauty. She opens the curtain hoping for some reason, that her new acquaintance will approve. Jennifer's eyes light up as Lucy appears from behind the curtain, holding her long blonde hair up with her hand.

"Well? Do you like it?" asks Lucy, clearly delighted with the dress.

"You look amazing" responds Jennifer, remembering how she felt on her own wedding day.

Jennifer stands up and walks over to her.

"Question is Lucy, do you like it?" asks Jennifer, with a smile.
Lucy is hit by a bolt of sadness, as she is reminded that she can't afford it. Before Jennifer let's Lucy's frown get any bigger, she smiles back at her.

"It's yours" claims Jennifer.
Lucy's face turns from confusion to shock, then shock to a dumbfounded smile, then back to confused.

"What do you mean it's mine?" Lucy asks, looking puzzled.

"I just paid for it for you" claims Jennifer, with an even bigger grin.
This time Lucy's face turns from confusion to shock, then overjoyed, then horrified.

"Hold on, why? Why would you? I don't get it" stutters Lucy, unsure of the generous offer.
Jennifer reassures her that she can accept the gift, but Lucy really doesn't know what to think.

"Trust me" says Jennifer.

"There's no catch, I just want to help" she adds, trying to convince the young girl she's genuine.
Lucy decides it's time to take the dress off, starting to get freaked out about Jennifer's over generous gesture.

"I don't know anything about you, how can I accept this?" Lucy asks, turning back to Jennifer.
Jennifer follows her over to the cubicle.

"My name is Jennifer. I am thirty years old and I just want to help you" she explains, continuing to wear her friendly smile.

"Yeah but why?" asks Lucy, opening the cubicle curtain.

"I saw you outside arguing with that guy before. I just wanted to make sure you were okay" explains Jennifer in more detail, trying not to offend her in anyway.
Lucy stands in the cubicle facing Jennifer outside, her hand ready to pull the curtain closed.

"That was my dad outside with me" Lucy tells her.

"We weren't really having a fight" she adds, telling Jennifer to give her a few seconds.
Lucy closes the curtain and starts to get changed out of the dress. Lucy explains that she is a live-in drama student at the school down the road and that her dad helps pay the fee's towards her studies.

"And he isn't happy about you getting married?" guesses Jennifer, outside trying to follow.

"No, that's not it" calls Lucy, slipping back into her jeans.

"He's okay about the wedding, he just can't afford the fee's and wedding together" she adds, pulling back the curtain whilst cradling the dress in her arms.

Lucy steps out of the cubicle desperate to accept the strangers gift, but still very unsure.

"So what do you do?" asks Lucy, trying to keep the conversation going.

Jennifer doesn't really know how to answer the question and the two girls stand outside the cubicle together whilst Lucy cradles her dress for as long as she can.

"I guess you could call me a life coach or something like that" Jennifer says.

Lucy's eye's sparkle as she starts to trust the female standing before her.

"I guess that pays you heaps of money then?" questions Lucy, showing an admirable interest.

Jennifer smiles and shakes her head.

"No, I don't profit or charge for my service, I just like to help people" explains Jennifer.

Lucy after hearing this feels that she can now accept the wedding dress as a gift from Jennifer and the two girls start to bond.

"Are you sure you don't mind paying for my dress?" asks Lucy.

"I will pay you every penny back" she adds, hoping Jennifer's offer is still there to be accepted.

Jennifer leans towards Lucy and runs her hand over the dress feeling the fabric.

"It would be my pleasure" Jennifer responds.

The girls spend another few minutes in the shop whilst the dress is packaged up and Jennifer explains exactly what her role as a life coach is. Not only does Lucy know she's got a new dress out of their meeting, but also feels she will be a good person to have around and invites her back to her room on campus for coffee. Jennifer accepts her invitation and the girls leave the shop together and head towards the drama school.

They arrive at the school entrance some ten minutes later and Lucy tells her to follow her in.

"Are you sure this is okay?" asks Jennifer.

"I don't want to get you into any trouble" she adds.

Lucy laughs and tells her she lives there and can have friends over to visit any time she likes. She explains that she has a room at the school, that she shares with a second year student called Rose and it's all really friendly and laid back. They walk down a long corridor and stop outside Lucy's door.

"Oh I hope my little sister is here, she will die when she sees the dress" says Lucy, pulling her keys from her pocket.

They enter what looks to be a stereotypical university flat, with a

small living area come kitchen and a tiny hallway leading off to another three rooms. Lucy heads straight over to the kettle and clicks the button before calling out to her room-mate Rose and her sister Tina. There is no response but she can hear music coming from one of the bedrooms, so knows somebody is at home.
Lucy tells Jennifer to sit down and make herself comfortable and then goes in search of the music. Jennifer watches as Lucy enters one of the bedrooms and closes the door behind her. Minutes later Lucy comes back out with another two girls. The younger one clearly in her teens, pushes past them in the hallway and races towards the living area and straight across to the packaged dress on the sofa.

"Be careful with that Tina" insists Lucy, re-entering the living area with the other girl.
Lucy makes a very quick introduction, in which Jennifer stands up to meet the two girls.

"This is my little sister Tina, Tina this is my new friend Jennifer" Lucy says.
Tina gives a quick hello over her shoulder, clearly more interested in seeing the dress.
Jennifer tries to enter into a little conversation with the young girl, but it falls on deaf ears. She watches as the black haired teenager unzips the dress bag and gasps.

"And this is my room-mate Rose" says Lucy, finishing off her introductions.
Jennifer turns to the curvy brunette to shake her hand, but again feels a little unwelcome as Rose just nods her head, making her way over to the kettle. In order not to let things get even more awkward, Lucy starts a conversation with Jennifer quickly as she sits back down.

"So you don't think that I am too young to get hitched?" Lucy asks Jennifer.
Jennifer feels a little put on the spot and doesn't really know how to answer the question.

"I guess if it's what you really want, then what is age?" answers Jennifer trying to support her, but not commit fully.

"What is age?" snaps a sarcastic Rose from the kitchen area.

"It's only your youth, the parties, the sex with loads of different guys she's giving up, oh nothing much" she adds, as Jennifer watches her make herself a cup of coffee, then walk over to join them both.

"It's okay Rose, I will make my own" laughs Lucy, getting up and walking over to the kitchen.

"I know you will" laughs Rose, making herself comfy and looking Jennifer up and down.

"So Jennifer, who are you and how did you and Luce meet?" Rose snaps arrogantly at Jennifer.
Jennifer turns to Rose to explain but before she can, Lucy interrupts bringing across the coffee that Rose didn't bother making.
"Jennifer is a life coach and helped me find the money for my dress" Lucy says smiling, trying to get Rose to back off slightly.
"Oh life coach" sighs Rose.
"Do gooder in other words?" she adds rudely.
Jennifer doesn't rise to it and just sits there trying to work them out, as Tina joins them finally putting the dress back down.
"What's a life coach?" Tina asks.
"It's someone that thinks they know it all" snaps Rose again rudely.
"So how much are you charging us then?" she asks, thinking she's marked Jennifer's card already.
Rose is soon put in her place when Lucy explains that Jennifer doesn't charge for her service and all Rose can do is sit back huffing and puffing about it. Although Jennifer is pleased Lucy is defending her against the unwelcoming Rose, she now sits there trying to do what she does best and work out who these girls are. She decides to start another conversation about the wedding and asks Lucy what is planned for her big day. Lucy spends a few minutes telling her although it's in a church, both her and her partner want to keep it relatively small.
"I wanted her to have a horse and carriage, but she won't" says Tina, trying to join in on the conversation.
Jennifer notices Tina paying close attention and looks over to her.
"And how old are you Tina?" asks Jennifer.
"Do you go to this school too?" she asks.
Tina tells her that she's sixteen in a few days and explains that she doesn't attend the school, but wants to once she's finished her exams.
"Careful Tina, she will be marrying you off too in a minute" snaps Rose, delivering another unwelcoming comment.
Jennifer, Tina and Lucy all seem to rise above it, but Jennifer is starting to feel the strain and is desperate to say something. Instead she composes herself and takes another look at Tina.
"You know, if you hadn't of told me, I would never have guessed you two were sisters" claims Jennifer.
Rose sits forward in her chair.
"What made you think that Sherlock? The blonde and black hair by any chance?" snaps Rose.
Jennifer again holds her frustration, but this time it's too much for

Lucy to take.

"Don't worry about grumpy over there" Lucy tells Jennifer with a smile.

"She doesn't mean it. Her nasty boyfriend hasn't answered her messages for a few days, that's all" she adds.

Rose takes one final mouthful of her coffee and throws the rest in the direction of Lucy, whilst jumping out of her seat.

"Excuse me" Rose snaps in Lucy's direction, as the coffee hits Lucy's shoulder.

"Don't be telling weird people my personal stuff" she adds, stomping to the kitchen area and throwing her cup in the sink.

Lucy tries to calm her down by telling her she was only joking, but Rose knows it's true and stomps back over to sit down again. Jennifer quickly thinks back to meeting her four friends on the other side of London and how on the first meeting, one of them acted the same way and how they became really good friends. She holds onto that thought and continues to wave Rose's sarcasm and behaviour aside.

"So let's talk about your future husband" says Jennifer.

"How did you know he was the one?" she asks.

Lucy goes a little shy and tells her they met at the supermarket where she works part-time.

"But what makes him the one?" Jennifer asks again.

Lucy has a little think about it.

"Is he good looking?" asks Jennifer, switching into teaching mode tactfully.

"Yeah" blushes Lucy.

"Is he honest and trustworthy?" asks Jennifer, trying to keep the line of questioning going.

"I guess so" answers Lucy.

"What about his sex? Is he good in bed?" asks Jennifer, losing her tactfulness when she realises what she's said in front of a fifteen year old girl.

"Oh I am sorry" claims Jennifer looking at Tina, showing them that the question was inappropriate.

Rose jumps up towards the kitchen area again.

"Don't worry about that Jen. Little Tina is a bigger slut than all of us put together" Rose declares in a nasty teasing way.

"No I am not" snaps Tina looking a little embarrassed, trying to defend herself.

Jennifer quickly tells them what she does with her lessons and explains it's already worked with many girls across the UK.

"Would you like my lesson on marriage?" asks Jennifer, hoping to get somewhere.

"And this won't cost us anything?" mumbles Rose, walking back over with a chocolate bar from the fridge.

Jennifer tells them again, she does what she does because she cares and doesn't want to profit from information that all girls should know.

"Go on then, educate us" laughs Rose, settling herself back into the sofa, clearly showing no interest.

Jennifer pauses for a few seconds and quickly goes into her lesson.

"What are the most important things to make a marriage work?" Jennifer asks them all.

Lucy and Tina seems to show great interest and sit there thinking, but Rose refuses to focus and jumps up again, making a joke out of it.

"Not getting married is the only way to make it work" she laughs, walking over to her music player and plugging it into her laptop sitting on the table.

Lucy and Tina still sit there thinking about the answer and waiting for Jennifer to answer it for them, but the atmosphere disappears when Rose presses play and lets her music drown out any conversation the girls might have had. Jennifer decides enough is enough and picks this time to leave. Lucy again tries to apologise for Rose's behaviour, as Jennifer says goodbye to Tina. Lucy walks her to the hallway and opens the front door.

"If you want that lesson on marriage Lucy, give me a call tonight" says Jennifer, handing her a piece of paper with her number on it.

Lucy thanks her for being so nice, for the dress and tells her she will definitely call her tonight. Jennifer says goodbye and leaves.

Half an hour later Jennifer arrives home, coming face to face with her new front door. She is greeted in the living room by her husband Bruce and can't wait to share the news, that she has three new girls to share her gift with.

"What have you done?" asks Bruce reading her smile.

Before she can tell him anything, he's already worked it out for himself.

"I know that face, you've gone and got yourself a new friend haven't you?" he asks.

His face then turns from happy to concerned when he remembers just how hard her task was a few weeks ago, when she took on four girls at once.

"How many?" he sighs, preparing himself for her answer.

Jennifer takes him by the hand and looks into his eyes.

"Three" she whispers, knowing that on one hand he is going to be concerned and on the other, she knows he will support her no matter what.

They take a seat on the sofa and Bruce tells her to tell him all about them. Jennifer tells him about the three new girls in her life and points out how nice fifteen year old and twenty year old sisters Lucy and Tina are, but how Rose could be a little harder to work with.

"So why don't you just take the two sisters and forget about this Rose?" asks Bruce listening intently.

Jennifer looks at him raising her eyebrows as if to say, you know me better than that. Bruce gets the message and shows his concern about Tina's age.

"Isn't this Tina a little too young to be sharing your talent with?" asks Bruce.

"After all, it is mostly relationship and sexual things you teach your clients" he adds.

Jennifer explains that Tina will be turning sixteen soon and how she is looking forward to helping someone with no experience for a change. Bruce accepts Jennifer's new challenge like the supportive husband he is and tells her to give him a shout if she ever needs his help. He then turns his attention to someone he himself has taken under his wing.

"I was thinking about meeting up with young Dave sometime over the next few days" he tells her.

"Oh Dave, isn't that the guy you met in the nightclub?" she asks him sounding really interested.

Bruce nods his head and looks for any words of wisdom, before he follows Jennifer down the path of helping people and becoming a life coach himself.

"You don't need any help from me babes" says Jennifer.

"You know what you are doing, you've been around me long enough now" she adds.

Bruce starts to laugh.

"What?" asks Jennifer.

Bruce reminds her that over the years he's been her demonstration doll when she's needed a male presence to help and teach her female friends.

"Do you know how many times I've had to drop my trousers" laughs Bruce.

"Loads" answers Jennifer, knowing she wouldn't be able to do what she does if it wasn't for him.

"But what's so funny?" she asks, trying to work it out for herself.

Bruce wraps his arm around her as they snuggle up on the sofa.

"Well if I start teaching guys like you do girls" he explains.

"You're going to have to be my demonstration doll and drop your knickers whenever I need a helping hand" he adds continuing to laugh.

"I haven't got a problem with that" Jennifer insists, telling him it would be for a good cause.

"Yeah, but all those young men getting horny at the sight of your naked body. Can you handle it?" he asks, waiting for her to assure him that she will do what he's been doing for years.

With that Jennifer lets out a naughty little moan.

"Oh no, there's no getting turned on by it" he says, playfully pushing her down on the sofa.

"You've got to stay completely professional like you've expected me to do" he adds, lunging towards her, tickling her until she screams.

"Okay, okay I will stay professional" she begs, wanting him to stop.

He stops tickling her and falls back into the sofa to catch his breath. Jennifer jumps up and heads into the kitchen, leaving him sitting on the sofa. She pops her head around the door.

"Just think about all those big cocks I'm going to be making hard for you" she teases him, disappearing back into the kitchen.

Bruce jumps up and playfully chases her.

"You can't do that" he insists laughing, wrestling her onto the sink counter.

"It's just going to take a little time to get used to the idea and get it out of my system" she claims, continuing to wind him up.

Bruce lifts her up onto the counter and immediately grabs at her jeans to rip them down.

"Let's get it out of your system now then" he insists, pulling her tight jeans down to reveal her red panties.

"Ooh that's cold" she yelps, as her bum makes contact with the kitchen counter.

"Yeah but your pussy isn't" he responds, pulling her knickers to the side and forcing a finger into her warm hole.

"Oh my god, this IS turning you on, isn't it?" he says, feeling just how wet the conversation is making her.

She forces herself off the counter and down to stand on the floor in front of him. With his finger still inside her, she lowers her hands down and quickly undoes his belt, letting his jeans fall to the floor.

"I see the idea turns you on too" she says, grabbing hold of his solid bulge.

He spins her round to face away from him, as she places her hands on the edge of the sink. He takes out his erect penis and quickly guides it into her from behind and starts thrusting.

"Mm-mm" she groans, as he pounds her hard from the very start.

"How big do you think young Dave's penis is then?" she flirts, trying to send him over the edge.

He doesn't respond and thrusts so hard that she cannot speak anymore. A few seconds later and he unloads his hot cream deep inside his wife's pussy, as she pushes it back out with her very own explosive orgasm.

"So when are you thinking about meeting up with young David then?" asks Jennifer, pulling her knickers back up.

"No time like the present" responds Bruce, tightening his belt again and heading into the living room with a smile on his face.

Bruce sits down on the sofa, takes out his mobile and calls Dave. Dave is overjoyed that Bruce kept his promise in the nightclub and has phoned him. Jennifer walks through to join him on the sofa and takes her phone out too. She sends a text message to Lucy telling her that she wants to continue the marriage talk tomorrow morning and types in her home address, so Lucy knows where to come.

CHAPTER 2
LOVE AND MARRIAGE, HORSE AND CARRIAGE

The next morning Bruce has already left home to run some errands before his meeting later tonight with Dave, in the same nightclub as before. Jennifer has just rushed out of the shower and is getting dressed fast, knowing Lucy should be knocking on her front door at any minute. She slips into some jeans, throws a white shirt over her head and runs downstairs into the kitchen to fill the kettle just as the doorbell rings. Fastening the buttons on her jeans, she makes her way back through the house to answer the door.

"Morning Lucy" says a flustered Jennifer opening it to her.

"You okay?" asks Lucy, noticing straight away that Jennifer has her shirt on inside out.

Jennifer catches on and explains that she woke up late and invites her in, whilst whipping the shirt off and putting it back on the right way. Jennifer tells Lucy how nice she looks today as Lucy stands there in her black leggings, a cropped top showing off her stomach with her long blonde hair bunched into a ponytail.

"Thank you" responds Lucy grinning, following her into the kitchen. Lucy takes a seat at the breakfast bar whilst Jennifer makes the coffee.

"So did you mean what you said yesterday about me not being too young to get married?" asks Lucy eager to get Jennifer's opinion.

Jennifer passes Lucy her coffee.

"In order for me to be honest with you Lucy, I need to ask you some questions first" says Jennifer, taking a seat opposite her at the breakfast bar.

"Is that okay?" she asks taking a sip of her coffee.

Lucy agrees to answer any question Jennifer may have for her.

"Okay Lucy" says Jennifer ready to get started.

"How many sexual partners have you had?" she asks, reaching over to a drawer and pulling out a notepad and pen to record Lucy's answers.

Lucy looks a little surprised at Jennifer's very first question but decides to answer it and show she is willing to help Jennifer, help her.

"There's been about fifteen" Lucy admits, expecting Jennifer to call her a slag or something.

Jennifer doesn't respond and starts writing on her piece of paper. Lucy relaxes quickly when she comes to the conclusion that Jennifer isn't going to judge her in anyway and she is ready for the next question.

"And how many of those fifteen have been one night stands?" Jennifer asks.

Lucy makes out she needs to think about it. Jennifer reassures her quickly, by telling her that whatever she says will never be repeated.

"Fourteen" answers Lucy, watching Jennifer choke on her coffee.

"Fourteen?" asks Jennifer, trying to make out it doesn't matter.

Lucy confirms that fourteen is the number of one night stands she has had and feels the need to explain herself. She tells Jennifer that she makes silly mistakes when she's drunk and also finds it hard to say no to guy's that are nice to her. Jennifer continues writing and unloads her next question.

"Tell me about your most favourite sexual experience to date" she asks Lucy.

Lucy starts to blush and finds this question a little bit too personal.

"With my partner now or in my life?" asks Lucy, trying to stay as open as she possibly can and delay answering the question itself.

"Both" answers Jennifer, coming across like a real life shrink in her office taking notes.

Lucy tells her that her best sexual experience was a one off threesome with her best friend and her boyfriend.

"Would you say you are bi-sexual, curious or part bi?" asks Jennifer, not letting her answer the question in full.

"What's part bi?" asks a confused looking Lucy.

Jennifer explains that part bi is a girl that is openly bi-sexual but still prefers a man to have sex with.

"Yeah I am probably the part bi type then" answers Lucy, relaxing even more around Jennifer's settling and friendly manner.

"And what about your best sexual experience with your current partner?" asks Jennifer.

Lucy needs a moment or two before answering and Jennifer shows a professional attitude and doesn't rush her at all. Finally Lucy has an answer and tells her it's probably the time they had sex in a public park at night time. Lucy watches as Jennifer continues to write everything she is saying down on the piece of paper.

"Last question" says Jennifer smiling across the breakfast bar.

"What do you think getting married means?" she asks, tapping her pen on the notebook.

Again Lucy needs a few seconds to answer.

"It's about two people who love each-other and want to make a further commitment" answers Lucy, very confident and sure of her answer this time.

Jennifer stands up signals Lucy to follow her through into the living room. Lucy quickly finishes her coffee and follows.

"Yeah but what is love?" asks Jennifer to Lucy behind her.

Jennifer sits down on the sofa and pats the cushion to invite Lucy to sit next to her. Lucy sits down, still pondering over the last question about love.

"Love is two people who want to share forever with each-other" Lucy answers.

This answer doesn't seem to be enough for Jennifer as she tells Lucy to go on.

"It's about being loyal and not cheating on each-other" claims Lucy, trying hard to elaborate on her answer for Jennifer's approval.

Jennifer isn't convinced Lucy knows what true love is but keeps the vibe very light and friendly.

"So what happens when a guy tries to sleep with you next?" asks Jennifer.

"I say no" answers Lucy confidently and abruptly.

"What if your husband ever cheated on you?" Jennifer asks continuing to probe her.

"He wouldn't" answers Lucy in the same manner as before.

Jennifer closes her notepad and places it on the table.

"Well?" asks Lucy.

"Am I ready to get married?" she asks, eagerly awaiting Jennifer's answer.

Jennifer looks into her eyes and tells her that she might be.

"Might be? I don't understand" claims Lucy looking somewhat concerned.

Jennifer stands up in front of Lucy and explains Lucy is right about marriage and making a commitment, but it's also so much more than that.

"What do you do when a random boyfriend cheats on you?" asks

Jennifer.

"Dump him" answers Lucy, without even having to think about it.

"And what happens when that random boyfriend lets you down or stands you up three or four times?" Jennifer asks.

"Dump him" answers Lucy again.

Jennifer sits back down beside Lucy on the sofa.

"And what about when you are married?" asks Jennifer.

"Would you divorce a cheating husband?" she asks.

Lucy for the first time doesn't know what to say. She wants to say he'd never cheat on her, she wants to say dump him, but she can't speak. Jennifer tells her that marriage isn't all about sharing the good times, but also sticking together through the bad.

"People make mistakes" explains Jennifer.

"But during a marriage you've always got to be prepared to forgive or work things out before considering divorce or dumping him" she adds.

Lucy quickly makes sense of what Jennifer is telling her and makes out that she knew that already with a simple nod of her head.

"It's about living two lives in one soul" Jennifer continues to explain.

"It's about him making a mistake and you both living and working through that mistake together" she adds, telling her exactly what marriage and love should be about.

Although Lucy agrees, she also sits there trying to work out if her and her man have that kind of relationship. Jennifer tells her she thinks she is ready for marriage, but should take a few more days to give her a real answer. Lucy accepts Jennifer's decision and the conversation starts to run dry. Lucy tries to keep the good feeling communication alive by asking how long Jennifer has been helping girls out for, in which Jennifer tells her a long time, but this line of question runs it's course too.

"So what about Rose?" asks Jennifer, sparking off a new topic of conversation altogether.

"Is she always that cold with people she meets for the first time?" she asks looking at Lucy.

Lucy explains that she's only known Rose for a short while, since she started sharing a room with her at drama school, but tells her she is a really a nice person with a wonderful kind manner. Jennifer looks confused knowing this isn't the feeling she received from their first meeting yesterday, but decides to listen.

"Rose is fun, looks out for me and also looks out for my little sister" Lucy tells her.

"What happened yesterday then?" asks Jennifer showing interest.

Lucy tells her that she doesn't know, but for the mood she was in, it could only be one of two things.

"What are they?" asks Jennifer, contemplating at the same time whether or not she can help Rose change her life too.

"It's either her boyfriend or her dad" claims Lucy, opening up fully on her friend Rose's private life.

Lucy tells her Rose's dad is okay but mingles with some very interesting people.

"Who?" asks Jennifer moving in closer to listen.

"He knows a lot of famous people and also a lot of not so nice people" Lucy tells her.

"What does he do?" asks Jennifer, trying to get a little more information.

"I don't know" answers Lucy.

"But he's always going to clubs and parties to mingle with all the people he knows" she adds.

Jennifer seems a little disappointed at the answer, because it doesn't help her find the root of Rose's attitude problem.

"And that's how Rose knows Whitney" Lucy tells her.

"Whitney?" questions Jennifer looking puzzled.

"Whitney the famous Hollywood actress" answers Lucy, clearly not impressing Jennifer as much as it does herself and going on to tell her how she's met her on three different occasions too.

"And what about her boyfriend?" asks Jennifer, not letting Lucy go off in her own little world about the famous celebrity in question.

"Oh him" Lucy says with a disgusted look on her face.

"He's just a shit head" she snaps.

Jennifer quickly picks up on the change in Lucy's mood and throws a question at her that sends shivers down her spine.

"Has Rose's boyfriend ever tried it on with you?" Jennifer asks, as Lucy's face falls through the floor.

"Nope" responds Lucy, hiding something behind the guilty look on her face.

Jennifer again reassures her the conversation will never leave the room and tells her about the importance of honesty in a new friendship. With that Lucy opens up...

"He was one of my one night stands" Lucy admits with a horrified look on her face.

"You don't need to tell me any-more" says Jennifer smiling and thanking her for being honest.

Jennifer comes to the conclusion that Rose has issues with her father and boyfriend and that's what makes her as rude as she is. She feels a desire to help her again, but puts it aside as she concentrates her efforts into getting to know Lucy's young sister Tina.

"So what about Tina?" asks Jennifer.

"Tell me a little about her" she adds, hoping that Lucy will continue to be honest with her.

Lucy has a little think to herself before opening up about her little sister.

"Well you know we are only half sisters" says Lucy getting started.

"She's the kindest, gentlest person I know" she adds with a proud look on her face.

Jennifer wants a little more information and again asks her to go on with a nod.

"She lives at home with our mum, her dad, who is my step dad" Lucy tells her with another strange look on her face.

"What is it?" asks Jennifer, picking up on the facial expression.

Lucy starts getting defensive and flustered.

"Your step father yeah?" asks Jennifer, working it out for herself,

"One of your fifteen?" she asks, not really needing an answer from Lucy as her red face confesses all.

Lucy starts to feel a little uncomfortable and her defensive attitude becomes more apparent.

"You can't say anything to anyone" insists Lucy, demanding Jennifer's trust instead of asking for it.

Again Jennifer tells her nothing will go any further and asks if she wants to tell her about it.

"It was a mistake, I came home late one night and he was waiting up for me" Lucy explains.

"It only happened once and I have told him no so many times since then" she adds.

Jennifer believes her and tells her to relax as she watches Lucy breakdown, as if Jennifer is the first person she's ever told.

"Why am I telling you all this? I hardly know you" asks Lucy, realising that she is telling Jennifer things she's never told anyone else before.

Jennifer just smiles at her and tells her it's a sign of a special friendship beginning.

"Do you still like me?" asks Lucy, fearing her confessions about her friend's partner and step-dad will put Jennifer off her now.

"Why?" asks Jennifer, not wanting her to feel that way at all.

"I've had a one night stand with my room-mate's boyfriend and my step-dad" Lucy tells her.

Jennifer once again reassures her she's not there to judge her and only wants to help. She also points out they'd have more of a problem if she didn't confess all this from the very start. Jennifer realises the conversation has taken a lot out of Lucy and decides to turn her attentions back to her sister Tina.

"What else do you want to know about her?" asks Lucy, happy to take the attention away from herself.

"Is she sexually active? Has she a boyfriend? Does she speak to you about boys?" Jennifer asks.

Lucy tells her that her sister does sometimes talk to her about boys and knows that she hasn't had sex. She also tells her that she's just stepped foot into her first real relationship and is considering giving him her virginity.

"Are you okay with that?" asks Jennifer, trying to find out how big sister feels about it.

Lucy tells her it's Tina's choice and that she lost her virginity at the age of fourteen, so can't really comment. With that Lucy has an idea and asks Jennifer if she wouldn't mind finding out if Tina is ready to have sex or not. Jennifer accepts the request straight away but wants a few things in return.

"What would you like from me then?" asks Lucy, willing to do anything for her new friend that could prevent Tina from making any unnecessary mistakes.

"I want you to come out clubbing with me tonight" says Jennifer, in exchange for helping Tina.

Lucy is pleased that the return request isn't an impossible task and tells her she could invite Rose along too.

"No don't do that" insists Jennifer, quickly shooting the idea down.

"Tonight is about you" she adds.

"And what was the other thing you wanted me to do?" asks Lucy, confirming the night out will be fine.

Jennifer tells her that she wants another meeting back at Lucy's home with Rose tomorrow morning. Lucy again knows she can handle the request and tells Jennifer to consider it done.

Lucy reaches into her bag, pulls out some keys and hands them to Jennifer.

"What do I need these for?" asks Jennifer, taking the keys.

Lucy tells her she could have a little chat with Tina after she's seen Rose in the morning.

"Yeah but she's going to be at home right?" asks Jennifer, unsure of why she would need keys.

Lucy tells her that her mum and step father are away for a couple of days on a trip to the countryside and that she will text Tina and tell her of Jennifer's visit.

"So why do I need the keys then?" asks Jennifer looking more and more confused by it all.

"If she isn't in, you can just let yourself in and wait for her" Lucy says, wanting Jennifer to keep the keys.
Jennifer still doesn't quite understand but decides to keep the keys and give them back at a later date.
Jennifer offers Lucy a final cup of coffee before they go their separate ways.
"So let me get this right?" says Lucy, sitting back down at the breakfast bar.
"We are going to a club later? Then In the morning you want to meet at mine with Rose and then after that, you are going round to have a chat with Tina?" she asks.
Jennifer turns, smiles and nods her head before switching the kettle on.
The two girls sit talking about the planned night out for a little while, as Lucy tries desperately to find out a bit more about Jennifer.
"So what's your husband like?" Lucy asks.
Jennifer answers every question with short answers, so as not to give too much away.
"He's the best" Jennifer answers.
Lucy continues to fire questions at Jennifer, where she does get answers every time, but not in any great detail. They finish their coffee and arrange a time to meet later.
"Shall we say about eight o'clock outside your school then?" asks Jennifer.
Lucy agrees and the girls part at Jennifer's front door with a hug.
As Lucy leaves and Jennifer closes the front door, Jennifer pulls her mobile phone from her pocket and calls Bruce.
"I need you to test someone for me tonight" she tells him.
"I wanted you to do the same with Dave for me tonight" Bruce tells her back down the phone, as though they are magically planning the same thing for two different clients.
"Good minds think alike" laughs Jennifer.
"I learnt from the best" Bruce says, asking where her test is going to take place.
Jennifer tells him to arrange the same night out she's planned with Lucy. Bruce tells her that he just wants her to go clubbing, flirt a little with Dave and find out just how talented he is on the pull. Jennifer tells Bruce that she wants him to find out if Lucy is ready to get married and to find out if she can say no and trust herself. The couple end the conversation and have planned their first joint lesson together.
Jennifer goes in search of something to wear tonight, but her phone rings again.

"Me and you tonight, Rose in the morning and Tina tomorrow afternoon" says Lucy's voice down the phone, showing Jennifer that she's sorted out things her end.

Jennifer confirms with a yes, but can't work out why she is telling her it all again.

"When are you going to tell me if I am ready to get married though?" asks Lucy, her real reason for the phone call.

Jennifer is horrified when she realises she completely forgot to give Lucy a little lesson on marriage. Being far too keen to get to know the three girls as quickly as possible and her huge interest in moody Rose, the lesson Lucy came round for in the first place simply slipped her mind. Jennifer quickly tries to rectify the mistake and asks Lucy if she wouldn't mind popping back to her house quickly. Lucy agrees and it's only a matter of minutes before she is knocking on her door again.

"I am so sorry" says Jennifer, opening the door to Lucy again.

"I am usually a lot more professional than this" she adds, inviting her back inside.

Lucy shrugs it off and tells her not to worry about it and it isn't long before the two girls are back in the living room, sitting together and going through what marriage means.

Jennifer's Lesson On Being Ready For Marriage

Most people when they get married end up wanting to do it for the right reason, but sometimes the occasion and other issues can get in the way. Nearly every girl out there wants the fairytale wedding and the planning of such a big day can sometimes overshadow what it all really means. Yes you are meant to enjoy your day fully and yes you are expected to get excited and nervous about the plans you are making, but this should never drown out what it all really means.

Getting married is not only about sharing a lifetime together, but it's about being ready yourself to stand by your man for the rest of your life, no matter what and vice versa.

It's no good having your big day, simply assuming that he's in it for a lifetime too and basing that all around the wonderful relationship you are currently sharing now. You have to consider the future too. Okay he may not cheat on you right now. He may not cheat on you in the next ten years, but the day will come where he is tempted by another, like you will also probably have lustful thoughts throughout your marriage.

The question should be... Are you and will you be strong enough to fight those temptations off, even twenty years down the line? Are you willing to listen, understand and maybe forgive mistakes if they are made?

So many people make the mistake of getting married because things have never been better for them in a relationship and the sex is the best you've ever had, but are they prepared for the day when he can no longer get it up or the spark goes out of your sex life?

To cut a long story short... Don't just base your plans to get married on the good times you are having currently or the fact he makes you orgasm more than you've ever done before. Be prepared for the future and the things that could go wrong and then ask yourself, are you ready?

If something happened to your partner and he had to spend the rest of his life in a wheelchair being nursed, would you honestly still be getting married? If your sex life became boring and he showed no interest in sex with you any-more, would you fight to put things right together? Has your partner ever let you down? Will it happen in the future? Or more to the point, can you stop yourself from blaming him, wanting to split up or can you share as one the mistakes he could make and work them out together? Would you honestly risk your life now and twenty years down the line to save your partner?

That's what marriage is... That is the kind of talk you should be having with yourself right now. Yes you may think it's irrelevant, it could also be considered shallow, but these are the things that make a marriage work. Does your man look good and hot right now? Course he does, you want to marry him right?

Now age him twenty years... A little saggy round the edges, losing his hair, hairier in other places, not making as much effort to impress any-more... Still want to be married to him?

Bottom line is, it's not all about the here and now... It's a long term thing and it's forever. You are only meant to get married once to your one true love and that's the way it should stay. Anyone can say they orgasm all the time, anyone can say they are happy and anyone can say I love you.

Not many people can say they've been hurt by someone, been cheated on in the past and are stronger than ever... That's what makes a solid marriage – The fight!!

After what is a long lesson to take in and one Lucy thinks she already knows most of the answers too, she still feels unsure of her own answer about being ready.

"Say I can forgive twenty years down the line, say I still can work at making my marriage work" says Lucy.

"That still doesn't answer the question of whether we are right for

each-other, does it?" she adds looking lost and confused.
Jennifer understands Lucy's concern straight away and knows how to answer it for her, but doesn't want to fill her head with too much information too soon.

"Would your man let you sleep with another guy and give you his blessing right now?" asks Jennifer.

"No way" answers Lucy abruptly.

"What about in ten years time?" asks Jennifer.

Lucy needs a few seconds to think this one over, but doesn't have an answer and just shrugs her shoulders with a little grin.

"Would you say your man is jealous or over protective?" asks Jennifer, continuing to fire questions at her.

"Maybe a little over protective" answers Lucy, trying to keep up.

Jennifer moves in closer and tells her before anyone gets married, the one thing both couples should consider is whether they can live as one.

"Like soul mates?" asks Lucy.

"Sort of" replies Jennifer.

Jennifer explains a marriage will never go the distance if a couple can't learn to live as one.

"Two different people in a single relationship, pulling in opposite directions, will always lead to divorce" insists Jennifer.

"Okay" replies Lucy, waiting for Jennifer to make her point.

Jennifer asks Lucy for complete trust and complete honesty, in which Lucy agrees to give it. Jennifer tells her to think about her partner and the sexiest woman she can imagine. She then tells her to think about him and the sexy woman having hot mind blowing sex together.

"Okay" answers Lucy again, trying hard to picture it happening.

"Be honest, is it turning you on at all?" asks Jennifer with a tiny glint in her year.

"A little" answers Lucy, trying not to blush or let her face overheat.

Jennifer tells her there's nothing wrong with her natural feelings, but asks her if she's ever shared them with her future husband or played them out during sex.

"I don't think so" laughs Lucy, as though Jennifer has said something really funny.

Jennifer asks her to switch roles.

"What me have sex with her?" asks Lucy.

"No" says Jennifer quickly.

"You have sex in front of your man with a stranger and a massive penis" she tells her.

"Okay" answers Lucy, as she tries hard to picture this image now.

Jennifer raises her eyebrows as if to ask, how do you feel?

"Yeah it turns me on" answers Lucy, enjoying this fantasy a little more than the last.

"Have you shared this one or played it out in a fantasy with your partner?" asks Jennifer.

Lucy doesn't respond and just shakes her head with a disappointed look on her face.

Jennifer explains whilst Lucy keeps these little desires and fantasies locked away, it's a part of their relationship that isn't living as one or being honest and the more they have of these individual thoughts during a marriage, the harder it is to make it work.

"But what if I tell him and he still doesn't like it?" asks Lucy, understanding the point made, but feeling a bit worried about the whole honesty thing.

"Well that's where you know if you are the right couple to be married or not" explains Jennifer.

"If you can never have another fantasy for the rest of your life, then you will be fine, but if you don't share everything with each-other, it's just another thing that could destroy your relationship in the end" she adds.

"I'm sure I can live without it" declares Lucy, choosing the safer option.

"Yeah, but you say that now" says Jennifer.

"That's because the sex is great. What happens when the spark goes and you start craving these desires more and more as you get older?" she asks.

With that Lucy understands the lesson, but still doesn't know if her and her future husband do live as one already or if they ever will. Jennifer tells her the answer won't come over night and that it will take a few days to sink in. Lucy appreciates Jennifer's advice and the two girls start talking about their night out again. They confirm their plans again and Lucy pops to the toilet before she sets off.

CHAPTER 3
JUST ONE WORD

It's seven o'clock at Jennifer's house and the couple are both in the bedroom getting ready for the night out. As Bruce grabs a shirt from the wardrobe to put on, Jennifer jumps in the shower quickly. Bruce follows her into the bathroom and stands in front of the mirror checking his shirt looks okay.
"So go over it once more. What do you want me to do tonight?" asks Bruce, as Jennifer stands behind the shower curtain in the steam filled room.
Jennifer tells him that she wants him to wait until she goes to the toilets in the club and then approach Lucy, flirt with her a little and offer her a drink.
"Is that all?" asks Bruce.
"No showing off my penis today then?" he asks, finding his job tonight a bit too easy.
Jennifer pops her head out from behind the shower curtain.
"No penis showing whatsoever tonight" she tells him, wiping the water from her face.
Bruce gets the message and knows the part he needs to play tonight to make Jennifer's test work.
"And you just want me to check out Dave's pulling skills for you tonight?" she calls over the noise of the running water.
"Yeah" Bruce answers, splashing some aftershave on his face.
"Mm-mm" Jennifer moans winding him up.
Bruce pulls back the curtain to find her standing under the shower, teasing him whilst rubbing her breasts.

"I told you, no funny business. You have to stay professional like I do" he tells her, laughing along with her playful antics too.
Jennifer stops messing about and continues to rinse the bubbles from her body. She then steps out of the shower and grabs herself a towel.
"What happens if this Dave is good with his chat-up lines? How far should I let him go?" she asks drying herself.
Bruce finishes up in the bathroom and heads for the door.
"Just make him feel he's pulled you and leave the rest to me" he insists, heading back downstairs.
Ten minutes later Bruce is sitting on the sofa in black jeans, a smart blue shirt and is ready to go. Jennifer walks downstairs and enters the room.
"So are we ready to paint this new part of London red?" she asks, wearing a short red dress that shows off her thighs, cleavage and back.
"Wow, you look great" gasps Bruce.
"I haven't seen that dress before" he adds, telling her to give him a spin.
Jennifer slowly turns around modelling the dress.
"Isn't it a little bit too revealing for a nightclub?" he asks, noticing the back of the dress is completely open.
She turns to face him and notices him starring at her thighs.
"What's revealing honey?" she asks, starting to tease him again.
He sits there stunned by his wife's beauty and knows deep down he wouldn't want her any other way.
"At least put a pap-strap on. You will get a cold" he tells her, picking up on her erect nipples through the dress.
"And what about my legs?" she teases some more.
"Are they too revealing?" she asks, hitching the already short dress up a little more.
Bruce swallows, as he watches her tease him.
"What if I do this?" she asks, carefully placing her hands up her dress in order not to lift it any higher and easing down her silky red thong.
Bruce grabs her by the waist and pulls her down and on top of him sitting on the sofa. She straddles his body as her knickers fall to her ankles.
"What are you doing? Don't we have to leave now?" she asks, not putting up too much of a fight as he starts passionately nibbling on her neck.
"Let's call it all off and do it another night" he mumbles, fondling her breasts out of the dress and nibbling on her nipples.
She lets him have is way for a few minutes and then starts to rock her

pelvis against his jeans.

"Bad boy" she snaps, jumping up and off his lap when she clearly feels his bulge hardening.

"That can wait till later" she laughs, pulling her dress down horny too, but enjoying telling him to be professional now.

Bruce knows she's right and knows he isn't going to get anywhere before they've completed their tasks, so he quickly composes himself, adjusts his jeans and stands up ready to leave.

Bruce grabs the front door key from the table and Jennifer picks up her bag. She drops her purse on the floor from her bag on purpose bending over in front of him. The dress rides up, giving him another glimpse of her warm, wet lips from behind. Bruce moves in for another go, but just as he gets near, she stands up, looks over her shoulder and calls him a bad boy again. With that they leave the house together.

Jennifer heads towards the drama school where she has agreed to meet Lucy and Bruce heads straight to the club to meet Dave.

Bruce reaches the nightclub first and is greeted by Dave who is already waiting for him outside.

"How you doing mate?" says Bruce, offering his friend a hand to shake.

"Nice to see you again" responds Dave shaking his hand.

The two guy's stand outside the club in light conversation whilst waiting to get in. Dave explains that he didn't think he would hear from Bruce again after their first meeting but Bruce puts him straight, telling him he never lets anyone down.

"So are you going to show me how to get the sexiest girl in here like you did last time?" asks Dave, getting excited knowing what Bruce is capable of.

Bruce standing beside Dave looks over at him, smiles and shakes his head to say no.

"So what are you going to teach me tonight then?" asks Dave, eager to learn something at least.

Bruce tells him on their first meeting he taught Dave how to pick out the right girl in the club.

"This time I will show you again, but I want to watch just how smooth you are at doing it" explains Bruce.

Dave looks a little stunned at first, but starts getting excited again.

"So I've got to do all the work, but you are going to show me who will say yes first?" Dave asks.

Bruce gives him the same look as before, smiles and nods this time.

"I can do that, I can do that" says Dave, bouncing around in the queue like a boxer.

Meanwhile outside the drama school Lucy is also waiting for Jennifer, but she isn't there yet. She starts to feel good about the attention she is getting from passer's by and male students from her school. She catches her own reflection in a parked car and takes a look. She quickly adjusts her knee length black dress and runs her fingers through her long blonde hair as Jennifer walks round the corner.

"You look amazing Lucy" says Jennifer, walking over to her looking at her really long legs.

"Me? Look at you" remarks Lucy back, as she is stunned by Jennifer's sexy red outfit.

Jennifer asks her if she's ready to go and Lucy smiles nodding her head. Jennifer leads her down the road and tries to get the somewhat nervous Lucy to lighten up, telling her it's going to be a great night.

Back at the club, the guy's have just entered to some Wham music pumping out through the main doors.

"You haven't brought me to a gay club have you?" jokes Dave, a little miffed by the music.

"Do I look gay?" asks Bruce, strutting towards the doors and checking out the first pretty female he looks at and getting a smile back as a reward.

Bruce explains that he knows it isn't a dance come rave club that Dave is used to, but explains it will be a lot easier for him to attract female attention as he opens the main door.

"Yeah attract my mum and her friends playing this 80's stuff" laughs Dave following on.

The doors open and the place is already alive.

"Do you see your mum and her friends?" Bruce laughs, showing young Dave the amount of talent already packed into the small area.

Dave can't believe his eyes as they make their way over to the bar.

"Look at all the fanny in here" shouts an excited Dave, over the music not knowing who to look at first.

Bruce grabs him by the arm as they arrive at the bar.

"Don't let me hear you talk like that again" Bruce snaps.

"See all those desperate fuckers over there? That's how they speak" he adds, pointing to the guys hovering around the edge of the dance floor sniffing out the easy targets for the night.

Dave doesn't like being grabbed and his facial expression tells Bruce just that.

"Do you want to go and stand with those losers or do you want to be a man?" asks Bruce.

Dave backs down, understanding Bruce was just trying to point out that only sad desperate guy's talk that way. Bruce orders a drink and tells Dave to have a look round with a new attitude.

"Don't look at all the FANNY in here. Ask yourself which one of these girls is going to have the pleasure of your company tonight" Bruce tells him.

A little unsure of what Bruce is telling him to do, Dave starts to scour the venue. Bruce takes the drinks from the bar and walks dumbfounded Dave across to a quiet corner and sits down at a table. He lets Dave continue to look for his dream girl for a moment longer and then asks him who he likes. Dave hesitates for a second and then points out a little blonde girl shaking her stuff on the dance floor in tight jeans and a backside to die for.

"Nice" Bruce tells him.

"Nice? She's HOT" responds an excited Dave.

"Just think, she could have anyone in this place tonight and even if she didn't want to, she still gets to go home and play with herself and that hot body" he adds in ore of the dancing blonde.

Bruce bangs the table to snap Dave out of his wandering thoughts.

"There you go again, childish remarks" shouts Bruce with a disappointed look on his face.

"What?" asks Dave looking concerned.

Bruce tells him that he thinks the girl in question is sexy too, but also points out that if he's got anything to offer her, she'd be the lucky one, not him and not her hands.

"But that's what all the guy's think" explains Dave, trying to fight his corner.

"Come on Bruce, you can't tell me you wouldn't want to be her hands in her bathtub tonight for just a few seconds, can you?" he asks, trying to teach Bruce what guy's talk about.

Bruce stands up at the table leaving Dave sitting there looking up at him.

"Do you want me to go home?" asks Bruce bluntly.

"Do you want to carry on struggling to attract hot women?" he asks.

Dave looks sorry and shakes his head, as Bruce takes his seat again.

"No Dave, I wouldn't want to be her hand, I want it to be my hand down her fucking knickers. No I wouldn't want to see her having an orgasm, I want to be the person giving her it" Bruce explains.

"And no I don't think she's the lucky one, because she hasn't met me yet" he adds making his point.

Dave understands, but doesn't fully know how to think like masterful Bruce. Bruce tells him that he isn't arrogant, doesn't think he's special in anyway but does believe in himself.

"Girls like funny, girls like charm, girls like compliments, girls like confidence and girls like a man to be different from every other knob-head that tries it on with them" Bruce explains.

Dave smiles and nods again.

"Just be different in a good way Dave and it will take you far" he adds, downing the rest of his drink.

Dave looks over at the sexy girl shaking her bum on the dance floor once more and notices one of the desperate guy's Bruce pointed out minutes ago, dancing in front of her. He keeps watching as Bruce heads back to the bar again for more drinks. Dave watches the girl continue to dance with the already drunk loser moving in closer and closer and just how bad it looks. Just then the drunken guy grabs her by the waist and starts talking and laughing with her. Bruce heads back with another few drinks.

"Look" says Dave, pointing at the girl and lucky drunk guy.

"He managed to get a dance with her" he adds, waiting for Bruce's next bit of advice.

Bruce places the drinks on the table and walks up behind Dave sitting down.

"He's a knob-head, you're not" whispers Bruce in Dave's ear.

"Be something different or you will find this happening to you" he adds, heading towards the dance floor himself as Dave watches on from the table.

Bruce struts over and stands right in front of the dance floor and leans onto the railing. Seconds later with Bruce standing there and Dave at the table in the corner, they witness the sexy girl shrug off the drunken guy and leave the dance floor. Bruce heads back to the table and sits back down.

"I don't get it" mumbles Dave unsure of what just happened.

"Did you say something to her?" Dave asks, looking really puzzled.

Bruce leans across the table and tells Dave he didn't say anything at all.

"Then how did you know she would do that?" asks Dave, thinking that Bruce is some kind of magician.

Bruce tells him he gave the blonde girl something different to look at. He explains that he could have gone on the dance floor, but then he would have just become another one of those predictable guy's trying it on with her. What he did was give her a sober smile from a guy clearly not interested in trying it on with her like all the rest.

"Does that mean you've stolen my thunder with her already then?" Dave asks.

"Sorry mate" Bruce laughs, but then points out that there are plenty more hot girls to do the same with.

"So is that all you really do, give them something different to look at?" Dave asks across the table, looking for a new girl to set his sights on.

"Yeah I guess it is, but there's many ways to be different Dave, you've just got to find the girl you want most" Bruce explains, as he notices his wife Jennifer and a hot blonde enter through the door.

"What do you mean?" asks Dave getting confused again.

Bruce explains that he's a happily married man, but he likes to flirt and look at other women.

"Okay" says Dave, following him so far.

"I offer a girl something different. In other words not a desperate drunken loser" Bruce tells him.

"Then once I have her where I want her or know she wants me, I tell her although I find her really hot, I wouldn't cheat on my partner" he adds, keeping his eye on Jennifer walking towards their table.

"Doesn't you being married scare them off then?" Dave asks, still a little confused.

Bruce explains that whilst girls out clubbing come across drunken married men all the time, those drunken married men are no different from the single drunken losers trying it on.

"I still don't get it" says Dave.

Bruce quickly tries to think of another way to explain it all before Jennifer reaches the table.

"Girls think married men in clubs are there to cheat. I give them something different" says Bruce.

"You tell them your wife lets you cheat" guesses Dave, shouting across the table over the music.

Bruce picks up his drink and takes a sip, before putting it back down again.

"No Dave, I don't cheat" Bruce tells him.

Dave looks more confused than ever now.

"So what's the point in being out on the pull then?" asks Dave.

Bruce nods his head in the direction of the two hot girls walking towards their table and Dave takes a look, unaware that one of them is Bruce's wife.

"Who said I'm out on the pull Dave?" Bruce leans in and whispers, before pointing his finger in the direction of Jennifer and waving her over.

Jennifer and Lucy walk over to the table as Dave and Bruce enjoy the vision in front of them. Both girls enjoy the attention from the boys entering the club and Lucy like Dave, has no idea that it's all a set-up by the married couple.

"Sorry to wave you over, but I need you to sort something out for us quickly" Bruce says to Jennifer, pretending he doesn't know her.

"What can we do for you?" asks Jennifer, playing along with it.

Bruce tells her what guy's say and think about women, being lucky enough to touch themselves... Whilst Bruce bluntly says it, Lucy takes an instant shine to him and Dave can't believe his nerve or what he's hearing him say to the two sexy strangers.

"So do you think it's true that women are lucky being able to go home and play with their bodies?" asks Bruce, catching Lucy's eye for the second time.

Jennifer leans over towards Dave in a flirty way.

"Is your friend always this refreshingly open?" she whispers in his ear.

"Always" Dave sniggers nervously, getting an eyeful of Jennifer's cleavage in that red dress.

"And what about you? Are you refreshingly exciting or just another boring lad on the pull?" Jennifer asks, making him notice her naked thighs too now.

Dave doesn't know how to answer and sniggers a little more. Jennifer then turns back to Bruce.

"I am sure most immature boys say it, but how can we be the lucky ones?" asks Jennifer.

"We've just got a vagina to rub, you've got a massive penis to stroke" she seductively whispers, turning back to Dave and looking down at his bulge.

Bruce thanks the sexy female for being so open and gives a little wink in Lucy's direction as the girls head to the bar.

"Why don't you come and join us?" asks Bruce, as they turn to walk away and before Lucy can come to terms with Jennifer's first encounter in the club herself.

"Okay" says Jennifer, smiling at them and telling the boys, she will buy the first round of drinks.

A cocky Bruce and a dumbfounded Dave sit and watch as the two hot girls and their legs head towards the bar.

"Not only did you say something no other bloke would dream of saying, but you got a dirty response, drink and them to join us in the process. You are a god Mr Bruce" boasts Dave in total ore of Bruce's stylish pulling power.

Bruce takes the compliment on the chin and doesn't give away the secret, that he is already married to one of the girls.

"So which one do you want to go home with tonight then Dave?" asks Bruce, rushing him to make a decision before they return.

"I don't' mind, they are both fit as fuck" stutters an over excited Dave.

"The blonde in the black is more my age, but the older one is just as sexy and says really naughty things" he adds.

Bruce takes another sip of his drink and watches the girls start walking back towards their table.

"Okay I will flirt with the blonde and you take the more experienced one" Bruce quickly says before they reach the table.

Bruce moves over, allowing the girls to put the drinks down.

"She's going to eat you alive" Bruce whispers, laughing whilst shuffling closer to Dave.

Jennifer sits on the end of the table next to Dave and Lucy sits the other end next to Bruce.

"So what are you two up to then? A night out on the pull?" asks Jennifer, getting the flirty conversation started.

Bruce quickly explains that Dave is the only single one at the table and that he himself is a happily married man.

"You're married? That's nice. I'm getting married soon" Lucy shyly utters, opening her mouth for the first time.

"So it's just me and you that are the single ones then babes" Jennifer says, moving in closer towards Dave and flirting with him a lot more.

Bruce leans in towards Dave from the other side as they all start to drink, smile and have fun.

"Did you hear that mate; the blonde one next to me is getting married?" Bruce whispers.

"Yeah I heard" Dave answers, trying to prise himself from Jennifer the older woman who has locked arms with him.

"Watch how much she wants me by the end of the night" Bruce smugly whispers again before standing up and telling them it's his round.

"I will help you" insists Lucy, standing up too as Bruce looks down towards Dave lifting his eyebrows to give another confident smirk.

Bruce and young Lucy set off to the bar leaving Jennifer ready to test Dave's pulling skills for Bruce. She moves a little closer but pulls down her dress, as not to flash him too much or make it too easy for him.

"So Dave, how often do you come here on the pull then?" flirts Jennifer.

Dave explains that it's his first time in the club. Jennifer makes out she doesn't know she knows he's already been there before and decides to make the conversation a little sexier.

"So do you think your bald mate will hook up with my friend

tonight?" she asks, looking at them standing at the bar.
Dave doesn't really know the answer.

"I'm not sure" he stutters.

"Bruce might flirt with women, but I know he loves his wife" he adds.

"How long do you believe oral sex on a woman should last?" she asks, licking her lips and flirting really hard with him now.

Dave starts to get nervous again and instead of answering, picks up his drink, smiles and takes a very large gulp of it.

"Sorry babes, I've embarrassed you haven't I?" claims Jennifer teasing him.

"No" he answers, trying to act more mature and not let this older woman have it all her way or call him "Cute".

"So what if I told you I didn't have any panties on under this dress and my pussy needed licking right now? Would you be the man for the job?" she unleashes on him, sending his new found maturity crashing down around him.

"Maybe, a little later" he stutters.

"Do you want to have a dance or something first?" he asks, knowing he can't dance but at least it will give him time to compose himself again.

Jennifer accepts and they stand up and head towards the dance floor as another 80's song blasts out from the speakers.

"Oh I love this one" shouts an excited Jennifer, taking him by the hand and rushing him down towards the dance floor.

Over at the bar, Bruce only orders two drinks for him and Lucy.

"What about the other two drinks?" asks Lucy.

Bruce tells her he doesn't think they will want another one just yet and points them out on the dance floor. Lucy looks over and laughs a little at Jennifer's stylish 80's moves and poor Dave trying hard to go with her.

"So when is the big day?" asks Bruce, turning to Lucy at the bar and giving her a drink.

Lucy tells him it's soon, but there's still a lot to organise first.

"Is he the one then?" asks Bruce, now doing the job he's there to do for his wife.

At first Lucy makes out she didn't hear the question over the music and when Bruce asks for a second time, she does it again but this time smiles, nods her head and makes out she's having a good time. Lucy wants to tell him her future husband is the one, but knows she has questions to answer herself first before she can be sure. Bruce tries for a third time.

"Do you love him?" he asks to the same reply as before.

Bruce knows he isn't going to get a straight forward answer and decides to change tactics. He moves in closer so she can hear him this time and he tells her how beautiful she looks. Lucy tries to hide her embarrassment and with that, she leans in and plants her lips against his lips and then backs off.

"I'm sorry, that was wrong of me" she utters, even more embarrassed with herself now.

Bruce just sits there smiling for a few seconds.

"What for? I haven't got a problem with a beautiful young girl kissing me" he responds, looking right into her eyes.

Again just like that, she moves in, kisses him and this time throws her arms around his neck.

"I'm so sorry, please don't tell my friend Jennifer" Lucy begs, after a few seconds and moving her lips away from his once more.

"I told you, it's fine" Bruce says.

"But I am not too sure your future husband will see it that way" he adds trying to calm her down.

Lucy lowers her head in shame at the very mention of her partner and starts to fiddle with her almost empty glass. Bruce waves over the bartender and orders another two drinks.

"Hey don't beat yourself up, I'd kiss me if I randomly met me in a club" Bruce laughs.

This lifts Lucy and she sees the funny side. Bruce tries to approach the situation a little more tactfully and asks her if her partner loves her.

"I hope he does" answers Lucy, still laughing about Bruce's joke and imagining him kissing himself in the mirror.

The conversation seems to come to an end and although Bruce is professional when it comes to helping Jennifer out, he is bewildered by Lucy's wandering lips.

"So Bruce, if I was single and you were too, would you go on a date with a girl like me?" asks Lucy changing the subject, but seeking a little more nice attention.

Bruce looks into her beautiful eyes, then lowers his eyes onto her petite breasts wrapped in the black dress and then finally her long legs.

"You are joking right? You really need to ask me that?" he responds with his eyes still fixated on her legs.

"I'd be all over you like a rash" he adds, looking back into her eyes.

Again Lucy throws her entire body in Bruce's direction and plants her biggest kiss yet on his lips. She keeps them held there until Bruce opens his mouth or kisses her back, but he doesn't. Once again, Lucy pulls herself away and tells him she's sorry. Once again, Bruce tells her it's fine.

"You don't understand" says Lucy.

"Every time a guy is really nice to me or I get nervous, I do things like this" she explains hoping he will understand.

"You've got the sexiest smile I've ever seen" laughs Bruce, knowing it should happen again and with that, it does...

Lucy plants her lips against his for the fourth time in as many minutes, then backs away and says she's sorry. Bruce hasn't seen anything like it before and starts playing around with her a little more.

"Lucy, can I kiss you?" he asks, holding back his laughter.

"Excuse me, I'm getting married and you're a married man" Lucy snaps back at him.

Bruce leans in towards her.

"What if I said you have the hottest body I've ever seen and I want to finger you right here and now?" Bruce laughs, trying to stay serious.

Lucy dives towards him and with the fifth planted kiss, lets one of her hands wander straight down to rub his bulge. Before it comes and Bruce knows she's going to stop and stay sorry, he continues winding her up.

"I want to kiss your sexy body from head to toe" he whispers in her ear.

Again this sends ripples through her body and she tries undoing the zip on his jeans.

"Please stop, please stop" she groans and begs, working herself up into a sexual frenzy.

Bruce decides enough is enough and stops winding her up thinking she will stop in a few seconds, but she doesn't...

"Please, oh please" she begs, rubbing him almost to erection standing there at the bar.

"Please what?" Bruce asks, ever so tactfully trying to ease her off.

"Please don't stop wanting to finger me" she begs, trying to press against his bulge with her groin.

Before it goes even further or Bruce himself starts to get tempted by her erratic behaviour, he again tactfully pushes her away and calms her down.

"I'm sorry, I'm so sorry, you must think I am a right slag?" she says panting and trying to take a drink from her glass.

Bruce doesn't want her to get the wrong impression and tells her he doesn't think she's a slag at all.

"I just think you like attention" he says with a shocked look on his face.
Before Lucy can predictably lunge for him again, Bruce is ready and holds her at arm's length. Lucy is kind of pleased he does it but doesn't understand why she's being rejected now.

"I have upset you haven't I?" she asks, wondering why Bruce is the first bloke ever to stop her when she's being like this.
Bruce tells her she hasn't upset him and feels the need to tell her the truth before things escalate. He takes her by the hand and walks her back over to the table in the corner. On the way he waves at Jennifer still on the dance floor and signals that they need to stop doing what they are doing. Jennifer nods her head to say she understands and the married couple put plan B into action. Bruce sits Lucy down at the table and tells her he needs to say something.

"It's okay, you don't need to explain" says Lucy, thinking she knows what's coming.

"You're married and I'm getting married" she adds.
Bruce takes her hand across the table and tells her again that he was being honest.

"If I was single, I would be in your knickers like a shot" he admits, holding her hand tightly so she cannot lunge again.

"My name is Bruce and I am here tonight simply to find out how good my friend Dave is at pulling and chatting women up" he adds.
Lucy looks baffled, but wants to understand.

"Well I guess he's done pretty well then" Lucy says, pointing out the fact he's with her friend Jennifer.

"If she was a normal woman, I would agree, but she's not" says Bruce.
Lucy takes her hand away and gets defensive, in order to protect her new friend.

"EXCUSE ME?" she snaps.

"What is that supposed to mean?" she asks in an aggressive manner.

"Your friend Jennifer is my wife Jennifer" Bruce explains.

"Is this some kind of sick twisted joke?" Lucy shouts.
Bruce just sits there, smiles and shakes his head. With that Lucy stands up and runs to the exit with Bruce giving chase.

Over in the other corner, the news that Bruce is in-fact Jennifer's husband has gone down a lot better and Dave is more embarrassed that he's now sexually attracted to Bruce's wife, not what the married couple have done.

"So why couldn't Bruce just tell me you wanted to put your friend and her wedding plan under the microscope?" Dave asks, trying to get his head round it all.
Jennifer explains whereas Dave knows Bruce the teacher, what he doesn't know is Jennifer's been teaching for year's too. Dave understands and they head to the bar for a quick drink and then back to the table to wait for Bruce and Lucy to return from wherever they've disappeared to.

Outside the club Bruce finally catches up with Lucy two streets away and gets her to stop.
"So what is this Bruce, some kind of seedy orgy?" Lucy bitterly lets out in anger.
Bruce again tries to explain she wasn't involved at all and that the night was based around helping Dave and his confidence.
"So are you one of these life coaches like Jennifer too then?" Lucy asks, trying to take it all in.
Bruce tells her he is a life coach, but it's in-fact his first night on the job.
"Not going very well is it?" says Bruce, looking for a vote of sympathy.
Lucy backs down trying to make sense of it all, but can't understand one thing.
"Why all the flirting at the bar then? Why not just tell me?" she asks.
Bruce tells her he was looking for the right time but before he knew it, her lips were all over his.
"Oh god, we kissed" mutters a horrified looking Lucy.
"What's Jennifer going to think when she finds out?" she panics, hoping he will have an answer.
Bruce reassures her that it will be fine and even if Jennifer did find out, she'd be okay with it.
"I don't understand, I thought you were married?" asks a puzzled looking Lucy.
"We aren't just married, we trust each-other and live as one" answers Bruce.
Lucy remembers the lesson on marriage Jennifer taught her and this seems to put her mind at ease.
"Besides, she has a wild fetish for watching me have sex with other women too" claims Bruce, getting a little personal and smiling at her.
"Oh does she?" smiles Lucy, happy that she's finally found

something personal out about her new friend Jennifer at last.
Bruce tells her everything will be okay as they stand in the middle of the street. Bruce asks her to return to the club with him and she agrees.

"Hold on" she says, before they start heading back.

"Does that mean all that flirting and winding me up in the club meant nothing then?" she asks.

Bruce moves in closer to stand next to her under the street lamp.

"If I didn't know you'd kiss and want sex again, I would be able to answer that for you" he says, trying not to give the answer away.

Lucy feels that she's in control of her emotions now and tells him to trust her and try. After a second of thinking it through and giving her the benefit of the doubt, he decides to give her an honest answer.

"No it didn't mean nothing. I was turned on by you the minute I saw you" he tells her.

He waits for her to lunge, but she doesn't, so he continues...

"If I wasn't married, you'd be top of my list" he tells her, very wary of the oncoming lunge.

Still Lucy stays rooted to the spot.

"You said Jennifer likes to watch, would you ever let her watch us?" she asks him standing there looking all innocent and feeling horny again.

"Without a doubt" Bruce responds with a big grin on his face.

"So you do think I am sexy then?" she asks, controlling herself really well.

Bruce wants to tell her just how sexy he finds her but can't find the words. He takes a step back to look her up and down and bites his lip. Just like that Lucy makes the lunge he's been waiting for, as she can't control herself any-more. She forces him against the lamp post and kisses him again.

"I didn't say anything, I didn't say anything" Bruce stutters in shock, trying to not let this new temptation beat him.

"You didn't have to say anything, your eyes did that for you" flirts Lucy, rubbing him to erection like there's no tomorrow.

"Kiss me, kiss me" she demands, trying hard to get her tongue into his mouth.

Bruce resists but feels himself weakening fast as the blonde bombshell tries all her best moves on him.

"I will talk to Jen for you and we can do this right" Bruce insists, trying hard to fight against her lips, wandering hands and now pelvis rocking against his bulge.

"But not like this please" he begs her to stop, knowing he is about to cave and be unable to stop himself.

She rubs harder and harder against his hard bulge and this sends her to heights where she just can't stop. With her other hand, she hitches up her black dress to reveal some white silky knickers. Bruce continues to grow weaker, as he tries to grab her waist to push her away but makes contact with the silk of her underwear.

"Get a fucking room" shouts a strangers voice from one of the houses on the street.

"Let us have your fucking room" shouts Lucy, as she manages to undo the zip on his jeans and unable to stop no matter who can see them.

Bruce doesn't want to get arrested and knows Lucy is unable to stop, which in turn is driving him wild, but he has to stop her somehow. He opens his mouth and lets her kiss him as their tongues meet for the first time. Now being able to determine the speed, Bruce starts to calm her down and control the situation. After a thirty second kiss, Bruce moves back as she floats off to heaven. She opens her eyes to look at him.

"Let's get back to the club before we get arrested" says Bruce, taking her by the hand and walking her back down the street.

Lucy just nods her head and agrees.

Minutes later Bruce and Lucy re-enter the club and walk back over to the table where Jennifer and Dave are waiting for them.

"Everything okay?" asks Jennifer, concerned that the situation didn't go exactly to plan for Bruce and noticing Lucy's somewhat distant glare into space.

"Yeah we are fine" smirks Bruce, looking at Lucy for her to agree.

Lucy nods her head, smiles and joins them sitting at the table. Bruce suggests they all have one final drink before calling it a night and they all agree. Bruce and Dave go to the bar, leaving the two girls sitting in the corner.

"You okay?" Jennifer asks Lucy, knowing her mind is now somewhere else.

Lucy tells her she is fine but can't get what just happened with Bruce out of her head.

"Did Bruce explain the situation?" asks Jennifer, trying to keep her attention.

Lucy looks over to the lads heading to the bar and then back at Jennifer.

"Yeah he told me you two are married and that you were asked to test his friend Dave" Lucy says, making out she understands it all.

Jennifer is pleased and says sorry for not telling her or warning her earlier. Lucy shrugs it off and tells her she's having a good night anyway. Over at the bar Bruce is going through the same routine.

Dave tells him he understands that they were there to test out Jennifer's friend Lucy, but only wishes Bruce had told him earlier.

"I can't believe I've been flirting with your wife for the last hour or so" Dave says.

"I'm really sorry Bruce" he adds, hoping Bruce isn't upset with him.

Bruce tells him it's fine and he hoped Dave learned something about women tonight.

"Yeah they are all fucking confusing and scary" laughs Dave, taking his drink from the bar.

The guys stand at the bar talking for a few more minutes as the girls across the club watch on waiting for their drinks.

"They look like they are deep in conversation" says Lucy, desperate for another drink.

"What do you think they are talking about?" she asks Jennifer, hoping Bruce isn't telling Dave about her strange sexual dispossession and behaviour.

Jennifer feels it's the perfect time to share a little lesson with Lucy and tries to work out how to deliver it.

"What do you think guy's talk about?" asks Jennifer getting it started.

Lucy has another quick look over at the guy's and tries to work out what they are saying.

"Don't they always talk about football, drink and sex?" asks Lucy.

Jennifer tells her they do sometimes, but that's not all there is to it...

Jennifer's Lesson On What Men Talk About

No matter how much you don't want to hear it or believe it, men talk.

Yes even you the person saying "My man doesn't tell anyone anything" Yes he does !!

Think about it... If your man played football and scored a David Beckham free kick or something like that, what would he do? He would tell the world about it wouldn't he? Well sex for him is no different than football in this case. If you've done something special or you've had the sex of your life, he is going to want to share it.

Go on say it... "My man would never tell anyone about our sex life" Yes he would !!

Turns out men aren't any different from us girls when it comes to talking to their friends... Yes even when they tell you they haven't told anyone anything. The question you really need to ask yourself is, how much has he said, not has he?

There are three ways to find out just how much your man tells his friends and they are...

1- It depends how close he is with a certain friend.
2- It depends whether or not he trusts that person not to say a word about it after.
3- It depends how confident and secure your partner is himself.

If your man has a friend that is just his football buddy and nothing else. If this friend drinks and opens his mouth at the wrong time and if you have a somewhat insecure partner, chances are something will be said about your night of passion, but it will be very very vague indeed.
However, if the two boys have a special bond. If your partner knows he won't land him in it or say anything about his confessions and if your partner is a confident and secure person, then you can consider the friend knows just as much about you as your partner does himself...
Go on, you want to say it again don't you?
    "He wouldn't"
Yes he would !!
Just think about the slut you turn into when you are drunk. Just think about that blow job you gave him out in public. Just think the sex you had on the trampoline. Your partner's friend could know the lot...
Before you freak out, don't. You can't stop someone talking no matter how hard you try. Again, just see it all a different way and know which friends know little and how many know everything. The manly bond he shares with one, might see him say we had sex on the trampoline, but his insecurity will stop him talking about you personally. If he shares a special bond with one, trusts him not to speak and your partner is completely secure in himself, then you can consider that friend doesn't just know about the sex on the trampoline, but what positions you are best at, right down to you licking on that smooth bit between his balls and crack or the design of your pubic area.
It's not about fearing him talking or trying to make him stop. Talking is a way of life. It's simply not to live life any more where you believe he doesn't talk, or feel guilty because you've said something to your friends you shouldn't have.
Put it this way... If he's telling some of his friend's private things. That means he's happy and proud of the things you do together. Wouldn't it be better knowing this than him not talking about you or your sex life at all? What does him **NOT** talking say?

With the guy's still at the bar, Jennifer feels pleased that she's managed to teach Lucy something quickly tonight. Although Lucy gets it all, she is now worried that Bruce will be telling Dave about the sexual encounter outside the club.

"So what would Bruce be saying to Dave about your sex life then?" asks Lucy, wanting to find out secretly how much Dave is going to know about anything.

Jennifer tells her Bruce is obviously very confident and secure which means he will be talking. Lucy's face drops a little as she lets her eyes wander back towards them at the bar.

"But Bruce doesn't know Dave that well, so there won't be much trust yet" explains Jennifer.

"So that means he won't say much then?" asks Lucy looking a little more relaxed.

"It means because of his confidence, he will say things about experiences, but because the trust isn't there yet, it won't be personal or graphic things he tells him" explains Jennifer some more.

Lucy still doesn't know if that means he will say things about her or not and just for Jennifer's sake, makes out she gets it.

"You could just do the other thing I do to find out" laughs Jennifer, understanding just how much Lucy really does get it.

"What?" asks Lucy, hoping this will give her the answer.

"I normally ask him" says Jennifer with a smile on her face.

Jennifer explains that Bruce and her share a marriage based on trust and that they tell each-other everything anyway.

"What even if that means him telling you what he tells his friends about your sex life?" questions Lucy in a little disbelief.

"Even that" laughs Jennifer, declaring she has the perfect marriage with no secrets at all.

Lucy now knows that even if Bruce isn't telling Dave about outside, there's now a chance Bruce will tell Jennifer anyway. She starts to panic and feels the need to tell her about her sexual problem and what happened outside before Bruce does. Just as she goes to open her mouth, Bruce and Dave return to the table with the drinks and Lucy tries hard to keep a smile on her face whilst they finish their last drink desperately trying to make eye contact with Bruce, but it fails. Bruce tells Jennifer he is going to see Dave home safely and Jennifer tells him she will do the same for Lucy and she will meet him back at home. The foursome leave the club together and say their goodbyes outside. Jennifer gives Dave a hug and tells him she will see him soon. Bruce gives Lucy a hug and a kiss.

"I want to see you soon beautiful" Bruce whispers in her ear, trying to wind her up one last time.

Lucy looks at him and bites her lip unable to jump on him right there in front of his wife. They watch the guy's walk off down the road and Lucy for a few seconds forgets she wants to come clean, thinking maybe Bruce won't say anything after the little whisper. She decides to keep it to herself and is for some reason confident that Bruce won't say anything.

The guy's set off on the London underground and head towards Bruce and Jennifer's old stomping ground where Dave lives. Bruce sees him to his door and the two of them make plans to meet up again soon. Bruce heads off back towards the underground through town.

"Bruce, Bruce" he hears a voice call from down the dark and busy street near the station.

He turns round to find out who it is and is really pleased to see Karen and Amy walking towards him. Bruce feels a sense of guilt, that he or Jennifer haven't spoken to the girls since they moved away, but this soon disappears when the girls wrap their arms around him.

"What are you doing here? Are you back? Why haven't you been in touch?" ask the girls.

Bruce explains they have only just settled in across the other side of London and that they've been really busy setting up home over the last twenty-four hours.

"Can we come visit? Where's Jen? When? How? Why?" are the next questions fired at him...

Bruce quickly explains he needs to rush off to catch the last train home and that they will all catch up again really soon.

"Don't go, you can stay at mine if you want" insists Amy.

"Or you can stay at mine" flirts Karen.

"After all, I am the single one" she adds, pinching him on the bum.

Although Bruce is really pleased to see the girls, he really feels the need to go. He places both hands on Karen's face and kisses her on the lips.

"I promise, I will give you a call tomorrow" he says giving her a hug and permission to grab his bum one last time.

He then places his hands on Amy's face and kisses her on the lips too.

"And you know what you mean to me Aims" he says, giving her a hug too.

Both girls look disappointed yet pleased they've seen him all the same and are glad the couple didn't move too far away when they did their moonlight flit. They agree to let him go and both get another kiss and hug before he sets off. Bruce enters the station and manages to hop on the last tube train back home. He sits there reminiscing about the four girls they left behind and starts to wish he could move back. Just then he gets a text message from Amy telling him not to forget them...

CHAPTER 4
OUTDOOR SEX

Bruce arrives home late to find Jennifer already in bed asleep. He is really excited to tell her about meeting Amy and Karen on his journey home, but decides to wait until morning.
In the morning Jennifer is first up and runs downstairs to make her loving husband breakfast and get ready to talk over their findings from the night before. Once she has his breakfast ready out in the kitchen, she calls him down. Bruce wakes up and immediately remembers last night, all the events and is still eager to share his news with her. He makes his way downstairs, enters the kitchen and sits at the breakfast bar where he is greeted with his food and a good morning kiss from Jennifer.
    "Are you ready to have a chat then?" asks Jennifer, placing her coffee down on the bar and sitting opposite him.
Bruce decides to put the Amy and Karen news on the back burner, noticing how animated and eager she looks to go first.
    "Okay let me have it" he says, taking a bite of his toast.
    "Can Dave cut it in the pulling department or not?" he asks looking over at her.
Jennifer starts to giggle to herself and takes pleasure in making him wait a few seconds...
    "Let's just say, you have your work cut out for you" she declares with a huge smile on her face.
Bruce starts to laugh knowing what he knows about her new assignment too.
    "So he needs a little motivation in the chatting up department then,

does he? Bruce asks, smirking back across at her.

"A little help?" giggles Jennifer.

"You're going to need a crane to lift young David I'm afraid Hun" she giggles louder, then stops herself knowing it's wrong to laugh at someone's slow approach when it comes to women.

Bruce takes another bite of his toast and smirks even more.

"No problem, I can train him up" he says confidently.

Jennifer can't hold it in any-more and although she knows it's not nice to laugh, can't help it.

"I don't think you understand" she tells him, starting to laugh a lot more now.

"I could have sat on his face and he still wouldn't have picked up on it" she adds, choking a little on her coffee in the process.

Bruce doesn't respond and lets her have her moment whilst holding onto his own information. Jennifer soon recomposes herself and decides it's time to find out about Lucy.

"So is my client Lucy ready to get married then?" she asks, still smiling.

Bruce gets up without answering and heads towards the kettle to make himself another coffee.

"I've never met someone so ready to get married" he claims, facing away from her, so as not to give his joke away.

"Really? She's ready?" beams Jennifer, knowing that her job as teacher will be a lot easier.

"Really" answers Bruce, heading back to the breakfast bar still avoiding eye contact.

"In-fact, she's going to make a great wife, almost as good as you are" he adds piling it on.

Jennifer can't keep her joy in and bangs the bar in delight.

"Yes" she shouts.

"Really, as good as me?" she asks, watching him sit back down and smirk at her again.

Bruce holds his smile a little longer before cracking.

"Not a chance. If you think Dave's going to make my job hard, you wait until you really find out who Lucy is" Bruce tells her, watching her face drop completely.

"Why? What is it? What makes you think that?" asks Jennifer, not knowing what to believe now.

Bruce tells her that Lucy is one of the nicest and kindest girls he's ever met.

"What's wrong with that then?" asks Jennifer, waiting for the punch line.

Bruce drags it out as long as he can, clearly enjoying winding her up.

"She kissed me" Bruce tells her.
"Okay" responds Jennifer, waiting for him to get to the point.
"Not once, not twice, but at least seven times" he tells her.
"Okay, so she likes you. It's not the first time one of my clients have taken a shine to you, look at Karen and Amy" explains Jennifer.
Bruce finds this the best time to mention last night.
"Talking of Amy and Karen, I bumped into them last night" he says. Jennifer although wants him to tell her about Lucy is also interested about their old friends.
"Wow, how are they?" she asks showing lots of interest.
"Were they angry about us leaving during the party?" she asks.
Bruce tells her they are fine and they all send their love. He also explains that he promised they'd catch up with them soon and how he didn't have time to talk to them because of the train home. He then decides to talk about a random person sitting on the train last night sleeping, which is irrelevant to the conversation and means nothing at all.
"I will have to give Karen, Amy, Jane and Michelle a call later this afternoon" Jennifer tells him.
"Yeah make sure you do honey" he responds before getting up, thanking her for breakfast and heading upstairs for a shower.
Jennifer does a little reminiscing of her own before suddenly realising Bruce didn't finish the Lucy story. She chases after him into the bathroom where he is taking off his shorts.
"Excuse me you shit" she playfully shouts.
"You didn't tell me why you think Lucy isn't ready for marriage" she adds, whilst he sniggers to himself.
He turns to her and asks her to tell him how hot she thinks he looks.
"Stop playing games" she responds wanting him to get to the point.
He tells her to do it, as she looks his naked body up and down and decides to play along. She moves in closer, places her hand on his naked bum and gives it a squeeze.
"You've got a sexy backside" she whispers.
With that Bruce lunges at her and forces his lips against hers. She pushes him away and tells him to stop playing games again.
"I'm not, just go with it for a few seconds" he tells her, before demanding she say something nice about his penis.
She looks at it getting a little horny herself and places her hand around it.
"I love your fat penis inside me" she whispers a little flirtatiously.
Again Bruce pushes her back, this time against the sink and kisses her. Jennifer manages to keep hold of his penis and feels it starting to

grow, so kisses him back. Before she can get into it, he pulls away.

"I don't get what you are doing" claims a confused looking Jennifer.

Bruce tells her to ask for sex.

"Fuck me" whispers Jennifer, getting a little bit bored and frustrated with his game playing.

"Fuck you" snaps Bruce to Jennifer's surprise.

Bruce finally explains that everytime he gave Lucy a compliment; she lost control and lunged at him. When he said something sexual without the compliment, she shot him down and that's how it went on.

"You telling me you've only got to pay her a compliment and she becomes sexual?" asks Jennifer struggling to believe it.

"That's exactly what I am telling you" Bruce laughs, finally pointing out that Jennifer's job to fix her client and get her married is a lot harder than Bruce training Dave's chat-up skills.

"How am I going to sort this one out?" asks Jennifer, totally puzzled by Lucy's behaviour.

Bruce explains it's amazing and he could hardly believe it himself, but agrees that this one will be Jennifer's hardest challenge to date.

"Just think" laughs Bruce jumping into the shower.

"If the best man tells her how sexy she looks at the wedding, she will be all over him at the altar" he adds, now crying with laughter.

Jennifer heads back downstairs and leaves him to shower with a horrified look on her face.

"How can someone like Lucy settle down?" she mumbles to herself on the stairs.

She gets to the bottom of the stairs and enters the front room deep in thought about her new friend and quickly remembers that she was meant to meet Lucy and Rose this morning. She bangs around quickly trying to get ready as Bruce comes back downstairs wrapped in his towel after his shower.

"Where's the fire?" he asks, watching Jennifer trying to get ready quickly.

She explains she forgot about their meeting this morning and how she's going to be late if she doesn't rush.

"That's not like you to forget something like that" he says, watching her in a flap.

"Don't forget when you get there, don't say anything nice to Lucy or she will be all over you" he jokes, watching her trip over whilst jumping into her jeans.

She quickly says goodbye to him and races for the door.

"Mobile" Bruce calls picking it off the table and tossing it in her direction.

"Keys" he adds, picking them up to and doing the same.
Jennifer leaves and rushes down the road towards Lucy's school.

Over at the drama school Lucy is already waiting for Jennifer to turn up and is trying to convince moody Rose to give Jennifer a chance.
 "I don't need a do-gooder in my life thanks Luce, but I will play along with you today" grumps the ever so cheerful Rose.
Ten minutes later and a dozen more sarcastic comments from Rose about Lucy's new friendship with the so called do-gooder and Jennifer knocks on the door.
 "Sorry I am late" says an out of breath Jennifer, as Lucy answers the door.
Lucy lets her in and plays the perfect hostess, whilst Rose sits slouched on the sofa.
 "Hello Rose, thanks for being here" says Jennifer, hoping that Rose is going to give her the time of day this morning, then quickly realising she isn't with another mumble about her being a do-gooder.
 "So what are you going to teach us about today?" asks Lucy, trying to lighten the mood and drown out Rose's cold comments.
Jennifer takes a seat on the armchair opposite Rose as Lucy joins Rose on the sofa. Jennifer places her bag down on the floor and tries to think of a lesson both of the drama students will be interested in. She can't come up with anything fast, whilst Bruce's voice echo's around her head telling her about Lucy's sexual issue.
 "How about we talk about sexual control?" asks Jennifer, trying not to make direct eye contact with Lucy at this stage.
Lucy immediately feels the heat from her blushing face and starts to wriggle around. Jennifer picks up on this quickly and decides to let the girls decide what they want to know about instead. Jennifer asks them to pick any subject they want and as Lucy recomposes herself and Rose sarcastically mentions the word spanking; thinking this will be a hard one for Jennifer the do-gooder to cover.
 "Yeah spanking" mumbles Rose smiling for the first time.
 "Why do girls enjoy something that is clearly painful?" she asks, hoping to stop Jennifer in her tracks.
But like a true professional Jennifer grabs the topic by the horns and tells Rose okay.
 "Why do you think girls enjoy being spanked then?" asks Jennifer, quickly getting started.
 "You're the do-gooder, I mean teacher, you tell us" snaps Rose, clearly not impressed by Jennifer's opening question.
Jennifer tries to start a conversation about the topic and goes into

what spanking means.

"Spanking is a form of S & M" explains Jennifer.

"Boringggg" mumbles Rose, noticing Lucy give her a funny look. Jennifer tries to continue but Rose is clearly going to ruin anything she has to say.

"Do you understand the difference between sadism and masochism?" Jennifer asks them.

"Do you understand the difference between boring and bored?" Rose mumbles, before getting up, walking through the hallway and into her room.

"Where you going Rose?" calls Lucy, feeling slightly embarrassed by her friends attitude once again.

Rose doesn't answer and closes the door behind her.

"I'm really very sorry about her" Lucy says.

Jennifer tells her it's not her fault and tells her not to worry.

"Okay let's try something else" says Jennifer, making out the Rose thing isn't going to bother her.

Lucy happily agrees and waits for Jennifer to suggest another topic.

"What about outdoor sex?" asks Jennifer.

"What about it?" responds Lucy.

Jennifer asks her to think of all the places she's had sex away from her own home. Lucy sits there trying to think of all the places she's had sex outside.

"What was your favourite?" asks Jennifer.

"I think I told you the other day, it was in a public park in the dark" responds Lucy.

Just then Rose storms back down the hallway and into the kitchen area.

"How's the spanking conversation going?" Rose snaps with her attitude.

"Has she told you how spanking leaves a red mark on your bum cheeks yet?" she asks rudely, trying to interrupt the flow of their conversation once again.

"You're such a bitch" snaps Lucy without confidence.

"And F.Y.I, We aren't doing spanking any-more, we are talking about outdoor sex" she adds, watching Rose with a face of thunder walk towards her.

Rose reaches the living room area as though she's going to unleash a mouthful on Lucy for her brazen speech, but doesn't. Instead she smiles and surprisingly shows a greater interest.

"Why didn't you say that? I love outdoor sex" beams Rose, sitting back down on the sofa.

Both Jennifer and Lucy smile at her and decide to give her another chance.

"Okay" says Jennifer.

"Where have you had sex outdoors? And which was your most favourite place?" she asks in Rose's direction.

Rose takes a few seconds to think it over, as the other two wait in anticipation.

"My most favourite sex outdoors. The one that got me cumin over and over again" says Rose before pausing for a few more seconds...

"Is none of your fucking business" she laughs, standing up and heading back towards her room.

This time Jennifer is upset by the outburst and Lucy really doesn't know where to put her face.

"Shall we just carry on with it ourselves?" asks Lucy, knowing that Rose has made yet another good lesson and topic pass them by.

Jennifer forces a smile but cannot continue sitting in the tainted room.

"I tell you what. Grab your jacket" says Jennifer, standing and picking up her bag.

As Lucy does what she is told, Jennifer tells her she will carry on the topic, but this time in the outdoors itself.

"I've got an hour before I need to go and visit your sister, let's go and explore the outdoors" Jennifer says to Lucy's delight.

Both girls head out the door and start walking down the street.

After a few minutes Jennifer tells her to stop in the middle of a random street. Lucy looks up and down the road, as if to ask why have they stopped.

"See this front garden right here?" asks Jennifer, pointing to the little fenced off area of grass in front of someone's house.

Lucy nods her head.

"Could you walk down this street with your partner, feel horny enough not to reach home and do it right here?" Jennifer asks.

Lucy takes another look at the garden, then looks at the house windows to find out what kind of view the home owner would have of the sexual situation.

"You know what Jen?" says Lucy.

"I think I would. In-fact I don't think I would personally say no anywhere once I am in the right mood" she adds, trying to be really honest with her.

Jennifer gives her a smile and then goes on to tell her most people would do it anywhere once they were in the right mood.

"Yeah but there must be places some people wouldn't do it?" asks Lucy trying to follow.

"Yeah some people will say they can't do it in certain places?" responds Jennifer, starting to walk away from the front garden.

"It's like me, I would say no to having sex on an aeroplane" she adds.
"Would you? Why?" asks Lucy, looking kind of shocked.
"I would say no but put in the situation where I couldn't control myself any-more, then I probably would" Jennifer answers.
Lucy starts to look a little confused as they reach the end of the street and into the local park through the main gates. Jennifer walks Lucy over to the park bench and sits her down.

Jennifer's Lesson On Outdoor Sex

It turns out everyone has their favourite places for outdoor sex. Be it in a public place, in the garden, in a car or somewhere else. It's not a question whether you like outdoor sex, because nearly every person on the planet will experience it at least a few times in their lives... It's whether you can let go and enjoy it fully.
Do you know how many times you've had outdoor sex in your life? Better still, do you remember how many of those times you really let go, enjoyed it and had at least one orgasm?
Just think of the couple that had sex in their own garden last week...
It was just sex away from the bedroom that's all, nothing special.
Just think of the couple that did it in a field in a tent...
It was the same sex they have at home with a little more fresh air, nothing special again.
These people although have outdoor sex, aren't making the most of it.
So here's how you should feel about outdoor sex?
Take a place. Let's just say for now the car.
Ask yourself two simple questions...
1 – Would you?
2 – What wouldn't you do during the sex?
Now you should be able to understand if you are having the outdoor sex the way you should.
The trick is to ask yourself question one...
Okay yes I would do it in the car **BUT** (Wait for your own BUT)
I wouldn't get out the car. I would only park the car in a place where there's no people around. I wouldn't ever get undressed during car sex. There are your BUT'S...
Now ask question two.
Your answers should be the same. Example... I wouldn't get out the car.
I wouldn't do it whilst other people could see us and I wouldn't remove any clothes.

The things you wouldn't do are okay. It's no good doing something that's going to make you feel uncomfortable after all. BUT, Push yourself in that direction. Try and get as close to those uncomfortable situations as you can. Instead of not wanting to be seen and blocking all the windows up and then staying fully dressed, push yourself a little.

Okay, don't get out of the car, but open all the windows instead.

Okay do it in the dark place with no-one around, but have the lights on when you do it.

Okay don't get naked, but try wearing a few less clothes before you start.

The benefits to outdoor sex and the benefits to your orgasm rest entirely on these little pushes you make. Anyone can have outdoor sex and nearly everyone will try... But are you pushing?

Are you enjoying it?

Are you a true outdoor sex person?

Do you like doing it outdoors in a tent?

Make that little push and don't zip the tent right up.

Like it in a shop changing room?

Leave the door slightly open which heightens the risk of getting caught.

Like to have sex in your garden?

Light up your garden by leaving a house light on.

Like sex on the beach in the dark?

Try it in the ocean during the day.

It's not about finding as many places as you can and ticking them off your list saying "Done that" or " Been there" You haven't done it or been there if you didn't push yourself.

Would you ever have sex on a public train?

No?

That's okay. Then make that little push and let him finger or play with you on the train instead. It's better than being an outdoor prude or nothing at all?

After Jennifer explains how to have outdoor sex to Lucy fully, she feels a little dejected.

"I don't think I've ever pushed whilst doing it outdoors" Lucy mumbles.

"And that's why you only have an orgasm outdoors one in every ten times you do it" responds Jennifer making her point.

"So do you push and have an orgasm every time then?" asks Lucy.

"An Orgasm?" smiles Jennifer.

"Only one each-time?" she asks, as though Lucy has said

something wrong.

Jennifer and Lucy decide the lesson on outdoor sex is over and walk away from the park bench towards Tina's house. Just then as Lucy goes through the whole subject in her head one final time, she stumbles on something that she just needs to ask.

"Is my biggest fantasy classed as outdoor sex?" she asks Jennifer.

"What is your biggest fantasy Lucy?" responds Jennifer.

Lucy tells her it's about her sitting in drama class and her partner giving her oral sex under the desk without anyone finding out.

"It's not at home, so yes it is classed as outdoor sex" explains Jennifer enjoying the idea too.

"But how can that ever happen and how do I push then?" asks Lucy.

They continue walking whilst Jennifer tries to find an answer for her. She explains that because of where it is, it would be highly risky.

"Are you telling me not to do it now then?" asks Lucy, looking a little disappointed.

"No" snaps Jennifer.

"You should respect the law fully but then find ways to bend those rules slightly" she adds.

Lucy doesn't understand and looks even more confused. Jennifer asks her what are the chances of them ever doing it or getting away with it.

"Pretty much none" Lucy sighs.

"Then you need to do the next best thing and improvise" explains Jennifer smiling.

"If you can't bring him to your desk. Bring your desk to him" she adds.

She tells Lucy to set up a make-shift school desk in her bedroom. Lucy doesn't look that enthusiastic about the idea.

"Then next time you are in class with the urge or temptation, masturbate without getting caught" Jennifer tells her.

"Okay" says Lucy listening, knowing she can let her hands wander a little in class and not get found out.

Jennifer tells her to go home, play out the school fantasy with him and then whilst he is down under the make-shift desk, tell him what you did in class.

"Ooh I like this idea now" Lucy groans a little.

"Saying that, use your mobile and record it or take pictures. That's better than words isn't it?" Jennifer says, getting into the fantasy herself.

Lucy can't wait to try this new idea out as Jennifer tells her never to let an urge, naughty thought or fantasy ever beat her.

Lucy feels so excited by this new idea, that it makes her horny and she finds herself with an uncontrollable desire to go and pay her future husband an unexpected visit at the supermarket where he is currently doing a nine hour shift. Lucy makes sure Jennifer knows where she is going and points her in the right direction to Tina's house. The girl's part ways with a hug and Lucy asks Jennifer to call her later and tell her how she got on with her sister. Jennifer heads off to Tina's house confident she will find it and pleased that at least Lucy has another worthwhile lesson under her belt.

Some twenty minutes later and after walking down a least one wrong street on the way, Jennifer finally arrives at the front door where Tina should answer. She knocks on the door and waits for her to open it, but Tina doesn't appear to be home. Jennifer quickly remembers the front door keys in her bag. She knocks again and listens carefully for any movement or noise inside, but there's nothing. She considers using the key but still doesn't want to. She quickly takes out her mobile phone and calls Lucy quickly to tell her Tina is not home. Like Jennifer expects, Lucy tells her to use the front door key and let herself in.

"She won't be long wherever she's gone" says Lucy's voice down the phone.

"Just let yourself in and make yourself a coffee" she adds, before saying goodbye and hanging up.

Jennifer takes the key out of her bag and puts it to the lock. The door opens and the house looks undisturbed. She closes the door behind her and slowly walks through the hallway. She comes to the first door and opens it. She walks into what looks to be the living room and has a quick look around. Just then her eye catches Tina lying on the sofa in a short black skirt, with her hand tucked down the top of it masturbating, whilst listening to an MP3 with her eyes closed.

Jennifer starts to panic and realises she can't be found standing there watching her. She has another quick look to confirm she is masturbating and heads straight out the door, closing it and stands in the hallway to think... Jennifer is faced with three options. She could just leave and tell Lucy that she didn't turn up. She could continue banging on the front door until Tina finishes and answers, or she could go back in and tap her on the shoulder. She considers the three options for quite some time and then works out that the first and second options wouldn't work. She couldn't tell Lucy she wasn't in, because Tina would say she was and she couldn't go and bang on the door, because Lucy told her to use the key. She places her hand back on the handle and carefully creeps back into the living room. Although she feels a little uncomfortable, she is happy at least that this young girl stayed fully dressed before deciding to masturbate. Jennifer walks up and stands beside her, hoping the shock won't make Tina scream. Things turn from bad to worse as Jennifer struggles to deal with the situation and Tina starts to fully let go and get into what she is doing. Before it can get any worse, Jennifer reaches out her hand and taps the youngster lightly on the shoulder.

"Oh my god" squeals Tina, taking her hand from the top of her skirt and removing her headphones with the other.

"Jennifer, I'm sorry I forgot what time you were arriving" she adds, sitting up whilst trying to compose herself.
Jennifer tells her it's okay.

"I can come back in twenty minutes or so if you want to finish off?" says Jennifer, trying hard not to look embarrassed herself.

"No it's okay, I am awake now" claims Tina, trying hard to convince her that she was sleeping, not masturbating.
Jennifer really wants to assure her it's okay to masturbate, but in order to do that, she knows she would have to teach her about honesty and masturbation first and doesn't want to avoid the job she's been sent there to do by Lucy.
Jennifer decides to give her a few minutes to compose herself fully and "Wake up". Then she sits down beside her and tells Tina she will come straight to the point. Tina sits up a little more and gets comfy in her seat.

"Question one Tina. Are you a virgin?" Jennifer asks, doing exactly what she said she would do.
Tina nods her head looking a little worried.

"Have you ever let a guy touch you in anyway?" Jennifer asks next, keeping it brief and to the point.
Tina this time gets a little flustered and doesn't know exactly what she means.

"I've had my boobs touched up a few times" Tina admits, hoping that's the correct answer.
Jennifer just smiles at Tina's truthfulness.

"I mean has a guy ever touched you sexually, like down below?" Jennifer asks, nodding her head towards Tina's short skirt.

"No, no never" Tina shrieks.

"Good, that's good" says Jennifer, reassuring her she's doing well, then moving onto the next question.

"Have you ever touched or seen a penis?" Jennifer asks.
Tina goes a little shy before answering the question, then smiles and nods her head to say yes.

"Which one? Seen one or touched one?" Jennifer asks, pushing for more information from Tina.

"Both" admits Tina, starting to feel this isn't a grilling but more of a grown up chat between two women.

"What have you done with a penis?" Jennifer asks.

"Touched it" Tina answers.

Jennifer knows with this answer, there's only been one guy involved in her life so far, but doesn't believe that's all she's done.

"Have you seen a guy cum before?" Jennifer asks.

Tina nods to say yes, biting on her bottom lip.

"Masturbated one? Watched a guy masturbate? Sucked one?" Jennifer extends the question.

"Played with it until he cum" answers Tina openly.

Jennifer is now confident and sure that Tina is sexually active, but still remains a virgin. She prepares for her final question.

"Do you think you are ready to have sex?" Jennifer asks her.

Tina doesn't take any time at all to answer the question and tells her she is ready.

"Are you sure?" responds Jennifer.

Tina explains how most of her friends have already had sex and that she knows her partner wants to do it with her.

"Yeah but do you know what you are doing?" asks Jennifer.

This seems to be the first question that offends Tina and she feels like she's being talked to like a child.

"I know how to have sex you know. They taught us that in second year at school" snaps the teenager, trying to show Jennifer she isn't a child any-more

Jennifer understands Tina's response but knows there is more to sex than just doing it.

"I'm sure you know how to open your legs and know where his thing goes and all that Tina, but do you know what you should be doing?" asks Jennifer.

Tina looks a little confused now.

"Yeah I am supposed to lie there and let him" she answers.

Jennifer stands up and walks across the room, whilst trying to think of what to say next. Tina's eyes follow her across the room and Jennifer knows Tina is losing interest now.

"Tina, have you ever had a real orgasm?" asks Jennifer, turning to face her.

Tina knows she masturbates but doesn't know what a real orgasm is meant to feel like, so shrugs her shoulders.

"Do you know if you like sex gentle or rough?" asks Jennifer, finally feeling she's getting somewhere.

Once again Tina cannot answer and shrugs her shoulders again.
Jennifer tells her she's been honest and thanks her for the chat. She then tells her she's going to pop round first thing in the morning to give her something.

"What is it?" asks Tina, who loves presents.
Jennifer doesn't tell her and makes sure this time, she will be up in the morning, not sleeping or got her headphones in. Tina agrees and Jennifer leaves things there.

Meanwhile over at the local supermarket, Lucy has been waiting in the staff canteen for her partner to get his break. She sits at a long table drinking a coke, when he walks in and smiles at her.

"What are you doing here on your day off?" he asks her, walking over to the table.
For a second Lucy doesn't remember why she's there. In-fact she's been sitting waiting for so long, that all the naughty thoughts have escaped her mind completely. She stands up, smiles and walks towards him. She wraps her arms around her man and gives him a kiss.

"Can't your loving partner come and tell you she's missing you any time she wants?" she asks, trying to cover up her real reason for the visit.
Out of the blue she then contemplates how well she really knows him and if they are ready to get married. She wraps her arms around him again.

"Tell me something really naughty about yourself baby" she says, looking straight into his eyes.
He is somewhat shocked by the inappropriate question in the staff canteen and looks back into her eyes, as if to ask her to repeat the question.

"When was the last time you played with your cock?" she asks him.
He doesn't understand and starts to feel uncomfortable.

"Can't we do this when I get home later?" he mumbles, trying to back away from her.
She quickly tells him she isn't angry or upset and just wants to know. She pulls herself back towards him.

"So, when was the last time you cum without me there?" she asks, starting to flirt a little more.

"No, I am not doing this at work" he moodily snaps.

"What's got into you?" he asks, removing her hands and backing away from her.

She looks into his eyes again, still trying to show she just wants to find a little honesty.

"Tell me something sexual that I don't know about you" she kindly demands.

"Don't you have an urge to fuck me on this table right now? I just want to know what's going on inside your head" she adds, trying to guide him towards the table.

"What's going on in my head? What's going on in yours?" he snaps again.

With that he backs away completely and tells her he will see her back at home later.

Across town Jennifer is walking away from Tina's house and decides it's a good time to say hello to her old friend Amy and have a quick catch up. She takes her mobile from her bag and dials her number. Amy is overjoyed when she hears Jennifer's voice say hello and just like she did when she met Bruce the other night, goes into overdrive.

"Jen, how are things? Are you coming to see me? When can we all come over and see your new place? Amy rattles off down the phone at speed.

It takes Jennifer a few minutes to calm her down before they are having a proper conversation. Jennifer tells her that they've only just got settled into their new home and that she has a few new clients she's trying to get to know.

"Oh that's not fair, I want to be your client again" moans Amy.

Jennifer then asks how all the other girls are doing.

"How's Michelle, Jane and Karen? How's Karen doing with the pregnancy? How are you and Dean getting on? Still fucking each-others brains out?" asks Jennifer.

Amy tells her that she hasn't really heard from Jane or Michelle since the party, but know they are both well and that her and Dean are fine.

"You don't sound it" says Jennifer, picking up on her tone.

Amy shrugs it off and just tells her that their sex life is still struggling without her help.

"It was great when you were here telling me what to do, but now you've left, it's just keeps going downhill" admits Amy, secretly hoping Jennifer will agree to pack up and move back across London.

"Although we've only been gone for thirty or so hours, it sounds like you need another lesson?" says Jennifer.

"I thought you were finished with us now?" asks a confused but delighted Amy.

Jennifer explains just because she's got new clients, it doesn't mean

that she's completely walked away from her old ones.
Amy goes into overdrive once more.

"When? Today? Tonight? Where?" she screams down the phone.
Jennifer tells her she will get something sorted very soon and let her know. She then asks about Karen and the pregnancy again.

"I hope you and Dean are looking after Karen for us" says Jennifer.

Amy tells her that it's only starting to sink in for Karen now but she will be there for her no matter what.

"But" asks Jennifer, knowing there's one coming.

"I am just a little worried about her" admits Amy.

She explains that Karen stayed over at her house after the party and had a nightmare when she was asleep.

"She was talking in her sleep about Tony being after her" Amy explains.

"Tony?" questions Jennifer.

"Yeah Tony, the guy we all set-up in the lap dancing club" Amy tells her.

Jennifer tells her she knows who Tony is and also says that she will talk to Karen about it and find out if anything is wrong. Jennifer then has to cut the conversation short.

"Sorry Aims I've got to go, someone else is trying to call me" says Jennifer.

Jennifer hangs up on Amy and answers her phone to Lucy. Lucy just wants to know how she got on with her sister Tina and Jennifer tells her that she needs to visit her again in the morning to find out anything for sure. Lucy then asks if Bruce would help out at Tina's sixteenth birthday party tomorrow evening and be the doorman. Jennifer tells her that it shouldn't be a problem and that she will ask Bruce when she gets home. Jennifer thinks the conversation is over but Lucy clearly wants to say something else.

"I need to talk to you about something that happened the other night" says Lucy, secretly starting to feel their friendship grow and the guilt about her and Bruce grow with it.

Jennifer asks her what it is but Lucy gets her knickers in a twist.

"It's not Bruce's fault, it's mine. But it wasn't really mine either" Lucy stutters all over the place down the phone.

Jennifer works out what she is trying to say, but wants Lucy to be honest with her, so doesn't put the words in her mouth.

Lucy continues to struggle to get it out over the phone and twists even more words into a jumbled up mess. Jennifer tells her they can have a chat about it tomorrow before Tina's birthday, but reassures her she can tell her anything.

CHAPTER 5
DADDY ISSUES

It's the next morning and Lucy and her partner are waking up in her little room at the school. He wasn't able to ask about her behaviour as Rose was around all last night, so decides this is the time to ask her what it was all about yesterday at work. He sits up in bed, as her eyes open and looks across at him.

"Morning baby" she grumbles, clearing her voice and smiling.

"Hey you" he responds, looking down at her head on the pillow.

He makes himself comfortable and gives her a few seconds to wake up fully before opening his mouth.

"So what was all that about yesterday at work Luce?" he asks, waiting for her to sit up and respond to the question.

She gets embarrassed and covers her head with the pillow.

"Is there something you want to tell me?" he asks, now waiting for her to take the pillow off her face.

"No there's no problem at all" she answers quickly, taking the pillow away, sitting up to stop him worrying.

She explains she really wants to marry him but needs to know that they are both ready first.

"Are you getting cold feet?" he questions with concern, putting two and two together.

"Because if you are, you just need to say" he adds, starting to worry even more.

She places her hand on his arm and explains again that it's nothing to worry about.

"I just want to make sure we are both ready" she explains.

"I want to be able to read your mind and you get inside my head too" she adds.
Finally he gets it and shrugs it off.
"Is that all you are worrying yourself about?" he sighs.
"We are fine Luce, we know each-other well enough" he adds smiling at her.
Lucy doesn't feel the same way and gets out of bed, wrapping a sheet around herself.
"I don't think we know each-other well enough" she tells him, with a worried look on her face.
"What are you saying then? Do you want to call it all off?" he asks, getting a little upset.
Lucy sits back down facing him on the edge of the bed and explains she doesn't want to call it off or delay the wedding at all. She goes on to explain she just wants them both to understand each-other fully.
"Do you think I would ever have a threesome with you and another female?" she asks him.
He feels a little uncomfortable by a topic that clearly turns him on but it's never been mentioned before.
"I don't know" he answers.
"Would you?" he asks, waiting for her answer first.
She looks down at the bed and then back at him.
"Yes I would" she answers, before explaining it's one of many things they don't know about each-other.
He finally understands the point she is trying to make and suggests they play an honest answer game right there and then to put it right.
"Okay" says Lucy ready to jump into it.
"Do you fancy a certain celebrity and who is she?" she asks, waiting for his answer again.
He feels a little uncomfortable yet again and rattles off something about only having eyes for her. She stands up, drops her sheet to the floor and reveals her naked body as she starts to put on her knickers.
"See you say that, but I don't believe it fully" she tells him, continuing to get dressed.
"What the fuck do you mean, you don't believe it fully?" he snaps, sitting there getting a little angry.
"Okay if you are so perfect, admit you fancy someone else" he grumbles, getting defensive.
She slips her shirt over her head and looks at him.
"Yeah I do" she admits with ease.
His face turns to thunder and he feels the jealousy build inside him.
"Who?" he yells.
"Who the fuck do you fancy?" he asks, getting animated sitting

there taking a tight grip of the pillow next to him.
Lucy doesn't react to his change of mood and continues to get dressed slipping into a pair of jeans.
"That's my point baby, you should know these things about me before we get married" she tells him.
With that she puts her shoes on and heads for the bedroom door.
"Where are you going?" he asks, backing down from his angry mood.
"To find out who I really am, so I can tell you" she says, opening the door.
"I suggest you do the same and bring some honesty back for me later too" she adds.
He jumps up from the bed in his boxer shorts and grabs his work uniform from the floor.
"Let's do it now, let's do it now" he calls after her, as she walks down the hallway and stops.
"Would you like to watch me fuck another guy?" she asks him, as he gets dressed.
"Fuck no" he snaps, giving her a dirty look.
"Yeah but do I or will I need that in my life at some point?" she asks.
"Will you?" he snaps again with another dirty look.
She walks back into the room, across to him and kisses him on the cheek.
"That's what we need to discover, find out and share together before we get married" she whispers.
"Luce" he calls.
"Lucy" he shouts, as she heads out the door and closes it.

As Lucy walks away from campus, Jennifer is just arriving at her sister's house for the second morning in a row. Jennifer knocks on the front door, hoping Tina will answer straight away today. In less than a minute the door is opened and there stands young Tina in her white fluffy dressing gown, looking like she's just got out of bed especially to answer the door.
"What did you bring me? What did you bring me?" Tina yelps like an excited child at Christmas, before Jennifer has a chance to set foot inside the door.
"If you don't mind Tina, I want to wait for your big sister to get here first" says Jennifer, enjoying her enthusiastic mood but trying to calm her down a little.
Tina's face drops and she looks disappointed.

"Why is she coming here?" Tina asks, feeling she's being treated like a child again.

"I am old enough to do this kind of thing without Lucy here, you know" she adds.

Jennifer quickly tells her it's nothing about letting her gate crash their chat.

"I just think Lucy can learn something from this lesson too" Jennifer tells her.

"Happy birthday by the way" she adds, trying to put a smile back on her face.

Tina tightly fastens her dressing gown and sits with her feet up, snuggled into a ball shape on the sofa. Jennifer doesn't think she's being rude and asks Tina if she could make herself a coffee.

"I will do that for you" insists Tina, smiling in Jennifer's direction.

Jennifer tells her it's okay and that she will do it. She offers Tina one too, which is politely refused.

A few moments later, whilst Jennifer waits for the kettle to boil, she checks to make sure Tina is okay. Tina is sitting there still wrapped in a little ball looking like she's going back to sleep. Jennifer decides it's time to get her going again and calls through to her from the kitchen.

"Yeah" Tina call out, lifting her head.

"Have you got any toys? You know toys to play with" calls Jennifer from the kitchen.

Tina knows what she's talking about straight away, but wants to make sure.

"Do you mean a vibrator?" Tina calls back.

Jennifer walks back in with her coffee and nods her head. She places her cup on the table and waits for Tina to answer.

"No I haven't got any yet. They are a little hard to buy before you are eighteen" Tina explains.

Jennifer quickly asks Tina where the bathroom is and tells her to have a look in her bag and choose one or two toys whilst she's using the toilet.

"Choose?" asks Tina, taking her feet off the sofa and watching Jennifer leave the room.

Tina stands up looking really intrigued, then looks over at Jennifer's huge handbag and walks over to it. She picks it up, takes it back across to the sofa and sits down with it. She opens it up to find five or six boxed sex toys. She wonders if that's what Jennifer meant by choose one and then comes to the conclusion that it must be. Tina takes the boxes out of her bag and places them on the sofa beside her. She takes a good look at all the toys, but wouldn't be able to pick a favourite even if she wanted to. Jennifer walks back into the room and is pleased that Tina is looking at them. Before she can say anything, there's a knock at the door. Tina panics and picks two of the boxes up and throws them back into Jennifer's bag.

"It's only your sister, don't panic" Jennifer tells her.

Tina can't hide her embarrassment and the thought she is doing something wrong by looking at them unsettles her. Jennifer tells her she will answer the door and to leave the toys where they are on the sofa. Tina takes the two boxes back out of the bag, as Jennifer answers the door. Seconds later Jennifer walks back in, followed by Lucy.

"What's going on here?" says Lucy, a little shocked to see sex toys on the sofa.

Whilst Lucy wishes her little sister a happy birthday, Jennifer tells her that she's letting Tina pick one or two toys for herself to try out. Lucy looks a little concerned that Jennifer might be pushing her sister far too quickly.

"At what age can Tina have sex Lucy?" asks Jennifer.

Lucy looks at Jennifer sitting next to Tina, the toys and tells her she's old enough now.

"Don't you think the law is a little messed up if she can have sex now with a real penis, but can't buy or use a toy for another two years?" Jennifer asks.

Lucy is stunned by something she's never really thought about before.

"That is so weird" utters Lucy, trying to get her head around it.

Jennifer says it again and tells her, porn is pretty much the same thing.

"You can suck a penis, sit on one at sixteen, but you can't watch porn until you are eighteen" Jennifer explains.

Jennifer's Lesson In Losing Your Virginity

Think about the first time you got drunk, how did you feel?

Did you have loads of questions to ask the morning after?

Questions like... Should you feel dizzy? Should you have this major headache? Should you have lost control like that when drunk?

How did you learn that all of these feelings were a normal process of drinking? We compared drinking notes with all our friends didn't we? That's how we learn in life !!

Those friends that are putting pressure on you to lose your virginity because they have already. Why are they doing it? It's not because they are bullying you, it's not because they feel like more of a woman and it's not because they are boasting. It's simply the same set-up as the drink explained before... Your friends may have lost their virginity before you, but whilst you sit there getting pressured by them now, they are simply waiting for you to share your stories with them too. That friend has loads of questions going around in her head and there's no-one she can talk to about them. Just think... Was it meant to hurt? Was that it? Did I need to do anything else other than lie there? How long should it have lasted? What part should I have enjoyed most? Did I have an orgasm? What does an orgasm feel like?

All these questions are hammering your friends head. She will not give up until you pop your cherry too and share your feelings.

Sex education at school just tells you where everything goes and how babies are made... That's even if everyone in the class is listening or paying attention over the giggles and boys acting immature.

Just imagine if during sex education, sixteen year old girls were given a vibrator and told to go and explore themselves and their own bodies first, before giving it to a random guy.

Just imagine if these girls could watch porn and understand it fully, before giving their virginity away.

What If girls were told to experiment first, find out what they like about sexual activity and know what an orgasm feels like before having sex? Surely this would stop girls rushing in or reduce the scale of teenage pregnancy.

Hey answer it for yourself... Was your first time, the best sex you've ever had? Did you know what you were doing? Do you remember having an orgasm? Then would you have rushed in if your school handed you a vibrator and told you to discover yourself and your orgasm first before having sex?

We might not be able to turn back time and change our first sexual experience, but we can spread the word and let the sixteen year old girls out there, not make the same mistakes everyone else makes.

Put it this way... Hand her some sexual information about the orgasm and a sex toy or hand her a pregnancy book, a sexual regret and a pack of nappies. Girls need to be told to explore more and understand it all fully before jumping in... Better sex, better first time and no mistakes !!

Tina sits there in total amazement after Jennifer's lesson on Virginity and feels great understanding why her own friends have been putting pressure on her to have sex. Lucy is stunned but makes sense of everything Jennifer has just said.

"So why don't the government have this opinion too, if they want to reduce teenage pregnancy?" asks Lucy.
Jennifer shrugs her shoulders and smiles.
"Politics is all about popularity" Jennifer tells her.
"Yeah but I've heard a politician tell young girls not to rush in or be pressured before having sex" claims Lucy.
Jennifer starts to giggle.
"Yeah me too" she responds.
"But they don't tell you to pick up a rampant rabbit and learn to orgasm first do they?" she adds.
Both the girls try to hold back their laughter as Tina watches on, still secretly pondering on the toys laid out in front of her. Jennifer turns to Lucy to ask if she can offer Tina a toy and Lucy smiles, nodding her head. Jennifer then turns to Tina and asks her which one she likes.
"I don't know, I don't know what they all do" responds Tina, trying to make up her mind.
"It's about going away with one and finding out sis" says Lucy, giving her verbal permission to pick one out.
Lucy picks up a little pink rampant rabbit and tries to explain what you do with it, without embarrassing her sister or herself in the process.
"This rotating bit goes inside. These ears press against your bud. And here's how you turn it on" explains Lucy, pointing it all out through the unopened box.
Tina quickly picks up another one that's much bigger and asks what it does. Jennifer stands back allowing Lucy to do what she was brought round to do.
"This one is just a vibrator. To turn it on, you just twist the button" Lucy tells her.
"And this one?" asks Tina, picking up another just as fast.
Lucy takes the box from her and looks at it.
"That's a dildo. It doesn't vibrate. It's just feels real inside you" Lucy explains.
Tina still doesn't know which one to pick and sits there looking at all six boxes again. She looks up to her sister.
"Which one would you pick?" she asks Lucy.
Before Lucy can answer, Jennifer steps in from the background and tells Tina she needs to pick for herself. Even Lucy looks a little confused by this comment. Jennifer explains Lucy's opinion and taste will be different to that of Tina's. Because she's had sex and because she knows what an orgasm feels like, what Lucy picks out, may not be best for Tina to try. Both girls understand but this just sends Tina back into her uncertainty.
"What I will do is leave them all with you" says Jennifer, knowing

they aren't getting anywhere fast.

"You can't do that" insists Lucy.

"This little lot must be worth over a hundred quid" she adds.

Jennifer tells her it's a small price to pay, instead of the big price Tina could pay if she rushes to lose her virginity. Lucy cannot argue and instead shows her gratitude with a simple smile. Tina starts to pick up all the boxes to take up to her room saying thank you.

"So all I need to do is try them all out" asks Tina, picking up the final box.

"Try them, enjoy them, find out what an orgasm feels like before you have sex" says Jennifer, reminding her of the lesson.

"But what if my boyfriend comes over tonight and wants to have sex?" asks Tina.

"Are you ready to have sex Tina?" asks Jennifer.

Tina looks at all the boxes in her arms and back at Jennifer.

"I'm not sure" she answers.

"Do you know what an orgasm feels like?" asks Jennifer.

"Do you know how fast, hard or slow you want the sex to be?" she asks.

Tina stands there taking in the questions and shakes her head.

"Your new friends, after a few days will tell you all you need to know" says Jennifer, referring to the toys.

Tina smiles and takes her new friends to her room to hide in her drawers. Lucy sits down with Jennifer and thanks her again for doing this for her sister.

"My pleasure" insists Jennifer.

"And by the way, in answer to your question the other day. No your sister isn't ready to have sex just yet, but hopefully she will be ready once she explores herself with those toys for a few days" she adds.

Lucy thanks her again and Jennifer quickly works out that Lucy has something else on her mind before Tina returns from her bedroom.

"Is everything okay?" Jennifer asks, giving Lucy the freedom to speak and open up.

Lucy tells her she needs to tell her something that happened involving Bruce the other day.

"Don't worry about it. I know" says Jennifer, with a friendly smile.

"But, I, I don't understand" stutters Lucy.

Jennifer pats her on the knee and takes hold of her hand.

"Bruce told me everything" Jennifer tells her.

Lucy doesn't know if she should feel embarrassed or relieved.

"And you are okay with it?" Lucy whispers, hoping Bruce has told her the complete truth.

Jennifer explains nearly every client she introduces Bruce to normally has some level of crush on him.

"Yeah but it isn't just a crush thing" admits Lucy.

"Things happened that night" she adds again, hoping Bruce has told her everything once more.

Jennifer tells her again it's okay and furthermore, she trusts her husband Bruce.

"And what about me?" asks Lucy.

"You're not going to be able to trust me now, are you?" she asks.

Jennifer smiles at her and squeezes her hand tightly.

"It's not your fault you cannot control your sexual urges babes" Jennifer tells her.

"And you've just told me the truth" she adds, putting an end to any doubts Lucy has.

Jennifer decides it's time to change the subject and asks her about the situation between her and her future husband.

"Have you worked out if you know each-other well enough to get married yet?" asks Jennifer.

Lucy tells her that she has spoken to him about it, but now believes they have a lot of work to do before they get married.

"How do I do it all quickly? What questions should I be asking?" asks Lucy.

Jennifer knows just how to help her and the questions she needs to ask, but decides to create an opportunity out of the situation.

"Why don't we head back to your place and go over it?" suggests Jennifer.

"I would love to get to know Rose a bit more in the process" she adds.

Lucy thinks it's a wonderful idea but doesn't understand her desire to help her room-mate, knowing Rose has been nothing but a bitch so far.

"Are you sure you want Rose there? She's not exactly been nice to you" Lucy claims.

Jennifer is adamant she wants Rose there too.

"Everyone deserves a chance to show their true colours" Jennifer tells her, as Tina walks back into the room.

Lucy stands up, smiles at her sister and tells them she is just going to make a phone call.

Tina sits back down beside Jennifer but doesn't know what to say. Jennifer explains they are going to leave her to it and that she must start exploring her own sexuality before she does anything else with a guy. Tina agrees by smiling and is secretly itching for them to leave, so she can head to her bedroom and open all her new toys. Lucy comes back into the room and tells Jennifer that Rose has agreed to

be there and is waiting for them now.
Jennifer and Lucy say a quick goodbye to Tina and set off. The minute the front door is closed, Tina dashes back upstairs towards her bedroom.

Soon enough the girls arrive at Lucy's and Rose's digs to find her in a better mood waiting for them. Noticing her unusual chirpy manner, Jennifer wastes no time and gets straight down to business. Jennifer tells Rose she doesn't think Lucy is ready just yet to get married and that Lucy agrees.
"Finally" smiles Rose.
"Maybe you aren't as bad as I thought you were Jenny" she adds.
It's not much of a compliment but Jennifer knows she must take what's offered from a girl like Rose and that's the nicest words she's spoken to her since they met.
Lucy walks over from taking her jacket off and sits with the two girls.
"So you've seen sense then have you Luce?" asks Rose.
"You're not going to marry that loser after all" she adds, with a little pleasure in her voice.
Lucy didn't hear what had already been said and looks a little bit confused.
"No, I am still marrying him Rose" Lucy confirms.
"I just need to sort a few things out first" she adds.
Rose's face turns to a face of thunder. She gets up, tells her she's stupid and storms out slamming the door behind her. A dumbfounded Lucy hasn't got words to say and Jennifer is left disappointed yet again. Jennifer decides it's time to call in Bruce and get him round. She tells Lucy what she's doing whilst summoning him over by text.
"Bruce's coming here?" yelps Lucy, panicking and forgetting that it's his wife sitting right next to her.
Jennifer spends the next ten minutes telling Lucy that she thinks Rose has a major problem.
"Yeah an attitude problem" snaps Lucy, really very disappointed with her friend.
Jennifer tells her not to be like that and she thinks her problems are a lot deeper than she's letting on herself. Minutes later there's a knock at the front door.
"That will be Bruce" says Jennifer.
"Would you like me to answer it or can you handle it?" she asks, laughing and smiling at Lucy's blushes.
Lucy gets up to show it doesn't bother her and walks across to the door and opens it.

"Hello Lucy, how are you?" asks Bruce standing there.
Lucy can't hide her bashfulness and turns all shy.
"I'm fine, come in" she stutters nervously, opening the door wider.
Bruce walks in and can't help but wind her up as he notices his wife across the other side of the room.
"I would tell you how beautiful you look Lucy, but I'm not sure how you will take it" he whispers loud enough for Jennifer to hear too.
Lucy doesn't know where to put her face, as she closes the door behind him.
"Stop teasing her, you mean sod" Jennifer calls out, laughing along with the awkward situation.
Bruce sits down allowing Lucy to recompose herself and letting Jennifer explain her concerns for Rose. Bruce doesn't quite know what his wife is asking him to do but decides to listen anyway.
"Sounds like she as a lot on her mind" says Bruce.
"Do we know anything about her parents or her partner?" he asks.
Jennifer tells him about her attention seeking father and that her boyfriend isn't very nice either. She then goes on to tell him she hasn't met either of them yet, but Lucy has managed to bed her current boyfriend.
"Does she know?" asks Bruce.
"No" replies Lucy and Jennifer simultaneously.
Bruce has a think about the whole situation for a few minutes...
"Did her boyfriend by any chance take advantage of your little sexual issue Lucy?" he asks.
Lucy again starts to blush, followed by a quick nod of the head. Bruce clearly works out what kind of person he is but doesn't know what Rose's problem is.
"Do you think it's something to do with the boyfriend?" Jennifer asks Bruce.
Bruce tells her it could be, but would start with the father to eliminate him first. Just as Lucy goes to say something and ask them not to land her in it, Rose walks back through the door.
"Still planning the waste of time wedding girls?" Rose laughs, closing the door behind her.
"Helloooo" she adds, looking over and making eye contact with Bruce for the first time.
Rose undertakes a personality transformation and becomes a really nice person. She walks over to sit with them with a smile on her face. She can't take her eyes off Bruce the whole time and just sits there checking him out.
"So is anyone going to tell me who this gorgeous man is then?" Rose asks, keeping full eye contact with him.

As Lucy and Jennifer both open their mouths to make the introduction, Bruce stands up and holds out his hand.

"I am Bruce. A friend of Jennifer and Lucy's" he tells her.

Rose shakes his hand and immediately starts flirting with him. Lucy however doesn't get it, as Bruce makes out he's not married to Jennifer at all.

"So what are we talking about then?" asks Rose, still giving Bruce the eye as though the two girls aren't even in the room.

"I will come straight to the point and get down to business Rose" says Bruce taking over completely.

"Ooooh down to business before offering me a drink. I like that idea" flirts Rose in response.

Bruce takes the comment on the chin and carries on.

"I am here to talk about your father and the problems you have with him" he tells her.

Rose's face drops and she stands up to storm out yet again, but this time Bruce grabs her by the wrist and stops her from leaving. She spins round to face him.

"What the fuck are you doing?" she shouts.

"Get the fuck off me" she adds, pulling her hand away from his.

Bruce keeps a tight hold and tells her he's here to help and listen.

"Listen? Listen to this you fucking shit head" she yells.

Bruce still doesn't let her go and she starts to shout abuse at the two girls sitting on the sofa.

"Why are you watching him hurt me? Get him the fuck off me" she yells again.

Bruce tells her again he's there to listen and help. He begs her to give him just one minute. After Rose tries to unsuccessfully pull away again, she grudgingly agrees and sits on the sofa.

"You have sixty seconds, then I want you and the do-gooder out of here" Rose demands.

Bruce kneels down in front of her and thanks her for giving him a chance to help her. Rose finally calms down and secretly hopes this new guy can help her after all.

"Tell me why you are so scared of your father Rose" demands Bruce.

"I'm not" she snaps, clearly covering something up.

"Yes you are and that's another minute you owe me for not telling the truth" Bruce replies.

After the same question going backwards and forwards a few times and Rose racking up a good ten minutes in honesty time, she snaps again.

"I fucking told you I haven't got a problem with my dad, so leave me alone" she shouts.

"LIAR" Snaps Bruce, with a tremendous roar to the shock of all three girls.

"Do you think I want to waste my time on an infantile bitch like you? I am here to help" he adds again at volume.

Rose doesn't know if to burst out crying or fight back.

"My father acts all nice, but the minute someone crosses him, he's not nice at all" she argues back.

Bruce tells her to keep going.

"You don't understand. He will kill someone for crossing him" she adds getting upset.

Bruce doesn't understand and asks what that's got to do with her.

"Because I've had sex with Tania" she shouts, before breaking down fully and busting into tears.

Bruce and Jennifer watch as Rose falls back into the sofa and sobs. They turn to Lucy for her to shed a little light on the situation, but notice Lucy's face has turned as white as a sheet.

Jennifer asks her what is wrong.

"Tania is Rose's dad's girlfriend. He will kill them both" stutters Lucy, realising why her friend has been such a bitch lately.

Just then another loud bang comes from the front door and all four of them jump, even Bruce...

Lucy gets up to answer it, as Rose wipes her tears away to find out who is at the door.

In walks Rose's boyfriend strutting through the door like he owns the place.

"What's up sexy?" he arrogantly says in front of everyone to Lucy.

"If she has to put up with that as the boyfriend and the father is just as bad, no wonder Rose is messed up" whispers Jennifer to Bruce, as they watch him walk in.

"Hello love of my life" he saying smirking at Rose, sitting on the sofa, then giving her a kiss on the cheek.

"And who are your friends?" he asks, looking across at Bruce and Jennifer sitting together.

Rose tells them they are relatives of Lucy's, not that he's really interested in listening anyway. Bruce stands up to shake his hand to be polite.

"Whatever man" Rose's partner says.

"I don't know you, so don't make out we are friends" he adds, refusing to shake Bruce's hand and walking right past him.

He arrogantly walks up to Jennifer and gives her a creepy smile.

"You however CAN shake my hand" he says, taking Jennifer's hand and holding it.

"Or shake and hold onto anything else you fancy" he adds, followed by another creepy smile.

Bruce loses his cool as he watches Lucy and Rose witness it all but do nothing.

"You seem to think you are some kind of big man" says Bruce, pulling Rose's boyfriends hand away from Jennifer's hand.

"Bruce" snaps Jennifer, telling him in one single word that she can handle it.

"No this BOY is fucking rude" Bruce tells her.

The boyfriend isn't bothered by Bruce's outburst and walks over to the kitchen. He takes the milk from the fridge and drinks it straight from the carton.

"Hey that's my milk" insists Lucy looking at him.

"Yeah whatever" he mumbles back, throwing the half empty carton on the worktop and dropping the lid to the floor.

He struts back across into the living room and over to Rose.

"So are we going to your room to have sex love of my life? I haven't come here for my benefit you know" he remarks, to which Rose stands up and nods her head.

"Hey you better get more enthusiastic than that in bed. There's plenty of other women out there that want a piece of me" he adds, taking her by the hand and giving Jennifer another one of his creepy smiles.

"Where are these women now then pal? Picking up their guide dogs?" Bruce says, trying to rattle the twenty seven year old pig.

"Whatever man" Rose's boyfriend utters again.

"That angry vein in your head popping out, is that there because your main vein isn't working any-more because you're too old?" he adds laughing, mocking Bruce and pulling Rose into the bedroom.

Bruce and Jennifer tell Lucy they think it's a good time for them to be leaving. Just then the bedroom door opens again and his head pops out.

"Hey old man" the boyfriend yells at Bruce.

"Shall I leave the door open, so you can see a real man in action?" he asks, laughing some more and slamming the door shut before Bruce can answer.

Bruce can't take any-more and stands up ready to go and kick the door open and beat the crap out of him, but Jennifer holds him by the arm and insists they are leaving again. Bruce and Jennifer leave Lucy and tell her they will see her soon.

Outside Bruce tells Jennifer that he likes Lucy but asks why she's wasting her time with Rose. Jennifer doesn't have a reason but tells him she wants to try at least once more at a later date.

Back inside the boyfriend's arrogant mood hasn't changed as he unbuttons his top and throws Rose to the bed. She falls backwards as he orders her to get undressed. She slowly starts unbuttoning her top, but this is obviously too slow for him. He pulls her up from the bed, wrenches her jeans down and spins her round and over the bed. He holds her down, pulls his already hard penis out of his trousers and aims it with his hand towards her vagina from behind. He thrusts inside her and starts to pump as hard as he can.

"Scream bitch" he aggressively demands, getting worked up already.

"Let sexy Lucy outside hear what I am doing to you" he adds, letting the sound of his own voice turn himself on.

Rose tries hard to get into it and tries a little to fake some kind of noise, but before she can do either, she feels him throbbing inside her like he's about to finish.

"Oh yeah" he groans, as the Forty-five second sex comes to an end and he simply pulls out and does his trousers back up.

Rose falls face first into the bed and starts to pull her bottoms up, trying to convince him that she really enjoyed what had just happened. Just then he snaps...

"How was that really good for you? It was only a quick fuck" he yells, standing over her.

"It was really nice" she responds, trying to convince him.

He grabs her violently by the hair.

"You were thinking about that old bald headed guy out there in the living room, weren't you?" he aggressively shouts, spitting a little in her face.

"No I wasn't. I was thinking about you the whole time" she responds, clearly in discomfort.

"You lying bitch" he yells again, slapping her really hard around the face.

"See you tonight at Tina's party" he adds, throwing her back onto the bed and storming out of the room.

Rose just lies there staring up at the ceiling, when Lucy comes in and sits beside her.

"Did he do it again?" asks Lucy, like she knows what has just happened.

Rose stays strong and refuses to cry as her eyes fill with tears and simply nods her head.

Back outside and on their journey home, Bruce still doesn't understand why Jennifer is bothered with the likes of Rose.

"Remember when we met the other girls across London and the problems I had with Karen at the start?" Bruce asks.

"Karen was hard but you got there with her in the end. This girl Rose doesn't need your help, she needs a personality transplant" he adds.

Jennifer understands her husband's concerns but tells him they've made a small breakthrough today.

"She was willing to talk to you, until that moron walked in wasn't she?" Jennifer tells him.

"Let me give it one more go" she adds, knowing her supportive husband is going to back her anyway.

"One last chance" insists Bruce.

"But don't forget you have Karen, Amy and the others across London to spend some time with, not forgetting the two new sisters. So don't push yourself with this Rose okay?" he adds.

The couple continue their journey home and start talking about Tina's sixteenth birthday party tonight. Bruce tells her he thinks he's going to ask Dave to help him out on the door.

CHAPTER 6
SWEET BUT SHARP SIXTEENTH

Early evening sets in, Jennifer and Bruce are getting ready to leave for Tina's birthday party. Jennifer is waiting in the living room for Bruce to come downstairs wearing her pink party dress. Bruce walks in wearing some black trousers, a white shirt and a short black bomber jacket.
 "You're only helping out on the door for an hour or so, not working there all night baby" says Jennifer, checking him out looking like a professional nightclub bouncer.
Bruce checks himself out in the living room mirror and tells her he needs to look the part.
Jennifer asks what time he's meeting Dave, when her phone bleeps and she starts to read it.
 "I'm meeting him at the front entrance" Bruce tells her.
Jennifer finishes reading her text.
 "Problem?" asks Bruce.
Jennifer tells him that Lucy has asked her to pick up Tina first, before heading over to the campus to meet her and Rose.
 "Oh dear, Rose" mumbles Bruce.
 "Just the sound of her name sends shivers up my spine" he adds, shaking the invisible bad feeling off himself like a wet dog.
Jennifer tells him not to be like that, when her phone rings.
 "Oh come on, we've got to go, not another phone call" says Bruce itching to leave.
Jennifer looks down at the phone and tells him it's Karen ringing. She picks up her bag, walks out of the front door and answers it. Bruce

follows closing and locking the door behind him.

"Hey Karen, how are you babes?" chirps Jennifer down the phone, starting to walk down the road towards Tina's house.

Bruce catches her up and walks beside her, trying to listen in on the conversation.

"What's wrong?" asks Jennifer, as Bruce shows some concern for his friend too, without being able to hear what is being said.

Jennifer listens to Karen for a while, then tells her she's on the way to a party with her new clients, but promises she will call her back in the next hour. Before Jennifer can put her phone away in her handbag, Bruce wants to know what's going on. Jennifer explains that Karen is fine but having some trouble with Tony.

"I thought that knob learnt his lesson before?" asks Bruce.

"What's he doing now then?" he asks, wanting to know his friends across London are safe.

Jennifer tells him Tony disappeared after they set him up in the lap dancing club, but Karen felt like she was being followed around London yesterday.

"Okay" says Bruce.

"I will hop on a train now and go and sort it out" he adds, ready to change his plans.

Jennifer tells him she needs him to watch the door at Tina's party tonight and that Tony and his wind up games can wait until tomorrow.

"Yeah but I've got Dave on the door" says Bruce.

"I could be back within a couple of hours" he adds, showing a greater concern for his real friends.

Once again Jennifer is adamant that Bruce sticks to tonight's plans, assuring him she will call Karen back in an hour to sort something out. With that Jennifer continues towards Tina's house and Bruce heads straight to the small community hall hired for Tina's sixteenth.

Bruce arrives at the hall five minutes later but clearly has his mind elsewhere as he meets up with Dave at the entrance.

"I thought I made the effort with my long doorman coat" laughs Dave, as he greets Bruce.

"But you look like you've joined the FBI Bruce" he adds in admiration.

It's not long before Dave realises that Bruce isn't in the mood to be playful and asks him what's wrong. Bruce tells Dave about Tony and what happened the other night, back across London.

"Sounds like you and the other girls got him good" says Dave trying to follow.

"Why would he start on the girls again a day later?" he asks Bruce.

Bruce explains that whilst he can handle Tony, the scum-bag also has a reputation to uphold and because they made him look bad, he could be out for revenge.

"So lets go and take him down then" suggests Dave, showing Bruce he's completely on his side.

Bruce tells him he wants to do that as well, but Jennifer needs to put her efforts into these new girls now and he cannot really sidetrack her.

"So what is the worst this Tony can do to your friend Karen then?" Dave asks, understanding why Bruce can't go and sort it out.

"If I was over there, nothing" says Bruce, confident he can deal with Tony.

"But without me, he loves to bully and pick on women" he adds in disgust.

Dave shows his disgust too, then comes up with an idea.

"Hey, I still live near there. Why don't I check out what this Tony is doing when we finish here and let you know how bad it is?" suggests young Dave.

Bruce agrees and tells Dave he will give him more information later, noticing the first party guests arriving at the door.

"Okay what do I do right now then?" Dave says, a little unsure of his role as doorman.

Bruce turns to him.

"Dave, you are a little girl with a tiny penis and I had sex with your ugly mother last night" Bruce quickly says to rattle him.

Dave's face hits the floor and a red mist rolls over his eyes. Bruce smiles.

"That's it Dave. Hold that face and look like you ain't going to take no shit from anyone" Bruce tells him, opening the door and welcoming the first party guest into the building.

Meanwhile a mile away, Jennifer is knocking on Tina's front door for the third time in twenty-four hours. An older blonde woman answers the door to Jennifer's surprise.

"You must be Jenny?" says the strangers voice at the door, before telling Jennifer that she's heard a lot about her from Tina and Lucy.

"I'm the girls mum" says the blonde women, before shaking Jennifer's hand and then being pushed aside by Tina trying to get out of the door in a hurry.

Before Jennifer and the woman can have any kind of conversation, Tina has wrapped her arm around Jennifer and is ushering her away in the direction of her party.

"Have a great birthday bash sweetie" calls the mum on the

doorstep.
The girls walk down the road together, Jennifer in a black jacket covering her long pink dress and Tina in a short black skirt and a low cut white top, showing off her generous cleavage for a girl her age. Jennifer wants to find out if Tina as had a chance to try any of her toys, but knows she's far too excited about getting to her party to have any kind of grown-up chat.
Minutes later they are at Lucy's school, waiting for her and Rose to join them.

Back over at the hall, Bruce and Dave are doing a great job on the door and have so far only turned away one little hooligan for being rude and an under aged drinker. Bruce then spots Rose's arrogant boyfriend heading towards them. Bruce gives Dave a quick nod to indicate trouble is approaching and Dave toughens his facial expression once again.
    "Okay Dave, I said look hard, not like you're constipated" Bruce laughs.
Dave's hard image goes out of the window when his toughness cracks and he laughs too.
    "Well well well, if it isn't Bruce, Bruce Willis and his sidekick Robin on the door" says Rose's boyfriend mocking them.
    "Name a Bruce Willis film" Bruce asks the boyfriend, as they come face to face.
    "Die hard" answers the boyfriend, unsure of why he's being asked the question in the first place.
Bruce gives him a little smile, then moves closer to whisper.
    "You will die harder if you fuck with me again, understand?"
For the first time the boyfriend seems scared and tries to pretend he didn't hear. Once Bruce and Dave let him past and into the building, he can't help himself and mocks Bruce again.
    "Yippee ki yay mother fucker" the boyfriend laughs, entering the building at speed.
Bruce watches him over his shoulder and simply gives him the look he gave him before.
Dave doesn't understand why Bruce has called him to help and points out that he could do this door watching thing on his own.
    "I know I could Dave" says Bruce with a cool smirk.
    "So why have you asked me to help you then?" asks a confused looking Dave.
    "You have access to a party that you weren't invited to, haven't you?" responds Bruce.

Just then the boyfriend pops his head out of the door again.

"Hey Willis" he calls in Bruce's direction.

Bruce turns round to find out what the annoying twenty-seven year old, going on thirteen dick-head wants now.

"Where's my bitch? I can't find her anywhere" the boyfriend calls.

Bruce gives him yet another stare and ignores the question.

"Fuck you then Willis" the boyfriend shouts so he looks tough in front of other party guests.

"If she doesn't turn up, I will just take that Jenny bitch who was with you yesterday" he adds laughing, then running inside as Bruce turns to go after him.

"That's just want he wants you to do" insists Dave, holding onto Bruce's arm preventing him from giving chase.

"That's want he wants me to do?" asks Bruce.

"That's what I am going to do very soon" he adds, trying hard not to get rattled any more.

Just then Dave and Bruce notice Jennifer's pink dress come round the corner with three other female's in tow.

"Which one's the birthday girl?" asks Dave, with his eyes wandering up and down the line of beautiful girls.

Bruce points out Tina followed by Lucy and then Rose.

"She's only sixteen today?" gasps Dave, looking at Tina looking all grown-up and sexy.

Bruce reminds him nicely to keep it in his pants as they reach the door. Jennifer says hello to Bruce quickly with a kiss, as Lucy tries to avoid any eye contact at all. Bruce makes a very quick introduction and Dave takes a shine to the birthday girl. Unfortunately she's too excited about getting inside and she doesn't even notice him.

"And this is Rose" says Bruce, finishing off the introductions.

"Yeah whatever, keep your eyes to yourself" mumbles Rose, in her orange leggings, black mini-skirt and black boob tube with nipples part of the deal.

"What's up with her?" Dave whispers to Bruce, as she completely blows him out and walks straight into the building.

"Remember that dick-head out here a minute ago?" Bruce asks him.

Dave nods.

"That's his girlfriend" declares Bruce.

Jennifer tells Bruce she will see him inside soon and the three girls rush inside after Rose.

As soon as the three girls catch up with Rose inside, Tina is greeted by all of her school friends and her young boyfriend too. It isn't long before one of her friends is hanging onto her arm and whispering

"Tonight's the night" in her ear.
Rose is off in search of her boyfriend. Tina can't escape her friends and boyfriend all making a fuss of her, so Lucy and Jennifer decide to go to the bar to get a drink. The party goes on for an hour or so without any problems, until Tina finds herself without her boyfriend nearby. She goes in search of him and finds him standing in a corner with one of her friends from school. She moves in closer to hear what they are talking about.

"You know, if Tina doesn't give out tonight, I am always willing to step in" the flirtatious school friend says to him.

Tina waits for her boyfriend to tell her to leave him alone or say something, but he doesn't. Instead the young sixteen year old is left devastated when he takes the girl up on her offer.

Tina walks away and is greeted by more well wishes from friends.

"Is it true tonight's the night?" another girl asks her.

Tina tries to stay strong and not let what she's heard affect her.

"I don't need to have sex just to make you feel better about being a whore" Tina snaps, then runs off looking for somewhere to hide.

Bruce and Dave have finished their duty on the door and enter the party. They quickly head to the bar for a well earned drink. They find Lucy and Jennifer still there drinking, enjoying themselves.

Jennifer and Bruce have a quick chat as Dave and Lucy stand in silence, unsure of what to say to each-other. Then they notice a commotion down at the other end of the hall, someone clearly has had too much to drink.

"You better go and deal with it baby. It is your job tonight after all" Jennifer tells Bruce.

"Oh but I've just got myself a drink" moans Bruce, wanting to enjoy the rest of the party himself.

Before he agrees to sort out the scuffle, they work out together that it's Rose's partner making all the noise. Bruce now wants to go and do his job, but Jennifer decides to hold him back.

"First you want me to sort it out, now you don't because it's him. Make up your mind" Bruce laughs, picking up his drink again and taking a sip of it.

Jennifer watches for a few seconds and tells Bruce that it's all gone quiet anyway.

Across the hall Rose has already said no to sex outside the hall to her trouble-maker boyfriend. She decides to head towards the toilets to escape him.

"Why can't we have sex outside?" he shouts at Rose, over the

music standing outside the toilets, before she enters.
Rose tells him she's there to enjoy the party and promises that once it's finished, he can have his wicked way however he wants.

"Yeah but by then you will be hammered" he argues, unhappy with the offer.

"You get hammered too then" she responds, trying to not let his demands ruin her night.

She enters the toilet, telling him she will be back out in a minute.

Back over at the bar area, Lucy notices her sister Tina running through the hall and out of the building. Lucy makes sure Jennifer sees her too and they both want to go and find out what is wrong with her or find out where she is going. Jennifer tells Bruce she will be back in a minute and the two girls set off in chase of Tina. Bruce and Dave grab two bar stools and order more drinks.

In the toilets, Rose is washing her hands and touching up her make-up at the mirror, before she has to go out and fight off even more sexual advances from her grumpy boyfriend. She delays leaving for as long as she can, when the door opens and he walks in.

"You can't come in here" she laughs, making out he's doing something really naughty.

"Who's going to stop me?" he laughs, walking towards her at the sink.

"Bruce Willis and Robin outside?" he asks, showing no fear.

He moves closer to her and places both his hands on her orange leggings. He runs his hands straight up her legs and lifts her short mini-skirt up to reveal her black thong.

"If not outside, then right here" he insists, lifting her onto the sink and parting her legs with his body.

"What if someone comes in?" she whispers, trying to stop him but feeling horny about the situation too.

Just then the door opens and in walks a fifteen year old girl. Rose tries to push him away and get off the sink, but he doesn't let her. Instead he holds her in position and tries to undo his jeans.

"Hey there little girl" he grunts over at the young female entering the toilet.

"Would you like to come and see a massive dick?" he asks, scaring the life out of the girl.

The girl runs back out of the door and once she has left he tries even harder to take his trousers down, but Rose isn't willing any-more.

"How could you scare her like that? That was fucking horrible" she snaps, trying to push him away again.

"She's gone, you want to get fucked, so what's your problem?" he grunts at her, still trying to undo his trousers.

Meanwhile outside the hall, Jennifer and Lucy have caught up with Tina outside. Tina is clearly upset and they ask her what's wrong. Tina explains that if she doesn't have sex with her boyfriend tonight, he's agreed to sleep with one of her school friends instead.
    "I will kill him" snaps Lucy, upset that he's upset Tina on her birthday.
Tina looks to Jennifer for some wise advice, but Jennifer doesn't give it.
    "You know what you've got to do" says Jennifer, trying to get inside her head.
    "Yes I do" Tina replies, understanding Jennifer's wisdom faster than anyone has ever done before.
Tina stands up, brushes herself down and steps back inside with a forced smile, as confused big sister Lucy watches on...
    "Did you just tell her to go and have sex with him?" asks Lucy.
    "I told her to go and dump him" responds Jennifer with a smile.
    "And Tina got that without words did she?" asks Lucy, looking really concerned.
    "She sure did" says Jennifer, with a really proud beam on her face.
Lucy tells Jennifer that she needs to use the toilet, so the girls go back inside. Lucy heads for the bathroom and Jennifer follows Tina who is now at the bar with Bruce. Tina asks him to make her now ex-boyfriend leave the party and Bruce doesn't need to be asked twice, following Tina through the packed hall in search of him. Jennifer joins Dave for a drink at the bar.

Back in the toilets Rose has managed to push her boyfriend away enough to lift herself off the sink.
    "I'm not playing Rose. If we don't have sex right now, it's over" he tells her, getting frustrated.
Rose is horrified by the way he's just spoken to the young girl and isn't interested in his sexual advances any-more.
    "If over is what you want, then consider it over" she snaps, trying to escape from the toilets.
He watches her walk towards the door, adjusts his jeans and warns her again. This time she doesn't even listen and storms out of the door as someone is walking in.
    "Rose, you okay?" says the voice walking past her into the toilet.
Seconds later she realises that they've both said it was over and it was her friend Lucy she just ignored on the way out. Rose quickly

turns and bursts back through the toilet door.
As he stands there looking at himself in the mirror, he can't believe his luck as Lucy walks in first, followed by Rose looking panicked. He works out what has just happened.

"Oh I get it" he laughs.

"You just dumped me but couldn't trust your school buddy to come into the toilet alone, knowing I was in here" he laughs, looking a really confused Lucy up and down.

"I don't get it" says Lucy.

"I only wanted to pee. I didn't' ask to walk in on one of your domestics" she adds standing there.

Rose ignores Lucy's comment and attacks him for what he's saying.

"Yes you are dumped you fucking shit-head" snaps an angry Rose.

"And don't for a second think that Lucy would ever lower herself to fuck someone like you" she adds in rage.

Lucy feels really uncomfortable and instead of leaving the bathroom quickly, finds herself right in the middle of the fight boiling over.

"Excuse me" snaps Lucy.

"Can I use the bathroom in peace please?" she asks, wanting them both to stop or better still, leave.

"What the fuck are you laughing at?" snaps Rose, towards her now ex-boyfriend and completely ignoring Lucy's plea again.

"You said Lucy wouldn't sleep with me" he says bending over, making out the laughter is hurting him.

"If only you knew how fucking dirty your room-mate really is" he adds to Rose's horror.

"Forget the toilet, I will leave" insists Lucy, knowing exactly where the conversation is going and trying to get out of the room fast.

"Stay where you are" orders Rose in Lucy's direction, as she fears the worst.

"Hey it's over, what the fuck do I care now?" he shouts, grabbing Lucy by the waist and pulling her over to him.

"Get off me you creep" snaps Lucy, trying to fight him off whilst Rose watches.

"Even if I tell you how sexier than Rose I think you are?" he whispers in Lucy's ear from behind, loud enough for Rose to hear.

Lucy quickly melts at the sound of his voice uttering those words, but starts fighting him off again.

"Are you telling me, you two have fucked?" snaps Rose, watching Lucy escape his arms and move away.

"We haven't had sex, have we Lucy?" he snaps back.

"But I am glad you care" he adds, making out he only said it to

make her jealous and it worked.
Rose snaps again knowing he's right and quickly heads for the door in her defensive manner.

"Fuck you both" she growls, leaving the toilet and Lucy alone with him again.

Lucy feels very uncomfortable and heads for the door too. He tries calling after her to stay but before he finishes his sentence, she's gone too. He chases after her and catches her outside the toilet. He grabs her and pushes her against the wall.

"Take your hands off me" Lucy orders, looking out for Rose who has disappeared into the crowd.

He forces her against the wall and gropes at her bum.

"Hey I could have told her the truth about us" he whispers in her ear.

"You should be thanking me" he adds, trying to get her to kiss him. Lucy continues to fight him off, but he easily overpowers her and keeps her pinned against the wall.

"Please, I don't want you" Lucy begs, trying to stop him moving his hand round to her front and between her legs.

"What not even if I tell you I want you more than Rose anyway?" he says, managing to get his hand onto her thigh.

Just then he feels his collar being grabbed.

"She said she doesn't want you stud" says Bruce's voice, as he throws him up against the wall, pinning him there by his neck.

"Where's your white vest Bruce?" the boyfriend mocks, struggling to get Bruce off him as Lucy watches.

The boyfriend manages to wriggle away from the wall and tries to quickly blend into the crowd, still mocking and threatening Bruce in the process. Bruce turns to Lucy and asks her if she's okay. Lucy nods her head and looks at Bruce as though he's her knight in shining armour. Bruce and Lucy go off in search of the other and finally Lucy finds some words to say, simply thanking him before they reach the others. Bruce explains he's just finished rescuing her sister, kicked her ex-boyfriend out and now is looking forward to doing the same with Rose's nasty boyfriend.

"Hey, maybe I should start wearing a white vest like Bruce Willis" laughs Bruce, making Lucy smile.

Bruce quickly explains to Jennifer, Dave and Tina what has just happened and tells them to look after Lucy whilst he goes looking for Rose's ex to throw out. Dave asks Bruce if he needs any help, but Bruce with a smile on his face has been looking forward to this moment all day and politely declines the offer. Bruce walks off into the crowd on his own personal mission and then Jennifer notices that

Rose is nowhere to be seen. She asks Dave and Tina to stay with shaken-up Lucy, whilst she goes looking for Rose.

"Where was the last place anyone saw her?" asks Jennifer, looking for a clue as to her whereabouts.

Lucy tells her, she saw her in the toilet ten minutes ago before downing a quick drink. Jennifer sets off on her search for Rose, but the toilets are empty when she walks in. As she comes out however, she sees Rose heading straight towards her. Jennifer backs herself into the toilets once more and runs into a cubicle. She stands there waiting for Rose to come in, so she can casually bump into her without Rose knowing she's been looking for her. Just then, in walks Rose shouting at someone...

"I told you to leave me alone" Jennifer hears Rose's voice shout.

It's not long before Jennifer can tell it's the boyfriend she is shouting at.

"Come on Rose, you know I love you" his voice says.

"Look, we are back where we started. Let's try and fuck again" he adds.

Jennifer listens from behind the door, as the boyfriend begs her to have sex and Rose keeps telling him to leave her alone. Now with the situation escalating and Jennifer listening from the cubicle, the life coach decides to sit it out and wait until they leave. Finally it sounds like Rose is leaving, but there's a huge crash and a loud bang...

"I didn't mean to push you over Rose, you forced me" he says, before getting angry again.

"Come on, get up. I said get up" he shouts at Rose.

Jennifer stands there anxious about the female outside the cubicle.

"I said leave me alone" grumbles Rose's voice, trying to leave the toilet once more.

Jennifer manages to find a small crack in the door and peers through it. She can see Rose grabbing the door handle... Now he's pushing her away from it and back down onto the floor again. Jennifer watches him pick up a chair and place it in front of the main door to lock themselves in.

"I told you, we are going to have sex in here and that's what we are going to do" he shouts, picking her up by her hair as dizzy and injured Rose gets to her feet.

Jennifer feels it's time to open the door and confront him. She takes a deep breath and peers through the hole once more. She can see him dragging her towards the sink and helping her up onto it.

"Please, I don't want to do this" grumbles Rose, in no fit state to defend herself now.

Jennifer hears Rose's plea fall on deaf ears and then she hears the zip go on his jeans. She places her hand on the lock of the door to open it.

"Bruce" calls Rose, in a massive effort to be heard.

"Bruce" she calls again, knowing it's her last chance to be rescued.

Jennifer slides the bolt across the door and opens it very slowly to witness him dropping his trousers to the floor and using his body to part her legs.

"Please, I don't want to have sex with you" Rose grumbles again, as he tears her thong away from her body.

"What's this fucking Bruce going to do?" he asks, preparing his erection for impact.

"If he comes to your rescue, he gets this" he adds, pulling a sharp bladed knife from his jacket and placing it down next to the sink where Rose is sitting.

Jennifer sees the knife and panics with fear. She backs into the cubicle, locks the door trying to think fast... She pulls out her mobile phone and considers ringing Bruce, knowing that the beast outside would then know she's in there.

"You ready for this?" his voice shudders, ready to have sex with unwilling Rose.

"Please don't do this" Rose's voice struggles to say.

Jennifer dials the number quickly and orders Bruce into the female toilets. The boyfriend unhands Rose and rushes to find out who's in the cubicle. Rose slides off the sink and onto the floor, as he starts to bang and kick the cubicle door. Jennifer holds her breath and hopes Bruce can get past the barricade at the door in time. With one mighty kick, the cubicle door rips off it's hinges and Jennifer finds the angry looking boyfriend towering over her. He grabs the mobile phone from her hand and throws it against the wall, then before he can drag her out by the hair, Jennifer decides to stand up to him.

"Do you really think you are going to get away with this?" she asks him, totally petrified.

"Get away with what?" he shouts.

"Trying to rape Rose?" she responds, hoping the words will make him realise what he's doing.

It doesn't and he starts laughing at her.

"Yeah you can laugh" says Jennifer, pushing past him and moving quickly to Rose on the floor.

"But I heard and saw everything you just did" she adds, helping injured Rose to her feet.

"There's one thing you are overlooking here Miss Know-it-all" he laughs some more.

"To accuse me of rape, you need a victim first" he adds.
Jennifer looks disturbed and confused at the same time. Finally he puts her out of her misery and tells her, Rose would never testify against him.

"Do you realise how many times a month this happens?" he asks her.

"You mean you've raped her before?" asks Jennifer, telling Rose to lie still and standing back up again.

"She loves the rough treatment, that's what gets her off" he tells Jennifer still laughing.

Jennifer goes to the door to remove the chair, knowing Bruce should burst in at any second. He walks up behind her, holds her by the waist and tells her she shouldn't do that.

"Why not? she needs medical help" insists Jennifer, trying to pull the chair away from the door and removing his hands at the same time.

"MM-mm that's quite a firm backside you have there sexy. Can I fuck you instead?" he asks, running his hands across her bum and trying to slide her pink dress up a little.

"Jen, Jen, are you okay?" calls Bruce from behind the door, as he starts to kick it in.

The boyfriend doesn't know if to fight back, touch Jennifer up some more or run and hide. Bruce starts to make his way through the door, as the boyfriend grabs hold of Jennifer from behind as though he is taking her hostage.

"Touch the door again and I will break her neck" the boyfriend yells to Bruce through the door.

Bruce doesn't stop, as he can see his wife through the door. With two more kicks the chair used as a barricade buckles and the door crashes open. The boyfriend panics letting go of Jennifer and makes a dash towards Bruce at the door in a rage. The men come together and fly back out into the hall and start scrapping on the floor, as the other party guests gather round. Jennifer quickly helps Rose to her feet and carries her out of the toilet to witness Bruce getting the upper hand as they roll around on the floor. Through the crowd Dave comes rushing over and helps Bruce hold the angry boyfriend down. Now in a mad rage the boyfriend starts to lash out and swings a fist straight into Dave's face. Dave falls back and the boyfriend manages to wriggle free and back into the toilet. Bruce goes in chase of him... Bruce takes a quick look around but has lost him, then from nowhere he flies out from behind one of the cubicle doors and knocks Bruce down onto the floor. Dave comes rushing across but the door is slammed shut in his face. The boyfriend quickly grabs another chair and re-barricades the door. Bruce gets to his feet and casually wipes some blood away from his mouth with a smile.

"Wrong move pal. You were meant to lock me in here and run away" laughs Bruce.

"Not lock yourself in here and get your head kicked in" he adds, watching the boyfriend back towards the sink.

Bruce moves towards him ready to kick the crap out of him.

"Bruce, he's got a knife in there on the sink" calls Jennifer's voice from outside, desperately trying to get the door open again.

Bruce hears his wife's call but it's too late... The boyfriend grabs the knife from the side and waves it around, moving towards Bruce.

"Who made the wrong move now Willis?" laughs the boyfriend, ready to attack.

CHAPTER 7
CHERRY PICKER

Whilst Bruce tries to plan a way out of the situation and Dave tries hard to kick through the door which has been barricaded again, the boyfriend seems to wind himself up more and more waving the five inch blade around in his hand. Now everyone is in a panic as they beg the madman not to do it from outside. Even Rose has come round from her injury and is calling for him to stop through the door. The boyfriend slowly moves towards Bruce, mocking him and telling him how badly he's going to get hurt. Bruce tries hard to work out a way to defend himself, but whilst he's swinging the knife in an erratic manner, even he can't see a way out of this one.

"Come on, put the knife down. You don't really want to do this" Bruce says, trying his best to talk him down.

"Don't do it. Don't do it" cries Rose from outside the door, where Dave has managed to fit his arm through.

"Yes I do" laughs the boyfriend, totally oblivious to the commotion outside in the hall.

Dave forces his arm through the gap to move the chair away, but can't quite reach it. He watches as Bruce backs himself into a corner and the boyfriend moves ever so closer.

"Okay put the knife down and fight me like a real man" Bruce shouts, changing his tactics.

Again the boyfriend doesn't rise to it and continues his slow movement towards him, ready to lunge at Bruce with the knife.

"Bruce" calls Dave from the gap in the door.

Bruce looks over to see a small skinny pole Dave has found and thrown through the gap. Just like that Bruce dives in the direction of the pole and picks it up. The boyfriend runs towards Bruce with the knife in a stabbing action and Bruce swings the pole across his abdominal area. The boyfriend drops the knife and drops to the floor clutching his side. Bruce makes a mad dash for the door, moves the chair out of the way and gets outside. Dave, Jennifer and Lucy try to comfort him, as he tries to get his head round what has just happened. Thirty seconds later Bruce remembers the knife on the floor and wants to go back in and pick it up, so no-one else gets hurt. Bruce tells Dave to call the police and he walks back into the toilet. He is stunned to find Rose on the floor with her man, trying to pick him up. Bruce wants to ask what she is doing, but it's clear she's trying to help him. Bruce turns to leave the toilet again.

"Hang up Dave" insists Bruce, before Dave talks to the police.

"It's not worth ringing them" he adds, as Rose tries to support and carry her man out of the toilet.

Everyone is shocked as they watch Rose and her man draped around her come out.

"What the fuck are you doing?" snaps a horrified Lucy.

"That nut job just attacked you, Jen and Bruce with a knife" she adds.

Rose doesn't respond and simply struggles to help her man towards the main entrance.

"Rose" Lucy calls, as the music is switched off.

Rose stops and looks at her friend without words and just as she does, the boyfriend looks over his shoulder winking quickly in the direction of Jennifer and Bruce, before playing the injured soldier again.

Lucy, Dave, Bruce and Jennifer huddle together and watch as Rose and her boyfriend leave the venue together.

"I guess that's my party over then?" says Tina, walking over to the group with a sad look on her face.

"Sorry sis, I guess it is" answers Lucy, putting an arm around her.

Tina's friends all start to come over and say goodbye before leaving, some even tell her just how cool her party was, with all the drama a teenager would enjoy.

"So Tina, now your party is over, are you going to do it with your boyfriend?" says one of her friends before leaving.

Tina turns to her and tells her she couldn't even if she wanted to, because she finished with him an hour ago.

"You frigid bitch" teases the other girl.

"You knew tonight was the night, so you dumped him" she adds laughing.

Tina tries to explain what she witnessed to the girl, but she's too busy laughing and mocking her to listen.

"You're never going to lose your virginity, virgin girl" teases the girl from school.

For some reason and the fact that her party has just been ruined, Tina snaps and tells the girl and others listening, that she isn't a virgin without thinking... As the words come out of her mouth, she already knows that this type of lie can only end in one place and it does with the following question.

"Yeah course you have Miss Virgin. If you've done it, who was he then?" the girl asks.

Tina feels trapped and put on the spot. She looks around and without thinking, points in the direction of Dave walking back to the bar with Bruce, Jennifer and Lucy.

"We will see about that" says the girl racing towards Dave and the others.

Tina doesn't follow and stands watching from afar, hoping a hole in the ground will swallow her up. She watches as the girl runs over to the group of grown-ups, asks Dave a question and what looks to be her laughing and him shaking his head to say no. Tina runs off out of the building again. What Tina didn't see is Bruce give Dave a punch in the ribs, as the question was asked and Dave in-fact cover her story up and make out he was her first. Bruce watches as Tina runs out the door and tells Dave to go and sort it out. Bruce turns to the bar for another well earned drink and the young girl walks away believing Tina is a woman who's had sex after all.

Outside, Dave manages to catch up with Tina as she runs past the cemetery gates and into the park. She sits down on the bench where she thinks no-one will find her and wipes the tears from her eyes. Seconds later Dave arrives.

"Thank god you stopped running" he says panting.

"What do you want?" huffs Tina, blaming him for the lie she just told.

"You don't understand, I covered for you" Dave tells her, sitting down next to her.

Although relieved, Tina starts to cry again. Dave tries to comfort her but is clearly no good at this sort of thing. He asks her what's wrong.

"Well where shall I start?" Tina mumbles wiping her tears away again.

"My sixteenth birthday party is a disaster. I dumped my boyfriend and most of my friends think I am still a virgin" she adds in one single breath.

Dave puts his arm around her, trying to think of how his mentor Bruce would handle the situation. All of a sudden Tina stops feeling sorry for herself and leans into Dave, feeling the full comfort of his hug.

"How old are you Dave?" asks Tina, with her face planted against his chest.

"Nineteen, why?" responds Dave, looking over at the cemetery gates to see if the others are coming yet.

As if by magic Tina perks up and swings her leg over him to straddle him on the bench. Dave starts to feel a little uncomfortable as he looks down and notices Tina's short black skirt riding up towards her knickers. He asks her what she is doing.

"You told my friends you were my first right?" she says, moving herself into position and pulling her skirt up from behind, so she can sit on his bulge.

Dave says yeah.

"Well why don't you be my first then?" she asks, starting to ride his bulge.

Dave although enjoying the advances from a girl he clearly fancies, tries to wriggle free and ease her off the top of him, but the more he resists, the more she gets turned on by the idea. She rocks backwards and forwards even harder, until she can feel his bulge hardening, then as if she doesn't know what to do next, stops...

"Isn't this the time where you do the rest?" she asks him, ready to have sex for the first time, easing herself off of him and relaxing back on the bench so he can get on top.

Dave stands up looking down at her and fights his own urges to pounce on top of her.

"Your first time shouldn't be like this" claims Dave, noticing her white knickers underneath the black skirt and fighting with his erection.

"It's fine, come on" insists Tina, still waiting for him to make his move.

"No it's not right" replies Dave.

"Your first time should be special" he adds, shocked that these words are coming out of his own mouth.

Once again Tina doesn't want to hear it and tells him it will be special. Finally Dave cracks and tells her the real reason he can't do it.

"Bruce told me to keep it in my pants" he utters, clearly getting weaker at the young girl throwing herself at him.

"Bruce? What's my virginity got to do with him?" Tina grumbles, sitting up on the bench, showing Dave that he's missed his chance.

Now Dave feels terrible, knowing just how much he wanted to do it. He sits back down beside her on the bench and tells her just how much he wants to have sex with her, but must clear it with Bruce first. The pair sit talking together for a few more minutes...

Back inside the hall Jennifer has started to plan everyone's departure and walks over to Bruce at the bar, who is now finishing his fourth quick drink with Lucy. Jennifer tells Bruce she will walk Dave to the train station with Tina, then walk Tina home and he is to escort Lucy home.

"Excuse me?" grunts Bruce, as Lucy chokes back on her drink, as the thought of her and Bruce alone together again hits her in all the right spots.

"What's wrong baby?" responds Jennifer, showing a great concern from her grumpy husband.

"I don't know if you just noticed, but your client Rose just left with the maniac that was going to attack you" he barks at her.

"Furthermore, that same maniac just waved a knife at me locked in a girl's toilet" he adds, ordering another drink from the barman at the same time.

Jennifer moves in closer and tells him she knows. She then tells him that they will talk about it when they are both back home and sticks to her original plan.

"Fine" snaps Bruce, taking the glass from the barman and downing it in one.

Bruce stands up but clearly isn't impressed by Jennifer's lack of concern. He turns to Lucy and asks her nicely if she is ready. Lucy gives him a smile back, saying she is and without another glance at Jennifer, Bruce chaperones Lucy out of the hall as Tina walks in with Dave. Dave catches Bruce at the door and quickly tells him he needs a word, but Bruce shrugs him off and tells him to text him once he's on the train home.

Bruce and Lucy walk down the road together and Jennifer, Dave and Tina follow on shortly after.

Lucy tries really hard to get a conversation out of Bruce the whole way home, but Bruce isn't in the mood to speak to anyone. Soon enough he's managed to chaperone the young blonde back to the school without a single word.

"You okay if I leave you here Lucy? it's been a long night" Bruce tries to say without grumbling.

Lucy knows she isn't going to get anywhere with him tonight and feels a little sorry for him, so tells him she will be fine.

Bruce starts to walk away and leaves Lucy.

"Bruce" calls Lucy.

Bruce stops and turns.

"What if he's inside with Rose? What do I do?" she asks, not wanting to burden him with any-more hassle but reluctant to go inside herself.
With that Bruce snaps out of the mood he's in and realises he's not being very nice.
"I'm sorry Lucy, how stupid of me to not think of that" he says, trying hard to smile at her.
Then he just stands wondering what to do.
"Couldn't I just come back and sleep over at yours and Jennifer's house tonight?" Lucy asks, not wanting to ask Bruce inside himself in-case it all kicks off again.
Bruce doesn't give it much thought and agrees.
"I won't be any trouble or get in your way" insists Lucy, seeming a little happier now.
Bruce just smiles at her.
"I don't think Jen would even notice us there" Bruce mumbles, starting off on the journey towards his house with the blonde now.
It doesn't take long for them to arrive at the house and Bruce welcomes her in, showing her to the living room.
"Fancy a drink?" he asks her, clearly wanting another one himself.
Lucy declines politely and sits herself down on the sofa waiting for him to return from the kitchen. Just then Bruce gets a text from Dave telling him he's on the train and still needs to talk. Bruce walks back through to the living room reading his message.
"It's okay. Just Dave telling me he's on the train now" Bruce tells her, putting his phone on the side without sending a message back.
"Does that mean Jen's on her way back then?" Lucy asks him.
"Who knows?" he responds, sitting down next to her and picking up the TV remote to switch it on.
Lucy realises not for the first time tonight, that Bruce is down on himself and asks if he's okay again.
Bruce just looks at her on the other end of the sofa and nods his head.
"I know what will make you smile" says Lucy, trying hard to cheer him up.
"Why don't you say some nice things to me, watch me go crazy and mock me like you do? That always makes you smile" she adds.
Bruce cracks a smile but doesn't take her offer that seriously.
"Come on Bruce, tell me how beautiful you think I look tonight" she flirts, adamant she can cheer him up by being naughty.
Bruce looks over at her again and can see naughty thoughts running through her mind.
"I'm not really in that kind of mood tonight Lucy" he tells her, trying

not to offend her at the same time.

"Come on. Have a laugh at how horny you can make me" she insists, moving across the sofa towards him.

"Really Lucy, it's not a good idea" Bruce says, leaning back into the sofa as she sits next to him.

"Why isn't it? You won't need to say much, I am already really wet" she teases, trying to tempt him.

"Because if I do, the mood I am in, I won't want to stop myself" he tells her.

With that she lets out a moan and leaps on top of him, planting her lips on his.

"I bet you want to rip my clothes off right now, don't you?" she whispers in his ear, whilst rocking herself against his bulge.

Bruce doesn't respond and for a few seconds, just sits there letting Lucy have her wicked way with his body.

"I bet you would love me to suck your dick right now?" she whispers, trying to get a reaction from his bulge.

"Please Lucy stop" he begs, knowing he's got no fight left in himself tonight.

She doesn't stop and continues riding against his soon to be interested penis. She lifts her top over her head and quickly ping's open her bra to show him her breasts. She leans in and brushes her nipples against his lips. Again he doesn't respond and just sits there trying hard not to become fully erect.

"Please Lucy, I won't be able to stop if you keep going" he begs again, feeling his trousers start to move.

Unfortunate for him, so does she... With that she lets out a small moan and starts to ride his solidness even harder towards a fully clothed orgasm. Bruce can't handle it any-more and places his hands on her backside to help her ride even faster. He leans forward to let her kiss him and they are disturbed by a key in the front door...

Lucy jumps off and leaps across the sofa trying to look all innocent. Bruce doesn't do a thing and just sits there waiting for someone to walk in.

"Hi gang" Jennifer says, walking into the living room.

"I thought Bruce might have used his brain and brought you back here for the night Lucy" she adds, putting her bag down and ignoring the sexual tension in the room and Lucy sitting there trying to casually put her top back on.

Bruce stands up, huffs and walks into the kitchen to fix himself another drink. Jennifer takes her jacket off and tells Lucy that she got Tina home safely. Lucy thanks her but is unable to hide the guilt written all over her face.

"I better go and cheer grumpy up" Jennifer tells Lucy, handing her the TV remote and telling her to make herself at home.
Jennifer walks out into the kitchen to Bruce standing over the sink with his head lowered.
"You obviously have things you want to say baby, so let them out" Jennifer tells him, sticking the kettle on and sitting herself down at the kitchen table.
Bruce turns round with a confused look on his face.
"Have you any idea what I've been through tonight?" he asks her standing at the sink.
"Yeah I do baby, I was there too" she responds, calmly.
Bruce reminds her that he had to play doorman when he didn't want to, he was attacked by a knife swinging maniac, is sick with worry about Amy and Karen having to deal with Tony across London and to top it off, his wife doesn't seem to care any-more
"Of course I care" she responds, after listening to him and then pausing in horror...
"What?" he asks, noticing her face drop.
She confesses that she forgot to ring Karen earlier.
"See, this is what I am talking about" he says with worry.
"My Jen would never forget a thing like that. I mean how could you?" he adds, looking really disappointed in her.
Bruce explains how he really feels about the Tony situation across London and tells her how they helped piss the dick-head off, how they've walked away and how they've left the girls to face it alone.
"You're right" sighs Jennifer.
"We will find a way of getting Tony off their backs once and for all tomorrow" she adds.
"And then what?" asks Bruce, as though he's lost all sense of direction with everything.
Jennifer looks into his eyes, but says nothing.
"Oh no" Bruce says.
"You aren't telling me you're going to carry on teaching these girls after tonight?" he asks, knowing exactly what her eyes are telling him.
Jennifer explains she's making progress with Lucy and her sister Tina and all Rose needs is a little more help than a normal person.
"Normal person?" he snaps, trying to keep his voice down.
"Did you see her pick the knife-lover up off the floor tonight and walk away with him?" he asks, getting a little upset with the conversation.
Jennifer doesn't respond and tells him again that they will help Karen and the others out in the morning.
"I want to go home Jen" he finally admits, with a home sick face

on.

"I know we've done a lot of travelling with your teaching in the past and I know we are only the other side of London, but I really loved life with the other girls" he adds.

Jennifer knows she's losing the one person that holds her together and decides to back down a little and understand how he feels.

"Tell you what" she says, reaching out for his hand across the table.

"If you still feel the same in two weeks time, we will move back" she adds, watching his face light up.

She stands up and tells him two weeks again, then with a satisfied look on his face, he feels that his wife does care again after all. She tells him she's going upstairs to bed and he tells her, he will join her.

"No that's okay baby" she says, walking towards the kitchen door.

"You go back to what you were doing with Lucy before I walked in" she adds with a smile.

Bruce can't deny the fact something was going on and is far too tired to explain that Lucy was just trying to cheer him up. He thinks it through for a few minutes and comes to terms that his wife wants to have some kind of threesome or watch them have sex. Just as he ponders on the idea or looks for the motivation to give her what she wants, she shuts down on him again.

"You don't even have to entertain me or let me watch this time baby" she whispers.

"You just enjoy yourself tonight" she adds, with the same loving and understanding smile.

Apart from being totally baffled by the words coming from his wife's mouth, he is left feeling again that she doesn't care.

"I can't do this" he snaps, still trying to keep his voice down.

"Do what?" she asks, turning at the door looking puzzled.

"I don't want Lucy or anyone else. I want my wife" he insists looking at her.

"Bet you wouldn't say no to Amy though?" she responds, trying to make him smile, knowing he has a soft spot for her.

"No not even Amy right now" he snaps back.

"I just don't understand you any-more" he adds, leaving the kitchen, walking straight past Lucy sitting in the living room and upstairs.

Jennifer follows him through, where Lucy senses something has just happened.

"Do you want me to leave?" asks Lucy, looking really concerned.

Jennifer tells her to relax, make herself comfy for the night and that Bruce is just stressing out because it's been a long day. Lucy feels a little uncomfortable, but does what she is told as Jennifer follows him up the stairs. Just as she reaches the first step, there is a knock at the front door. Jennifer opens it.

"Rose, what are you doing here?" asks Jennifer, surprised to see her standing on the doorstep.

"Fucking great" Bruce's voice echo's downstairs, as he pops his head round the corner to find out who it is.
Rose explains she's really sorry for what happened and tries to justify helping her boyfriend after what he did.

"You know, he didn't cheat on you Rose. He didn't fuck one of your best friends" Bruce says butting in, coming back down the stairs.

"He tried to rape you and kill me" he adds, reaching the bottom as Rose begs him too for forgiveness.
Just when Bruce thinks he's heard enough, Jennifer's phone bleeps. Bruce looks over her shoulder to see who it is.

"It's only Karen. I will ring her back later" says Jennifer, trying to welcome Rose in.

"Don't you fucking dare" snaps Bruce.

"Take your phone upstairs and talk to Karen. I will make Rose a cup of coffee" he demands, ushering his wife towards the staircase.
Jennifer tells Rose not to leave and tells her she just needs to make a quick phone-call. With that Bruce lets Rose in and through to the living room, as Jennifer runs up to her bedroom to talk to Karen on the phone.

Through in the living room Rose doesn't hang about telling Bruce and Lucy how sorry she is and inviting them to her drama workshop tomorrow to make it up to them. Like a true friend or one that knows a few well known celebrities will be there, Lucy is quick to accept her room-mates repentance and accepts the invitation. Bruce however isn't so impressed.

"Is that all you think you have to do Rose?" he grunts at her.

"A party will make me forget about a knife in my face, will it?" he adds, standing there as Rose sits down on his sofa next to Lucy.
Rose again tries to bribe him and make him forgive her, but Bruce isn't having any of it and tells her he's going to make her a coffee.

"With some fucking rat poison in it" he mumbles under his breath, walking towards the kitchen.
He goes into the kitchen and Rose smiles at Lucy, telling her to stay there. Rose stands up and follows Bruce.

"Bruce isn't going to be that easy to convince Rose" whispers Lucy, trying to advise her.

"He hasn't met me properly yet though, has he?" Rose whispers, with a flirtatious smile, standing at the kitchen door.

"We aren't all that different you know Bruce" she says, placing her foot up behind her against the door frame in a seductive manner.

Bruce spins round and takes a look at her.

"Go back through there little girl, there's nothing similar about us" he tells her, with a disgusted look on his face.

"Really?" she asks, slowly walking towards him, shaking her seductive attitude as she walks.

"The way I see it Bruce, is you want me and I want you, so that makes us similar" she adds, reaching him and whispering her dirty words towards him.

Bruce starts to laugh.

"I might be attracted to other women. I might even be able to look at other women, but you would be the last girl I would ever consider wanting" he tells her adamantly.

"Stop fighting it Bruce" she tells him, standing right in front of him licking her lips and fluttering her eye lashes.

Bruce laughs again and backs away towards the kitchen table.

"You don't love yourself much do you?" he says, trying to ignore her seduction.

"I know my man must have given you a scare earlier" she tells him, standing in front of him.

"Scare my knob" Bruce laughs, walking towards the sink and away from her again.

"Your boyfriend is nothing but a dick-head who needs weapons to fight his battles" he adds, turning to face her.

"MM-mm, I love to give dick HEAD Bruce" she utters, with a horny expression on her face.

"Yeah well if you think I am stupid enough to fall for this, then you can suck mine" he barks, showing her there's no way he's going to back down.

Just as Bruce starts to think he's got her backing down and giving up, she falls to her knees.

"Get it out then" she orders, showing him she wants to suck it for him.

"I bet your dick is nice and fat" she flirts, waiting for him to deliver.

He walks over to her, grabs her by the arm, pulling her to her feet.

"I thought you told me to suck your dick?" she asks, making out she is innocent.

Bruce ever so gently pushes her in the direction of the kitchen wall.

"I don't know what your game is Rose or why my wife would even bother with someone like you, but I can't stand you, so stay out of my way" he threatens her, with anger in his voice.

She turns her head away, then over his shoulder and nibbles on his ear.

"I always get what I want and your dick is it" she whispers, before turning and going back into the living room.

Jennifer walks back in at the same time and Bruce shows more interest in the phone-call, instead of what Rose has just whispered to him.

"How did it go? Are they okay?" he asks Jennifer.

Jennifer tells him everything is fine, that Tony is becoming a pest but nothing they can't handle. She then tells him she's planned to go over in the morning and see her. Bruce is pleased about something at last and then remembers what Jennifer had promised him.

"Two weeks, two fucking weeks" he mumbles under his breath, as Rose gives him a wink across the room.

Rose again invites them to her drama workshop tomorrow afternoon and tells Jennifer that Lucy and Bruce have already agreed to come. Jennifer looks over at Bruce for his answer and watches as he smiles and shrugs his shoulders.

"Two fucking weeks. Fourteen days" he mumbles, with the same forced smile.

"Well I guess if these two have already said yes, then I will be there too" says Jennifer, smiling at Rose, unaware of the mind games she's playing with her husband.

CHAPTER 8
TOYBOY THIGHS AND NASTY EYES

It's the next morning and whilst Lucy sleeps on the sofa downstairs in the living room, Jennifer is waking up next to her husband in bed upstairs in the bedroom. She lies there for a few minutes just watching him sleep and smiles, gently running her hand over his face as he makes funny noises. Suddenly she stops touching him as his eyes open.

"Morning sexy" she whispers smiling at him.

"Yeah morning" he grunts, as he turns over facing away from her, not in a great mood.

She leans in towards him and snuggles up behind him.

"Hey mister grumpy pants, don't you feel like having some fun with your beautiful wife this morning?" she whispers, trying to run her hand under the cover towards his shorts.

Bruce quickly sits up, so she is unable to make contact and throws the covers back to get out of bed.

"Oh dear, we aren't in the best of moods this morning are we?" she softly says, trying not to rattle him.

He stands up, jumps straight into a pair of jeans from the floor and turns to face her.

"Sorry, have I got something to smile about this morning?" he grunts again.

Jennifer doesn't answer and starts to get out of bed too.

"I mean, who would smile being me?" he mumbles, loud enough so she can hear.

"I have a knife waved in my face. I am sexually threatened by a

strange girl called Rose. That same strange bitch whose man it was that waved the knife only hours before. The strange bitches' roommate is trying to bed me and my own wife for some reason is making out nothing is wrong" he adds, getting more and more worked up as he mumbles.
Once again Jennifer doesn't respond and starts getting dressed on the other side of the room.
"Nothing to say about nothing Jen?" he asks, trying hard to get something out of her.
"That's not like you. You've always got something to say about everything" he adds, putting on his top.
The more Jennifer doesn't take him on, the more aggravated he seems to get. Jennifer tries calming him down by reminding him she's going over to visit Karen this morning and that everything is going to turn out okay.
"Would you like to come with me?" she asks.
"I know she would love to see you there too" she adds, searching for a top to wear.
Now it's Bruce's turn to ignore her as he puts his shoes on and leaves the room to go downstairs.
Bruce walks into the living room to find Lucy waking up on the sofa under a duvet. She sits up and smiles at him as he apologises for disturbing her.
"I was just waking up anyway" Lucy says in a soft voice, whilst having a stretch.
Bruce heads into the kitchen to put the kettle on and minutes later, Lucy follows him through. He turns and asks her if she would like a cup of coffee and notices her standing there in one of his shirts, only partially buttoned.
"Nice shirt" he says, trying to take his eyes from her long legs.
"I hope you don't mind. Jen let me borrow it last night" she tells him, trying to do up the rest of the buttons, not to show off too much cleavage.
Bruce notices her cleavage before she manages to do the buttons up and drops the spoon he is using on the floor. Both of them make a mad dash towards the floor to pick it up and meet each-other. They gaze into each-others eyes for a few seconds before laughing about the situation and standing up again. Bruce can't help but notice her white knickers underneath his shirt as she hands him the spoon and she can't help but take a quick glimpse towards the package area of his jeans. Just then Jennifer walks into the room.
"Hope there's a cup for me too" she chirps, walking over towards them.

Bruce turns and hands her a coffee, telling them he needs to go.

"You not coming to see Karen with me then?" Jennifer asks him, as he approaches the door.

"Maybe next time" he responds, forcing a smile and leaving.

Jennifer and Lucy sit around talking for a little while and drinking their coffee. Jennifer asks if she's going home today but Lucy tells her that she thinks she's going to take the day off and asks her if she could hang around the house for the day.

"Sure thing, stay as long as you like" responds Jennifer, explaining that she needs to pop out in a little while too.

An hour later Jennifer has made her way across London and is quite excited to be visiting her other friends. She arrives at the coffee shop where they have planned to meet and is the first to turn up.

She enters the shop and can't help but reminisce about all the times she spent with the girls sitting at the same table. Minutes later her friend Karen walks through the door.

"Look at you. Sexy, confident and glowing" Jennifer proudly claims standing up and waiting for a hug.

"Don't stop there, you've got a lot of compliments to give before I forgive you for leaving us like you did" laughs Karen, reaching her and giving her a massive cuddle.

The girls sit down and the smiles beam across the table for everyone to see. They catch up a little in light conversation, before Jennifer decides to touch on the subject of Tony.

"So what's been going on? What has he been doing?" asks Jennifer.

Karen explains that he hasn't done much, but she knows it's only a matter of time before he does. She explains how he has popped up in random places over the last twelve hours or so.

"It's as though he enjoys scaring me and it's just a taste of things to come" explains Karen.

"And what about the other girls? Have they experienced it too?" asks Jennifer.

Karen tells her that Michelle and Jane haven't been around since the party the other night so doesn't know, but it's just starting to happen to Amy now.

"Maybe he won't do anything then" says Jennifer.

"He might just be chasing you for the scare. We did humiliate him after all" she adds.

Although Karen is grateful of Jennifer's listening ear, she doesn't think it's as clear as she is making out.

"I'm not sure" says Karen.

"He's got this nasty look in his eyes, like he's going to kill me or something" she adds, taking a long sip of her coffee.

Jennifer finally understands just how scared Karen really is. She knows that Karen won't take any kind of abuse from anyone and to scare her, it must be pretty serious. Jennifer tells her not to worry and that she will get Bruce to come across and find out what is going on. Karen feels relieved.

"It's not me I am worried about, but now I am expecting, I can't risk anything happening" Karen tells her.

Again Jennifer understands her concerns and tells her Bruce will sort it out nevertheless.

Karen smiles and decides to jazz up the conversation and get off the subject of Tony. First she asks her how the new clients are doing, then she asks when herself and Amy can come visit. Jennifer tells her about Lucy, Tina and Rose and what has just happened at Tina's birthday party.

"Is Bruce okay?" asks Karen, with concern all over her face.

Jennifer tells her he's fine and explains how home sick he is at the moment.

"Hey you can't blame him" Karen says giggling.

"Once you've had Karen in your life, nothing else ain't quite the same" she adds laughing.

This comment seems to lighten the mood and Jennifer quickly asks if the last forty-eight hours and if the pregnancy is sinking in yet. Karen tells her that the morning sickness is a bit of a shit, since she got out of hospital but that's about it really.

"I imagine morning sickness is a tough thing to cope with?" asks Jennifer.

"No not really. Just like a normal night out on the town with you girls. Without the same fucking hangover in the morning of course" Karen responds making Jennifer laugh again.

For a few seconds everything goes silent and the girls run out of things to say. Karen then asks another question she feels she needs to know the answer to.

"Seeing as you've moved away and you left us so suddenly, does that mean we are not your clients any-more?" she asks.

Jennifer explains that no matter how long passes; she will always have a connection and friendship with the girls.

"Yeah but does that mean no more lessons for us?" Karen asks, unsure of what she means.

Jennifer tells her she must put most of her time and effort into her new clients, but it doesn't mean that they can't have a lesson every now and again too. Karen's eyes beam with joy as she hears the words come out of Jennifer's mouth and has an idea already.

"I've been struggling with masturbation and having an orgasm since this morning sickness started, but I have had a really strong desire for bum fun. Is that normal?" asks Karen.

"Do you mean anal sex?" asks Jennifer.

"Yeah you know, sex up the ringer" responds Karen, showing no shyness about the topic at all.

Jennifer asks if she's ever done it before.

"I might have once" answers Karen.

"What do you mean, you might have once?" laughs Jennifer.

"Well it happened so quickly. He sort of missed the hole at the front and slipped up there by mistake" Karen tells her.

Jennifer explains that isn't what she really meant by having anal sex and tells her the desires and cravings she's having are normal.

"Really?" asks Karen.

"Really" answers Jennifer.

"In-fact many pregnant women get the urge to do a sexual thing they wouldn't normally do during the nine months" she adds.

"Thank fuck for that" signs Karen.

"I thought the baby had already put my vagina out of business and this was just of taster of things to come" she adds, wiping her relieved brow.

Jennifer tells her that her vagina and urges will go back to normal once she's had the baby.

"So what should I do then?" asks Karen.

"Should I find a guy that likes to fuck up the little brown hole all the time? Or should I just make a normal guy miss the hole and do me up there instead?" she asks, trying to get as much information out of her friend and coach as possible.

Jennifer doesn't really know how to answer the question and looks a little confused, so Karen tries to explain herself again.

"There's someone I like and kind of been shagging, but I don't think he's the kind of guy to be into anal sex" Karen says.

"Should I make him miss my hole or should I just find someone that likes to do it?" she asks.

Jennifer listens to the question again but still doesn't really have the answer, so decides to give her the whole anal lesson.

Jennifer's Lesson In Anal Sex

There are so many stories out there about anal sex, that none of us seem to understand what it's all about, why men enjoy it so much and how it's meant to feel.

Ask yourself this question right now... What stories have you heard? Have you heard it hurts?

Fact is... Anal sex if done correctly, shouldn't hurt at all and believe it or not, can lead to a great orgasm if performed correctly.

For men it's one of three things.

1... It could be the fashionable trend he wants to jump on. A little like his desire to have a threesome with two female's at once, anal sex is the same. He hears stories from friends and other men doing it and simply wants to see what all the fuss is about.

2... It could be that he's into anal, which means this is a part of his sexuality.

3... It could be that he simply needs a change and the different feeling and tightness gives him what he craves.

Although it might be your first time trying anal sex and you would normally stay clear of the anal kind of guy, it works out that if you are ever going to try it, you will always be better off with someone that enjoys it or has had previous experience. With someone like this, he should already know now to put it in, how to do it and how to help you relax and enjoy it.

The stories that you hear about anal sex being painful come from those women that have either the fashionable guys or the one's that fancy a change. With no previous experience, he will most probably try and squeeze it in, forget the foreplay or lube and start hammering at you, which can be painful. Although the experienced guy will hammer you too, he will make sure you are ready for it before doing it.

When it comes to trying anal, it's really no different from losing your virginity. Yes it feels strange at first, yes it might take time to start enjoying it, but you can in the end.

My personal tip is... Find out if your man has ever done it before and just how experienced he is, then whatever happens next, RELAX !! Relaxation is the key to enjoying anal sex. If you don't relax, it's always going to feel uncomfortable.

If you really do have your doubts, use your fingers or sex toys to try it out on your own first. Failing that, ask him to finger you, or even better use his tongue. Men that won't do either show their inexperience and unwillingness to make it great for you too. Failing everything and if you want a man off your back when it comes to anal, just say

"Yes I will let you fuck my rear, as long as you let me use a strap-on up your bum first"

Remember, anal sex is no more designed for a woman than it is a man, so if he wants it, he should be prepared to take it too.

Anal sex can be very pleasurable... Some women enjoy it more than normal sex. In moderation and in the company of a caring, considerate and experienced partner, you will enjoy it too. Remember – Relax.

"I guess I won't be trying it after all then" Karen says, looking a little disappointed after the quick lesson.

"Why not?" asks Jennifer.

Karen explains that the bloke she had in mind isn't all that experienced in the bedroom department anyway, so there's not much chance anal will be his thing.

"Yeah but don't forget, it's not always about having an experienced partner Karen" says Jennifer.

"You can experience it yourself with toys and then let an inexperienced man at you too" she adds.

"Oh yeah, I forgot that bit" giggles Karen.

Jennifer explains once more, that it is better to have an experienced man perform anal on you, but if you learn how to relax by yourself and what you like inside you, then any man will do.

"Anyway, enough of that. Who's this guy? I thought you said you didn't have time for a man in your life the last time I saw you?" asks Jennifer, wanting to know all the gory details.

Karen sits and ponders on her answer for a few seconds then goes to open her mouth. As she does Amy walks into the shop.

"I hope you haven't started a lesson without me" says Amy, with a big smile on her face, walking over to them waiting to be greeted.

Karen and Jennifer get up and welcome Amy to the table.

"You look as stunning as ever" says Jennifer, looking at Amy in her tight white jeans, light blue figure hugging top and short blonde hair.

"Why thank you Jen" Amy says smiling back.

"Yeah and still a big tart" laughs Karen, teasing the blonde bombshell.

Amy takes a quick look around.

"No Bruce?" she asks.

Jennifer tells her he's not with her this time but he sends his love.

"Anyway, forget about Bruce, how's you and Dean doing?" Jennifer asks.

Amy gives a little smile.

"Yeah me and Deano are good" she responds.

"Good, is that it? No sex on trains or buses of late then?" Jennifer asks, remembering their phone call the other day.

Amy only answers with a smile again, then sits down with them at the table. She asks what she's missed and what they are talking about.

"Oh yeah that's right Miss Karen, who is this man then?" Jennifer asks, nearly forgetting about the mystery man.

"Man? Are we talking about Karen's new crush?" laughs Amy, as Karen tries to kick her under the table but misses.

"Boy you mean" she adds, laughing at Karen's face and the fact she missed and kicked the table.

Jennifer looks at the two of them laughing and wants in on the joke.

"Come on, don't keep me hanging. Boy? Man? Who?" insists Jennifer.

As Karen tries to hide her blushes, Amy takes great pleasure in giving Jennifer all the gory details.

"She has a major crush on a seventeen year old boy" laughs Amy.

"Mm-mm toy boy" responds Jennifer, giving her approval.

Amy doesn't understand the support Jennifer is giving her.

"You don't understand" says Amy.

"She must be fifteen years older than him" she adds, calling Karen a MILF.

Jennifer quickly explains that age is nothing but a number.

"You are only as old as you feel or the penis you are feeling" laughs Jennifer.

"Yeeaahhh, I feel a lesson coming on" Amy laughs, clapping her hands, getting excited.

Jennifer's Lesson On Age And Fetish

As long as two people are legally at an age to both have sex, then there's nothing wrong with the age of your partner. Whether it's older men that do it for you or younger, it doesn't matter.

Many women have one or both of these fetishes and some even keep it to themselves all their lives. There is not one single reason why a woman will find either older men a turn on or a younger guy sexier, but either way it is not perverted in any way, shape or form.

For the women that are turned on by a younger guy. People normally put it down to the fact she feels that she's getting older and wants a young man to make her feel young again, or that her experience now wants to teach a younger guy how to do it all. These are the two main reasons women think they desire younger men. In most cases this is true, but you are missing one honest secret ingredient... You want young because you remember just how good it feels.

Pushing aside the prudes out there and the married women that still claim they only have eyes for their husband... How many of you would turn your nose up if a sexy, fit, good looking eighteen year old wanted sex with you?

Yes you might hear yourself saying "I'm old enough to be his mother" or

"You're just a kid" but how many pairs of knickers would it warm up?
I tell you how many... All of them !!
If we are honest, we would all love to let this young guy have his wicked way with us. Just think... Firmer body, different sized penis, a mentality that is eager to please, the energy levels of a horse, the list goes on...
But it's only those women with nerve that can admit to these desires. The rest of you feel perverted and guilty.
So which are you? If the sexiest man in your eyes claimed to be only eighteen years old, who would honestly say the thought didn't turn them on?
Okay it's not just about the desire for a younger guy. Younger women have the same fetish for older guys too. Why?
Many say it's because they want to be protected and search out a father figure. Now personally, this is something that sounds really wrong to me. Father figure? No... The answer is simply because these young girls are already sexually active and know what they like. The young sex starved teenager that the older women craves, isn't good enough for the younger girl as she seeks out someone that can make her orgasm over and over again with his experience.
What it all comes down to is age is a strange thing. When you are younger, you want older and when you are older, you desire younger. There's nothing wrong with this fetish, there's nothing wrong with this fantasy and if you can get yourself a piece of the action, good for you !!
Don't let age or what people think of you get in the way of your true feelings. If you are the younger girl craving an older man, go for it. You are more likely to have a full-on multiple orgasm before any of your friends still having sex with boys their own age. And if you are an older women craving a young man, go for it too. You know what an orgasm feels like, so go and enjoy those lustful thoughts running through your mind. Soon enough the age of your younger man will rise and you won't be able to even consider an eighteen year old again.
Remember there's no such thing as us getting younger, only older.
The more you hold back, the more you miss out on, the more you don't enjoy yourself when the time is right, the older your younger man gets.
Don't cheat on your partner with a fetish, but don't cheat yourself out of a certain craving.

"See Aims, I told you there was nothing wrong with me" laughs Karen, enjoying the lesson.
"I still find it wrong that you're chasing someone nearly half your age" laughs Amy.

"Why?" asks Jennifer, trying to work them out at the same time. Amy doesn't have an answer and instead, just screws her face up and makes a vomiting noise.

"That's because you are still a little girl" laughs Karen, trying hard to tease her.

"That's right Amy. You are still very young" says Jennifer, backing Karen up.

"That's why you have the hots for my Bruce, the older man" she adds.

Amy doesn't respond just giving them both a funny look, then Jennifer finishes off her lesson...

"Your honest age fetish says a lot about your sex life believe it or not" Jennifer tells them.

"How?" asks Amy, waiting to hear what Jennifer has to say about her.

Jennifer explains that Karen is looking for a younger guy because she hasn't got a man, doesn't want any commitment and wants to be ravished.

"Yeah so what about me then?" asks Amy, still waiting for it.

Jennifer explains that Amy has enjoyed sex with guys her own age and younger, but now she knows what an orgasm feels like, she wants an older man to take her further. Karen gets the point but Amy still struggles with it a little. Jennifer decides to write it down at the table.

She writes:

Teenage virgin having sex with guy her own age =
Inexperienced in sex and to the orgasm.
Teenage virgin craving an older man for first time =
Enjoys masturbation correctly.
Girl aged 18-29 craving sex with younger guys =
Hasn't experienced a real orgasm yet.
Girl aged 18-29 craving sex with guys her own age =
Still learning.
Girl aged 18-29 craving sex with older guy =
Craves more than the single orgasm now.
Girl aged 30-39 having sex with guys her own age =
Experienced.
Girl aged 30-39 craving sex with older guys =
Hears sex stories, but rarely sees the action.
Girl aged 30-39 craving sex with younger guys =
Knows the orgasm inside out.

Girl aged 40+ craving sex with older guys =
A wasted youth. Never had a real man satisfy her.
Girl aged 40+ craving sex with younger guys =
Wants to teach or feel young again.

Amy and Karen read what Jennifer has written down for them and tells them it's only a rough guide, but there is some logic behind it all.
　"Yeah baby" shouts Karen.
　"I know the orgasm inside out" she adds, trying to quickly read what Amy's says about her.
Amy starts to blush as Karen and Jennifer look at her.
　"Amy and Bruce sitting in a tree" sings Karen, in a childish manner then stops...
　"Sorry Jen, I still forget that you and Bruno are married" she adds, covering her face.
Jennifer tells her it's okay and asks the girls if it sounds about right. They both quickly agree but Amy still has her doubts.
　"I know what an orgasm is. I've had many. So why am I still searching for the older man?" asks Amy.
Jennifer explains although she's experienced and had many orgasm's, Amy's sexuality is still searching for that little bit extra.
　"I don't understand" says Amy looking confused.
　"Would you still like to have sex with Bruce?" Jennifer asks her.
Amy knows that she can be totally honest with her friend and nods her head.
　"Why?" asks Jennifer.
Amy shrugs her shoulders.
　"Is it because you want an older, not so firm body on top of you? Or is it because you believe it would be the best sex of your life?" asks Jennifer, coming to her point.
Amy doesn't need long to think it over.
　"The sex" Amy answers.
　"That means you still feel there's something out there to be discovered" explains Jennifer.
Amy seems a little more satisfied with the answer now and Karen looks a little more interested.
　"Are you saying Aims is wrong to look for an older man then? Or could Bruce do the business hypothetically speaking?" Karen asks.
　"Oh Bruce could do the business" responds Jennifer, with a huge grin across her face, knowing she's experienced it over and over again in the years they've been married.
With that all three girls drift off into space for a few seconds...
As they one by one come round from their own sexual visions of

Bruce doing the business, Karen and Jennifer notice Amy still out of it. They laugh about the blank look on her face and try to get her attention back.

"Aims, come back to earth Aims" laughs Karen.

Still nothing, as the blonde just stares out of the shop window in her daydream.

"Amy are you okay?" asks Jennifer, getting a little bit concerned now.

"She's fine" laughs Karen.

"She will start having a Harry met Sally orgasm at the table shortly" she adds.

"No look" snaps Jennifer, noticing her eyes staring out the window and her white face.

"Aims" shouts Karen, trying to keep her voice down in the shop as Jennifer tries to see what she's looking at outside.

Just then Jennifer spots it and there across the road leering at the three of them is Tony...

It takes Jennifer a while to come to terms with it, until Karen finally spots him too.

"There's that bastard" Karen yells, getting up from the table and heading straight to the door to confront him.

Jennifer gives chase and Amy panics about being left alone.

The three girls run out of the shop and try crossing the busy road where he stands still staring at them.

"What's your problem?" screams Karen over the traffic, as she gets half way across the road.

Tony doesn't move.

The three girls manage to get across the road as he starts to laugh.

"Do you know how easy it would have been to get one of my drivers to run you down just then?" Tony asks, as they walk over to him.

"But that would be too easy. I want you all to suffer first" he adds, with a nasty glint in his eye.

Although they are scared, the girls seem stronger as a unit and stand their ground.

"What do you want Tony?" asks Jennifer, speaking for all three of them.

"Remember what you did to me in the lap dancing club a few nights ago?" asks Tony.

"It's payback time" he adds, not giving them a chance to respond.

Karen knows there's not much she can do in her condition, but her fierce manner doesn't take too kindly to being threatened.

"What are you going to do Mr Cum in your pants?" Karen laughs,

hiding her fear.
Tony moves closer to the girls and points them in the direction of an alleyway.
"Once you are alone. Once you walk down the wrong street. You will die" says Tony, like a villain out of a film.
The girls look towards the alleyway where Tony is pointing and notice a big black car with five or six large looking men staring at them.
"Somehow, some way, you will all pay for what you did to me" Tony laughs once more.
Jennifer decides she's heard enough and tries to usher the girls away. Not even loud mouth Karen is brave enough to stand up this time. The girls start to walk away, making sure he isn't following.
"You won't always have each-other. At some point you will all make a bad move on your own" Tony calls out.
Jennifer continues to usher the girls away from the street as Amy starts to get really emotional.
"Say hello to Bruce for me too Jennifer. Tell him I love the new house" calls Tony, sending a shiver of fear down Jennifer's spine.
Jennifer manages to get the girls out of sight and round a corner. They stop and panic but Jennifer keeps it together more than the other two. She quickly feels it would be safer if they all stay together from now on and invites Karen and Amy to stay with her and Bruce.
"You heard what he said. He knows where you live too" says Amy, still panicking.
"Yeah but Bruce won't let anything happen to us, would he?" Karen says, trying to calm her down a little but looking petrified herself.
Karen agrees to take Jennifer up on her offer but tells her there's something she needs to do first. Amy wants to say yes but knows she has her man Dean at home. Jennifer tells Karen to do what she needs to do quickly and ring her later, before making her way across London.
"In-fact I will get Bruce to come meet you the minute you ring" says Jennifer, trying to cover every angle.
Karen says goodbye to the two girls and quickly jumps on a bus that's stopped beside them. Jennifer waves her arm out and stops a taxi passing by. She puts Amy in it and tells her to go straight home.
"Any problems, just ring" Jennifer tells her, as the taxi driver starts to drive off.
Now all alone, Jennifer looks up and down the street for another taxi but can't see one. Then she gets really scared as Tony reappears from around the corner and stands staring at her again. Jennifer knows what Tony said about making a wrong move, so decides it's

safer to stay on the main high-street where there are plenty of people around. She slowly walks away from Tony and keeps checking to make sure he isn't following her. On the third look however, Tony has vanished. She spots a minicab coming towards her with it's light on and waves her arm, jumping in the car before it even comes to a halt, frantically looking out the back window.

"Where to sexy? Tony's place?" Jennifer hears the driver in front of her say.
Her heart stops beating as she hears the cab drivers voice repeat the question in slow motion. She panics and gets ready to jump back out.

"What did you say?" she stutters, trying to work out what the safest option is and making sure she can pull the lever on the door to open it again.
The driver turns to her.

"Sorry, I can't help flirting with the hot women that get in my cab" says the driver.

"My name is Tony, Where would you like to go?" he asks.
Jennifer gives him her home address and feels her heart pounding in her chest. Soon enough they are travelling away from the busy high-street and Jennifer doesn't seem to be bothered by the perverted driver giving her the eye in his rear view mirror. At this moment in time, one perverted driver is safer than what is back there...

Meanwhile back at Jennifer's house. Bruce has just walked back in to find Lucy still sitting on the sofa and Jennifer not home.

"Nice to see you dressed" says Bruce, in a much happier mood than he walked out in.
Lucy moves her hand and picks up his shirt sitting beside her.

"Here's your shirt back" she says smiling, quickly sniffing it and handing to him.

"I love the smell of you on it" she adds, closing her eyes taking in the scent.
Bruce takes the shirt from her, looking a little baffled.

"What do you mean it smells of me?" he asks, putting it up to his nose and getting nothing from it but a waft of her perfume.
She asks him to sit down beside her and he reluctantly does wary of her sexual behaviour.

"Can I quickly try something on you please Bruce?" she asks, looking right at him.
Bruce smiles and nods his head.

"Could you tell me how sexy you think I am?" she asks, keeping eye contact with him.

Bruce tries to shuffle further up the sofa, knowing exactly what is coming but she doesn't react.

"Please Bruce I want to show you something" she says again, pleading with her eyes.

Bruce explains he does find her attractive and on a normal day would flirt, tell her these things and have some fun.

"Isn't this a normal day then?" she asks, still wanting him to do it.

Bruce smiles again but shakes his head. He tells her that on a normal day he would flirt, even do a few naughty things with Jennifer's clients just to make a point or help make a lesson work.

"Oh yeah" she responds, looking very interested.

"How many girls have you flirted with then?" she asks.

Bruce smiles at her again, leans back on the sofa and tells her loads.

"What about kissed, how many?" she asks, with a flirtatious look on her face.

"A few" answers Bruce.

"Shown your dick to?" she asks, fidgeting on the sofa, allowing the conversation to wind her up.

Again Bruce smiles and tells her loads.

"Fucked?" she asks, as her mouth goes dry desperate to hear the answer.

"None" Bruce answers.

Lucy finds this really hard to believe and moves in a little closer to ask him again.

"There have been times when I've been tempted. There have been many offers, but none" he tells her again.

Now Lucy doubts his words.

"So you've never fucked another girl in front of Jen? Not even in a threesome?" she asks.

"Yeah we had a threesome years ago but never when it comes to her work" he explains.

It goes silent for a while as they look at each-other and smile.

"Come on" Bruce says.

"I know you've got something else to say" he adds.

Lucy sits forward on the chair, bites her lip and looks at him.

"Have you ever wanted to have sex with any of Jen's clients?" she asks him, getting horny.

Bruce doesn't want to say too much but doesn't like to lie either.

"Yeah" he answers, hoping this will be enough for her.

"Who?" she asks, stroking her leg through her jeans, praying for the answer she wants.

Just then Bruce jumps up off the sofa and starts laughing.

"This is making you horny isn't it? You just want me to tell you how sexy I think you are, don't you?" he asks, looking at her.

"Please" she begs, looking up at him.

"No way" Bruce laughs, knowing she will jump on him the minute he utters the words she wants to hear.

"Please Bruce. I need to hear it" she begs again.

Bruce gives in and sits down beside her. He takes her by the hand, looks into her eyes and smiles.

"I think you are really sexy and you have a smile that could make me hard in a second" he tells her.

"And yes there are two girls I've been attracted to over the years and you are one of those girls" he adds, bracing himself, closing his eyes and waiting for her to jump on him.

He opens his eyes and can't believe that she hasn't moved from her spot. He can't work out how she can be that horny, hear those words and not react. She keeps eye contact and just smiles at him.

"I've learnt how to control it" she boasts, with the grin on her face getting bigger and bigger.

Bruce still can't believe it, so he tries harder.

"You are the most sexist woman I've ever set eyes on" he tells her. Still she doesn't move...

"I want to have sex with you right now" he stutters, waiting for the immanent eruption from her, but still nothing...

Soon enough he gives up and tells her how happy he is that she's learnt about self control so fast.

"Now I want you to fuck me" she says, wiping the smile straight off his face.

"What?" he stutters, feeling himself lose control of a situation for the first time ever.

She moves closer to him on the sofa and places her hand on his leg.

"I said I want you to fuck me right now" she repeats, slowly moving her hand towards his inner thigh.

He places his hand quickly on top of her hand to stop her and tries to work out what's going on.

Finally she explains she's managed to master the self control bit, but still wants to have sex with him.

"I really need to know if I want to get married or if I need to sleep around a little more" she tells him.

"And sleeping with me will do that?" Bruce asks, trying to understand what she's asking him.

Lucy tells him she would rather take the chance with someone she trusts, than find herself a one night stand and risking it. Finally Bruce understands but doesn't quite know what to say.

"So will you sleep with me?" she asks, ready to lunge at him and

rip his clothes off.
Just as he goes to answer, they hear the front door go.

"Wow, the same thing happening to me twice" she mumbles, as this time he gets up, panics and looks all flustered.

Jennifer walks in with a face like thunder and heads straight to the drinks on the sideboard. She pours herself a straight vodka and downs it in one as Bruce and Lucy watch.

"What's happened Jen? Are the girls okay?" asks a concerned looking Bruce.

"Maybe I should go?" says Lucy, feeling the couple need space to talk.

Bruce tells her she's more than welcome to stay but gets no response from Jennifer when he asks her to tell Lucy the same. Lucy stands up, thanks them both for their hospitality and leaves.

"Well that was fucking rude" Bruce snaps, joining her at the sideboard for a drink.

"You want to tell me what's going on?" he adds, pouring himself a drink.

Jennifer slams her glass down and turns to walk away.

"There's nothing wrong. I am going for a bath" she responds, heading straight upstairs.

Bruce watches his wife leave the room and clearly knows something is very wrong. Knowing that he doesn't want to get into a fight or force it out of her, he pours himself another drink and sits back down on the sofa. Ten minutes pass and he doesn't hear a peep out of Jennifer upstairs. All he can hear is the water filling up the bathtub and the silence of his own thoughts. Suddenly his phone rings. He takes it out of his pocket and looks down to see who it is.

"Hey Aims, how's things with you?" Bruce says, answering the phone to his friend.

Amy tells him she's fine but then goes into detail about the days events with the girls and Tony.

"Didn't Jen tell you then?" asks Amy, realising it's all new information to him.

Bruce makes out he hasn't seen Jennifer yet, but will be talking to her soon enough.

"So is that all that happened then, Tony just gave you all a fright?" asks Bruce, wanting the whole story with nothing left out.

"Yeah but the strangest thing about it all is Jen" she says.

For the second time during this short conversation, Bruce doesn't know what she's talking about and has to ask her what she means.

"Jen offered me and Karen a chance to stay over with you because it would be safer. Before I got home I got a text from Jen telling me I couldn't stay after all and Karen got the same" Amy tells him.

"What the fuck is going on?" asks Bruce, getting really confused.
He tells her that she's welcome to come and stay and to tell Karen the same thing. He then needs to cut the conversation short as he hears Jennifer coming back downstairs. He quickly tells her to pass the message onto Karen and tells her he will ring her back once he's found out what's going on. He quickly hangs up and hides the phone under his leg. Jennifer walks back into the room fresh out of the bath wearing a big pink fluffy towel. Bruce stands up ready to explode in a bewildered rage...

CHAPTER 9
"OUCH" MISS WHITNEY

"Do you feel better after your bath?" asks Bruce, holding his temper back for a few more seconds.
"Yeah funny enough I do" answers Jennifer, sitting down on the sofa ready to watch some TV with him.
"And don't you feel you were a little rude to Lucy before she left?" he asks, sitting down at the other end of the sofa, knowing that one way or another he will get to the bottom of everything.
Jennifer admits she may have been a little hard on Lucy and promises she will talk to her in the morning and put things right.
"And what about Amy and Karen, how are they?" he asks, knowing this is the question that could send him over the top if not answered honestly.
Bruce waits for an answer as she starts flicking through the channels on the TV.
"JEN" he snaps a little, trying to get her full attention.
"Sorry what?" Jennifer answers, making out she didn't hear the question whilst playing with the remote control.
Bruce asks the question again, to which she tells him they are both fine.
"They both said to say hello" she adds, still paying more attention to the remote in her hand.
Bruce quickly reaches over and snaps. He pulls the remote from her hand and throws it across the room in the direction of the wall.
"What's wrong with you now?" snaps a very distant Jennifer.
Bruce stands up and tells her he can't take much more.

"Much more what?" she answers, with a moody attitude turning back to the TV.
He walks over to the TV and switches it off and stands in front of it.
"Stop running away Jen, I can't help you if you do" he begs.
"Running? Who's running, I am sitting right here" she responds sarcastically.
"You know what I mean" he says.
"You've never lied to me about anything before" he adds, crouching down forcing her to look at him.
She looks at him and quickly gets up and heads towards the kitchen.
"What have I lied about?" she asks, swinging the kitchen door open and leaving the living room.
Bruce follows her into the kitchen knowing she is avoiding him for some reason.
"You won't tell me why you've changed over the last few days. You won't explain why there's an obvious divide between Amy and Karen across London and the girls here and why you've become so obsessed with this Rose girl after all she's done" he tells her.
Jennifer isn't doing anything in the kitchen, but staring out of the window into the back garden. She listens to what he has to say and knows he's speaking the truth. She thinks about backing down and telling him what's on her mind, but decides to be funny about it again.
"I know all this is happening but where did I lie?" she asks him, not even having the decency to turn and face him.
Bruce snaps into a full-on rage.
"That's it, after all we've been through, after everything I've done to help you and your teaching. Well that's it, you're on your own from now on" he shouts to the back of her head.
Something he said hits home and she turns with tears in her eyes. Bruce quickly hides his rage and walks over to comfort her.
"Come on baby, this isn't you" he whispers, giving her a cuddle.
She hugs him back continuing to cry.
"Tell me what's going on" he begs her for the final time.
She lets go of him and walks to the table ready to speak. She wipes away the tears and sits down. He follows her and sits opposite, waiting for her to open up.
"It's Tony" she tells him.
"I don't think I've ever been so scared" she says, before unloading the whole story on him.
Bruce listens to the events of the day carefully and is really pleased that she isn't hiding any-more
"The girls need me to be strong for them, but I was so scared" she goes on to tell him.

"He's not going to walk away or leave us alone until someone gets really hurt" she adds, starting to cry again.
Bruce takes her hand across the table and tells her he won't let anything like that happen.

"I think it's time I paid Tony another little visit" he says, ready to put all his rage to some good use.

"No you can't" snaps Jennifer sitting there.

"There are a lot of large men with him now. Not even you will be able to take them all on" she adds, asking him not to do it.
Bruce tells her no matter what happens, he won't let anything happen to her or the girls. Although he is still concerned about the whole Tony thing and the fact she didn't tell him straight away, he feels this is the most honest she's been with him for ages. This feeling doesn't last long however, when he suggests they pack up and move back across London.

"What about Lucy, Tina and Rose? I can't leave them now" she tells him.
Bruce explains it's better to walk away from girls she hardly knows, instead of something really bad happening to the one's she has real friendships with. He goes on to make the decision for her, by telling her he can't protect them living this side of London anyway.

"Okay" she tells him sighing, backing down and agreeing with him.

"But first I want to attend this drama workshop this afternoon and tell them we are leaving" she adds.
Bruce understands her request but reminds her Rose's nut-job boyfriend will probably be there. She tells him she knows, but really needs to do this.

"Fair enough, but just a warning" Bruce says.

"If he kicks off this time, I won't be holding back" he adds.
The couple agree that after the drama workshop and Jennifer has had a chance to say goodbye to the girls in person, they are moving back across London to their real friends and to sort the Tony thing out once and for all. The couple decide to relax and take it easy for a few hours at home before they are due at the drama workshop. Jennifer watches TV and passes out at times on the sofa. Bruce sits with her most of the time, but does manage to send a few reassuring text messages to Karen and Amy. Then out of the blue a music video comes on the TV and Jennifer jumps up.

"Look Bruce" she tells him.

"That's this girl that will be at this workshop thing in a few hours" she says, watching the celebrity sing one of her songs.

"I thought it was a drama school, not a music one?" asks Bruce.
Jennifer explains this famous girl called Whitney is a singer but has

just shot her first film over in America.

"Listen to you knowing everything about the world of celebrity" laughs Bruce, watching the blonde girl strut her stuff on the screen.

"You read far too many of these celebrity magazines you know" he adds, trying to dance along to the song and make Jennifer laugh in the process.

They watch the end of the music video and Jennifer feels it's time to start getting ready.

"So is she English or American then?" asks Bruce.

"Don't you know anything?" she laughs, claiming Whitney is a massive American star.

"Even bigger than Madonna some say" she adds.

"Oh Madonna, he's that footballer that cheated years ago isn't he?" Bruce says joking.

The couple go upstairs and into the bedroom. Jennifer starts going through her wardrobe for something classy to wear. Bruce stands in front of her, spins round in his jeans and top that he's been wearing all day and tells her he's ready.

"Suit and tie for you mister" she demands laughing at him again.

Although Bruce doesn't want to make the effort, he decides to dress accordingly, just because things seem fine between him and his wife again at last. They get dressed, Bruce wearing a dark blue suit and a pink tie, Jennifer wearing a pink dress and dark blue shoes. They stand together in front of the mirror and are pleased how they both look with the perfect colour co-ordination that seems to connect the strong couple once again.

An hour later Bruce and Jennifer have arrived and hardly recognise the school in front of them. There are cars everywhere, lights beaming out across the sky and even a red carpet placed in front of the entrance. The couple try to get in but are stopped by a doorman claiming they need someone to meet them from inside before they can enter.

"Oh well, we tried" laughs Bruce, spinning around and making out he wants to go home now.

Jennifer tells him to behave and quickly calls Lucy on her phone. Minutes later Lucy and Tina arrive at the entrance to welcome them to the school and workshop. Jennifer asks where Rose is and Lucy tells her with a disappointed look, that she's gone to meet her horrible boyfriend.

"Are you going to tell them that we are leaving yet?" Bruce whispers in Jennifer's ear, away from the girls waving at friends and

the crowd trying to get inside.
Jennifer tells him to wait until Rose is there and then suggests they move inside the building.

"What are you looking for?" Jennifer asks Bruce searching all his pockets and stalling entering.

"Hold on, here it is. No it isn't" Bruce says, continuing to search his pockets.

"Sorry we are late guys" says Karen's voice appearing from behind them.
Jennifer spins round shocked to see Karen and Amy all dressed up ready to join the workshop too.

"Oh here they are" Bruce says, making out Amy and Karen were what he was looking for in his pockets.
Bruce turns to Lucy and asks her if she would mind getting the two girls in too. Although Lucy looks a little confused, she has built a nice relationship up with Bruce and agrees.

"Looks like you've got competition" sniggers Karen in Amy's ear, noticing the sexy smile directed in Bruce's direction by Lucy.
Jennifer and Bruce make the introduction between the four girls and they all seem to greet each-other with warmth and kindness.

"Any other little surprises?" whispers Jennifer to Bruce.

"Is Dave going to pop out of your trousers now?" she asks, smiling and happy that her new and former clients have all bonded really well.
Bruce places his hands on Jennifer's shoulders and spins her round.

"Dave's already here I'm afraid, love of my life" he whispers to her, before explaining he's there as Tina's guest.
The gang are all ready to step inside, when they hear another voice.

"Nice suite Willis, have you got your vest on under there?" Rose's nasty boyfriend sniggers, walking up behind them.
Bruce turns to face Jennifer and asks without words, if he can do something now, but she tells him to smile using a hand signal. Bruce forces a smile in the direction of Rose and her man standing there waiting for them to say something else.

"I was really out of order the other day and I am sorry" the boyfriend says to Bruce, holding out his hand to shake.
Bruce looks at Jennifer and once again her facial expression tells him to do the right thing.
Bruce holds out his hand and they shake hands. The girls all huddle together as though everything is forgotten, but the boys have different ideas when the girls are not looking.

"Yeah I am sorry. Sorry I didn't finish you off the first time Willis" the boyfriend whispers in Bruce ear, holding his hand tighter and more aggressively.

"Try it again big man and I will make sure you don't walk again" responds Bruce, before the girls notice them squaring up to each-other.

They part and follow the girls inside giving each-other daggers. It's not long before Rose stops thinking about herself and notices there are two new female's latching onto them. Instead of saying something like she usually would and being a bitch, she gives them daggers too. Luckily for the entire group, the intense unfriendly atmosphere that is building doesn't last very long when Rose and her man separate from the group to mingle with the big wigs inside.

"Where are they going?" asks Bruce to the group.

"Probably off to find her dad" responds Lucy.

"You think she's been a bitch up until now? Wait until she's been with her dad for a few minutes" she adds, ushering them towards the hall where the big production is about to take place.

"What's happening over there?" asks Amy, pointing in the direction of a big gathering of people and what looks to be a load of security guards.

"That's probably Whitney's lot" answers Lucy, not fazed at all by the famous celebrity in the building.

"Not Whitney, Whitney?" says Amy getting excited.

"Don't be stupid, why would she be at a drama school in London?" asks Karen, telling Amy not to be silly.

Bruce walks up behind both of the girls.

"It is that Whitney" he whispers in Karen's ear, so Amy can hear too.

Both girls try to get a better look over into the crowd and are a little disappointed when Lucy carries on walking them past and towards another large hall filled with people starting to take their seats.

"Okay, I need to go and get ready for my production" says Lucy.

"Tina will stay with you and help if you need anything" she adds, walking into yet another crowd.

"I want to go back and meet Whitney" Amy grumps.

"I want to go home" whispers Bruce in Jennifer's ear.

"Don't worry, you will meet her later" Tina tells Amy casually.

"My sister Lucy knows her" she adds, to the surprise of Karen and Amy.

Jennifer, Bruce, Tina, Dave, Karen and Amy take their seats to watch the first of three mini productions today. The audience goes silent and the show begins... They all try and show an interest in what's going on but it's only really Tina that gets fully into it. They wait for Lucy to come on stage and do her part. Just then Bruce looks towards the exit leading into the other hall and notices Rose standing there by herself looking lost. He tells the others that he is just popping to the toilet and gets up and walks across to the door.

"You okay Rose? Aren't you meant to be getting ready to do your show too?" he asks her, as people struggle and push past them still piling into the hall where the others are sitting.

"You haven't seen my man have you?" Rose asks him, clearly not bothered by anything else going on around her.

Bruce feels this is his opportunity to have a little alone time with her boyfriend and tells her he will find him for her.

"That would be really nice of you Barry" she says, not even taking him on or getting his name right.

Bruce tells her to go and get ready and that when he finds her boyfriend, he will send him straight over.

Rose takes one final look around and disappears behind the stage to get ready. Bruce wanders off in search of her boyfriend and walks through into the next huge hallway and notices the Whitney clan still huddled together. He takes a wander over towards them to find out what is going on and manages to squeeze past a few people in the celebrities entourage. Just then he comes face to face with the superstar sitting on a chair, with four or five different people working on her make-up and hair. He looks her up and down and stares at her bugs bunny top thinking, she's not much of a glamorous star wearing something like that.

"Hello" says blonde Whitney, with her American accent.

"Are you a reporter from the tabloids?" she asks smiling at him.

Bruce gives her a smile and takes a look at the amount of chaos for just one person. There are people everywhere... Reporters, managers, stylists and performers and this Whitney woman has them all chasing after her.

"EXCUSE ME" snaps Whitney, with a diva tone in her voice.

"I asked if you were a reporter?" she adds, without the smile this time.

Bruce turns to her and simply shakes his head to say no, then starts looking around again.

"Then who are you and how did you get past my people?" she asks him.

"Got you" mumbles Bruce, leaving the diva waiting for an answer and heading off in pursuit of the boyfriend he's just spotted in the background flirting with a hairdresser.

He follows the trail of people leading backstage and watches the boyfriend and the random girl step into a dressing room.

"Double-Whammy" chirps Bruce smiling, as he knows what he's

going to find behind the door when he opens it.

He takes out his mobile phone, sets it to record and opens the door very slowly. He moves inside as he can see the boyfriend in front of him draped over the girl on a dressing table kissing her neck. He hides himself behind a curtain, holds the phone up and starts to watch as the action unfolds.

"I've really missed you my darling" groans the girl, as Rose's boyfriend nuzzles on her neck.

He moves his head down, nuzzling on her nipples, removing her bra at the same time.

"It's been so long since we last saw each-other. Tell me you've been faithful" she groans, enjoying his touch but clearly wanting a conversation too.

"I only have eyes for you" the boyfriend tells her, as he quickly reaches down and undoes her trousers.

"I think that's you done Mr Fucking Twat" whispers Bruce, under his breath, knowing he's got enough to end his relationship with Rose once and for all.

He pulls the phone back towards him and presses the stop button.

"Who was that girl I just saw you walking in with and what's her name?" Bruce hears the girl ask from behind the curtain.

Bruce quickly switches the record button back on and records him telling her she's a neighbour that can't get a date and that he offered to escort her to the event because he felt sorry for her. With that Bruce gives him enough time to lose his trousers and let his buttocks smile for the camera before turning it off again. Bruce creeps out from behind the curtain as the boyfriend starts to have sex with the girl. He opens the door very slowly and squeezes out of the gap, so not to be caught.

"Oh, here it comes" the boyfriend shudders to Bruce's delight, knowing he only lasted ten seconds.

Bruce fights it but can't resist, spoiling it for the boyfriend whilst he's in mid orgasm.

"Now that's how a real man fucks" Bruce calls out, watching the girl start screaming, cover herself up and the boyfriend looking furious as he doesn't get to cum properly.

"I'm going to kill you" the boyfriend calls out, as Bruce laughs and opens the door fully.

"That's if you pull your trousers up fast enough to catch me" Bruce sniggers, leaving the door open for everyone to see.

"What the fuck is going on in there?" calls diva Whitney, from her stool as everyone turns to see the couple in the room.

"Aren't you my friend Rose's man? And Donna, how could you?"

she adds, ordering her managers and other staff around her to make him leave and fire her on the spot.
Bruce races back through the hall and to the spot where he left Rose ten minutes ago. He steps backstage and asks someone if they know where she is. Another random girl shows Bruce to the changing room and Bruce walks in.
　"Sorry" Bruce says, as he walks in on Rose and a few other girls semi naked.
Rose wraps a towel around herself and walks over to him, telling the other girls to finish getting ready.
　"Did you find him?" Rose asks, holding her towel so it doesn't fall down.
Bruce a little flustered by the half naked women around him, nods his head to say yes.
　"Where is he then?" she asks, getting impatient knowing that she needs to get dressed.
Although Bruce is secretly going to enjoy his next confession, he knows it's never nice breaking someone's heart, so tries to be as tactful as he can. He pulls out the phone and tells her to watch it.
He presses the play button and her face turns as white as a sheet as it shows her, what he's been doing and saying behind her back. Rose fills herself with hatred, sorrow and then doesn't know if to go mental or breakdown and cry. She only watches half of the video and refuses to watch any-more but Bruce tells her she needs to hear what he says about her next... She takes a deep breath and looks down at the phone again, watching as her boyfriend refers to her as a sad neighbour and makes out she is no-one special to him.
　"Where is he now?" she grunts, ready to explode.
　"I am going to rip his balls off for this" she adds, getting animated in her towel.
Just then the door of the changing room opens again.
　"Knock knock, where's my buddy?" calls Whitney, entering the room with two large bodyguards and the celebrity changed into a short silver sparkling dress.
Whitney notices Rose in the corner with a guy and then quickly places Bruce's face.
　"Hey are you the same guy that was standing beside me earlier?" Whitney asks looking at him.
　"And aren't you the guy that just ran from the seedy sex going on in one of my dressing rooms?" she asks, ordering her bouncers to move in and take him away.
Rose quickly changes her rage into a diva acting up and tells Whitney that Bruce is with her.

"Bruce was just catching an ex of mine in the act for me" Rose tells Whitney, as she glides towards them in the sparkly dress and orders her bouncer's to wait outside.

"So you're not a stalker or a sex pest? That's a shame" Whitney says looking at Bruce.

"Then who are you?" she asks, standing right in front of him.
Before Bruce can answer, Rose does for him.

"He's my new man" Rose tells Whitney, rubbing her hand up across his chest and holding up her towel with the other.
Bruce doesn't know how to react, so decides to find out where it's all going.

"I didn't think you were a reporter anyway" flirts Whitney.

"Too rugged looking for a nerd" she adds, holding her hand out to shake his.
Bruce takes the superstars hand and shakes it with a little smile.

"I didn't think you were a celebrity sitting there in that bugs bunny shirt before" Bruce cheekily responds.

"But now you've lost your clothes, WOW" he adds, flirting back with her.
Whitney lets go of his hand, laughs at his comment and watches Rose give him a playful slap for flirting with her famous friend.

"I like him Rose" Whitney tells her, giving him a real once over with her eyes.
Just then the dressing room door springs open again with a lot more force.

"Tell them who I am Rose. Tell them" shouts an angry boyfriend, wrestling with two big bouncers against the door frame.

"I told you, it was over weeks ago you loser. I am with Bruce now" shouts Rose, holding onto her new make-believe partner by the arm tightly.

"Get him the fuck out of here or lose your jobs" Whitney demands of her bouncers, as they wrestle him to the floor and start punching him.
Rose watches as the bouncers give him a real good kick-in.

"You know what? I can't do this" says Bruce, uncomfortable with the lie he's being dragged into.

"What are you doing baby?" whispers Rose, forcing a smile and trying to hold him tighter by the arm and flirt at the same time.
Bruce shrugs Rose off his arm and quickly tells the celebrity the truth. She looks at Rose for her to confirm his story and she does with a sorry looking nod.

"It was lovely to meet you Whitney but I've got to go" Bruce says, smiling at her and making for the door where the bouncers are

removing the boyfriend by force.
Whitney takes a quick look over her shoulder at Bruce leaving and pouts her lips.

"Fuck me Rose, if you don't want him, I will" she says, eyeing up his backside as he leaves.

Bruce makes his way back through the crowd and watches as the bouncers make their way to the main exit with the now ex-boyfriend under their arms. Lucky for Bruce he turns up again just as the show finishes next door and watches Tina with tears in her eyes, looking so proud of her sister Lucy's performance.

"Where have you been?" asks Jennifer, standing up and giving another clap to the performers on stage.

"Ah you know, hanging with Whitney a little. Making Rose dump her boyfriend" he responds with a smirk on his face.

"Yeah right" responds Karen.

"Probably masturbating in the toilet knowing you Bruno" she adds laughing.

The group slowly exit the hallway together as the main lights turn on. Then Tina, Jennifer, Amy and Karen all notice a commotion over near the changing room area and watch as Rose comes out in tears, cuddled by superstar Whitney in her sparkly outfit.

"Bruce" says Jennifer, as they all look over to him to ask what he's done now.

"Hey, it's not my fault none of you believed me is it?" he responds, walking off to find a drink.

Jennifer and Tina rush towards the changing room. Karen follows Bruce, claiming she needs a drink to end the dullness of the event and Amy just stands in the middle of the hallway, unsure of which direction to take... She wants a drink with Bruce and Karen but on the other hand, there's her idol Whitney. As Jennifer and Tina finally reach Whitney and Rose through the crowd, Jennifer takes over with Rose whilst Whitney greets Tina with a big hug.

"I am really sorry" cries Rose on Jennifer's shoulder.

Jennifer isn't sure what's happened or what she's sorry for, so asks her why.

"For being a complete bitch to you and Bruce since we met" Rose tells her.

Jennifer still doesn't get it but knows whatever her husband has done, it worked.

Rose wipes the tears from her face and quickly makes a formal introduction between Jennifer and Whitney.

"Jen this is the ever so talented Whitney. Whit this is my life coach Jennifer" Rose claims.

Jennifer glows with delight and shakes the superstar by the hand.

"I tell you what Rose, this is the last time I fly over to the UK to attend one of your productions" says Whitney.

Rose, Tina and Jennifer all look worried.

"There's far too much drama at one of these things" Whitney jokes, making them all laugh.

With that Amy runs over like a child and bounces on the spot waiting for an introduction too.

Jennifer puts her arm around Amy and introduces her to Whitney and Rose, as a good friend and a former client.

"I love you Whitney, you are so talented and beautiful" mutters Amy, mixing her words and getting them nervously in the wrong order.

"Nice to meet you too Amy. You look absolutely stunning" Whitney says, greeting her like a fan.

Then Bruce and Karen appear, failing to find anywhere to have a drink. Again Jennifer makes the introductions for Whitney, Rose, Karen and Bruce. Whitney says hello to Karen and then looks at Bruce.

"Yes we've met already haven't we Bruce?" says Whitney, flirting with him again.

"Looks like you've got even more competition for Bruce now Aims" laughs Karen, whispering in Amy's ear.

"That's Whitney. She can do whatever she wants" whispers Amy, getting excited again.

"What?" asks Karen, trying to get her to stop dancing around.

"Me, Bruce and Whitney in a threesome" Amy whispers a little too loud, as Bruce overhears and smiles at them both.

"Hi I am Bruce. I am Jennifer's husband" he says, taking Whitney by the hand for the second time and shaking it.

"And the plot thickens" giggles Whitney, shaking his hand and winking at Jennifer.

Finally as the group of girls, Bruce and the superstar bond, Jennifer has never been happier or smiled so much. They all stand around for a few minutes sharing conversation and jokes, before one of Whitney's bouncers interrupts and tells her they must leave right now.

From out of nowhere cameras start flashing, an argument and chanting starts to come from the entrance.

"That will be for me then" Whitney laughs, knowing trouble is coming her way.

Two bouncers put their arms over the celebrity and start moving her towards the door. Lucy comes out just as Whitney starts to leave the building and the rest of them follow on close by. Jennifer and Bruce try to see past the crowd to find out what all the fuss is about but can't make it out. Just then and as they move closer to the exit, the chanting gets louder and some abuse is targeted at Whitney.

"Is this what you call being a good role model Whitney?" shouts one voice.

"This is the last place you should be dressed like that, you slut" shouts another.

"Smile for the camera Whitney" calls a guy, pushing past everyone trying to get a picture.

"Try and get it up her skirt" says another guy with a camera.

They all exit the building, faced with fifty or so people all shouting abuse at the blonde superstar. There is chaos everywhere... Jennifer looks over at Whitney and watches her heavily protected like a caged animal, not like the confident girl on screen, but petrified.

Jennifer ducks out of the group and sprints in front of them all. She climbs up onto a wall and whistles really loud over the screams, chants and noise. Everything falls silent as the bouncers usher the superstar towards a waiting car.

"Whitney. Whitney" calls Jennifer from the wall.

"It's me Jennifer the life coach" she adds at the top of her voice.

Whitney tells her bouncers to stop and she looks towards the wall. The people stop and face Jennifer, except the photographers who keep flashing, now at Jennifer too.

"Don't keep running" Jennifer calls to the celebrity.

"These people aren't going to listen, they hate me" responds the American superstar.

Jennifer calls out to one of the chanting women and tells her to say her bit. The woman tells them that Whitney has no right being here dressed like a slag and that she sets a bad example for young girls today. As the woman finishes her speech, it seems to rattle the chanting crowd again and Jennifer struggles to get them all to settle down again.

"Whitney, come up here with me" insists Jennifer, standing on the wall.

Whitney wants to but her bouncers refuse to let her go it alone.

"No, leave your bodyguards there and show these people that you are human" calls Jennifer.

Whitney tells her bouncers to back away and then Jennifer then calls Karen to the wall too.

"Fuck no" mumbles Karen, still standing with the others.

"I ain't letting these dick-heads take photo's of me looking this fat" she adds, refusing to do what Jennifer asks.

Karen doesn't want to go but with a push from the others and

knowing Jennifer needs her up there, Karen makes her way through the crowd and up on the wall too.
Jennifer, Whitney and Karen stand together on the wall with everyone looking at them and flashes from cameras going crazy.

Jennifer's Lesson In Celebrity Role Models
How many of you have heard women attacking a female celebrity?
For what reason have you heard it? Does the celebrity dress like a slag? Does she smoke? Does she have her photo taken without any knickers on? Who are you and which side do you stand on? The parents that think these celebrities are bad role models or the celebrity?
All I have got to say is, get a life to all these people that run celebrities down for acting like human beings. Yes they drink, yes they smoke, yes they dress sexy to sell a product, so what !!
The only REAL reason this kind of person attacks a celebrity is because they need someone else to blame. Most of the time it's their own kids that have gone off the rails and started smoking or dressing like a slut. Who can they blame? They don't want to take the responsibility for it themselves? Oh no, lets blame the famous person and make her feel like shit for working hard at her job.
If you are a good parent, then you should know before anything else, there's only one role model a child needs and that's you !!
What if your daughter decides to go out without any knickers on? Superstars fault right? What if she then robs a bank? Did the celebrity do that? Oh no, that was uncle Norman who you didn't protect your children from? And what about sister Alice that binge drinks every other night? Or cousin Vince arrested last week for assault? I guess these people in most families don't face an attack like the celebrity does from you.
YOU as a parent are responsible for your child.
YOU teach them right from wrong.
Don't blame a celebrity for things you failed with as a parent, these celebrities are entertainers, no-one pays them to bring up your kids or be their role models. If you are completely set in your way and prudish when it comes to a certain superstar, switch the TV off, even you can do that !!

Whitney stands beside Jennifer on the wall and can't believe her eyes as Jennifer manages to silence nearly all the crowd, except one mouthy parent at the front. Jennifer looks down at the woman and asks her what her problem is.
"How much is the slag paying you to do her P.R for her?" shouts

the woman.

"I don't work for Whitney, I ain't getting paid and I only met her today" Jennifer responds, before the the woman rattles the crowd again.

Jennifer explains Whitney wasn't running away from the scene because she feels guilty, she was running because people don't want to listen and that if people let her entertain, she would be more than happy to sing them all a song or two instead of disappearing.

"So what about the pictures in the papers?" the mouthy woman asks, continuing to probe the superstar.

"Why does she feel the need to go out in public without knickers on?" she adds once again, trying to unsettle the crowd.

Jennifer turns to the two girls on the wall and asks the crowd which one they think isn't wearing any knickers. This question from Jennifer herself does rattle the crowd again and the over excited people start chanting Whitney's name once more. Jennifer whispers in Whitney's ear and with that she shows off the string of her underwear from the top of her silver skirt. The men in the crowd go wild cheering her and the flashes start to illuminate the sky once again. Jennifer then turns to Karen.

"No fucking way" says Karen, standing on the wall knowing what is coming,

"There's no way I am getting my bits out and having them all over the papers" she adds.

Jennifer whispers something in Karen's ear and with that Karen turns around and flashes the tiniest bit of her naked bum as possible. Once again the cheers go up and Karen turns round enjoying the attention. She gives the photographers a cheeky smile and a curtsey.

The woman in the front row starts to get angry and shouts abuse towards Jennifer. Jennifer looks down at her.

"Have you ever smoked a cigarette?" Jennifer asks the aggressive woman below.

The woman nods her head.

"Have you ever had sex in a car with a partner?" Jennifer asks her next.

The woman gets defensive and tells her to mind her own business.

"You say Whitney runs from personal attacks on her personal life but who's running now?" Jennifer explains out loud, so that everyone can hear.

The woman feels she's being put on the spot and the photographers start snapping away at her too.

"Okay then, yeah I've had outdoor sex, so what?" the woman responds, getting into a conversational war with Jennifer.

"Do you love your partner more than anything?" Jennifer asks her. The woman sighs like she's getting bored and nods her head again.

"Have you ever gone out in public without any knickers on for him?" Jennifer asks, as the crowd go completely silent waiting for the answer.

"Yes" mumbles the woman under her breath.

"Sorry I didn't hear that" shouts Jennifer, ready to make her point.

"Yes" the women calls out, as the crowd erupt.

The woman feels helpless as all of the other women in the crowd acknowledge Whitney and this woman on the wall as the winner, but the mouthy woman isn't done fighting yet.

"Okay we do the same things and I guess it's not her fault these dirty perverts with their cameras take pictures of her, but she's paid a lot of money to do what she does, I ain't" argues the woman, with her last breath and shooting herself in the foot in the process.

Jennifer looks down at her, around at the crowd and they all start to cheer again. Jennifer quickly tries to hush them down again, as Whitney starts to feel sorry for the woman below.

"Answer honestly now" says Jennifer.

"Does your partner think Whitney is sexy?" she asks, watching the woman not even stick around to answer and the crowd erupt once again.

Whitney can't help but be impressed by Jennifer's lesson and gives her a quick hug, which the photographers love again.

With that all three girls go to jump off the wall very pleased with themselves, Jennifer blows a kiss in the direction of Bruce leaning against the entrance wall watching his wife and her talent.

"BRUCE" Jennifer screams, as she then sees a baseball bat appear from behind the wall and smash him across the back of the head.

There is a panic as women scream and the photographers have something else to point their cameras at. Jennifer fights her way through the crowd and Dave leaves Tina to run to his aid. Amy and Karen panic as the crowd try to escape and Whitney is ushered away and into the car by her bouncers.

"Somebody call an ambulance" cries a woman, watching the blood seeping from his head.

"Bruce" cries Jennifer, rushing to his side, lifting his head up onto her lap.

Jennifer sits there cradling her husband. Tina, Lucy, Dave, Rose, Amy and Karen all gather round.

"Come on, you will be okay" cries Jennifer, trying to wipe the blood from his face.

"He's opening his eyes" says Dave, willing his mentor to wake up. Bruce slowly opens his eyes and looks at Jennifer.

"You will be okay Bruno, stay awake" says Karen, as Amy bursts into tears.

"Did you see who it was?" asks Dave.

Bruce tries to open his mouth as Jennifer tells them all to be quiet.

"What is it baby? Come on speak to me" Jennifer begs, wiping more blood from his forehead.

"What? Who did this?" Dave asks, bending over him and Jennifer. They all listen intently...

"Ouch, that hurt" Bruce mumbles, before closing his eyes again.

"Come on baby, keep your eyes open" Jennifer begs, shaking him. Bruce struggles to open his eyes again.

"Who did it mate, was it Rose's ex again?" Dave asks trying to get an answer.

"Of course it was him" insists Karen.

"Bruce just proved that he's a lying cheating scum-bag, didn't he?" she adds, wanting Rose's ex for herself or more importantly, his blood.

"I know who it was" Bruce mumbles, before closing his eyes again. Jennifer, Dave and Karen try and get an answer out of him, but he doesn't give one. Seconds later the ambulance turns up and the paramedics rush to his aid.

One of them usher a blood stained Jennifer away from Bruce, whilst the other paramedic starts to treat Bruce. Bruce is lifted on to a trolley and put in the back of the ambulance as the driver takes his position in the front cab. The other paramedic asks if anyone wants to go with him, but a shocked and confused Jennifer has shut down from everything that's going on around her.

"Bringing in one male, mid thirties with a serious head injury" says the driver over the radio.

Karen wants to go with Jennifer in the back of the ambulance, but Amy begs her not to leave her alone. Karen then suggests that Dave accompanies Jennifer. Dave puts his arms around Jennifer and helps her into the ambulance. Dave jumps in too and the second paramedic closes the doors.

The ambulance takes off at speed with the sirens blaring and the lights flashing. Everyone huddles together as they fear the worst for Bruce.

"Did you hear what the paramedic said?" asks Lucy in tears.

CHAPTER 10
DOCTOR WHO AND THE DYING WISH

As Bruce lies in the back of the ambulance and the female paramedic checks his pulse, Dave and a shell-shocked Jennifer sit beside him and watch. Suddenly Bruce comes round again and tries to sit up and remove the mask from his face. The paramedic tells him to stay still or he could make his injuries worse. Bruce doesn't listen and still tries to pull the mask off and wriggle about.

"Are you okay baby?" asks Jennifer, coming out of her shocked state of mind and leaning towards him.
The paramedic tells her to sit back and try not to talk to him too much.

"What is this a flash back to play school or something?" grumbles Bruce from behind his mask, as the paramedic tries to get Bruce to stay still again.
Dave and Jennifer watch again as a hysterical Bruce doesn't know whether he should laugh or cry, as he again tries to pull himself up on the trolley.

"Please stay still sir. We need to get you to hospital first" pleads the female paramedic.
Jennifer leans over and tells him to do what the paramedic is telling him to do, but Bruce isn't listening and pulls the mask off his face and laughs.

"We've got ourselves a delirious" calls the female paramedic to the male driver speeding down the road.
The driver calls back and instructs her to use the restraints. With that she pulls out some belts from under the trolley and starts strapping them across Bruce to keep him still.

"Are you watching this baby? I'm getting some bondage" Bruce laughs in pain, as the blood starts to gush from his head again.
Finally Bruce is strapped down and cannot move. He starts to lose consciousness again, when the paramedic injects him with a sedative.
"What's going on? Is he okay?" panics Jennifer, watching his eyes close yet again.
The paramedic tells her she's given him something to calm him down and take the pain off a little. A few minutes later they arrive at the hospital and the ambulance comes to a halt, which brings Bruce round again. The paramedics jump out and run round to the back, opening the doors.
"It's okay baby" Jennifer says reassuring him.
"We're at the hospital now and they will make you all better" she adds, rubbing his arm and still covered in blood herself.
Bruce opens his eyes wider, feeling the pain easing off.
"That was a nice sleep" he grumbles with a dry mouth.
Jennifer tells him they gave him something for the pain and that in an hour or so, he will be back home as good as new. Bruce then struggles in discomfort again.
"What is it?" panics Jennifer.
"I just woke up" says Bruce, making no sense at all.
"I know you have baby, don't worry" answers Jennifer, rubbing his arm again.
"I'm strapped down" he grumbles again, as she leans over to hear him speak.
"It's okay, they will be taken off in a minute" she tells him.
"It's not that, I've just woken up" says Bruce again, confusing Jennifer a little more.
The paramedics start to free the trolley for transportation into the hospital.
"What if I get morning glory? How will I hide it strapped down?" he whispers, laughing.
Jennifer gives out a big sigh of relief and follows the trolley into the hospital.
"Blow to the head, managed to stop the bleeding but lost a lot of blood at the scene. Given five of morphine for the pain and vital statistics are good" says the female paramedic, handing the trolley over to the doctor and nurses in the hospital corridor.
As Bruce is rushed through to get checked over, Jennifer and Dave are shown to the waiting area by another nurse.
After an hour of waiting and two cups of coffee, Karen and Amy turn up.

"Where is he? How is he? Is he okay?" Karen and Amy both ask. Jennifer tells them she thinks he's going to be okay and that he's being checked over now.

"Is he awake? Have you seen him yet?" Karen continues to probe, until she has all the facts.

Jennifer tells them he did wake up a few times in the ambulance but she really doesn't know anything yet.

"Stop panicking you two, he will be fine" says Dave, trying to calm them down.

"Bruce was worried about having an erection whilst lying on the bed" Jennifer says, making them both laugh, knowing that he must be fine if that was all he was concerned about.

"That's our Bruce, cock always comes first" laughs Karen.

They spend another half an hour waiting together before Dave asks if he should go and fetch Bruce some fresh clothes. Jennifer really appreciates the offer and hands him her door key without a seconds thought. Dave tells them he won't be long.

"Dave" calls Jennifer.

"Could you go and check in on Tina, Lucy and Rose at Karen's house before you come back here?" she asks, hoping that he won't mind.

"Already on it" Dave says smiling, walking out of the exit.

The three girls sit waiting to hear some news on Bruce's condition for another twenty-five minutes, when a doctor finally comes out to speak to them. He tells them Bruce is doing well and he was very lucky.

"Can we take him home?" asks Amy, before Jennifer can open her mouth.

The doctor tells them they are waiting for one final scan result to come back and that he will have to be kept in overnight just as a precaution.

"Can I see him?" asks Jennifer, eager to see her husband smile again without all the blood.

"I should only let one of you in at a time, but if you promise to be very quiet, you can go in now" says the doctor, a little unsure of which one is his wife anyway.

The doctor leads the way and opens the door to a private room.

"You're a lucky boy Mr Bruce, three lovely ladies are here to see you" the doctor says, letting them in and telling them he will be back with his scan results shortly.

Jennifer enters the room followed by Karen and Amy. Jennifer looks at him and soon enough sadness fills her heart as she sees him on the bed looking so helpless.

"Nice hat Bruno" laughs Karen, picking up on the big white

bandage wrapped around his head.

"Nice knickers" Bruce responds, pointing down at her jeans as though she has her buttons undone.

Karen quickly moves her hands down to fix the problem and finds nothing is showing and all four of them share a laugh.

"So did you see who it was?" Karen asks, as they all take a seat.

Bruce sits up and tells them he doesn't remember a thing.

"Don't you remember about the morning glory comment in the back of the ambulance then?" asks Jennifer, seeing if he remembers anything at all.

"Remember it? When they wheeled me through and some sexy nurse started taking off the straps, I got one" he tells them, sending laughter around the room once again.

"I bet she didn't even notice it" laughs Karen, keeping the joke going.

Just then Bruce starts to feel dizzy and throws his head back into his pillow. Wincing in pain he struggles to catch his breath and the three girls gasp and ask him what's wrong.

With that Bruce sits back up, showing them he was faking it and tells them nothing.

"You shit" snaps Jennifer, slapping him on the arm and telling him not to do it again.

This time her playful slap does hurt him and he sits back nursing his arm.

"I'm sorry baby, I didn't mean it" begs Jennifer, knowing that she did hit him kind of hard.

"That's okay, I didn't feel a thing" Bruce says, sitting up again and playing with them some more.

"Who would have guessed being in hospital could be such fun?" says Bruce, tempting to play another joke.

"You are cruel" laughs Karen, shaking her head at him.

"I tell you what will be cruel" responds Bruce.

"When I buy all the newspapers tomorrow and plaster your bum up all over town" he adds laughing again.

They four of them sit there for nearly an hour winding each-other up and having a laugh.

"Knock, Knock" says a voice, as they all turn to see who it is, but can't see anyone.

"Who's there?" calls Bruce from his bed.

"Doctor" responds the voice, as everyone bursts out laughing.

The Indian doctor walks in and asks them to share the joke.

"Knock, Knock, Who's there" says Karen, trying to make him understand, whilst still finding it funny herself.

"I don't get it" says the doctor, with a confused look on his face.
He tells them that Bruce's scan result came back clear and he will be able to go home first thing in the morning.

"We will have to have some kind of party ready for you then Bruno" says Karen, overjoyed by the good news.

"I don't think you should be partying too much in your condition" says the doctor walking out of the door again.

"Doctor" calls Karen after him.

"Can I have a quick word with your about my pregnancy please?" she asks, chasing him out of the door with a naughty look on her face for the others to see.

As Karen runs out, Dave walks back in with a bag of clean clothes for his mentor. Bruce greets Dave with a smile, a thank you and Dave just looks really relieved that he's okay.

"Did you look in on the other girls for me?" Jennifer asks Dave.
He tells her they are all at Karen's house eagerly awaiting news of Bruce's condition. Jennifer takes it upon herself to do this and leaves the room, taking her mobile out of her bag. Bruce takes the chance to get rid of Amy, by sending her for some fresh water and having a little chat with young David. Bruce tells him quickly he needs him to stay at Karen's with the others tonight and watch out for them all.

"Why? Do you think something is going to happen?" asks Dave.
Bruce tells him no, but he will be able to sleep easier if he knows someone is looking after them. Dave doesn't have to be asked twice and accepts the mission from his mentor.

Seconds later Amy returns with the water, Jennifer from making the phone-call and Karen wearing a massive grin.

"You didn't?" says Bruce, knowing that face all to well.

"Didn't what?" answers Karen, trying not to make it so obvious.

"You dirty bitch. Whilst I sit here in hospital too" responds Bruce looking disgusted.

Karen tries to hide her guilt again and starts to blush as everyone realises what he's talking about.

"Come on then" says Bruce.

"Did he have a big needle then?" he asks, showing Karen he's actually proud of her.

"More like a stethoscope" beams Karen, to everyone's laughter.
They all sit around trying to get more information out of her about the doctor but she doesn't give anything else away.

"I can't believe you've just gone out there and blatantly had sex with a doctor?" says Amy.

"What can I say, all this worry and stress makes me horny" Karen responds laughing.

"Where did you do it then?" asks Jennifer, shocked at Karen's nerve too.
Karen looks out the window and points to an empty room across the corridor smiling.

"Fuck me Karen, I haven't even got the balls to do that" gasps Bruce.
They sit around laughing for a few more minutes, then suddenly it all turns very serious when the police turn up to take a statement from Bruce. The police knock on the door and Bruce looks at everyone's worried faces.

"You would think I'd done something wrong, the way you lot look" he says, telling them to all wait outside.
Karen, Amy and Dave stand up to leave, Jennifer wants to stay with him.

"It's okay, you go with them, this won't take a second" Bruce tells her.
They open the door, letting the police in as they leave.

"Hey Karen" calls Bruce.

"I bet him outside has a bigger truncheon than your doctor" he laughs.
Karen makes sure to get a good look down at their trousers as she leaves the room. The two police officer's walk over to Bruce and say hello. Just then Karen catches Bruce's eye through the window and signals to him that both policemen are small down below. Bruce tries to hold his laughter in as the two officers stand next to him and ask if he remembers anything. Bruce spends the next five minutes telling the police that he didn't see anything and that he was hit from behind. They try to quiz him and help him find answers but in the end, he does enough to convince them he's telling the truth. After another few minutes a female nurse walks in to check Bruce's blood pressure and that his head wound is not bleeding. The police leave it there and tell him they will be in touch, as the nurse starts to do her job.

"Did you tell them anything?" asks Amy, walking back in and sitting back beside Bruce.

"What could I tell them Aims? I got hit over the head and that's all I can remember" explains Bruce, paying more attention to the hot nurse standing in front of him.
Just then Bruce sits back and smiles deliriously.

"What?" asks Karen, looking at him as she takes a seat on the chair next to his bed.

"Are you okay baby?" asks Jennifer, noticing his eyes staring into space.

"Nurse is he okay?" asks Karen, growing more concerned.

The nurse looks into his eyes and asks him if he's okay. Bruce doesn't respond, so she tries waving her hand in front of his face and clicking her fingers in front of his eyes, but still nothing...

"I'd better go and get a doctor" claims the nurse, looking just as worried as the others are now.

Just as she turns away and the rest watch over him to see if he even blinks, he snaps out of it.

"Don't go nurse" he tells her.

The nurse walks back over to him and asks if he is okay.

"Course I am" he answers.

"I went to heaven for a few seconds" he adds.

"What does that mean?" asks Amy, showing her concern too.

"A tiny little room, me wearing nothing but this hospital gown and four beautiful, sexy female's around me. I thought it was my dying wish coming true" Bruce tells them with a silly grin on his face.

"You dirty bastard" laughs Karen.

"I was just waiting for the big white fluffy clouds to appear and I would have been set" he tells them with a smirk on his face.

Jennifer laughs knowing her husband is already on the mend, Karen shakes her head at him and calls him a sex maniac and the nurse doesn't know where to put her blushes as she tries to finish her job. Jennifer doesn't hear Amy laughing and turns to her. Amy has turned white again, looking petrified.

"What is it Amy?" asks Jennifer, worried about her this time and telling her again that he was messing around and is okay.

"She's probably off to heaven with me too" laughs Bruce, still acting up.

"Wait, I've seen her look like this before" claims Jennifer, taking it more seriously than everyone else.

Suddenly Jennifer realises what it is and looks out of the window to feel her own heart stop... There's Tony standing across the corridor.

"It's him" shouts Jennifer terrified.

"Who? What? Where?" stutters Bruce, trying to see past the nurse.

"It's Tony" screams Karen, standing up to see for herself.

Jennifer panics, Karen does too. Amy stands silently mortified and Bruce makes eye contact with him outside.

"Nurse, call security" Bruce insists, staring straight into Tony's hateful eyes.

The nurse presses the alarm above the bed and Tony slowly walks away from the door.

Bruce tries to get out of bed to go after him but the nurse won't let him get up.

"Stay there" panics Jennifer.

"You are in no fit state to be fighting" she adds, trying to watch where the blackmailer goes.

Two big hospital security guards enter the room and the nurse tells them to go after Tony, only able to give them a vague description of him. One of the guards radio the other security guards at the hospital entrance to watch out for him leaving the building. They then set off in search of Tony around the hospital. It takes the gang a good few minutes to settle down and stop panicking and when they do, Jennifer has an idea. She pulls out her mobile phone and calls Rose to ask for Whitney's number. She then calls Whitney herself and asks a favour from the superstar. Jennifer asks the celebrity if she could lend her some muscle to chaperone everyone back to Karen's house safely. Whitney agrees but tells her she's leaving to go over to Ireland in a few hours, so it would have to be quick. Whitney sends one of her bodyguards to watch the others at Karen's house and two towards the hospital, one to chaperone the three girls and Dave back to Karen's house and the third to watch over Bruce's room whilst Tony is still around. The gang say their quick goodbyes to Bruce.

"Don't worry baby, I've got someone to come and watch over you for a few hours too" says Jennifer, giving him a kiss on the nose and telling him she will see him in the morning.

"You didn't have to do that, I can handle Tony" responds Bruce, acting all macho but knowing deep down he really isn't fit right now.

The girls leave him to rest for the night and cautiously move towards the main entrance, knowing that Tony is still at large. Just as they reach the elevator, Amy turns white again.

"Is it Tony?" asks Jennifer, noticing her freeze on the spot.

"No look" stutters Amy, pointing her trembling finger to a trolley wheeled in by paramedics.

"Look at what?" asks Jennifer, still trying to work out what is scaring her this time.

"There" points Amy, starting to get very upset.

"Where?" snaps Karen, trying to see what Amy is looking at.

"On the trolley with the paramedics" shouts Amy.

"It's my Deano" she adds, swaying in the direction of them, whilst the hospital staff rush him to the treatment area.

The three girls and Dave rush over to hospital staff, trying to find out what has happened to Amy's boyfriend Dean. One of the paramedics tell them the victim has been beaten up quite badly.

"Why do you know this man?" asks one of the doctors, as they try to work out who he is.

"He's my boyfriend" whimpers Amy, trying to get close enough to

say something to him or hold his hand.
Just then Jennifer spots Tony casually standing at the doorway entrance in front of them smiling. As the doctors wheel Dean towards the treatment area, Jennifer makes Karen notice Tony standing there.

"Did you do this you fucking coward?" shouts Karen, as they all rush past him.

"You three are next" Tony threatens, loud enough for Jennifer and Karen to hear with another smile.

Amy doesn't even see Tony, as she keeps her mind and eyes focused on her man. Karen and Jennifer are stopped at the door by a nurse telling them, only his partner can go in. Jennifer and Karen stand watching through the window as Amy and the trolley fade into the distance and know they've got to turn back round to face Tony again. They look at each-other, catch their breath, take each-others hand and slowly turn round.

"He's gone" says Karen, shocked but relieved looking at where he was standing.

"Hey you two, I thought I said meet me at the main entrance?" calls one of Whitney's bodyguards, walking towards them.

"Come on, time to go" he adds, waiting for them to make a move.

"Hold on" calls Jennifer to the bodyguard.

"Our friend has just gone through those doors, we can't leave her here" she adds, trying to stop the massive man from exiting the building.

"We go now or not at all" claims the bodyguard in a really deep voice.

"I've got to be on a plane with Whitney in less than three hours" he adds, telling them to make a decision.

Jennifer explains they need to go with him in order to stay safe, but Karen doesn't want to leave Amy behind. Jennifer tells her she will probably be there a while and they can phone the hospital or Amy when they get home safely.

"Yeah but then what? Does she have to cross London on her own?" asks Karen.

"No, she can go and stay with Bruce in his room. That's IF she gets out at all tonight" Jennifer answers, knowing Dean is in a pretty bad way.

Karen knows she's right and they follow the big bodyguard out of the hospital.

As the two girls arrive back at Karen's house safely and are greeted by the others, Jennifer decides it's time to call Amy and find out what's happening with Dean before the two bodyguards at the house have to leave. The group wait in anticipation to hear the news, hoping that Amy will pick up her phone. All of them are tired and hungry but food and sleep are the last things on anyone's mind...

CHAPTER 11
DUMPED AND A LAST FLING

It's early evening and everyone is on edge after a very eventful and emotional day. Lucy, Karen, Tina, Dave and Rose sit round waiting for Jennifer to give them some good news about Amy's partner Dean. They watch her hang up her phone and tell them that Dean is going to be fine.

"So are they coming out tonight? Shall I go and meet them?" asks Karen, still very wired about the whole Tony situation.

Jennifer tells her that Amy has agreed to jump in a taxi and come straight over the second Dean is discharged. Just then Jennifer notices Rose putting on her jacket.

"Where are you going?" asks Jennifer, concerned for traumatized Rose.

Rose tells her she just needs some air and a walk to freshen up.

"You're going to find your ex aren't you?" asks Lucy, showing her concern too.

"Are you crazy babes? There's a mad man out there" Karen interrupts, suggesting it's a good idea for them all to stay together tonight.

Rose has other things on her mind and doesn't really listen to the groups concern about her safety. Jennifer asks Dave to chaperone Rose to wherever she is heading but Dave refuses.

"Bruce instructed me to stay here and watch out for you all, not go walkabouts" he tells her, adamant he is going nowhere.

Before Jennifer can come up with another plan to keep the wandering wannabe safe, Rose is heading towards the door...

"Wait" calls Jennifer, trying to think fast.

"No mad man scares me. After all, if he messes with me, he messes with my dad" Rose says, opening the front door and leaving. Jennifer, Lucy, Tina, Karen and Dave can't do anything about Rose walking out, so they all try and relax.

Over at the hospital Amy has just been let in to see Dean. She walks in and over to his bed. She looks at him with a few cuts around his face, a black eye and a plastered wrist.

"Oh baby, what did they do to you?" she asks, guessing that Tony is responsible before finding out the facts.

"I guess by that you know who did this to me already then?" grumbles Dean from his bed, feeling sorry for himself.

Before Amy can admit she thinks she knows who hurt him and says sorry again, Dean stops her.

"It's over Aims" he tells her, without another minutes thought.

"It's okay baby, I know you are upset but it's just the shock talking" responds Amy, taking his hand and holding on to it.

Dean pulls his hand away.

"It's not the shock Aims, we both know it's over. We've both known it for a while" he tells her, sitting up in his bed and trying to show her it isn't hurting him.

"What do you mean, it's over?" she responds, starting to struggle as her bottom lip quivers.

Dean explains they've had a good relationship and great sex life, but since Bruce and Jennifer left town two days ago, things haven't been the same. He goes on to tell her they haven't been together really for awhile now and he's been thinking it for weeks anyway.

"We can get it back" she responds, trying to hold his hand again and starting to cry.

Dean finally lets her hold his hand.

"Get what back Aims? Our relationship or Bruce and Jennifer to move back?" he asks her.

"Why do you keep mentioning them? This is about us, me and you" cries Amy, showing her frustration but trying to keep the noise down for the two other patients on the ward.

Dean looks deep into her eyes and takes her other hand.

"We both know you have feelings for Bruce" says Dean, starting to struggle now.

"Yeah but it's just a crush and we've both known that for ages" she answers quickly, wondering why this is an issue now.

"Me or him Aims, who would you pick?" he asks, knowing the

answer might destroy him.

"You" she answers without a seconds thought.

Dean sighs in relief but can't let it go.

"But do you have feelings for him? If me and Jen weren't around, would you want to be with him?" he asks, knowing this is the make or break part of the conversation and their relationship.

Amy sits there and thinks for a few seconds. She knows the answer already but knows the truth will hurt him.

"If it was just me and Bruce then yeah, I would want to be with him" she answers, going for the honest approach knowing Dean already knows the answer anyway.

"But it doesn't matter because I am with you" she adds, trying to make the truth less painful for him.

His eyes start to fill up, as he appreciates the truth from his beautiful partner.

"You aren't with me right now, because it's over" he tells her one final time, then lowers his head fighting back his own tears.

"Don't do this to me" begs Amy in floods off tears, not caring about the other patients in the ward any longer.

"Sorry I've made my mind up" Dean responds.

"We can move away and start again" she whimpers, in her final stage of begging.

Finally for his own sanity and to end it once and for all, he snaps.

"Look at me Aims. Your fight did this to me" he yells.

"This isn't my fight. This shouldn't have been OUR fight" he adds asking her to leave.

With that, the high emotions and the fact other people are starting to notice, a nurse walks over and tells Amy it's best if she leaves. Amy doesn't argue with the nurse and stands up.

"I will be right outside waiting for you" Amy mumbles, wiping the tears from her face.

"Nurse can you please bring me a phone" asks Dean, making Amy wait for his response.

"Goodbye Aims" he adds, looking at her one final time and his eyes saying the rest for him.

Just a few yards down the corridor, Bruce is in his private room watching TV. He sits there flicking through the channels trying to find something to take his mind away from everything worrying him. He switches the TV off using the remote and sits there in silence, just thinking about everything with the weight of the world on his shoulders.

Over at the house the others are doing pretty much the same thing. Lucy sits staring into space on the armchair, Karen and Jennifer still sit in silence on the sofa and Dave and Tina sit snuggled up at the other end. The mood is really low but not lower than Amy in the hospital waiting room, watching Dean through the window on the phone.

Back in Bruce's room nothing seems to make sense in his head and he is about to become even more confused with a surprise visitor.
 "What are you doing here?" says Bruce, sitting up looking at the door.
Rose walks in and asks to sit with him.
 "I just wanted to find out for myself how you are" she responds, with a sense of guilt written all over her face.
 "You've come here alone? Don't you know there's a lunatic out there hell bent on hurting us all?" Bruce says, disappointed with her irresponsibility.
Rose doesn't seem to care about herself and changes the subject into something she wants to talk to him about.
 "Earlier today you told Whitney that I'd be the last person you would ever consider being with, why?" she asks, like it's the only question that matters in the world to her.
Although Bruce is a little put out by the question, he knows his reaction earlier has upset her and tries to explain what he meant.
 "You are so all over the place Rose. No-one ever knows where they stand with you" he tells her.
 "I don't understand" responds Rose looking confused.
Bruce explains he's seen a really nice side to her, but then horrible too.
 "What about the sexual threats in my own kitchen the other day? What was that all about?" he asks.
 "That's why you don't like me? Because I said I wanted to have sex with you?" she asks, trying to understand.
 "No" answers Bruce.
 "I don't like you because you think you can take what you want when you want it" he adds.
Rose stands up in her skinny jeans, baggy white jumper and walk towards the door, making him think she's going to leave. She reaches for the blinds and closes them.
 "What are you doing now?" Bruce asks, starting to get a little

scared, as he hasn't got the strength to fight anything she's going to throw at him tonight.
Rose turns and walks back towards the bed. She throws her hands up in the air and whips off her jumper, claiming that the room is really hot. Bruce watches as she slowly moves towards the bed in her bra and then undoes the top button of her jeans.

"We aren't going to do this again are we?" he asks, knowing that's exactly what is on her mind.

"If I stopped messing around and started being honest with everyone, would that make you like me?" she asks in a soft voice, unclasping her bra and letting her petite breasts free.

"It would be a great start" mumbles Bruce, trying not to look at her hard nipples.

"But not to do this" he adds, getting more nervous as she stands beside his bed playing with her nipples and covering up again.
She leans in towards him and softly asks him to kiss her. He turns his head and makes out he can hear someone coming.

"There's no-one CUMIN Bruce" she responds, moving one of her hands into his blue hospital gown and running it across his chest.

"Well, that's excluding me and you of course" she adds, running her hand right down towards his stomach continuing to flirt.

"That's enough" snaps Bruce, before she manages to make him hard under the covers.
Rose refuses to listen and tries to carry on by tugging at the covers.

"Come on; just let me get you off. Let me suck it for you" she flirts.
Again Bruce snaps and this time pushes her back into the bedside chair.

"What the fuck is wrong with you?" he growls, getting angry with her.

"One minute you're a bitch, the next you are nice, then you turn into this. Why can't you be just one person?" he asks.
Although she is adamant she's going to please him, Bruce's attitude makes her feel slightly uncomfortable and she puts her jumper back on to hide her breasts. She stands up, as Bruce thinks he's convinced her to stop but moves in closer again.

"I said no" snaps Bruce again, taking her hand away from under the covers where his semi hard penis is.

"Fine" she strops, picking up her bra and putting in her pocket.

"But tell me just one thing then Bruce. Was it my ex that did this to you?" she asks standing over him.
Bruce looks at her and cannot think of words to say. He takes his time and tries avoiding the question.

"Is that what this is all about? Your man hurts someone, so it makes you horny?" asks Bruce, looking confused by the question that just came out of his mouth.

"No" she snaps back.

"Was it him?" she asks again.

Bruce struggles to work out why she's asking, so decides to play along with her.

"If it wasn't him that did this, would you still be trying to fuck me?" asks Bruce.

"No" she snaps back.

Bruce is now baffled.

"So why are you trying to fuck me then? Because you think he did and you feel sorry for his victim?" he asks, trying to find something out about her at least.

"No" she snaps once more, not really giving any clues behind her sexual mood.

Finally Bruce works it out and leaps off his bed.

"You're fucking protecting him again aren't you?" he grunts at her.

"No" she answers for the fourth time.

"So what if I said I've already told the police who did it then?" he says.

Rose panics and runs to the door, opens the blinds and looks outside.

"Please tell me you haven't. Please Bruce. Please. He will blame and kill me" she stutters, looking very nervous now.

"Who will kill you? What's going on? Your boyfriend?" asks Bruce, feeling he's nearly got her.

Suddenly she snaps, walks over and grabs him by the arm.

"Tell me you haven't said anything to the police" she demands, getting aggressive now.

Bruce makes out she's hurting him, then he twists her arm back round and holds her against the side of the bed. She struggles to free herself but can't.

"Get off, you're hurting me" she yells, struggling some more.

"Who's going to kill you and what for?" Bruce asks her one final time.

"Okay, okay I will tell you" she moans in pain.

Bruce lets her arm go and watching her composes herself and sit back down in the chair. He waits for her to speak and finally she opens up and tells him everything.

"Ages ago I slept with my dad's partner, if he finds out he will kill me" she tells Bruce.

"My ex knows and has threatened to tell my dad about this many times" she adds.

"So that's why you always go back to him?" Bruce says, understanding it all now.
Rose nods her head ashamed of herself.
"And that's what all this sex offering is about? To buy my silence right?" Bruce asks.
Rose nods her head again as Bruce puts all the pieces of the puzzle together.
He lets her get it all off her chest and although she feels better for it, Bruce is in no fit state to be offering protection of any kind and knows he's got enough to deal with in Tony, without taking on Rose's dad too but still manages to offer his services.
"If you start telling the truth more often. Start respecting the people that care about you and stop protecting your maniac ex-boyfriend, I promise I will never let anything happen to you" says Bruce.
Although she knows there's not much he can do from his hospital bed, this is the first time anyone has ever offered to protect her and she is very grateful.
Whether Bruce knows who attacked him or not, he continues to let Rose believe it was her ex-boyfriend, just so she can finally change and maybe trust the people who care about her the most. He tells her to get a taxi back to Karen's and do everything Jennifer tells her to do. Rose agrees and furthermore, tells him that she's going to be a better person from now on.

Back down the corridor, Dean made his phone-call about half an hour ago and is waiting for the doctor to discharge him. Amy still waits outside ready to beg him for another chance. She watches him through the window stand up, thank the doctor and walk towards the door.
"We need to talk baby. I can change" begs Amy, trying to get his attention, whilst he tries to walk straight past her towards the exit.
"That's the problem Aims. You are perfect, so there's nothing to change" he tells her.
Before Amy can take a positive from it or say anything else to change his mind, he tells her he's been on the phone to friends out of town and they are on their way to pick him up.
"Who's coming? Where are you going? When will you be back?" Amy asks, panicking that this will be her last few minutes before she is officially single.
"Away from here and I am never coming back" he mumbles, before turning and walking out of the exit.
She gives chase but he doesn't stop. As Amy tries desperately to fight

back even more tears and get his attention, she realises he's gone and slows her jog into a walk. She comes to a standstill and watches her now ex-boyfriend Dean exit the hospital. She prays that he will take one final look at her, but he doesn't and soon disappears out of sight. Amy breaks down in the hospital corridor knowing that her relationship with him is now over. She doesn't dare following him out, knowing that Tony could be out there, so turns and walks back into the hospital to find a phone to ring a taxi to take her back to Karen's house. She walks slowly around the hospital trying to get her head together for a good twenty minutes, before remembering Bruce is still there. She knows it's not the exact comfort she wants right now, but knows at least with him she will be safe. She makes her way towards his private room and looks at him through the window. She watches Bruce on his bed looking out of the window, places her hand on the door, but takes it off again walking away.

Five minutes later there is a knock at Bruce's door. Bruce sits up expecting it to be Rose back for another chat, as he isn't aware of what's happened with Dean and Amy.

"Can I come in?" he hears an American accent ask from the door.

Bruce is shocked to see Whitney stick her famous head around the door to say hello.

"What are you doing here? Where's are those big body builders you carry around with you?" he asks.

Whitney explains that she needs to get to the airport in less than an hour but wanted to check that he was okay before leaving.

"You didn't have to worry about me" says Bruce, pleased that the superstar has made the effort anyway.

Whitney sits down on the chair next to his bed and tells him she shouldn't really be here.

"If I am spotted after the trouble you've just had, the paparazzi will love it" she tells him.

"As I said, a phone-call would have been fine. I didn't expect you to come in person" responds Bruce, somewhat star-struck that this could mean he's now friends with a famous superstar.

It's not long before Bruce is however knocked off of his perch, as Whitney tells him the real reason she is there to see him.

"I know you and Jen are married" she tells him.

"But after seeing her in action today defending me, I want her with me all the time" she adds.

Bruce is shocked by the celebrity's admission but knows everyone in the world would want his wife by their side, so asks her what she means.

"I want Jen to work for me and move over to the States" she tells

him.
Bruce doesn't know what to say.

"Of course I want you to come as Jen's partner too" she goes on to tell him.

"To do what?" asks Bruce, waiting for his job offer.
The celebrity wasn't prepared for this question and delays answering.

"I don't know, live the high life" she says.

"The money I am going to offer your wife, means you will never have to work again" she adds, hoping this will make him smile.

"That's not a job Whitney" he responds remaining friendly.
Bruce looks confused about it, so Whitney decides to tell him to think about it for twenty-four hours.

"When I come back from Ireland, I will be offering her the job" she confirms, before telling him to get better soon and quickly leaving him with even more to consider overnight.

Back at the house, Rose has just turned up to the relief of the group and asks to have a private word with Jennifer. The two of them move through into Karen's kitchen, where Rose tells her she's going to change her attitude from now on and listen to life coach Jennifer. This is the best news Jennifer has had in ages and her smile tells Rose just how happy she is about her admission.

"So where have you been?" asks Jennifer, testing the water with Rose and her new attitude.

"I just had to go for a walk to clear my head and make sure my relationship is over for good this time" she tells her, forgetting to mention her visit to the hospital.

"And is it finally over between you two now?" asks Jennifer looking concerned.

"For good" responds Rose, with a big smile across her face.
Just then Karen walks into the kitchen and hands Jennifer her phone. Jennifer takes the phone and says hello.

"Amy, where are you? Are you and Dean getting out of hospital?" asks Jennifer.
Amy explains that herself and Dean have split up and that he's left town. Jennifer tries to comfort Amy but there's not much she can do over the phone. She tells Amy to jump in a taxi and come over for a proper chat, but Amy declines.

"I just want to be on my own tonight" sniffs Amy down the phone.

"How about me or Karen come and stay with you then? Where are you now?" asks Jennifer.
Amy tells her she will be fine, that she's booked herself into a hotel

and again, she just needs a night alone. Jennifer knows she cannot do any-more for her friend and tells her to come to Karen's first thing in the morning. Amy distantly agrees and the conversation comes to an end. Just as Rose gets herself a drink and Karen takes her phone back, Lucy comes through to the kitchen, leaving just Dave and Tina alone in the living room.

"Can I have a quick word Jen?" asks Lucy.

"Wow, it's all go tonight isn't it?" responds Jennifer, telling Lucy to meet her upstairs in Karen's bedroom.

The two girls go upstairs and sit together on Karen's bed.

"So what's on your mind Lucy?" asks Jennifer ready to listen.

Lucy doesn't know where to start and tells her she's been doing a lot of thinking over the past few hours.

"I think I am ready to get married now" says Lucy, looking a little unsure of herself.

"What makes you say that?" asks Jennifer, knowing there is far too much emotion in the air at the moment and it could be the result of this.

After a little chat Lucy really does convince Jennifer that she is ready and knows what love is. Jennifer is pleased about it but isn't quite fully there at the church with her yet.

"What about your sexual self control issue though?" Jennifer asks.

"If you can't say no, how are you going to stay faithful in a marriage?" she asks.

Once again Lucy manages to convince Jennifer that she has her self control mastered and that is thanks to her. She then claims to understand how to deal with temptation and more importantly, how to say no. Jennifer tells her she thinks she is ready too and gives her a hug.

"I am pleased you got there in the end" says Jennifer smiling.

"I wouldn't have been able to do it without you and Bruce" says Lucy smiling.

With the mention of Bruce, Jennifer says something Lucy wasn't expecting at all. She asks her if she would like one final fling before getting married.

"I don't need to have a one night stand with some random bloke, I really am ready" insists Lucy, worried about where the offer has come from.

"I know you don't Lucy, but just to be REALLY sure. How about one last fling with someone you know and can trust?" offers Jennifer.

Although Lucy knows her own mind and knows she doesn't need it, she doesn't want to shut down on the person that has already taught her so much and asks her who she has in mind.

"Bruce" answers Jennifer with a smile.

"You're Bruce? Your husband?" stutters Lucy in shock.

Jennifer tells her it's the best way of knowing for sure she really is ready and it would be good to have one final night of freedom.

"You want me to go to bed and have sex with your husband?" Lucy asks again, baffled by the strange but interesting offer.

"I will lend you him for one night and ask no more questions about it. If you enjoy yourself and still think you are ready to get married, then we are good to go" explains Jennifer.

"And what if I am not?" asks Lucy following so far.

"If not, then you have the best sex of your life and move on" explains Jennifer.

With that Jennifer congratulates her again and tells her to give her an answer in the morning.

"All you've got to do is say yes. I will do the rest" explains Jennifer, hugging her again and walking out of the door.

"Jen" calls Lucy still sitting on the bed.

"I already know my answer" she adds, with a worried looking smile.

CHAPTER 12
CHOOSE

Jennifer walks back over to Lucy sitting on the bed and waits for her to speak.

"If it's okay with you and Bruce, I would love to have a last fling with him" admits Lucy, hoping the offer from Jennifer was genuine and not some kind of test.

"That's great news" says Jennifer.

"I will sort it out with Bruce and all you've got to do is be ready when he gets here in the morning" she adds, with a big smile on her face.

Although Lucy wants to give it a go, she still looks a little concerned about the whole idea and thinks Jennifer might be losing the plot.

"What about Bruce? Is he going to be okay with it after his stay in hospital?" asks Lucy.

Jennifer tells her that Bruce could break both of his legs and still manage to have sex. This makes Lucy feel a little more comfortable with the whole thing, but she has more questions to ask first...

"Have you ever done this before?" asks Lucy, knowing Bruce told her only days ago that he'd never gone as far as sleeping with one of Jennifer's clients.

Jennifer confirms what Bruce told her and goes on to say that it will be a first for Bruce.

"So why me? Why do you want to do this for me?" asks Lucy, feeling a little overwhelmed.

Jennifer tells her she really likes her and thinks she's a very kind and caring person. Lucy starts to blush a little.

"I just know that one night with Bruce could be the making of your marriage or the making of you" says Jennifer, trying to say all that she can to make Lucy feel at ease with the idea.

"And YOU will definitely be okay if I do it?" asks Lucy, wanting to be one hundred per cent sure.

Jennifer tells her no more questions.

"I will have Bruce ready for you. All you've got to do is enjoy your last night of freedom" says Jennifer, telling her to get some sleep and have sweet dreams.

The morning arrives and Jennifer is the first one up in the morning. Karen is upstairs sleeping in her own bed. Tina, Dave and Lucy are all snuggled up on the sofa under a single duvet and Rose is draped over the arm chair with a sheet covering her. Jennifer opens the living room curtains to let the sun shine in through the windows. Dave is the first to come round and tries to untangle Tina and Lucy from his body.

"I bet you had a nice sleep in there?" laughs Jennifer, watching him struggle and fight his way off the sofa.

This then wakes the two girls and Jennifer decides to get breakfast started in the kitchen. Seconds later Lucy joins her in the kitchen wiping the sleep from her eyes.

"Are you ready for your big day with Bruce then?" asks Jennifer, putting some bread in the toaster.

"Are you sure you and Bruce are fine with this?" asks Lucy, trying to answer the question and wake up fully.

Jennifer tells her it's sorted out with Bruce already and that all she has to do is go and meet him at the hospital this morning.

"Wow you don't hang around, do you?" giggles Lucy, looking at the clock on the kitchen wall.

Jennifer hands her a piece of toast and tells her to go and shower.

"Whilst you are in there, I will get Karen to lend you something sexy to wear and order you a taxi to take you to the hospital" Jennifer adds, hurrying her along.

Once again Lucy is a little overwhelmed by the whole thing but wants to do what's right for her relationship and what's right by Jennifer. She drags herself still half asleep towards the staircase in the hall and makes her way up to the bathroom.

Jennifer goes upstairs and into Karen's room, she walks over to the curtains and opens them.

"Oh this better be fucking good" mumbles Karen, under her duvet as the sunlight blinds her.

Jennifer tells her to go back to sleep and that she is just borrowing

some clothes for Lucy to wear.
Karen jumps up and tries to focus her eyes towards her wardrobe where Jennifer is looking through it.
    "What do you mean you are borrowing some of my clothes?" grunts Karen, not impressed by the idea.
Jennifer explains that Lucy needs to be somewhere important and hasn't got time to go home and pick up her own clothes.
    "Anyway, it's not like any of what I am borrowing for her will fit you soon, will they fatty?" laughs Jennifer.
    "You cheeky bitch" snaps Karen, throwing one of her pillows at Jennifer's head.
The girls playfully argue until Jennifer has found something for Lucy to wear. She picks out a very short denim skirt, matching waistcoat, some black leggings to go underneath the skirt and a pink boob tube. Jennifer tells Karen to go back to sleep for a little while longer and steps out on to the landing towards the bathroom. She knocks on the door to hear the shower being turned off.
    "It's open" calls Lucy from inside.
Jennifer walks in on blonde Lucy standing wrapped in a long towel and hands her Karen's clothes. Lucy takes a quick look through what Jennifer has picked for her and is pretty pleased with the outcome.
    "Oh but I haven't any clean undies" Lucy says, noticing that there isn't a pair of those to borrow in the pile.
    "You don't need knickers on Lucy. You'll be taking them off once you meet up with Bruce anyway" responds Jennifer smiling.
Jennifer leaves the young blonde to get dressed in private and heads back downstairs to join the others, where she is met on the stairs by Karen who has dragged herself out of bed.
As many of them have breakfast together, Rose finally wakes up to join them and Lucy comes back downstairs looking and feeling really hot.
    "Wow you look amazing" gasps Jennifer, as Lucy walks into the kitchen wearing the little denim skirt.
    "Have you got a date or something?" Rose mumbles, still trying to wake up, totally oblivious as to what is going on.
    "I don't like it" snaps Karen, looking Lucy up and down.
Karen's comment wipes the smile from Lucy's face and it's seconds before they all turn to her to ask why.
    "What's wrong with it?" asks Lucy, getting paranoid and trying to pull the skirt down a little.
    "I'm bisexual" responds Karen to everyone's confusion.
    "And that means a bi-curious girl like Lucy can't pull off your outfits?" asks Jennifer, trying to work out what she's talking about.

"No" sighs Karen.

"It means I think you should go back up to my bedroom, get undressed and jump under my covers" giggles Karen.

"I don't understand" Lucy says, standing there looking worried.

"Don't worry Lucy" says Jennifer.

"That's just Karen's sexual way of saying you look really hot" she adds, explaining it to her.

Lucy feels hot again as the taxi pulls up outside the house. Jennifer walks her to the front door, giving her some final instructions.

"Remember, just tell Bruce I said you could do this" Jennifer says, opening the front door.

"I thought you said you would tell him first?" Lucy asks.

"It will be fine. Who wouldn't want you dressed like that?" says Jennifer, ushering her towards the taxi waiting in the street.

"What are you up to Jen?" says a suspicious Karen, walking up behind her.

"Hey, we can't let this Tony thing stop us when there's lessons to be taught" answers Jennifer, giving her a little wink and waving Lucy off as the taxi sets off towards the hospital.

Over at the hospital a groggy Bruce has woken up and has been given the all clear by the doctors to be discharged. He rings Jennifer and tells her the good news, to which she tells him that Lucy is on her way to meet him. Bruce is a little confused as to why she is sending Lucy to pick him up, but Jennifer makes an excuse that they need to go to Karen's via their own house to pick up some clean clothes first. Bruce goes along with it and it's only a matter of minutes before Lucy enters his room.

"Well aren't you a sight for sore eyes" says Bruce, checking her out in the short skirt.

Lucy walks straight up to him smiling and wraps her arms around him before kissing him on the lips.

"What are you doing?" Bruce asks with a smile, knowing that the kiss is a little too friendly for an innocent hospital pick up.

Lucy wraps her arms around his neck and gives him a hug.

"I'm not wearing any knickers underneath this skirt. Does that turn you on?" she whispers in his ear, wanting to get things started as soon possible.

"Of course it does, but what's this all about?" he asks, unwrapping her arms from his neck.

"I want you right now. Take me somewhere and let's do it" whispers Lucy, looking down at his bulge and tugging gently on his belt.

Bruce hasn't a clue what is going on and tries to deal with the situation as best as he can.

"I know we've talked about doing it before Lucy, but this isn't the time or place" he tells her, trying to make her hormones calm down a little.

Now Lucy looks confused.

"I thought you wanted me too?" Lucy asks, looking deep into his eyes.

"I told you the other day that I liked you, but also said that this wasn't a good idea" he explains.

Lucy only listens to what she wants to hear and grabs at his bulge, starting to rub it with her hands.

"Please Lucy, this really isn't a good idea" he tells her again, fighting off his hardening bulge as she rubs it getting hornier.

She takes his hand and places it up her short skirt and onto the leggings where her pussy is dripping already.

"Can you feel how wet I am just wanting you?" she whispers, trying to rock her pelvis against the reluctant touch of his hand against her.

Bruce can feel the warmth of her pussy through her leggings and knows she was telling the truth about having no underwear on. His bulge starts to grow as she starts to rub harder and harder against it.

"Let's lock the door, close the blinds and do it right here on your bed" whispers Lucy, desperately trying to motivate his hand to her inner thigh.

Bruce knows it's only a matter of seconds before he cracks, so pulls his hand away, backs across the room and away from the already groaning Lucy.

"Look, we can't do this here" says Bruce, trying not to offend her but getting a little fed up now.

"Okay, we will go back to your house then" says Lucy, ready to do whatever it takes to get into his pants.

"I think I should go and check everyone is okay first and talk with Jennifer about this before we take it any further" he tells her, still trying to be tactful and calm the lump in his shorts.

"But Jennifer knows, it was her idea" says Lucy, looking really confused.

Bruce takes a seat on the edge of the bed and realises what has happened now. He shakes his head feeling really upset but for Lucy's sake, holds onto his emotions and anger building inside.

"Did she tell you to come here and do this?" he asks her.

Lucy pulls her skirt down a little, crosses her legs and nods her head to say yes.

"A last fling before you get married by any chance?" guesses Bruce, looking a little disappointed.

"She said you were expecting me" Lucy tells him, feeling like she's done something wrong.

Bruce picks up on her mood and quickly tries to reassure her she's done nothing wrong.

"Believe me Lucy, I would love to have sex with you but not like this" he tells her.

"Like what? In a hospital?" she asks, unsure of what he means and why she is being rejected.

"No, it's being ordered and told to do it by someone else" he tells her.

"You mean by Jen?" she asks.

Bruce nods his head and finally cracks.

"I can't believe she would send you here to try it on" he mumbles, throwing his rucksack on the bed.

"Don't be too hard on her with everything that's going on Bruce" she begs, trying to calm him down now.

"What's been going on? I'm the one in hospital, not her" he snaps, clearly upset that Lucy is trying to defend her.

"Yeah but it's not just you, is it Bruce?" she says.

"The attack on you unsettled everyone yesterday and now with Amy's lad Dennis in here as well" she adds.

Bruce looks over at her.

"You mean Dean?" he asks.

"Yeah that's right, Dean" she confirms, claiming she didn't know his name.

"What about Dean? What are you talking about?" asks Bruce, sensing that more has happened since yesterday that he doesn't know about.

Lucy knows she's put her foot in it, but also knows that Bruce isn't going to stop until she tells him. She decides to tell him the truth about Dean being attacked yesterday too and that Amy and Dean have broken up.

"Why has nobody told me about this?" he asks, looking really miffed.

"Maybe Jen wanted you to get better first?" answers Lucy, trying to guess.

"Where are Amy and Dean now?" asks Bruce.

Lucy tells him that Amy spent the night in a hotel and that Dean left hospital yesterday and moved away. Bruce decides enough is enough and picks up his bag from the bed. He tells Lucy that he needs to speak to Jennifer urgently and that they need to get back to Karen's place. The two of them race out of the hospital and jump in a taxi.

Twenty minutes later they arrive at Karen's house.

"Bruce, it's good to see you back on your feet mate" says Dave with a smile, as they walk through the door.

"Did you have nice wet dreams about all those nurses last night?" jokes Karen, as Tina and Rose try to get a closer look at his wound.

"I will talk to you all in a minute okay" Bruce says smiling.

"But first I just need a quick word with Jen" he adds, heading into the kitchen.

Everyone looks towards Lucy, as if to ask her what's going on, but Lucy just sits on the edge of the sofa and shrugs her shoulders.

"Baby your back" beams Jennifer, turning round from the washing up.

"You did wait for Lucy to get there first, didn't you?" she asks, hoping that everything went as planned with her last fling idea.

"Yeah I waited for Lucy to turn up" Bruce says, sitting down at the kitchen table.

"So do you want to tell me what the hell is going on now?" he asks, waiting for her to join him and explain at least.

Jennifer knows something has gone wrong with her plan but doesn't know what. She sits with him at the table.

"What do you mean, what's going on?" asks Jennifer, keeping her cards close to her chest.

Bruce rolls his eyes looking tired.

"Why have you told Lucy to have sex with me and why did no-one tell me about Amy and Dean?" he grumps, not in any kind of mood for her games this morning.

Jennifer sits there looking lost for a few seconds and then tells him she didn't want to worry him while he was in hospital.

"And the Lucy thing?" he snaps, losing his patience with his wife again.

She doesn't answer the question and they sit there throwing the conversation backwards and forwards for a few minutes... Finally after getting no sense out of her, Bruce snaps again.

"I just don't understand you anymore. We used to work at these things as a team, now it seems that all you do is shut me out" he argues.

Again Jennifer doesn't respond and Bruce gets even angrier.

"That's it, I'm going home and I want you to stay here and look after everyone else" he demands.

"When you want to tell me the truth, call me" he adds, before standing up, knocking his chair over and storming into the living room.

Jennifer stands up, picks his chair up and leans against the table looking like she's going to cry. Bruce doesn't stop to speak to anyone and storms out of Karen's house.

Karen runs straight into the kitchen to see if Jennifer is okay. Jennifer quickly composes herself, as though nothing is wrong but her good friend Karen knows otherwise.

"So you didn't tell him then, I take it?" asks Karen.

"Tell him what?" responds Jennifer, pretending she doesn't know what she is talking about.

"You didn't tell him the whole truth?" Karen asks, showing Jennifer she isn't taking any shit and it's Karen she's talking to now.

Jennifer shakes her head and walks back over to the sink.

"If you don't tell him soon Jen, you will lose him" Karen says, feeling sorry for her.

"And look at the damage it's already causing. Bruce's upset, Amy gone walkabouts. It's not right you should be doing all this alone" she adds, before Tina comes through for something to drink and blows the conversation out of the water.

"Why is everyone so mad at each-other?" asks young Tina, looking confused by everything that's going on.

Jennifer and Karen try to tell her there's nothing to worry about but Tina doesn't believe it.

"Why do you all keep treating me like a little girl?" Tina snaps, getting upset herself, then running upstairs into Karen's spare room.

"See Jen, another person affected" sighs Karen, going back into the living room.

Bruce arrives home to his empty house and unlocks the front door. He walks inside and feels a little lost on his own. Just then he hears a noise coming from upstairs in his bedroom. He thinks it's Tony or his goons, so picks up his baseball bat conveniently hidden behind the living room door. He creeps upstairs with the bat held in a striking position and makes his way towards the noise. He waits outside his bedroom door and can hear movement. He tightens his grip on the bat, takes a deep breath ready to enter the room...

He rushes in hoping to surprise the intruder, before he needs to start swinging his bat.

"BRUCE" screams a voice behind the wardrobe door.

"It's me, It's me" squeals Amy, emerging to show her face.

Bruce drops the bat and bends over to catch his breath.

"Amy what the fuck are you doing here? You nearly give me a heart attack" he claims, trying to calm himself down.
Amy explains about the break-up with Dean and that she didn't have anywhere else to go.
"Why not Karen's place?" Bruce asks, trying to understand.
She explains she needed some time alone and couldn't take everyone feeling sorry for her.
"And how do you feel about Dean going?" he asks, sitting down on his bed.
"Fine" Amy answers, picking up the clothes she dropped from the wardrobe when he burst in.
"Really?" asks Bruce, wanting to believe her but knowing himself heartache can be a painful thing.
She tells him she's never felt better and realises now that it's been over between them for a while.
"Hey that means me and you can run away together now" giggles Amy, flirting with her dream man.
"Don't tempt me" he mumbles, just loud enough for her to hear.
She walks over to the bed and sits down next to him.
"Do you remember what happened in the hotel room in Spain?" she asks him.
Bruce thinks about it for a few seconds...
"Yeah, wasn't that when you thought I was trying to get you drunk but I just wanted a coke?" Bruce asks, with a smile of the fond memory.
She tells him that since meeting, they've had so many opportunities to have sex together.
"What about in Spain when Jennifer locked us in the bathroom together, remember that?" she laughs, remembering how nervous she was.
Bruce remembers again but starts to wonder where this is all going.
"How nervous and scared I was of you back then" she tells him, taking his hand and holding it.
"And now, how I can sit here alone and feel so relaxed with you" she adds, looking into his eyes.
The sexual tension builds as the couple sit on the edge of the bed smiling at each-other.
"You can talk to me Bruce. I know something is wrong" she says, remaining deep in his eyes.
Bruce pulls his hand away from hers and places his two hands gently onto her face.
"Right now everything feels just fine" he whispers smiling, before kissing her on the lips.

Amy melts in his arms as they fall back on the bed and for the first time ever, share a passionate kiss that wasn't ordered by Jennifer and was just about the two of them.
Before it goes any further he slowly pulls away and leans back to look at her again. Just then, a tear rolls down her face.

"Hey what's wrong?" asks Bruce looking worried.

She explains she's only just lost Dean and that it feels a little wrong to have such strong feelings for someone else this soon. With that she gets really emotional and lunges towards him. Bruce lies on the bed as she leans back down for another kiss. Bruce allows her to kiss him but soon tries to calm her down, as she starts to lose control of her emotions completely pulling at his trousers.

"We can't Amy, not like this" he says, as she straddles him, trying to ride his trousers and persuade him to get harder.

Bruce explains that once she is fully over Dean and he has a chance to work out what is going on with Jennifer, then maybe the time will be right. Amy doesn't listen and wants to have sex.

"Amy" Bruce snaps, trying to stop her from going any further.

"Do you care about me?" he asks, as she finally stops.

"Of course I care about you" she responds, looking at him looking a little confused about the question.

Bruce tries to sit up a little but she is still straddling him.

"Do you want our very first time to be amazing? Or do you want it to be rebound sex?" he asks her, clearly explaining that she means more to him than just a quick fuck.

Amy gets the message and the idea of sex goes out of her head completely. She wraps her arms around him, letting him cuddle her as they lay together in silence.

Back at Karen's house, Jennifer sits around worrying about her relationship with her husband and that she isn't ready to tell him the big secret that Karen keeps talking about. Karen knows there's no more she can say to Jennifer to change her mind, so switches her attention to her other friend Amy. Totally unaware that Amy is currently across London in Bruce's arms, Karen worried about her tries calling. Amy's phone keeps going straight to voice mail and soon enough Karen decides she wants to go in search of her friend. She puts the idea to Jennifer but Jennifer wants them to all stay together for at least one more day.

"But I know for a fact there's only two hotels Aims would use" Karen tells Jennifer, saying that she just wants to make sure she is okay.

Jennifer tries to fob Karen off again by asking her to go upstairs and cheer up Tina, but suddenly Karen snaps.

"Bruce's walked out because you can't tell him the truth. Tony wants our blood and my best friend is out there somewhere heartbroken" Karen shouts.

"Do you really want me to go upstairs and babysit, when her sister is in the next room watching TV? Besides Dave's up there with her anyway" she adds, making it clear that all she cares about right now is Amy.

Jennifer knowing that stress is no good for Karen in her condition backs down, telling her to go and check the hotels if she wants.

"But then it's straight back here okay?" insists Jennifer not best pleased but feeling she has no alternative.

Within a few seconds, Karen has ordered a taxi for herself and is off in search of her friend.

Upstairs Tina sits on her bed upset with the whole situation and tells Dave just how angry she is with them all for treating her like a child. Dave sits on the edge of the bed with her and tries to make her understand the dangers around them right now.

"How old are you again Dave?" asks Tina, not enjoying being patronised by him now.

"Nineteen" Dave answers, wondering why she is asking this question again.

"That means you are only three years older than me and considering girls mature quicker than boys, we are the same age really" says Tina, making her point.

Although age is age and Dave knows he's clearly older than sixteen, he understands her point and knows when to back off. He decides to change the subject all together and asks Tina if she's got any music. Tina jumps up from the bed and puts some chart music on her MP3.

"Not too current for you, is it old man?" giggles Tina, turning it right up.

She walks over to the wardrobe and hides behind the door to get changed. Dave tries not to let his eyes wander, but still starts to think about sex with Tina. Every now and again Tina pops her head over the door, just to make sure he's still sitting there. She emerges wearing a yellow Yogi Bear T-shirt and some jogging bottoms.

"I know it's not really sexy but I don't care" says Tina, referring to her outfit as Dave looks her up and down and she pushes her dirty clothes into her rucksack on the floor.

"You would look amazing in anything" stutters Dave, trying to escape an erection staring at her big boobs through her T-shirt.

"Do you like Yogi or something Dave?" she asks, knowing exactly what he is looking at.

Dave turns away making out he's looking at something else.

"Pervert" mumbles Tina, loud enough for him to hear.

She bounces across the room and jumps back up on the bed to join him.

"So Dave, do you want me then?" asks Tina, stretching out on the bed, parting her legs and undoing the string on her jogging bottoms.

Dave turns to face her, knowing he's been warned by Bruce not to do anything with Tina already.

"What do I have to do to make you have sex with me?" flirts Tina, sitting up quickly and taking her shirt off to show him her firm breasts.

Dave's jaw hits the floor and his eyes roll uncontrollably around in his head as he is now unable to hide his erection.

Tina lies back down and shyly covers herself with her arms. She shows him with the other hand that her bottoms are loose enough for him to remove, as she waits for him to crumble.

"Well, what you waiting for?" she asks, giving him another glimpse of her nipples.

Dave without giving Bruce another thought, removes Tina's jogging bottoms and throws them to the floor, as he stands up and removes his trousers and boxer shorts.

"Oh my god" gasps Tina, staring at Dave's enormous erection.

"How do you fit that into a condom?" she asks, wondering whether he will fit it inside her.

"Shit" utters Dave.

"I haven't got any condoms on me" he adds, already throbbing at the thought of having sex with the virgin.

"Oh well then" sighs Tina clutching at her tiny knickers, whilst Dave tries to remove them.

Dave knows he can't continue and tries to calm himself down.

"What's wrong with you? There are other things we can do, you know?" says Tina.

With that Dave like a kid in a candy store starts sucking at her nipples and runs his hand straight into her knickers. Tina lies there not quite sure what to do or how it should feel, so tries grabbing at his huge penis.

"Oh yeah, play with it" demands Dave, struggling with her knickers.

She helps him out by taking them off herself and throwing them to the floor to join her jogging bottoms. He takes a look at her hairy little bush as she holds onto his big throbbing stick, rocking against her hand. He reaches down and eases a single finger inside her pussy sending different thoughts and feelings rushing through her mind. She starts to enjoy his fingering action and starts to moan.

"MM-mm stop now" she tells him, feeling her first male fingering experience and not sure what to do.

Dave gets on top of her as she spreads her legs and starts rubbing his stiff manhood against her pubic area.

"Don't put it in me, don't put it in" she moans, although really wanting him to.

He thrusts away rubbing against anything that comes his way until, unknowingly she moves to the side a little and before they know it, the top of his penis is inside her tight wet hole.

"We can't, we can't" she panics, desperately trying not to crave another inch of his penis.

"I know, I know" he grunts, past the stage of no return and unable to stop himself now.

Four inches of his penis penetrate her pussy for a few seconds and both of them know she isn't a virgin anymore. Then five inches, as she starts to enjoy it... Six inches, as he starts to throb inside her... Then the full nine inches, as Tina manages to take his full length.

"Whatever you do, don't cum inside me" she begs, moaning louder than the music playing in the background.

"I won't, I won't" he grunts, desperately trying to hold it back.

Then he starts to explode inside her, quickly trying to pull out. His spunk fires out all over Tina and he collapses beside her on the bed as she recovers from her first sexual experience and doesn't quite know why it ended so fast.

"You didn't cum inside me did you?" she asks, looking down at her spunk covered pubic hair.

"No" mumbles Dave, knowing there's a small chance that he did.

They lie there for a few minutes before Tina knows she needs to tidy herself up and get dressed before anyone comes in to the room.

"So was that okay for your first time?" Dave asks, clearly showing her he enjoyed it but looking for an ego boost.

"Yeah" sighs Tina, happy but a little concerned.

"Yeah but what?" asks Dave, knowing that she hasn't got anything to compare it with, so his ego should remain in check.

"It started really good, the middle was nice, but what happened at the end?" she asks him.

Dave doesn't know what she means.

"It's as though it was building up and building up, then it was over. Shouldn't there be a thirty second warning before it finishes or something?" she asks being honest.

Dave doesn't know how to answer the question and changes the subject, by telling her they'd better get dressed.

Back downstairs and unaware of what's been going on in her spare room, Karen is in the kitchen starting to put together some tea for everyone, whilst Lucy is on the sofa trying to hear the TV over the music Tina is belting out from the spare room. Jennifer and Rose are having a heart to heart about her father again and for the first time, are really bonding.

Meanwhile over at Bruce's house, he and Amy have managed to calm their sexual urges for each-other and lie on his bed in a tranquil bliss.

Meanwhile Karen has already visited one hotel in her search for Amy and has just turned up at the second. She walks in and walks over to the reception desk, to ask them if she is staying there. Then out of nowhere a man in a suit walks over to her and asks if he can help, claiming to be the assistant manager of the hotel. Karen asks him if her friend Amy is staying there and he tells her that the information is confidential. Karen quickly thinks of an excuse and lies about an aunty dying and how she desperately needs to find her. The manager softens and offers to help her.

"Yes, I think your friend is saying at our hotel. Tell you what I will do" he says, smiling with compassion.

"I will take you to her room myself and if she confirms that she knows who you are, we have lift off" he adds, walking her towards the elevator.

The manager and Karen enter the elevator and he presses the fourth floor button. Just as the doors go to close, three large men appear from nowhere signaling to hold the doors open. They enter the elevator with Karen and the manager, as Karen starts thinking naughty things about the four of them, herself and the elevator breaking down.

"So how long to go before you are due?" asks the manager, with the three men towering behind him.

Karen tells him she's not due for ages and he goes on to question her about the father.

"Is he still around and supporting you, like a man should?" he asks.

Karen feels this is a little inappropriate but tells him nevertheless that the father isn't around anymore, as she watches the light reach the third floor.

"And what about your little friend Jennifer? Is she sticking around to help you?" asks the manager, in a creepy voice.

Karen realises she's in trouble.

She turns to the three guys behind her to ask for help, but realises they are part of the deal too.

"We've been following you Karen and now it's your turn" the manager says, as two of the men behind, grab her arms as the elevator door opens.

Karen panics and thrashes, trying to take them all on at once. They wrestle her to the wall of the corridor, as she manages to make contact with one of men with a kick in the balls.

"We can do this the easy way or the hard way" says the manager, getting right in her face as she is pinned to the wall by the others.

Karen doesn't like being threatened and spits in his face.

"MM-mm Karen's saliva" says the man licking his face, like something out of a horror film.

"I wonder if Tony will let me taste your other juices too?" he adds, smiling at her.

Karen screams for help and struggles even more when she hears Tony's name mentioned. The manager slaps her across the face, as she screams and then punches her straight in the ribs as the other men restrain her.

"I said we can do this the easy way or the hard way" says the manager again, leaning over and telling her to be quiet.

"The easy way you will get shaken up and the hard way, you will be leaving here in a box" he adds, punching her in the ribs for a second time.

Karen drops to the floor and the three big guy's pick her up, as the so called manager leads them down the corridor to an empty hotel room. Karen can hardly stand up as the pain cripples her body and they have to drag her inside the room.

"Hello Karen. I guess it's your turn today. Nothing to say?" asks a smiling Tony, standing in the middle of the room.

"Shame, I've always been secretly turned on by your filthy mouth" he adds, telling the big men to put her on the bed.

The so called manager leaves the room and tells Tony he will keep watch outside, in case the noise raised anyone's suspicions. The three big men throw Karen on the bed and Tony walks over, stopping at the sideboard to pick up a sharp knife.

Karen doesn't want to think about what is coming next...

"You've been a very bad girl Karen. Did you enjoy making me cum when you did?" Tony asks, approaching the bed and leaning over her waving the knife in the air.

"Please, I will do anything" she begs, now in tears.

Tony takes pleasure in running the knife up Karen's leg towards the buttons on her jeans.

"You teased me until I cum in my shorts" says Tony, pinging off one of the buttons on her jeans with the knife.

"You didn't see my cum personally, did you Karen?" he asks, pinging another button.

"Please, I'm begging you. I'm pregnant" she utters, hoping this will stop him.

"Now you will see, smell and taste my cum" he tells her with anger, as he pings off the final button so that her jeans fall open revealing her black knickers.

Tony takes a step back and demands the goons remove her jeans.

One guy holds both of her arms down and the other two try and take off her jeans. Karen with all of her strength tries to kick out at them, so Tony tells one of them to hurt her if she moves again. Karen lies still as Tony uses the knife to cut her jeans off, leaving just her thong.

"Okay who wants her knickers to wank over?" Tony asks the others, as the knife cuts through the elastic with ease.

"And who wants her mouth? And who wants her butt?" he asks, running the knife over her shaven pubic area, down towards her pussy.

Karen realises she's going to be raped and that's if they don't kill her first. She starts to struggle again and with that Tony undoes his trousers and pulls out his dick. He lowers himself on top of her and tells her to be a good girl. She pleads once more for him not to do it, but this only seems to make him hornier.

"You can fuck me but your small dick will never make me cum" she shouts, spitting and struggling all she can to get free.

"Fuck her, fuck the nasty whore good" yells one of the men, holding her down and egging him on.

Just then Karen has an idea, in hope it will stop him.

"You want to make me wet? Hows this?" she cries, as she starts to urinate on the bed.

The plan doesn't work and it only works Tony up more, as he falls to his knees, telling her to urinate all over his face.

"Yeah baby, soak me" he laughs, standing back up and telling the other men to turn her over.

The goons flip her over and pin her to the bed again, so she still can't move.

"A dirty whore like you doesn't like to be fucked the normal way, does she Karen?" Tony asks laughing.

"You like it up your bum, don't you?" he says, lowering himself into position.

Hours later Amy is still in Bruce's arms, completely unaware of what her friend is going through. Bruce's land line rings...

"Don't move, it will probably be Jen checking up on me" he tells her, making sure Amy doesn't get off the bed.

Bruce picks up the phone and Amy watches as the colour drains from his face. She sits up on the bed, waiting for him to hang up.

"What's wrong?" asks Amy, as he hangs up.

Bruce starts dialling and doesn't answer her question.

"Hi Lucy, it's Bruce. Stick Jen on the phone quickly for me" he says down the phone.

Amy knows there is something wrong and waits to hear what he has to say to Jennifer over the phone.

"Jen" says Bruce down the phone.

"Where's Karen?" he asks in a calm voice.

Bruce has just received a phone-call from the hospital, telling him that Karen has been attacked but because of everything going on, he won't believe the call until Jennifer confirms it. Soon enough Bruce's worst nightmare is confirmed, when Jennifer tells him that Karen went to look for Amy.

"And you fucking let her?" snaps Bruce down the phone.

"What is it? What's happened to Karen?" panics Amy.

"Amy's here at our house with me" says Bruce.

"What's she doing there with you?" asks Jennifer, a little miffed.

It takes a while for Bruce to explain Amy's been there all along and that she was there when he got back. Then Jennifer wants to know what's happened to Karen.

"Nothing" answers Bruce, blatantly telling her a lie.

"Amy just wanted to know if Karen was okay, that's all. So what have you been doing today?" he asks in a calm voice, noticing the confusion on Amy's face.

Jennifer tells him Lucy is making them all supper and that she's been bonding with Rose really well.

"Oh that's nice for you" says Bruce still remaining calm, then snapping again.

"So whilst you have your nice cosy chat about nothing, our poor friend Karen is being attacked because you let her out of your sight?" he shouts, getting really angry.

"I don't understand. She only took a taxi to two different hotels" stutters Jennifer, as Amy bursts into tears.

"All you do these days is interfere in things that ain't your concern" he tells her.

"When are you going to put the people that matter most, first Jen?" he asks, waiting for her to realise her mistake.

"But Rose IS important to me" Jennifer says, trying to defend herself.

Bruce takes a deep breath and goes silent for a few seconds...

"I'm taking Amy up to the hospital to see our friend Karen now" he says.

"You decide what you are doing and choose. Karen or Rose, who is more important?" he asks, before hanging up on his wife...

CHAPTER 13
CHEER ME UP YOU MISERABLE SOD

Bruce hangs up on Jennifer and is faced with having to calm down a now hysterical Amy.

"What's happened? Why aren't you telling me anything? How badly is Karen hurt?" Amy blurts out in tears.

Bruce sits Amy back down on the bed and explains that Karen has been attacked.

"Why? How did it happen? Why weren't the others with her?" she asks, trying to understand it all.

Bruce knows that Karen was out looking for Amy when it happened, so tactfully tells her they will know more when they get to the hospital. Amy starts to calm down.

"I thought we had a connection Bruce?" she says looking at him.

"We do Aims" he responds, sitting next to her, then taking her hand.

She jumps up, pulling her hand away from his.

"Then don't lie to me, tell me the truth. What has happened to Karen?" she shouts, demanding an answer from him.

Bruce tells her to sit back down and he will tell her. She sits down and he takes her hand again.

"Karen went looking for you and was attacked" he explains, knowing it's going to hit her hard.

"Don't be stupid" she snaps, standing up again as her bottom lip starts to quiver.

"She knows I was safe because I told her" she adds, before breaking down completely.

Bruce knows he needs to get over to the hospital fast, but also needs Amy to come to terms with what has happened first. He tries to comfort her again but this time there is no stopping her tears.

"It's my fault, it's all my fault" she whimpers in floods of tears.

Bruce tries telling her it's no-one's fault and explains that they need to go.

"First you get hurt, then Dean leaves me and now Karen" she stutters, trying to catch her breath as she chokes up.

Bruce knows there is no way she can go to the hospital in this state and suggests that she gets some sleep and he will go alone. Amy doesn't argue and no quicker than the suggestion leaves his mouth, she is on the bed covering herself with the duvet. Bruce gives her a couple of minutes to settle down and kisses her on the head.

"I will be back soon. Don't get out of this bed until I get back" he tells her.

"Don't turn any lights on, don't answer the door and don't go out" he adds.

Amy manages to stop sniffling just enough to tell him she will be fine and that she stayed here last night on her own anyway. Bruce leaves her in bed and makes his way to the hospital.

Bruce and Jennifer arrive at the hospital at the same time, both looking totally distraught.

"No Rose with you? I am surprised you could drag yourself away" Bruce sarcastically snaps, whilst entering the hospital with his wife.

The bitchy comments from Bruce keep coming as they walk through the hospital and towards Karen's private room. Suddenly Jennifer has had enough of listening to him and puts a stop to it before they get there.

"I know you are angry with me Bruce, but can we stop until we've made sure Karen is okay first?" asks Jennifer, trying to reason with him.

"You were supposed to be protecting your friends, not picking the one's more important to you" he snaps, showing he's in no mood to forgive her.

Suddenly Jennifer feels anger build inside her and turns it back on him.

"If you told me Amy was at home with you, Karen wouldn't have gone out looking for her" she snaps back, placing the blame on him.

It hits him hard and all of his anger subsides as he realises he's as much to blame as she is. Instead of continuing the blame game, he changes direction with the conversation and asks her if she's made her choice.

"What choice?" she snaps, eager to see Karen and stop the bickering.

"I told you to choose. Karen or Rose, who's more important to you?" asks Bruce, still boiling over inside.

Jennifer tells him she refuses to pick between the two girls and that is her final word.

"Then why don't you just go back to your precious friend Rose and leave us alone?" he snaps, making it clear he isn't going to let it drop and doesn't want her there.

He is stunned when Jennifer tells him she will do what he requests and turns to walk away. Without another word from either of them, Bruce watches as Jennifer walks towards the exit of the hospital. Totally stunned that she's gone, he turns to enter Karen's room and walks in feeling his tears welling in his eyes as he looks at Karen in her bed.

"Oh Karen, what have they done to you?" he says, walking over to her bedside.

"It's not as bad as it looks" Karen says smiling, pleased to see him.

"A few cuts and bruises, two broken ribs and a few burns to my wrists" she claims, trying to force a smile.

Bruce sits down and holds her hand without any words to say...

"Just think, only a few hours ago I was visiting you in here" says Karen, still trying to force her smile out.

"Yeah having sex with the doctor" Bruce responds, trying to force a smile himself.

They sit in an uncomfortable silence for a few minutes as Bruce can't even bring himself to look at her.

"Come on Bruno. You were meant to come here and cheer me up you miserable sod" she says.

"I'm sorry, it's just a lot to take in" he responds.

"What about the baby? All fine?" he asks, trying to put a positive spin on the whole thing.

Karen doesn't respond and although she is still smiling, Bruce notices her eyes fill up.

"What?" snaps Bruce.

"There's nothing wrong with the baby, is there?" he asks, fearing the worst.

The strain starts to show on Karen's face.

"The babies gone" she answers, trying to hold back her tears.

Bruce looks into her eyes, unable to speak as a lump builds in his throat.

"I had a miscarriage" she tells him.
Bruce's eyes fill with tears as he listens.

"Was it the attack? How? Why? What did they do to you?" stutters Bruce, trying to come to terms with the news.
Karen can't hold back her tears any longer and starts to cry.

"I don't know Bruce. Maybe it was when they were dragging me into a hotel room. Maybe it was when three of them held me down and hurt me. Maybe it was when I was punched in the stomach. Or maybe it was when the fucking shit-head raped me" Karen blurts out.
Bruce sits there and listens to the details of the horrible ordeal she's been through and knows he's got to stop pitying her now and get her through it. He stands up and tries to comfort her, as she gets more and more animated.

"Why Bruce why?" she cries, banging her fists against his chest.

"Why would they do something like this to me?" she asks, before letting him cuddle her.
Once Karen calms down, Bruce sits down on the edge of the bed. He takes her hand and tells her she's going to get through this and that he will be there for her every step of the way.
Karen doesn't respond and just nods her head, trying to force another smile.

"I promise you Karen, I will find Tony and kill him for this" he says, like his life depends on it.

"You can't" says Karen, trying to calm him down now.

"What do you mean I can't? After what he's done to you, yes I can" Bruce claims, adamant that it's as good as done.
Karen this time takes his hand, sniffles and tells him to listen.

"I can kick your butt right" she tells him.
Bruce humours her and nods his head with a smile.

"I couldn't beat them, so someone soft like you stands no chance" she tells him, cracking a joke.
She goes on to tell him that these aren't the kind of people you go after and they are a dangerous gang.

"I don't care" snaps Bruce again.

"I am still going to kill them all" he adds, as his face looks like it will explode with rage.

"There's only two outcomes if you go after them Bruno. One you get yourself killed or two you kill them and end up in prison. I don't want any of them to happen" she tells him, trying to make him understand her concerns.

"Promise me you will go home and keep the rest of the girls safe, especially Amy for me" she adds, watching him take a deep breath and nod his head.

"I will look after you too and never let anyone hurt you again once you get out of here" he claims, agreeing to not go after them.

"Just look after the girls, Amy and most importantly, Jen" she tells him to his confusion.

"Believe it or not, she really needs you right now" she tells him.

"Jen won't talk to me about anything anymore, so you tell me what's going on?" Bruce asks, still holding her hand.

"Just trust her judgement" she demands, giving him a smile and sinking back into her pillow.

"Trust her with what?" asks Bruce.

With that Karen shuts down on him and tells him she's really tired.

"Bruno, I don't mean to be rude but it's time for you to fuck off" she says laughing and trying to be her old self.

Bruce doesn't want to argue with her and if he's honest, is getting a little claustrophobic. He stands up and says goodbye, moving towards the door.

"Hey shit face" calls Karen from her pillow.

"Don't I even get a kiss goodbye?" she asks, pouting her lips at him.

Bruce walks back over to the bed and gives Karen a kiss goodbye and tells her to rest. Then for the first time ever, she tells him she loves him.

"Who is the soft one now?" laughs Bruce, giving her another kiss on the forehead.

"Love you too Karen. Now get some sleep" he says, leaving her room.

Bruce leaves the hospital and the first thing he wants to do is ring Jennifer to tell her what's happened, without getting angry with her. This doesn't last for long as Jennifer tells him she's back at Karen's house safely and the others are fine.

"So everyone's fine then?" says Bruce down the phone, with a grunt.

"Snuggled up safe and sound in Karen's house, whilst the poor bitch lies in hospital in her condition, are you? That's good" he grunts again, with a little sarcasm in his voice.

Jennifer asks him what's happened to Karen and how is she, with some concern in her voice.

"You know, badly beaten up, raped and lost her baby, nothing much" he tells her.

"Where are you now?" asks Jennifer, listening to the desperation in his voice.

"Walking home" answers Bruce with attitude.

Jennifer knows that Tony is still out there somewhere and also knows there's a chance that Bruce will now want revenge for Karen.

"Why don't you jump straight in a taxi, pick up Amy from home and head back here to us?" Jennifer suggests, knowing she needs to keep an eye on him now too.

"As long as you've got your new friends Jen, you don't care about us" he snaps, not willing to do what he is told and with that, tells her he will call her in the morning and hangs up.

Over at Karen's house Jennifer knows there's no point ringing Bruce back, but can't help worry about him with the mood he's in. A million thoughts race through her head as she sits alone at Karen's kitchen table. Rose walks in and notices a worried looking Jennifer at the table.

"Are you okay?" asks Rose, sitting next to her at the table.
Jennifer tells Rose what has happened to Karen and that she is worried about Bruce's mentality. She opens up and tells her she feels her marriage is in trouble because of everything that is happening.

"Why would this man try to hurt you all like this? What did you do to him?" asks Rose, concerned for their safety.
Jennifer explains about the nasty man and the lap dancing club. Then about how he was blackmailing a friend of hers and what they did to stop him.

"Sounds like he's a nasty piece of work and deserved all you gave him" responds Rose, showing she's fully on their side.
Rose tells Jennifer not to worry about Bruce.

"He loves you" Rose tells her.
For the first time ever, Jennifer doesn't believe in the strength of her own marriage and the words from Rose are of no comfort.

"How do I know that? I haven't seen love in his eyes for so long now" sighs Jennifer, looking a little upset.
Although Rose doesn't want to say anything or land herself in any trouble, she feels that she must say something.

"You know he loves you, because I know he loves you" says Rose across the table.
Jennifer looks at her to ask what she's talking about and Rose unloads the guilt built up inside her own thoughts.

"The other day when Bruce was in hospital, I tried it on with him" admits Rose, ready for Jennifer to lunge at her across the table or something.
Jennifer doesn't respond or show any emotion at all.

"You've got to understand, I wasn't moving in on your husband" insists Rose.

"I was just protecting myself" she adds, worrying about Jennifer's silence.
Jennifer tells her it's okay and believes her, but still doesn't understand what this has to do with Bruce loving his wife.
"He didn't want me and he said he loves his wife" Rose tells her, hoping that the truth will make her smile at least.
Jennifer does smile and thanks Rose for her honesty, but then has a new plan. She asks Rose if she fancies Bruce.
"It's okay if you do, everyone else does" says Jennifer, reassuring her before she answers.
Rose sits there for a few seconds before answering...
"I guess he's kind of cute in a rugged kind of way" answers Rose, sticking to the new truthful attitude she's adopted.
Jennifer tells her the plan and makes it clear she wants Rose to go and have sex with him.
"But I told you, he isn't interested in me" responds Rose to Jennifer's crazy idea.
Jennifer tells her she will sort it out and help her bed him.
"I'm sorry Jen but this is too weird for me" responds Rose.
"You're his wife and you are begging me to sleep with him?" she adds, looking worried now.
Jennifer decides to tell her the truth and be completely honest with her too.
"I need to keep everyone together and safe through these tough times" explains Jennifer.
"Bruce really adores Amy and Karen" Jennifer says, trying to be tactful but Rose gets it.
"But he hates me right?" responds Rose, knowing it's not rocket science.
Jennifer tells her Bruce doesn't hate anyone but believes in real friendships.
"And I haven't exactly been a good friend have I?" responds Rose, understanding now.
Jennifer reaches across the table and tells Rose that she really cares about her and really wants her to stay in her life.
"If you have a little flirt with Bruce or things happen between you, then you will be on the same playing field as Amy and Karen" Jennifer explains, which makes sense to Rose.
Rose still has one major concern.
"Even if I said yes, he still might not be interested" Rose claims, still not feeling confident about the whole set up.
"If I can help you turn him on, will you do it for the sake of the group?" Jennifer asks bluntly.

"Sure, why not" responds Rose, like there's nothing to lose.

Back over at Jennifer's house, Bruce has just arrived home and heads straight into the bedroom where Amy is still sleeping in his bed. He walks over and disturbs her, as he sits down on the edge of the bed to take his shoes off.

"How's Karen?" grumbles Amy, trying to wake up.

Bruce decides not to hide the truth from her, but keeps reminding her that she was well enough to joke with him and slag him off from her hospital bed. Although Amy is still clearly very upset with the incident, she remains in bed and lets Bruce comfort her. She lies in his arms on the bed and asks about Jennifer.

"How was Jennifer? Is she okay with what's happened to Karen?" asks Amy, with her head resting on his chest.

Bruce doesn't answer at first and doesn't want to tell her that Jennifer didn't go to see Karen.

"Bruce" mumbles Amy, looking up at him.

"Is Jen okay?" she asks a second time, sensing that something is wrong.

Bruce avoids the question and tells her he doesn't know how she's feeling.

"What do you mean, you don't know how she feels?" probes Amy, sitting up next to him.

Bruce tells her he doesn't understand his wife anymore, so Amy tries to reassure him and blame what's going on, being the reason Jennifer is acting strange lately.

"No, there's something not right with it all" says Bruce, still trying to work out his wife's feelings as he speaks.

"I think it might be over between us" he adds, showing Amy he isn't that concerned and gives her another hug.

Amy rests back on his chest with many emotions running through her mind. She is firstly worried about her friend Karen. Then she's worried about Bruce and Jennifer's marriage and this then might mean she could finally have Bruce for herself.

The couple remain in each-others arms thinking their own thoughts until they fall asleep together...

CHAPTER 14
THREE NOTES AND A SCARE

It's morning and emotions are still running extremely high as the two households wake. Over at Bruce and Jennifer's marital home, Bruce wakes up on top of his bed covers, snuggled up with Amy under the covers. Over at Karen's house, Lucy thinks she's first up and heads into the kitchen, where she is surprised to find Jennifer and Rose already up, deep in conversation at the table.

"Wow, you two are up early" says Lucy, looking a lot fresher after a good nights sleep.

"How long have you two been up?" she asks, opening the fridge for a glass of milk.

Jennifer tells her they've been getting to know each-other properly and chatting nearly all night long, as Rose lets out a yawn.

"You know what, I think I will go and grab a few hours sleep before the day really starts" says Rose getting to her feet and thanking Jennifer for the night.

"I would make that five or six hours" laughs Lucy.

"You can't be too careful when it comes to beauty sleep" she adds, starting the day with a positive joke at Rose's expense.

Rose laughs along with the joke and leaves the kitchen in search of somewhere to crash out. Lucy is really pleased she's got her old friend back in Rose and that the grumpy one seems to have disappeared for good.

"You two seem to be getting on really well now" says Lucy, with a smile on her face.

"Yeah it's great isn't it" responds Jennifer yawning too.

Lucy suggests that Jennifer should get a few hours sleep too, but before Jennifer can agree to the suggestion, her phone rings. Jennifer picks her mobile off the kitchen table and answers it to Bruce at the other end.

"Please don't tell me, you're going to have another go at me?" says Jennifer, making it clear from the start that she is too tired to be fighting this morning.

"Late night was it?" asks Bruce down the phone.

"Partying all night with your new friends, whilst your old friends don't matter anymore?" he asks, showing he hasn't forgiven her yet.

They toss the same conversation backwards and forwards over the phone for a few minutes longer, until Jennifer decides she has had enough.

"Look baby, you either come over here and have a chat or I am ending this conversation right now" she tells him, trying her best to sound approachable.

"No, you meet me at the hospital and visit Karen with me in the next hour" Bruce bluntly tells her, showing her he isn't going to jump through any hoops for her this time.

Jennifer mumbles and grunts about the suggestion for a few seconds, but realises how adamant he is.

"How about at lunchtime then?" suggests Jennifer, knowing that she needs to sleep first.

"How about in twenty-nine minutes? Or you can safely assume our marriage is over" Bruce snaps back down the phone, without giving her the chance to agree.

Jennifer looks shell-shocked as she presses a few buttons on the phone to confirm he's just hung up on her.

"Did he hang up on you?" asks Lucy, being a little nosey standing at the toaster.

Jennifer turns to her and nods her head, still a little shocked.

"You guys are so strong together, what has happened?" asks Lucy looking concerned.

"You know what Lucy? I am not sure, but I am going to sort it out once and for all" Jennifer claims, before grabbing her jacket and leaving the house.

Within the hour, Bruce, Amy and Jennifer are meeting at the hospital entrance.

"Wow, it seems you were partying with the others last night, look at the state of you" says Bruce, greeting his wife with these words and pointing out that she looks rough.

"You don't look too great yourself" replies Jennifer.

"You and Amy do anything special last night?" she asks, implying they've been at it behind her back.

Bruce knows things are going to boil over again and turns to Amy, who Jennifer hasn't even bothered saying hello to and tells her to go and visit Karen first. Amy knows that the couple need space to talk and agrees.

"I will see you inside soon then?" Amy says, heading into the hospital alone.

Bruce takes Jennifer by the arm and ushers her round to the side of the hospital building.

"What the fuck is going on with you Jen?" he asks, with a desperate look on his face.

"You couldn't even be bothered to say hello to Aims before you turn into a bitch" he adds, throwing himself up against the wall as though he wants to bang his head against it.

"Aims now, is it?" Jennifer snaps.

"Nickname terms, she's moved into my bed, what next?" she adds, giving as good as she gets.

Bruce sits himself on the grass bank, holding his head in his hands. He looks at Jennifer and wonders if she cares at all.

"Is our marriage over?" he asks, looking worried about the answer.

Jennifer sits next to Bruce on the grass.

"No, our marriage isn't over. I really hope not anyway" she answers with only a look of love in her eyes.

He takes a look into those eyes and immediately knows she still loves him.

"So what's going on? Why is everything so messed up?" he asks, hoping that the two of them can figure it out together before it's too late.

They talk together for awhile and about the enormous pressure they are all under and end up blaming a few things other than themselves.

"But you've been so shut down on me lately" he claims, still not fully believing that it's all about the situations around them.

Finally Jennifer opens up and tells him just how much she really does love him. Bruce listens to her, as she promises to fix everything and make it all better.

"You do trust me, don't you baby?" she asks him.

"With my life" Bruce answers, hoping she is right or at least telling the truth.

Just as the couple seem to be making a breakthrough for the first time in ages, Jennifer says something that shatters the world around him again.

"I need you to do one last thing for me, before I can fix everything" she tells him.

"I need you to have sex just once with Rose" she adds, hoping that he will agree.

"What is it with you and this girl? When does this joke end Jen?" he fumes, before calming down again.

"Just tell me why you need me to do that for you?" he asks, trying hard to understand without getting worked up again.

"I can't tell you why, but I need you to trust me like you say you do" answers Jennifer, knowing herself she's asking a lot of him.

"If you can't tell me why, then you don't trust me, do you?" he answers, totally deflated by the request and poor reasoning behind it.

"Please Bruce, I really need you to do this" she begs him.

"We are almost there" she adds, pleading with him to accept.

"We are almost where?" snaps Bruce.

Before Jennifer can answer, Amy comes running out of the hospital screaming for them both in tears.

Bruce and Jennifer run to Amy.

"What is it?" asks Jennifer, watching Amy in a panic.

Amy somehow manages to explain through her frantic behaviour that Karen isn't in the hospital.

"What do you mean she isn't there? Of course she is" says Bruce, thinking Amy has entered the wrong room or something.

"The doctor said she discharged herself late last night and that she left us these three notes" Amy explains, waving the envelopes in front of them.

Bruce takes the envelopes from Amy's hand and notices they are addressed individually. He gives Amy hers, hands Jennifer her one and starts to rip his open.

"What does yours say?" Jennifer asks Bruce, reading her own.

"It just says she needs some space, that she's fine and to never change, calling me a sex animal" Bruce responds, reading his note out loud.

"What about yours Amy?" asks Jennifer.

"It just says I love you and will come back soon" says a dumbstruck Amy.

"What about yours?" Bruce asks Jennifer.

"Oh pretty much the same thing as yours" responds Jennifer, folding it quickly so he doesn't ask to read it.

Bruce knows that she is hiding something and asks if he can read it himself. Jennifer gets protective of her envelope and tells him no. Bruce tries to grab it from her, but Jennifer is too fast and puts it in her handbag.

"What the fuck are you hiding now?" he yells, as Amy confusingly watches Jennifer's strange behaviour too.

"What did she say to you?" he asks, not being able to take much more of his wife's secretive behaviour.

Jennifer palms him off and tries to change the subject quickly, telling him she needs to go.

"What did she write in your note Jen?" Bruce asks again.

"Are you going to do the Rose thing we spoke about?" asks Jennifer.

"What did the note say Jen?" Bruce asks again, as they get into a tug of war conversation.

Finally Bruce snaps and tells Jennifer he will talk to her later, when she decides to trust him again. He then tells the upset Amy that they are going home, leaving Jennifer standing outside the hospital pondering on her own thoughts. Jennifer stands there for a good ten minutes trying to piece everything together, then decides she needs to use the toilet. She runs into the hospital to use the toilet and then back outside to find a taxi. She stands at the entrance waiting for a cab.

"Hello Jenny" says a voice from behind her.

She spins around to face Tony.

"You stay away from me or I will scream" she threatens, knowing exactly what has just happened to her friend Karen.

She walks backwards towards the hospital door again, hoping to get inside and around plenty of people where it is safe. She keeps walking backwards with Tony still in her sights, making sure he isn't coming any closer.

"Sorry Miss" says a man's voice, as she backs into someone.

She turns to find two big men standing there, but they don't grab her because there are lots of people around. Instead they prevent her from moving any further as Tony approaches her.

"Don't look so worried Jenny. I got Bruce, the boy and Karen the other day" he tells her.

"Next it's skinny little Amy and then it's your turn" he adds.

Jennifer although scared, tries to fight back verbally.

"What's wrong with you? Why are you doing this?" she snaps, trying not to tremble.

Tony moves closer and gets more in her face, as she stands there starting to tremble.

"Oh Jennifer, don't you remember what you did to me?" he whispers.

"Exactly" she argues.

"What I did, which means you can leave the others alone" she

demands, thinking of all the terrible things he's already done.
Tony starts to snigger, as he signals to the men behind to grab her arms.

"Hitting your husband was boring and as for as the other lad, I wasn't even there" Tony laughs.

"Karen was great fun but I've been looking forward to fucking Amy, don't take that away from me" he adds, licking his lips.

"You sick bastard" she screams in his face, trying to free her arms and hit out at him.

"Karen lost her baby because of what you did to her" she adds, as the men restrain her.

"I know and don't you find it ironic" laughs Tony.

"I fucked Karen and she lost a baby and I am going to make sure I give little Amy one of her own shortly" he adds.

Jennifer struggles again and looks for a member of the public to call out to, but no-one is around.

"Please Tony, this is my fault, don't hurt anyone else, you can do what you want to me" she begs, knowing she isn't going to get anywhere struggling or fighting.

Tony steps back and gives her a dirty look from head to toe, then gets back in her face.

"Tell you what I will do for you Jenny" he whispers.

"Remember how you made me cum in my boxers and humiliate me? If you cum in your knickers standing right here in the next sixty seconds, I will leave the rest of them alone" he adds, knowing that with the fear running through her body, it would be impossible to achieve.

"Okay, okay, I will do it" Jennifer answers to the shock of Tony and the goons behind her.

Tony is impressed with her nerve and decides to give her a chance to prove herself.

"You do realise that you need to have an orgasm right here?" he says, checking that she understands the request in hand.

"Yeah" answers Jennifer, knowing that she hasn't got a problem with masturbation and if it keeps him away from the others, it will be worth doing if she can.

"And you do realise my guys behind you, will be checking with their fingers to make sure you are wet enough after" he laughs, trying to put her off.

Jennifer thought all she had to do is masturbate and fake an orgasm for a few seconds to save Amy from being attacked, but now she knows she can't get away with it.

"You know what Tony? Fuck you" she snaps.

"What makes you think I won't go straight to the police right now?" she asks, trying to wriggle free again.

"Do it" laughs Tony.

"See where it gets you" he adds, stepping away from her and telling his men to let her go.

The men behind, release her arms.

"Tell Amy to book her anti-natal classed now Jenny" Tony laughs walking away from her.

"And once she's pregnant, then I have special plans for you" he adds.

Jennifer stands up strong until they are out of sight, then slumps against the hospital wall unable to stop shaking. Not only is she petrified, but she knows that they are going after Amy next. She manages to find herself a taxi and go straight home. As she pulls up outside Karen's house, a big black car pulls up in front of the taxi. It crosses Jennifer's mind that it could be Tony again come to scare her, so jumps out of the taxi ready for another fight.

"Jenny" calls a friendly American voice.

She turns round to see superstar Whitney sitting in the driver's seat of the black car.

"I didn't think famous people like you drove yourself around?" asks Jennifer, trying to stop her shakes and welcome Whitney.

"I've given my people a few days vacation and I want to spend a few days getting to know you" Whitney tells her.

She puts a cap on her head and some big sun glasses on her face to disguise herself and asks if she can stay with her for a few days.

"I would have stayed at the drama school, but people always make too much of a fuss there" Whitney tells her.

"I need somewhere that I can keep my head down and get to know you better" she adds.

Although Jennifer has a million and one other things on her mind, like the imminent attack on Amy and the fact it's Karen's house, she welcomes the superstar inside with open arms and tells her she can stay as long as she likes.

"Rose is staying here with me for a few days anyway" smiles Jennifer...

CHAPTER 15
THEY CALL ME MISTER WIT

It's evening again and it's been another long day for Jennifer as she tries desperately to come up with a plan to sort everything out in her head and entertain the American superstar who has now latched onto her.
  "I didn't say a proper thank you for what you did for me the other day" says Whitney, sitting with her on the sofa trying to get to know the new life coach, she secretly wants to hire and take back to the USA.
  "It's what I do" responds Jennifer, trying not to be rude but sitting there deep in thought.
Suddenly she has a plan and tells Whitney what she needs to do.
  "I know you've come to get to know me Whitney, but right now Amy needs me and I am going to have to give her all of my attention" Jennifer tells her.
The superstar isn't too happy about being left on the shelf, but doesn't dare show her diva side just yet and responds with an understanding smile.
  "I will dedicate all my time to you once I am sure Amy is okay" promises Jennifer, making Whitney happy.
With that Jennifer stands up and tells everyone in the room that she needs to go home and look after Amy for the night.
  "What's wrong with her?" asks Dave, sitting on the floor playing a card game with Tina.
Jennifer tells her about Karen going away and explains how upset Amy is, forgetting to tell them the truth about the imminent danger she is in.

"Now I've just got to convince Bruce to swap places with me" Jennifer mumbles, picking up her phone and walking into the kitchen. Jennifer calls Bruce and gets a very frosty reception.

"How is Amy? Is she with you?" Jennifer asks him down the phone.

Bruce tells her that Amy is fine and just a little upset about her best friend leaving.

"You wouldn't know how that feels being so cold with everyone that loves you lately" he remarks, having another dig at his wife.

Jennifer doesn't react and gives him the chance to get it out of his system.

"Bruce, I need you to do something for me and it's very important" she tells him.

"I know, you want me to sleep with Rose" he huffs.

Jennifer explains that idea was a mistake and tells him, this thing is even more important and it doesn't involve him sleeping with anyone else.

"Okay I am listening" says Bruce, pleased that it's not sex at least. She explains she needs to swap places with him for the night.

"You want to swap places with me and stay here with Amy?" he asks, sounding suspicious.

"Yeah and when I get over there, Rose will conveniently try it on won't she?" he asks, thinking he knows her ulterior motive.

"I promise you, Rose won't try anything" Jennifer tells him.

"I just need some time alone with Amy" she adds, begging him to accept.

Bruce thinks it over for a few minutes before she tells him his friend Dave is there and would love to spend some time with his mentor.

"What for?" asks Bruce, still sounding suspicious.

"Why do you need time with Amy alone tonight?" he asks, begging her to be honest with him.

Jennifer lies again and tells him she needs to teach her a lesson quickly to help her come to terms with Karen leaving. Bruce can't argue with this reason and accepts. The couple make plans for Jennifer to get a taxi first, then for Bruce to leave as soon as Jennifer arrives. The phone-call comes to an end and Jennifer starts to get ready for her night back in her own house with Amy...

Over at the house, Bruce puts his mobile in his pocket and walks through into the living room where Amy is sitting on the sofa not watching the TV she's staring at. Bruce tells her the plan expecting her to kick off or get upset, but she just shrugs her shoulders and says it's okay. He clearly knows she is depressed and feels maybe Jennifer is showing some sign of normality by doing this for her. An hour passes before the doorbell rings and Bruce and Amy haven't spoken a word to each other.

"Is that Jen home already?" Amy asks, telling Bruce she will miss him before he opens the door.

"Just one night and I will be home" he tells her, kissing her on the head and opening the door to his wife.

Jennifer walks in to a smile from Amy on the sofa and a grudged kiss on the cheek from Bruce.

"Okay baby, you can leave me to it now. I will ring you in the morning" whispers Jennifer in Bruce's ear, giving him a hug.

He picks up his jacket, says goodbye to them and sets off for Karen's house. As soon as Bruce is gone, Jennifer gets to work and sits on the sofa with Amy.

"So how are you Amy?" asks Jennifer, hoping she takes her on.

Just then Amy sits up.

"I'm Okay Jen but Bruce has gone, so let's have an honest chat, shall we?" says Amy, to Jennifer's surprise.

"Why did you hide Karen's note from Bruce and what did it say?" she asks, making it clear that she wasn't happy with Jennifer earlier.

Although a little gob-smacked, Jennifer tries to be honest with Amy and pulls Karen's note out of her bag. Amy takes the note and reads it.

"Keep doing what you are for everyone Jen. It might be a messy right now but it will all turn out for the best in the end" Amy says, reading the note out loud,

"I promise I will be back once it's all done with but can't stand by and watch you lie to Bruce" she adds, reading the final words of Karen's letter and looking back at Jennifer.

Amy spends thirty seconds looking into Jennifer's eyes waiting for her to say something, but she doesn't...

"You know Karen is coming back? You know where she is? And what lies are you telling Bruce?" Amy asks, without taking a breath.

Jennifer spends the next twenty or so minutes explaining in detail the secret she's been keeping from her husband. Although Amy finds it hard to follow, she does understand why things have turned out the way they have.

"I don't get it" utters Amy.

"Why don't you just tell Bruce the truth?" she asks, looking really concerned.

Jennifer just tells her, she can't right now but will very soon.

"Yeah but Bruce is really struggling with all of this" Amy tells her.

"He knows something isn't right and it will be worse if he finds out from someone else" she adds.
With that Jennifer makes Amy promise not to say anything to him.

"I don't know" utters Amy again, knowing that she is loyal to him.

"I can't lie to him" she adds, with a sense of guilt already sketching over her face.

"Then don't lie, just say nothing" Jennifer tells her.
Amy sits there thinking about Jennifer's request and then is totally blown away by Jennifer's next question.

"Do you love him?" Jennifer asks, throwing a smile her way.
Amy sinks into the sofa and gets a little flustered.

"Love who? Bruce? No, why would you ask that? He's your husband?" Amy stutters.
Jennifer puts a hand on her leg to calm her down and tells her it's okay.

"Me and Bruce are coming to the end of the line" she explains.

"He deserves someone that adores him like I do, he deserves nothing but the best and I would like that someone to be you" she adds, truly meaning the words she is saying.

"Yeah but if you told him the truth about everything, you could save your marriage" insists Amy, trying to prove she isn't trying to steal her man.

"Bruce and I WILL break-up shortly. It's just whether you want him or watch him walk away with someone else" Jennifer tells her.
Amy can't believe what she is hearing and really wants to tell Jennifer just how much she does love Bruce, but can't. Instead she tries to push Jennifer a little further.

"Don't you love him anymore then?" Amy asks.

"Course I love him, I always will" Jennifer responds.

"You just don't want him anymore then?" Amy fires another question straight at her.

"Want him, I can't live without him, but I know once this is all done with and the truth comes out, he will never trust me again" says Jennifer, finally showing some emotion with her eyes welling up.
Amy decides to stop probing her now and simply tells her she will think about it properly, but only once or if they ever break-up and not until then. Jennifer smiles at her and says thank you.

"If I can't have him, then I want you to look after him" Jennifer says, holding back her tears.
Amy decides it's time to change the subject and she knows, not only is Karen coming back soon but Jennifer's wants her to be with Bruce. She is really very happy inside.

"So is that why you came to stay with me then?" asks Amy,

perking up.

"No" answers Jennifer, then pausing...

"What?" asks Amy, knowing there's more to tell her.

"Tony is coming after you next" Jennifer tells her bluntly.

Amy panics...

"How? How do you know?" she stutters at breaking point.

Jennifer tells her not to worry and that whilst she is there, she isn't going to let anything happen to her.

"But you sent Bruce away. I want him here" insists Amy, getting herself all worked up.

Over at Karen's, Bruce has just turned up and walks through the front door. He walks into the front room where he is greeted by Lucy, Rose and the surprise addition to the group, Whitney, all sitting watching TV in their pyjamas.

"Whitney, what are you doing here?" he asks, shocked by the superstar sitting with the others like a regular girl.

Whitney tells him she's back for three days to spend some quality time with her friends and to get to know Jennifer a little better.

Bruce isn't really in the mood for a long conversation and remembers what Whitney told him about offering Jennifer a job on her return. He budges the three of them up and throws himself in the middle of Lucy and Whitney, with Rose on the end.

"So Bruce, I bet you never thought you'd be snuggled up on a sofa with a famous celebrity?" asks Lucy, knowing him well enough to know dirty thoughts will be running through his mind.

"I can't say I've ever thought about it before" he responds, not rising to the question and grabbing the TV remote from Rose's hand.

"Yeah but she's Whitney, a worldwide sex icon" says Lucy, trying to tease him again.

"F.Y.I Lucy, she was voted world's sexiest female two years in a row" beams Rose, getting involved too.

Bruce just sits there and smiles, as Whitney is somewhat taken back by his relaxed manner.

"You are not intimidated by me sitting next to you in my pyjamas then Bruce?" asks Whitney smiling.

"Nope" he responds, flicking through the channels.

The three girls then seem to telepathically connect with each-other and have the same desire to tease and wind him up before they go to bed.

"How do you feel with all those men out there fancying you Wit?" asks Rose, in a flirtatious voice.

"I guess it sometimes makes me kind of hot" Whitney teases, with her sexy American accent.

"Have you ever had sex with a fan?" asks Lucy, joining in with the flirtatious conversation, whilst Bruce pretends he isn't listening.

"No I haven't" answers Whitney.

"But if these guy's didn't try so hard around me and relax in my company, then maybe I would" she adds, looking right at Bruce knowing she's talking about him or at least trying to wind him up about his laid back manner.

"So have you ever been to bed with another girl?" asks Rose, keeping the wind up going.

Whitney feels the heat radiating from Bruce's body next to her and delays answering the question until she's sure he's listening...

"Only once with another celebrity but you can't beat a real man in between your legs" she answers, as his face turns red.

"Stop it" giggles Lucy.

"All this talk is making me horny" she confesses.

"Horny?" giggles Whitney.

"I want to have sex right now" she adds, moving her hands between her thighs.

Bruce jumps up from the sofa and tells them he can't take anymore. With that, the three girls burst out laughing, showing him they were playing with him.

"You bitches" laughs Bruce, stepping into the kitchen to pour cold water over his head.

The girls continue wetting themselves on the sofa, when there is a knock at the door. Bruce quickly notices that Dave isn't there and asks where he is.

"He's probably upstairs in the spare room watching a film or listening to music with Tina" Lucy tells him, still unaware that her sister is no longer a virgin.

Like the protector he is, Bruce goes to the door worried about who it is. He opens the door and not like him, pins the guy on the doorstep up against the wall.

"Who the fuck are you?" Bruce asks, making it clear he's ready to fight but knowing himself, he hasn't recovered from his head injury yet.

"I'm Lucy's future husband" stutters the scared guy, cowering against the wall.

Bruce says sorry, introduces himself quickly and lets him go.

"Oh yeah, I've heard a lot about you from Lucy" the guy says.

Lucy walks out hearing her man's voice and invites him in. She quickly makes her excuses and tells the others she is going to have

Karen's room tonight. With that she takes her man by the hand and directs him upstairs, saying goodnight to everyone.

Bruce walks into the living room where Rose and Whitney are still having a little laugh at his expense. He tells them he's going to have a coffee before he settles down on the armchair for the night and asks if they want anything. Rose declines politely and tells him she's going to get some sleep but Whitney takes him up on his offer. Rose curls up on the sofa as Bruce and Whitney go into the kitchen together.

"Oh it's a lot cooler out here, isn't it Bruce?" she says, before saying sorry for the little escapade.

"Tea or coffee?" Bruce asks, telling her that he loves a good joke and the next one might be on her.

"I would rather have something stronger" she responds, showing him her celebrity partying lifestyle normally starts when people go to bed.

"Good idea, I think I will join you" says Bruce, opening Karen's cupboard and pulling out all of the bottles of alcohol in the house.

Bruce puts all the bottles on the table with two glasses.

"Help yourself, worlds sexiest woman" he says grinning, sitting down at the table.

Whitney joins him and starts searching through all the bottles until she finds something she wants to drink.

"You famous people are not fussy much, are you?" Bruce laughs, watching her turn her nose up at five or six of the bottles.

"Once I have the right drink, I am set for the night" claims Whitney, pouring herself a glass of Bacardi.

"Set for the night did you say or an hour?" Bruce laughs again, implying that girls can't drink all night.

Before he knows it, Whitney is challenging him to a drinking contest and they don't hang about getting to grips with the game...

They sit drinking for around twenty-five minutes insulting each-others drinking skills, genders and accents before things really get going...

"So what's your surname?" Whitney asks him, starting to relax with the fast consumption of alcohol.

"I can't keep calling you mister Brit guy can I?" she adds, pouring herself another drink.

Bruce takes a quick swig of his next drink.

"They call me Brit, Bruce Brit" he tells her, doing his best James Bond impression.

Whitney just sits there looking confused and gives him a funny look.

"You've never seen a James Bond film?" quizzes Bruce, horrified at her reaction.

"No" responds Whitney.

"Have you ever seen the film I was in?" she asks, moving her chair around the table to sit next to him.

Bruce tells her he only found out days ago that she could sing and didn't know anything about her acting career before that.

"Well it just so happens, I have it on my mobile" she says, pulling her phone out of her bag.

She presses a few buttons as Bruce pours himself another drink. She waits for the screen to load,as he looks at it ready to watch.

"Nope, you don't want to see this part" she insists, trying to hide it from him and press the buttons again.

"Yes I do, what is it?" he asks, taking it from her and getting a good look at it.

He watches for a few seconds before realising it's a bedroom scene in the film.

"Ah look at you with your boobs out and sexy knickers on" laughs Bruce, not quite connecting the actress on the screen and the girl sitting next to him.

"Okay that's enough" she laughs, trying to pull it away from him.

"Wow, now you are taking off your knickers" he tells her, messing about as she gets all flustered.

She snatches the phone away from him and turns it off.

"You do realise I can go and download it for myself right now and watch it" he tells her.

"Why can't I watch it now?" he asks, pretending to sulk.

Suddenly he looks at her putting the phone away and makes the connection between the film and the woman sitting in front of him. He stares at her in her white and red spotted pyjamas and can vision her taking them off in the film.

"That's why I didn't want you to watch it" she says smiling at him, knowing exactly what he's thinking.

Bruce tears himself out of his thoughts and downs another glass of vodka, as they plan to carry on with their game. Whitney decides to tease him some more, in hope it puts him off and she wins the challenge.

"So what did you think of my film then?" she asks, putting the naked image of her back in his head.

"I didn't get to watch it, did I?" he mumbles, pouring another drink.

"I don't use any stunt doubles you know? That was all me" she tells him, hoping he will choke as he tips his head back and downs yet another drink.

Bruce doesn't react to her obvious flirtations and tells her she's falling behind with the drinking challenge. She pours herself another drink and watches him do the same.

"Come on Mr Bruce Brit, tell me, what do you think of my body?" she asks, knowing that he's drinking a lot more than her now and she can't keep up.

Bruce looks over at her again in the pyjamas and takes them off in his head. Instead of saying anything, he just sits there staring at her...

"Hey snap out of it Mr Brit" she demands, knowing his mind is wandering again.

"Mister Brit, Mister Bruce Wit, Mr Whitney" she adds, laughing at her own drunken wording.

Suddenly she leaps up from her chair, knocking some of the bottles over.

"Hey that would be a great headline for the paparazzi, if we were ever spotted together out in public" she says, dancing around as though she needs the toilet.

"Whitney and Mr Wit the Brit" she adds, laughing again at her own joke.

Bruce bemused with the whole thing sits there wobbling on his chair a little, but managing another glass.

"Come on Bruce let's get married" she says, falling to her knees in front of him.

"Take me now Mr Wit the Brit, I know you've been thinking about it" she adds, pulling open her pyjama top to reveal her large firm breasts cupped perfectly by her silver bra.

Whilst the hour of drinking has taken Bruce's mind off of his problems with his wife and the worry of Amy, he now faces the dilemma of fighting off a sexy blonde celebrity on her knees in front of him, with her erect nipples showing through her bra.

"Come on Bruce, one night" she drunkenly stutters.

"One night to fuck a world famous superstar. You'll never get this opportunity again" she adds, placing both of her hands on his knees to steady herself.

Bruce grabs her arm and stands her up. For a split second he is tempted to make contact with her big boobs right in front of his face, but decides against it and sits her back down on her chair.

"You not going to fuck me then?" she stutters, trying to look into his eyes.

"Fuck, that's never happened before" she adds, trying to come to terms with her first ever sexual rejection.

Bruce tells her he thinks she's had enough to drink and that she should probably go and crash out on the sofa, whilst he tidies up the mess.

"I know you want to fuck me" she sings, standing up and steadying herself against the table.

"I could snap my fingers and you would want to fuck me" she giggles, falling towards him so he will catch her.

Bruce does catch her and she wraps her arms around his neck.

"Come on Mr Wit Brit, one night, what do you say?" stammers Whitney right in his face.

Bruce picks her up and cradles her in his arms. He walks her through into the living room, where she thinks he's finally giving in.

"I knew you wanted me" she mumbles, letting him carry her around.

"I am going to show you how an American girl can fuck" she adds, holding on tightly around his neck.

Bruce lowers her down onto the sofa and removes her arms from around his neck. Whitney looks over and notices Rose asleep at the other end of the sofa.

"Ooh kinky" she whispers.

"Are we going to do it and try not to wake her up?" she asks, waiting for him to take his penis out.

Bruce crouches down beside the sofa, next to her head.

"You are just another hot blonde with a pussy. I could have one of them any day of the week" whispers Bruce in her ear, kisses her on the head as he watches her pass out.

The next morning Bruce is up first after spending an uncomfortable night on the armchair. He pulls out his mobile and calls Jennifer to make sure both girls are safe back home. Jennifer tells him everything is fine and that they might venture over to Karen's house at some point today. After the short phone-call he starts tidying up in the kitchen, where him and Whitney had their own special little party last night. Whitney wakes on the sofa through in the living room to the loud clanking of empty bottles.

"What the fuck?" she grumbles, waking with an almighty hangover.

"I knew I should have stayed at a fancy hotel" she moans, mumbling to herself.

This wakes up Rose the other end of the sofa and both girls try to be pleasant to one another, even though it's too early for either of them to be smiling. Whitney drags herself off the sofa and puts her sunglasses on to block out the light. She stumbles into the kitchen to find a fresh faced Bruce putting the final sparkle to the clean and tidy kitchen.

"Hangover?" Bruce asks, watching the superstar walk through the door looking terrible.

Whitney can't even function or talk properly yet and just nods her head from behind her glasses. Then she sits down at the table as Bruce pours her a strong coffee and hands it to her.

"So did you have a fun time last night?" he asks, knowing she's going to struggle to answer anything.

"And by the way, who drunk who under the table?" he asks, laughing at her.

Whitney holds her head in her hands.

"Please Bruce, stop talking" she grumbles kindly, as her head throbs.

"Sorry superstar, I just wanted to see if you remembered anything about last night" he responds with a smile, continuing to purposely clank the bottles around some more.

She takes a few sips of her coffee and stands up.

"I can't deal with your noise right now" she grumps.

"Oh FYI, I remember everything about last night thank you Mr Wit Brit" she says, smiling in his direction as she leaves the room.

As Whitney walks back into the living room, she sits back down on the sofa and covers her head with the duvet. Dave and Tina come downstairs and head straight into the kitchen.

"Bruce mate, what are you doing here?" questions Dave, expecting to find Jennifer there.

"If you two had bothered to drag yourself away from your music last night, you would have discovered I've been here since then" responds Bruce in a fatherly way.

Bruce asks if they want any breakfast but Dave tells him they are going for a morning walk. As the pair of them step out into the back garden, Bruce calls Dave back. They meet on the doorstep as Tina continues walking down the pathway. Bruce leans into whisper something to Dave.

"Remember what I said Dave, hands to yourself" Bruce kindly reminds him, still unaware that they've already done the sexual deed.

"Of course Bruce, perfect gentleman me" laughs Dave, covering up his guilt.

"Gentleman my knob" laughs Bruce, watching him catch up with Tina and walk out of the garden gate.

Bruce decides he's bored and he's going to piss off the girls in the living room by switching on the TV. He walks through and looks over at Whitney and Rose, both fighting for the duvet as they try to get back to sleep. He puts the TV on and switches to a music channel.

"Hey look Wit, you're on TV again" he says, sitting on top of their legs.

"What's wrong with you Bruce?" grumps Rose.

"You Brit's are such morning people aren't you?" grumps Whitney, trying to free her legs.

Whitney wriggles free, stands up and tells him she's going for a shower.

"Don't try and drink the water, I know how much you American's like to drink" calls Bruce, still teasing her about winning the drinking challenge last night.

"Fuck off Mr Wit Brit" says Whitney, giving him the middle finger and walking up the stairs.

Bruce flicks through the channels, as Rose tries to make out he's not there and go back to sleep. He turns it up a little louder to try and get her to move.

"You're a dick" snaps Rose, throwing the duvet over herself and ignoring him.

He sits there watching the TV for about half an hour before Whitney walks back into the room. He looks her up and down and can't believe the transformation. Whitney has gone from looking rough in her pyjamas to stunningly beautiful in the matter of half an hour. She stands at the door and fastens the belt on her figure hugging jeans.

"Full English breakfast please Mr Wit Brit" she orders, as clear as day without a hangover in sight.

Bruce steps back into the kitchen with her to make her some breakfast. She sits at the table and goes through some paperwork that she has pulled from her handbag. Two minutes later, Bruce slaps down a plate of toast and another cup of coffee.

"Is this what you call a full English?" asks the diva, expecting some kind of five star treatment with strawberry's.

"No I call it toast" responds Bruce, making it clear that he isn't her servant.

Bruce sits down at the table with her and shares a few bits of toast.

"There's something we need to talk about" says Bruce, trying to get her attention away from her paperwork.

"How you are the first guy to ever turn me down?" responds Whitney, picking up a piece of toast and giving it a funny look, before returning it to the plate.

"I'm sorry about that" says Bruce, not sure whether she's upset about it or grateful.

Whitney doesn't want him to apologise and tells him he's the first guy to ever have refused sex with her, when it's offered on a plate.

"I mean it Bruce, thank you for not taking advantage of me" she says, dropping her diva attitude completely and being honest.

"You know what Whitney. When you stop being the pop star, film star and the diva everyone thinks you are, you're a nice girl" Bruce tells her, as though it's him that approves of her and not the other way round.

She responds with a smile and picks up a piece of his toast again. Just then he notices a really nice smell wafting from her and asks what it is.

"It's me" responds Whitney, with another grateful look on her face.

"Fuck me, you've got the lifestyle, the success and even your body odour smells great" he responds, trying to be funny.

She looks over at him looking a little confused by the comment, then gets it.

"No, IT'S ME" she tells him.

"That's the name of the perfume I am wearing, it's my own brand" she explains, thinking he doesn't understand.

Bruce just smiles at her, as if to say he knows and then asks her a personal question about her fortune and how rich she is. The superstar doesn't like to boast about her fortune and explains that she could comfortably buy anything she wants. With that she finds it an appropriate time to ask him whether he's decided to follow Jennifer over to the states, if she accepts her offer. After escaping any worries for the last twelve hours, the state of his marriage, the Tony situation and everything else, it all comes crashing down on top of him again. A little shrug of his shoulders is all she gets as a response to her question and then he fires one back asking her if she's propositioned his wife with an offer yet.

"No I haven't yet, but I want to soon" responds Whitney.

He asks why the superstar wants him and Jennifer in her life so badly.

"With everything I've got Bruce, the only thing missing is real people" declares Whitney.

Bruce doesn't fully understand what she means, so she explains. She tells him that her money could buy her anything she wants and that her fame could let her have a choice of friends.

"But it's real and true people I need in my life" she tells him.

"Isn't there anyone else out there that could be your life coach?" he asks, as he watches her take one bite of her cold toast and put it down on the plate again.

"I've had six life coaches in my life and paid them an absolute fortune" she tells him.

"Your Jenny is different" she adds, waiting to see if he understands.

"You mean she's cheap?" he responds.

Whitney is somewhat put out by this comment but keeps her cool.

"Although I plan to pay her a lot of money, I don't see Jenny working for me" Whitney tells him.

"Yes she can help sort out my life, but I see her more as a friend" she adds with a smile.

"And where do I come into it all then?" asks Bruce, understanding where she's coming from now.

Whitney looks over at him and focuses on his eyes.

"You are not only the first person to reject me sexually Bruce, you are the first guy ever not to want something from me" she tells him.

Bruce smiles.

"If that's not a future friend, I don't know what is" she adds, tugging on his heart strings.

Bruce can't respond and sits there wondering how so many people get the superstar so wrong.

"Besides" she says.

"Money can't buy your toast making skills" she adds, laughing and making him smile.

The pair of them sit talking a little longer and share a few witty comments. Just then, out of the blue Dave comes bursting through the back door.

"What's going on?" Bruce asks.

"It's Tina" Dave gasps out of breath.

"She's been taken" he adds, leaning against the sink to steady himself.

Bruce's face turns to horror.

"What do you mean taken Dave? Who by and where were you?" Bruce huffs, demanding answers from him fast.

"I couldn't do anything, there were too many of them" pants Dave, looking worried about Tina or worried that Bruce is going to blame him.

"Who took her and where?" Bruce bluntly asks again, still waiting for answers.

"I don't know, they took her and pushed her into a car" Dave says, avoiding eye contact with Bruce's furious face.

"DAVE" shouts Bruce, for the whole street to her.

"Who took Tina?" he asks one final time, grabbing him by the arm and spinning him round to face him.

"Tony" Dave mumbles, looking into Bruce's eyes for the first time with fear.

"Tony and his big men took Tina" he adds...

CHAPTER 16
BETRAYAL

Bruce orders Whitney to go and fetch Dave some alcohol to calm him down, then he sits Dave down and asks him to go through everything that happened again. As Dave takes the drink from Whitney's hand, Lucy saunters down from the bedroom to make a coffee for her partner still in bed. Lucy knows something is wrong, as she looks at Dave shaking like a leaf.

"What's happened and where's my sister?" asks Lucy, standing there.
Bruce, Dave and Whitney all look at Lucy but say nothing...
"What's going on?" snaps a more irate Lucy, wanting an answer.
Whitney takes it upon herself to tell her friend what has happened.
"It sounds like Tina has been kidnapped" Whitney says, not very tactful, placing an arm around Lucy as she screams.
With the scream, Rose rushes into the kitchen. With far too many hysterical people in the room, Bruce can't hear himself think or what Dave is trying to say.
"Shut the fuck up everyone" Bruce shouts in a loud voice, as the room falls silent.
Bruce asks Dave to start from the beginning and everyone stands around as he tells them again that Tina was taken and shoved into a passing car.
"Where the fuck were you?" screams Lucy, worried sick about her little sister.
"Three of them grabbed me and pinned me against the wall, whilst they took her" Dave explains.

"I couldn't stop them, I am really sorry" he adds, getting emotional. Bruce puts his hand on his shoulder and tells him it's okay.

"Where did this all happen?" Bruce asks, trying to find a clue as to their whereabouts.

"We were walking towards the high-street, that's all" Dave tells him.

Dave's facial expression changes.

"What?" asks Whitney, noticing the change.

"Tony was in the car and said something about getting Amy too and taking her to her favourite booth" Dave tells them, trying to remember every little detail.

Bruce knows exactly where they are going and worries about Jennifer and Amy's safety at his house.

"Where are they? Where is my sister?" cries Lucy, still in the arms of Whitney.

Bruce quickly pulls his mobile out of his pocket and calls Jennifer for the second time this morning.

"Tina's been snatched out walking with Dave. I think they are coming for you two next" Bruce tells Jennifer down the phone.

Bruce tells her he thinks he's taken her to the booth at the lap dancing club and that he is going to have a look, but needs her and Amy to come over to Karen's house first. Bruce doesn't give Jennifer time to think or argue about it and she agrees. He turns back to the emotional group in the kitchen and tells them that Jennifer is on her way over and that he's going to get Tina back.

"I will come with you" insists Dave, still looking rather shaken up.

Bruce tells him that he needs him to stay in the house and protect everyone else, knowing that he's in no fit state himself to be playing hero. He then starts searching through Karen's kitchen drawers and cupboards for something...

"What you looking for?" asks Rose, offering to help him find whatever it is.

Bruce doesn't know, but feels although he hates weapons, even on this occasion, he might need something to defend himself. In the end and after raking through every cupboard and declining the offer of a big shiny meat cleaver, he ends up arming himself with nothing.

"Okay Dave go over it all again. Tell me everything one more time" Bruce says nervously, gearing himself up and getting ready for the fight of his life.

Dave tells him exactly the same thing again.

"How many blokes were there?" asks Bruce, bouncing on the spot like Rocky the boxer.

"Five including Tony in the car" Dave answers, like he's taking an exam at school.

"Did you see any weapons?" asks Bruce ready to leave.

"No, but that doesn't mean that didn't have any" answers Dave, as Amy and Jennifer rush in.

Amy stands at the kitchen door trying to take everyone's mood in, then notices her idol Whitney standing there. Jennifer walks over to Bruce.

"Oh no you're not" she tells him.

"Your head hasn't even healed properly and you are going out to fight" she adds, adamant that he isn't going anywhere as she watches him put his jacket on.

"The longer you hold me up, the more chance something is going to happen to that girl" explains Bruce.

"If I don't go and get her, who will?" he asks, zipping up his jacket.

Jennifer knows he is right but also knows that there's a chance he won't come back alive.

"Why don't you just ring the police department?" asks Whitney, in a sensible grown-up manner.

Bruce looks at Jennifer as though Whitney might have a point.

"No, you do it Bruce, but be careful" Jennifer responds, as though there's something wrong with calling the professionals to Bruce's bemusement.

Bruce walks towards the front door, being wished good luck by the others.

"Bring my sister back for me Bruce" begs Lucy, as Jennifer follows him out.

Bruce turns to Jennifer at the front door and whispers some orders.

"If I ain't back in exactly two hours, call the police?" Bruce demands.

Jennifer nods her head but looks confused.

"What is it? What aren't you telling me now?" Bruce snaps, knowing there's something wrong again and not wanting to risk his life if his wife's information might help.

"Oh it's nothing" sighs Jennifer.

"It's just Tony said Amy was next" she adds, knocking Bruce sideways with this new bit of information.

"Who said that? Tony?" Bruce asks, looking really baffled.

"Why would you be having a conversation with him?" he asks.

Jennifer quickly tells him he was at the hospital and what happened outside when they were there to visit Karen.

"It's okay, he didn't hurt me" claims Jennifer, so as not to worry or anger Bruce anymore than he already is.

"It's okay? It's okay?" snaps Bruce.

"Is it okay that everyone around us is getting hurt and you have a nice conversation with him?" he asks, getting really animated now.
Bruce desperately wants to get to the bottom of this but knows he needs to leave.

"Another fucking betrayal Jen. How many more things are you going to keep from me?" he grumbles before leaving and slamming the door in her face.

As Bruce makes his way towards the high-street and plans out an attack on Tony and his goons to get Tina back, Jennifer and everyone else sit around in the living room, waiting for Bruce to return with some good news. Five minutes later Rose is the next to crack and stands up declaring that she is going back to the school.

"I've been here days and missed loads of course work" Rose tells them.

"None of this is anything to do with me and I don't want to be next" she adds, clearly showing them all she's scared now.

"You selfish bitch" snaps her roommate Lucy.

"My little sister is out there and all you can think about is yourself" she adds, fuming at her.

"You understand, don't you Wit? You surely can't be caught up in this kind of trouble, can you?" Rose asks her celebrity friend, looking for some support.

"I am here aren't I? And I ain't going anywhere" responds the superstar to Rose's horror.

Rose already knows that she is defeated and falls back into the sofa as if to say, okay then, I am staying.

Nearly two hours pass as Bruce's search of the high-street and lap dancing club continues with no sign of Tina or Tony and his gang. Bruce's feet are tired and he is starting to fear he was wrong about knowing where they were heading. Just as he contemplates giving up, he notices a car screech towards the back of the lap dancing club. Bruce recognises the car knowing that it's one of Tony's vehicles and gives chase. He runs up the alleyway of the club, towards the back entrance and hides himself behind the wall to have a look. He watches as the driver, Tony from the passenger seat and two other big guys get out of the car. The two guys that get out of the back leave both doors open and there he can see Tina sitting in the back. He thinks about bolting towards the car to jump in the drivers seat and speed away, but thinks again when Tony waves two of his men to follow him into the club. Bruce crouches down behind the wall in the car park, as Tony and the two guys step inside. He now contemplates running over and taking on the only guy left guarding the car, but knows even one of them will be a tough call with his injury.

Bruce realises time is running out and soon enough Tony will be emerging from the club. He watches as the remaining guy walks round to the front of the car, sits on the bonnet and lights up a cigarette. This is his chance...

With the back doors of the car open, Bruce can sneak up and rescue Tina. He creeps towards the car some five hundred yards away and can't work out why Tina isn't jumping out herself or trying to escape.

Bruce arrives at the back of the car and quickly checks the guy is still smoking at the front. He crouches right down and shuffles towards the back door. Tina jumps as Bruce's head appears from nowhere and he tells her to be quiet. He tells her to put her head down and follow him out of the car. Tina does what he tells her and they both manage to get to the back of the vehicle safely without being seen.

"When I say, I want you to run into that alleyway and out into the high-street as quickly as you can" whispers Bruce to Tina.

Tina nods her head and Bruce takes one final look to make sure it is clear...

"Okay go" says Bruce, ushering Tina towards the alleyway as fast as she can while he watches.

Bruce watches Tina disappear down the alleyway and is relieved that she is safe.

"Now to rescue myself" Bruce mumbles to himself, knowing this will be a little bit trickier, with no-one watching his back.

Bruce stands up behind the car and peers through the window at the guy still there.

"Bollocks" Bruce grunts, as his zip clanks against the car and the guy hears, walking to the back of the car.

Bruce stands up to find the big towering guy standing over him.

"What the fuck are you doing here Bruce?" snaps the huge goon.

Bruce stands, facing facts that he might have to take on the big baboon in a fist fight but is then really shocked as he walks away finishing his cigarette. Bruce decides with a lot of confusion, that it's time to get away and he backs away from the car keeping his eye firmly on the guy. Slowly but surely Bruce is almost near the safety of the alleyway, where Tina is standing telling him to hurry. Bruce keeps one eye on the goon and one eye on the nightclub back door for Tony. Just then the goon from the front of the car, turns round and points a gun straight at Bruce. Bruce freezes, throws his hands in the air and knows he is in real trouble now... Bruce knows that he should try and run but for some reason, would rather see a bullet coming towards him than be shot in the back. The two men stand face to face in the car park like two cowboys drawing pistols at dawn. Except in this case, one has a gun and one doesn't.

"Bang" shouts the goon, pointing the gun at him.

"Your'e dead" he adds, laughing at Bruce.

The goon lowers his gun and puts it away, Bruce realises that it was just another ploy to scare him and have a laugh at his expense. He continues to back towards the alleyway and is soon out of sight of the club.

"I thought he was going to shoot you" says Tina hysterically, as she greets him in the alleyway with a big hug.

"Come on, we've got to go" says Bruce, totally baffled by the situation but grateful to still be alive.

Bruce ushers Tina onto the high-street and hails down a taxi. They jump in together and he tells the driver to take them back to Karen's house fast.

"Did they do anything to you? Did they hurt you in anyway?" Bruce sits questioning Tina in the back of the car, which has now set off on it's journey.

"They didn't do anything" Tina tells him.

"They just told me to do what they said and I wouldn't get hurt" she adds, shaken a little by her ordeal.

Bruce can't figure it out and doesn't understand what is going on. He sits in silence for the remainder of the journey, trying to work out what Tony's next move is going to be. Soon enough they turn up at Karen's house and jump out of the car. Bruce knocks on the door and within seconds it's opened by Lucy greeting her little sister in tears.

"I'm so happy you are okay little sis" cries Lucy, giving her hugs and kisses at the door as Bruce walks in.

"So you did it then? You managed to be the hero?" says Whitney, walking over to him with a glass of vodka, as if she's read his mind.

"Nice one mate" Dave greets Bruce with a pat on the shoulder.

Amy hasn't the words in her mouth to speak and runs over to give him a massive hug and multiple kisses on his cheek.

Bruce downs his drink in one to take the edge off of his shock and asks where Jennifer is.

"I think she's in the kitchen with Rose" says Dave, making his way towards Tina as she manages to escape the fuss of her big sister.

Bruce walks into the kitchen and sees Jennifer sitting at the kitchen table whispering with Rose.

"Did you find her?" asks Rose, looking at Bruce.

Bruce nods his head and smiles before turning to his wife.

"How long have I been out there Jen?" he asks, not looking best pleased.

"About an hour" guesses Jennifer, looking up at the clock and back at him.
Bruce walks over to the table and reminds her what he said before he left, before telling her he's been out there well over three hours.

"So where are the police then? I asked you to call them after two hours" he grunts at her.

Jennifer explains she is sorry and lost track of the time talking to Rose. Bruce isn't shocked by his wife's concern for him, but is now sick of being the only one that seems to find everything a little bit too odd.

"Do you know what I've been through to get Tina back here safely?" he asks her.

Jennifer looks across the table at Rose and then back at him with a shake of her head. The kitchen door opens and in walks Tina for some water, followed by the rest of the group.

"I had a gun pointed at my head, whilst you sat here giving Rose another little chat" he tells her, feeling really hard done by.

"It's true" boasts Tina listening and welcoming herself into the tiny spat.

"I thought that guy was going to shoot him" she adds, walking over to the sink.

Jennifer turns to him and tells him she is sorry again.

"Sorry, what for? Not caring about your husband again?" snaps Bruce, letting the situation sink in after his ordeal.

"What do you want from me?" Jennifer snaps back to his surprise.

"I am sorry a gun was pointed at you, but how's that my fault?" she asks, with an out of character outburst that shocks most of the group.

Bruce's face drops and he clearly feels this is yet another nail in the coffin of his marriage.

"Sorry Jen" his broken heart and beaten face says.

"I thought you cared" he adds, stepping into the living room, pushing his way through the group and letting his rage get the better of him by punching at the wall a few times on the way.

Everyone follows Bruce through into the living room and there's a horrible atmosphere, where no-one knows where to put themselves.

"I am trying my best" Jennifer tells him, as she watches him pour himself another drink.

"Yeah I know. Trying your best to be a teacher, whilst ignoring the dangers around us" he grunts, downing the drink in his hand.

"What do you want me to do? Tell me and I will do it" says Jennifer, almost begging him to understand her, whilst looking the innocent one in front of everyone else.

Bruce turns to face her and thinks about it for a few seconds, as everyone stands waiting for him to speak.

"I want no secrets, no lies, no lessons and most importantly, a wife" says Bruce.

"Seeing as I haven't got any of them, I want this to be over" he adds, turning back towards the drinks and pouring himself another one.

"So do we all baby, but how?" asks Jennifer, trying to sound understanding again.

Bruce turns to her with his glass in his hand.

"By going after Tony myself" Bruce says, with a dangerous look in his eye, then downing his fourth drink.

"You can't" insists Jennifer.

"You aren't going out there again" demands Amy.

"Come on Bruce, this is crazy, even for you" says Whitney.

Bruce looks at them and tells them he needs to end this tonight, but none of them will agree. Finally his friend Dave shows his support.

"I know where Tony will be tonight, if it helps? I overheard them speaking earlier when they took Tina" Dave tells him.

"Where?" snaps Bruce, looking pleased that someone agrees with his idea.

"I heard them say seven o'clock down by the lake in the park" Dave says, giving Bruce all the information he needs.

Bruce tells them he's made his mind up and this time tells Whitney, not Jennifer, that if he isn't back in three hours, to call the police. With that Amy bursts out crying and runs upstairs and Jennifer just stands there knowing she isn't going to be able to stop him now.

"Jen, can I do this?" Bruce asks, looking over at his wife for her approval.

"I don't want you to go out there and I won't agree to it" she answers, before turning her back and stepping into the kitchen.

Minutes later Dave, Tina, Lucy, Rose and Whitney all follow her.

"He's gone then has he?" asks Jennifer, sitting at the table.

They all confirm that Bruce has left and is going after Tony.

Tina, Lucy and Rose can't stand still as they wait for Bruce to return. Whitney sits at the kitchen table with Jennifer and Dave searches through the cupboards for something to eat.

"I know this might not be the right time" says Whitney, looking at Jennifer.

"But it may help throw a little happiness your way" she adds, as Jennifer tries to look interested in what she's got to say.

Whitney finally tells her she wants her to move over to America with her to become her life coach. Although Jennifer is overwhelmed by the offer, she sits there with lots of reservations about the idea.

"You do know I don't do this for a living?" Jennifer tells her.

"I don't ask any of my clients for money" she adds.

Whitney knows exactly how Jennifer works, but tells her it won't be a problem. Jennifer looks a little confused by the offer.

"Well if I don't earn money, how can I afford to stay over there?" Jennifer asks, showing the superstar she is flattered by the kind offer but has no intention of accepting it.

Whitney picks up on Jennifer's concerns and decides to cut to the chase.

"Here it is Jen" says Whitney.

"I want you back home with me and I am willing to do anything to get you there" she adds.

Jennifer listens, whilst the superstar tells her about what she can offer her and the job she wants her to do.

"You want to offer me twenty thousand dollars a week to make tough decisions for you?" asks Jennifer.

"And what would that work out in UK money?" she asks, considering the offer now.

Whitney tells her that it works out about seventeen thousand pounds a week and then seals the deal by offering to buy her an LA apartment and a car. Jennifer is completely dumbfounded by the proposition and seeing how life isn't exactly going to plan right now, considers accepting the offer that second, but needs time to think it over. As she sits contemplating the offer, she thinks about what Bruce will say and then leaving Amy and the others behind.

"Dam" Jennifer says, remembering her friend upstairs in a state.

Jennifer looks at Dave, making himself a sandwich and asks him if he can run up and check on her. As usual Dave doesn't have to be asked twice and tells her he will in a few minutes, once his eggs for his sandwich have boiled.

Jennifer turns to Whitney and says sorry.

"It's a really great offer Whitney, but I am not sure and I would really have to speak to Bruce about it first" she tells her.

Whitney keeps the bit about Bruce already knowing to herself.

"Just think though" says Whitney.

"You and Bruce starting over in America. New car, new apartment and only me as your client" she adds, trying to tempt her some more.

Dave walks past them to carry out Jennifer's request and check on Amy upstairs.

"If Bruce doesn't want to go with you, I will" laughs Dave, cheekily showing them he was listening to their private conversation.

Whitney and Jennifer just laugh at Dave's nerve and watch him leave the room.

"Just think it over" says Whitney, really wanting her to accept.

"New life, none of this trouble and a client willing to listen to your every word" she adds.

Once again Jennifer thanks her for the offer and tells her she needs a little time to think it over.

"If Bruce is okay with it and all this trouble with Tony has settled down, that is when I will accept your offer, but I really need to deal with a few things first" Jennifer tells her.

The two girls sit at the table for a few minutes longer, talking about Bruce and what he's gone to do. Whitney is a little concerned that he will get into trouble and not be able to move to America, but Jennifer is confident she knows her husband and assures her he will just try and resolve it, more than anything else.

"Although Bruce is tough, he's not a fighter" Jennifer tells her.

"He hates weapons and violence with a passion" she adds, as if she feels Whitney may retract the offer if she worries too much.

In the living room Dave is being taken advantage of by Tina, Lucy and Rose making him do things for them.

"Oh and Dave, before you go upstairs, can you switch the TV on?" giggles Lucy.

"Daveeee, would you be a love and rub my feet?" teases Rose on the sofa.

Once Dave has completed the first few requests, he realises he's being taken for a fool and tells them he's got to go check on Amy upstairs with a friendly smile.

"Fucking whores" he mumbles outside the room, walking up the stairs.

He stops half way up the stairs and takes out his mobile phone and starts dialing a number before holding it to his ear.

"Hello Tony it's me David" he says down the phone.

"Bruce is on his way to the lake as planned" he adds...

CHAPTER 17
48 HOURS

After Dave has made his traitorous phone call he quickly continues upstairs to check on Amy. He calls out to her but she doesn't respond. He looks in the spare room, but she isn't in there. He walks into Karen's room but she isn't in there either, so he tries the bathroom. He walks over to the bathroom and calls out again. His search is complete, when she calls out to him that she is in the shower and will be out in a minute or two.

"Okay" Dave calls back, placing his hand on the door knob.
He is expecting it to be locked and is totally amazed when the door starts to open. He opens the door just wide enough so that he can have a quick peek. He peers through the door and witnesses Amy with her back towards him, standing under the shower letting the water trickle down her body. He stares at her, paying much attention to her bum, as her cheeks wobble around as she washes. Dave's heart starts to race and the imminent erection in his jeans is not so imminent anymore. The dirty traitor starts to fiddle with his penis as he watches Amy shower and he pulls it out on the landing as Amy starts to wash her hair. Dave wills her to turn round but at the same time, does not want to get caught. He starts to stroke and masturbate his full erect nine inches, getting more and more excited by the second, as he dares himself to open the door wider. Suddenly his mind works overtime as he considers walking in and letting her see what he is holding in his hand. He turns himself on even more, contemplating just how she would react seeing his young hard cock standing there masturbating thinking about her. He pushes the door

open an inch wider, as he watches her bend over to pick up her shampoo.

"Part those legs, part those legs" he says under his breath, desperate to get a glimpse of her pussy from behind.

He feels his cock throb hard in his hand, then starts to worry about where he's going to cum as he feels his veins pulsate. He watches Amy stand up ready to turn round and his heart stops beating, quickly closing the door so she doesn't see him. Now with his cock pulsating rapidly in his hand, he desperately feels the need to cum. He needs just one final look at her before he can send himself over the edge with his orgasm and dares himself to open it once more. His beating heart is deafening in his ears and will get him caught for sure, but he places his hand back on the doorknob nevertheless and slowly starts to turn it again, knowing Amy should now be facing him the other side. He desperately wants a quick glimpse of her pussy, he desperately wants her to see his hard cock, but he just can't push the door open again. Just then he hears Tina calling to the others, telling them that she is just going to the toilet. Dave acts fast, tucks his penis back inside his jeans and hides himself in the spare room.

"Dave are you up here?" calls Tina, looking for him.

Dave walks out of the spare room looking innocent and tells her that he was listening to some music, as he gets the urge to have sex with her, grabbing hold of her outside the bathroom door.

"Let's make our second time more special" he tells her, wrapping his hands around her waist.

"Let me go to the toilet and we can talk about it" responds Tina, trying to escape his hold, giggling to herself.

"No, I want it to be dangerous" he says, still holding onto her.

"We can do it right here on the landing" he says, trying to pull Tina's black leggings down and get at her vagina.

"Dave I am bursting" she claims, dancing around and preventing him getting any further.

Dave lets her go, knowing that she is about to enter the bathroom but grabs her again as she puts her hand on the doorknob.

"We can do it in the bathroom then" he whispers, making out he's following her in to do just that.

Whilst feeling his own secret throb going on in his jeans, he takes out his massive penis again to show Tina he is ready. The door swings open but luckily for Amy, she is quick to react when Tina enters and grabs a towel, before Dave has his wish come true. He looks at her just as the towel covers the last bit of her body and Amy looks at Dave and then down at his massive nine inches.

"I'm sorry, I didn't know you were in here" blushes Tina, the only

one to get a full view of the blonde beauty.
Although Dave is gutted and being ushered back out of the bathroom by Tina, he loved the sight of Amy's face as she noticed him standing there to attention. He can't help himself anymore and as the door closes to give Amy some privacy again, he grabs hold of Tina once more and pulls her through into the spare room.

"What are you doing?" giggles Tina, knowing exactly what her new secret boyfriend is up to.

"I still need to pee you know" she adds, not putting up too much of a fight as he closes the door behind them.

Downstairs Lucy, Jennifer, Rose and Whitney sit in the living room where Whitney has just told the others about offering Jennifer a chance to move over to America with her.

Back upstairs Amy has finished drying off, has put her pyjamas on to go downstairs, as Dave continues to tug at Tina's leggings in the spare bedroom.

"Dave I really need to go" Tina utters, clearly enjoying his roaming hands but bursting for a pee nevertheless.

Dave doesn't listen and manages to tug her bottoms down to feel his throb even harder. When he notices Tina isn't wearing any knickers, he lets out a groan, turns her round and bends her over the bed. He pulls her leggings down to her ankles and quickly takes aim with his huge penis.

"I'm sure it was a lot slower than this the first time" Tina says, bending over the bed not sure what to do next, as he holds the lower half of her back down in position.

He quickly guides his long cock between the parting of her butt cheeks and aims it towards her foreplay lacking vagina. He rubs his solid helmet against her tight lips and quickly thrusts it deep inside her.

"OUCH" Tina squeals, as she is forced to accommodate the full length of his enormous penis from his very first thrust.

"Stand still" he grunts, trying to stop her from wriggling around.

No sooner than he thrusts for a second time, he explodes deep inside her. Tina still wriggles around in discomfort as he thrusts every last drop out of himself.

"Fuck that was good" he mumbles, finishing off and falling onto the bed next to her.

Tina stands up feeling a little confused. She doesn't know if that was real sex or whether she should have enjoyed it more.

Back downstairs Amy has gone into the kitchen to make herself a drink and the other three continue to talk in the living room. Suddenly Jennifer, Rose and Lucy all stop when they hear simultaneous screams...
　"What was that?" Whitney gasps.
　"I think it was Tina upstairs" claims Lucy.
　"No, that was Aims in the kitchen" claims Jennifer.
All four of them jump off the sofa. Jennifer, Rose and Whitney run straight into the kitchen, whilst Lucy races upstairs to her sister.
Lucy gets upstairs in record time and bursts into the spare room, where Tina is sitting by herself on the bed looking terrified.
　"What is it?" says Lucy, looking over to the window.
Tina tells her that she is bleeding.
　"What's bleeding?" asks Lucy, looking a little confused.
Tina doesn't answer and just points towards her vagina.
　"Why are you bleeding?" asks Lucy, even more confused knowing her little sister surely understands what a period is.
　　"It's not my period" Tina declares, admitting that Dave is in the bathroom washing it off himself too and that it happened after they had sex.

Meanwhile back downstairs Jennifer, Whitney and Rose are trying to calm Amy down standing in the kitchen, with her mobile phone in her hand.
　"What's happened?" asks Jennifer, trying to give her a cuddle.
Amy is far too scared to talk and shakes like a leaf. Instead of opening her mouth, she quickly hands Rose the phone. Rose looks at it and notices she has just been sent a message.
　"Loved watching your naked body in the shower just then, can't wait to fuck you" Rose reads out aloud to the others.
　"I don't understand" stutters Whitney, looking scared and grossed out for the first time.
　"Why are they watching me all the time?" cries Amy, claiming she wants Bruce back at the house now.
　"Hold on" says Rose, thinking of something.
　　"If this madman is watching you right now, then who is Bruce out there chasing?" she asks, confusing the whole group.
Jennifer decides enough is enough and pulls her mobile phone out of her pocket and calls Bruce.

She tells him about the text message and how someone has been watching the house. Bruce in return tells her that he's been sent on a wild goose chase and hasn't seen anyone in the vicinity of the lake. Jennifer tells him it's best if he returns to Karen's house, but Bruce wants to question Dave about what he heard again first. Jennifer calls Dave down from upstairs and hands him the phone. Bruce questions clandestine Dave about the situation and Dave only relays what he may or may not have overheard earlier in the day. Bruce knows he isn't going to get anywhere, so tells him to tell the others that he's on his way back.

Half an hour later Bruce walks back in to a calm house. He checks everyone is okay before going into the kitchen to have a private word with his wife.
   "Everything seems to be okay now and there's no sign of anyone outside" Bruce tells her, sitting at the kitchen table.
Jennifer explains that Amy's message couldn't have been a hoax and that the message was sent just after she got out of the shower. She then suggests that Bruce takes Amy back across London to their home. Not for the first time over the past week, Bruce is stunned by Jennifer's request.
   "First you want us here concerned about Amy, then you want us to leave" he says, trying to make sense of it all, or at least let her explain herself, but as usual, Jennifer doesn't have anything to say.
Bruce knows he's not going to make any sense of her and like an easily defeated husband, he just huffs and puffs a little, then agrees to follow her request. He walks into the front room to make sure everyone is okay and to double check the house is secure. He checks upstairs to make sure the windows and the bathroom in particular is secure, but nothing seems to worry him, until he arrives outside the spare room. He finds an upset looking Tina on the bed being cuddled by her sister Lucy.
   "Everything okay in here?" he asks, realising something has upset the teenager.
   "Nothing to worry about, just a sex, no, I mean girls problem to sort out" whispers Lucy, telling him she has it under control.
Bruce is shocked by the revelation but pretends he isn't concerned, checks the window is securely locked and heads back downstairs. He walks into the living room again and looks straight at Dave who is sitting flirting with Rose and Whitney.
   "A word now Dave, in the kitchen please" Bruce bluntly demands, ignoring the three girls and walking straight into the kitchen.

"I thought you taught Tina not to rush into having sex?" Bruce asks Jennifer at the table, before Dave joins them.
Jennifer once again doesn't respond and just tells him she did. Dave walks in and asks what Bruce wants.

"What did I ask you to do Dave?" Bruce asks, not looking happy.

"I told you to keep it in your pants with these girls" he adds, before Dave has a chance to answer.
Dave knows he's broken Bruce's rule but doesn't want his mentor to lose trust in him.

"I'm sorry, it just happened" responds Dave, trying to hide the fact he doesn't care anymore, or that he is a surreptitious traitor.

"It just happened?" snaps Bruce.

"Don't tell me, you walked into her room, slipped and put you dick in her, did you?" he asks, clearly disappointed with Dave's excuse.
Dave tries to wriggle out of it again and make good the bad atmosphere stewing in the room, but Bruce doesn't blame him and tells him to leave. Dave walks out of the kitchen and Bruce turns back to his wife just sitting there.

"What? How was I supposed to know they were having sex upstairs?" she utters, trying to defend herself but horrified she's let this happen.

"Having another cosy chat with Rose were you?" Bruce responds sarcastically.

"You need to get it together before you lose everything baby" he tells her, getting ready to leave with Amy.

"Excuse me" calls Jennifer from the table.

"What is that meant to mean?" she asks, looking a little put out by his comment.
Bruce tells her she keeps messing up and Tina going missing and losing her virginity, or Karen leaving and losing her baby is no coincidence.

"What has happened to you Jen? Since you've been obsessed with this Rose girl, you've forgotten everything good about yourself. If you're not careful you aren't just going to lose Karen, you will lose everything" he tells her, storming out the room.
Amy is sitting waiting to leave and Bruce wastes no time in doing just that. Bruce and Amy say a quick goodbye to the others and leave without uttering another word to Jennifer still in the kitchen.

An hour later and after a long, silent taxi ride across London, Bruce and Amy arrive at the house. Very paranoid, they take their time entering the house and settling down, feeling safer behind the closed front door. Still with a million things on his mind, Bruce for the first time feels he can't cope anymore... As Amy gets changed back into her pyjamas, Bruce sits in the living room thinking hard about everything. His marriage, the problems with Tony, the betrayal by Dave and the blossoming relationship with Amy all make his head spin in circles. Amy joins him in the living room and snuggles up with him on the sofa.

"I feel so much safer with you around" she tells him.

She snuggles up with him for a good ten minutes, before she realises he hasn't spoken once since they left Karen's house.

"Is everything okay?" she asks him, realising he has a lot on his mind.

Bruce tells her without even thinking, that he thinks his marriage is coming to an end.

"Sorry I shouldn't be telling you this, knowing that is exactly what you want" he tells her.

She explains it's not her intention to break up his marriage and no matter the outcome, all she wants is for him to be happy, because he truly deserves it. This makes him feel special and that's something he hasn't felt from anyone in a long time. He wraps his arm round her and hugs her tighter.

"No matter what happens, if we end up together or not, you will always be special to me" he tells Amy, making her smile.

They sit in silence for a few minutes, taking comfort that they have each-other, before he starts getting upset again.

"I just don't get it, me and Jen used to be so close. It feels like we are strangers now" he tells her.

Amy sits up, looks at him and knows he's hurting because of the secret Jennifer is keeping. For a split second she wants to open up and tell him everything, but also remembers she made a promise to Jennifer not to say a word.

"Maybe Jennifer has a lot more on her mind than we think" says Amy, trying to be of some comfort to him.

"Why? What has she said to you?" he asks, thinking she can shed a little light on it.

At first Amy doesn't want to put her foot in it or say anything she shouldn't, but as she looks into his eyes and notices the pain he's in, feels she has to say something.

"Me and Jen had a little talk the other day" she tells him.

"And what did she say?" Bruce responds, unwrapping his arm and bracing himself for the news coming his way.

Amy tells him Jennifer said, she wants them to become a couple.

"My wife Jennifer said those words to you?" he asks in disbelief.

"She wants me and you to get together?" he asks.

"That's what she said" Amy answers, hoping it's what he wants to hear too.

Bruce doesn't respond and lets her snuggle back into him again. Then Amy with a positive response from the admission, gets carried away and does say too much... She tells him Jennifer has a plan to sort Tony out once and for all. Bruce again takes his arms from around her and sits up to find out every last detail.

"I don't know" claims Amy, realising she can't tell him the whole truth a little too late.

"She just told me she has a plan, that is foolproof" she adds, hoping she can cuddle back into him now.

Just as Bruce reaches to put his arm around her again, they hear a noise from outside the front door. Bruce leaps off the sofa, Amy looks terrified following right behind him, as he goes to investigate the noise. Not wanting to take anymore shit, Bruce swings open the front door and steams outside looking for a fight. He doesn't see anyone in the dark but knows someone is messing around with them.

"Come out and face me like a man" he calls, whilst Amy stands at the door refusing to go any further.

"Come on, let's see who is scared now" he adds, sounding like he would take on the world right now and win.

No-one comes out of the dark and there is complete silence, as Bruce waits for something to happen. He turns to go back inside with Amy.

"I am fucking sick of this sitting round waiting for something to happen" he snaps, showing Amy he's really angry now.

Maybe Bruce is angry about the whole Tony intimidation thing or maybe some of that rage has come from Amy confirming that his marriage is doomed, but he isn't backing down. He picks up his phone and dials a number.

"Who are you ringing?" asks Amy, a little scared of his rage.

"Jen" he responds, sounding really pissed off.

"This shit needs to stop tonight" he barks, placing the phone to his ear.

Amy tries to tell him Jennifer told her those things in confidence, but he is too far gone to care about anything now.

Jennifer answers the phone and he quickly tells her what is happening.

"I know you have a plan of some sort, but I think it's time to call the police" Bruce tells Jennifer down the phone.

Jennifer listens to his request and isn't too bothered about Amy outing her secret at all. She knows that if Amy told him the whole truth, he would be going mad right now, so she tries to calm him down and suggests the noise outside may have been cats.

"Cats? Don't be so fucking stupid Jen. I know someone is out there trying to piss me off" he snaps at her, getting frustrated by her laid back response once again.

Just then they hear the noise again and Amy panics even more than she did before.

"Did you hear it? Cats my knob" Bruce snaps, rushing back towards the door with an even bigger sense of rage building inside him.

"Don't open it" demands Jennifer down the phone, before he goes outside again.

He stops to listen as Jennifer assures him, nothing will happen if he just ignores it for the night.

"Just give me forty-eight hours to sort this out" she begs, hoping he won't fight her on this.

"Tell me the plan and I will think about it" responds Bruce, with his hand on the door handle.

She explains that if he goes out there now, someone might get hurt or even killed. She then repeats her request for forty-eight hours again and promises him, it will all be over by then.

"Whatever you have planned Jen, you have forty-eight hours to get it sorted or I will be calling the police" he tells her, before hanging up and heading back into the living room to settle down with Amy for a night in front of the TV.

Over at Karen's, Jennifer hangs up the phone and takes a huge sigh of relief but is it a sigh of relief that Bruce has given her the extra time to sort things out? Or is it a sigh, simply because she has a lot to do in the hours left?

Either way she doesn't worry about it and steps into the living room, where Whitney has been trying to convince her to accept the American job offer again.

"Okay I will take the job" says Jennifer, walking into the room.

"But first I need you to do a few things for me" she adds.

"Anything" claims Whitney, ready to do whatever it takes.

Jennifer sits down and tells her first that she can't go anywhere for the next fifty or so hours. Whitney is okay with that, claiming that her flight home is in seventy-four hours anyway. Then Jennifer tells her she will only go if Whitney herself can convince her husband Bruce to go with her. Whitney listens to the request and is a little confused by this request.

"Sure I will, but why can't you just ask him yourself, surely it would be better coming from you?" the superstar asks, treading carefully so as not to change Jennifer's mind.

Jennifer explains she has had to be a little secretive with Bruce of late and he won't decide as quickly as Whitney would want him too.

The superstar still doesn't quite understand what she is being asked to do but accepts the challenge anyway.

Whitney turns to Jennifer and asks her, when would she like her to talk to Bruce about it.

"It's up to you, but as you said, we've only got seventy-four hours to get him on board that plane with us or I don't go" Jennifer responds.

"I could call you a taxi now and get you across there with him for the night" she adds, secretly wishing the superstar would do it tonight. Whitney accepts the offer and tells Jennifer to give her half an hour to get changed. Jennifer tells the superstar she will order a taxi and Whitney knows, Jennifer's final decision depends on her own persuasions on Bruce over the next few hours...

CHAPTER 18
I DIDN'T SAY A FINGER TOO

As the evening slowly draws to a close and another eventful day is nearly over, Lucy decides the mood at Karen's house needs lightening and she suggests that Rose, Jennifer, Dave and Tina have a discussion about her wedding day.
    "Oh well, I think that is where I should call it a night" says Dave, sitting on the sofa with Tina now that she's recovered from her bleeding experience.
Tina asks Dave if he wants her to join him upstairs, but Dave tells her to stay with the others and help plan her sister's wedding. He says goodnight to the girls and walks out of the room clutching his mobile. Lucy's plan works, as the four girls start to relax and Jennifer smiles for the first time in hours. They sit around talking about where the reception should be held, the first song and more importantly to most, the up and coming hen night.

Across London Bruce and Amy have finally relaxed and forgotten about the prankster who was outside the house an hour ago making noise. They sit together on the sofa watching a film on TV. Just then Amy hears something at the front door again.
    "Bruce" she whispers, nudging him in the ribs as he keeps drifting off to sleep.
    "I think that person outside is back" she whispers, as he grumbles waking up.
Bruce tells her to ignore it just like Jennifer told them to do and with

that he turns the TV up louder to drown out anymore strange noises. Just when they think they've got the noise beaten, they both jump when they hear a really loud bang on the front door. Bruce leaps up.

"You can't" says Amy, sitting there looking at him.

"Jennifer told us to ignore it remember?" she adds.

Bruce isn't in the mood to listen anymore and tells her to stay on the sofa. He storms into the hallway and heads straight for the front door. He pulls open the door with purpose, amazed to find superstar Whitney standing on his doorstep.

"Is a high profile celebrity like yourself meant to be lurking around London on her own in the dark? What are you doing here?" Bruce asks, relieved in a way that he doesn't have to fight anyone.

Whitney tells him they need to talk and before being asked to come in, invites herself inside.

"Besides" says Whitney, letting Bruce close the door behind her.

"I missed Mr Wit Brit's toast, didn't I?" she adds, making him smile as she strolls into the living room.

As she enters the living room and takes a look at Amy snuggled up on the sofa watching a film, she notices Amy's eyes light up with joy.

"Hello, it's Amy, isn't it?" says the superstar being friendly.

Amy somewhat dumbstruck just smiles, nods her head and is overwhelmed that she would remember her name. Amy sits up to find out why she has come round, as Bruce walks in and sits next to Amy.

"Well isn't this cosy Mr Wit Brit? I won't ask what's been happening here" Whitney says, thinking that they look like a couple sitting together.

"No, it's not like that" stutters Amy, trying to convince the superstar that she isn't a home wrecker.

"That's a shame" giggles Whitney.

"I was going to ask if I could join in" she adds, sending shivers of joy and sexual thoughts through Amy's mind.

Whitney doesn't sit down and comes straight to the point. She asks Bruce whether she can talk to him about the America plan.

"What America plan?" asks Amy, finding the nerve to butt in on a conversation that has nothing to do with her.

Bruce feels a little uncomfortable knowing Amy doesn't know anything about it and shrugs the request off.

"How about you go and make Whitney a cup of coffee and I will fill you in later" suggests Bruce, ushering a confused looking Amy off the sofa and into the kitchen.

When Whitney and Bruce are alone in the living room, Whitney can't help but tease him about what she thinks she's walked in on.

"No wonder you knocked me back" she says, shaking her head

and smiling,

"Mr Wit Brit has already two women on the go" she adds, giggling some more.

Bruce isn't in the mood for mind games with Whitney tonight and asks her politely, what she is doing there again. Whitney tells him that Jennifer will only agree to the job offer, if he agrees to go with her. Bruce listens to her tale and the shock knocks him sideways.

"Bruce, did you hear what I said?" asks the superstar, when he doesn't respond".

He can't get his head around it and asks if she could have been mistaken. Whitney tells him again, word for word what his wife demanded but it doesn't help.

"I don't get it" says Bruce, looking totally baffled.

"Only an hour ago, she was pushing me and Aims together and now she wants me over in America with her" he adds.

With no answer, Whitney and Bruce are left baffled by it together. Amy walks back in with Whitney's coffee and with her hand trembling, hands the cup to her idol with a thanks as a reward. She looks at the cup and at Bruce as if to say, do I really have to drink this.

"Bacardi is on the sideboard" Bruce says, reading her mind and making her smile.

Whitney tells Amy that she will enjoy her coffee and thanks her again, but needs a stronger drink. The superstar moves across to the sideboard, realising she can't ask the question again and pours herself a drink. Just then Amy decides she wants to join her idol and hurries into the kitchen to fetch herself a glass.

"Bruce" whispers Whitney, turning to face him.

"Are you going to come with us?" she asks, sipping her drink.

Bruce walks over to her before Amy returns and tells her quickly, he will give her a direct answer in the morning. Amy walks across to the sideboard with her empty glass.

"Well I think I will leave you girls to it" says Bruce, not bothering to have a drink himself and telling them he's really tired.

"I will be up in a little while" claims Amy, before she can feel Whitney's eyes staring at her with raised eyebrows.

Amy tries to tell the superstar that she didn't mean anything by it and there's absolutely nothing going on between her and Bruce. Bruce says goodnight and goes upstairs and Whitney tells her nervous fan to relax, she isn't there to judge her.

"Hey if I had my way" whispers Whitney, with a naughty smile.

"I would follow him right up those stairs too" she adds, relaxing tense Amy.

The girls take a seat on the sofa together and start bonding as though they were best friends. Whitney initiates most of the conversion as Amy sits there in ore of her idol.

"This is not how I imagined meeting you" says Amy, plucking up the courage to say something.

"I had so many questions to ask you but can't think of any now" she adds, getting a little frustrated with herself.

Whitney understands and tells her she's felt the same way before.

"Really?" asks Amy, doubting that someone like Whitney would ever have this problem.

"Yeah, when I met your Queen and the Royal family" the superstar claims, as Amy's jaw hits the floor.

The two girls have a few more drinks and have a good laugh in the process. They sit chatting for another hour or so, until Amy feels she should go and check if Bruce is okay.

"Do you want me to come up with you?" asks the superstar, putting naughty thoughts into Amy's head again.

"No it's okay, I won't be a second" Amy tells her, adding that she wants to put her pyjamas on anyway.

Whitney tells her she hasn't got any pyjamas with her and Amy quickly tells her she will lend her something to wear for the night. Amy heads upstairs leaving Whitney to flick through the channels on the TV and pour herself another drink. Amy walks into the bedroom to find Bruce just sitting on the bed deep in thought.

"Can you believe I am downstairs with Whitney?" Amy boasts.

"And now I'm going to lend her some of my pyjamas" she adds.

She turns to Bruce from behind the wardrobe door, where her bag of clothes are and notices he isn't listening to her. She picks up her bag and takes it over to the bed to sit with him. She asks him if he's okay and is knocked sideways by what he says next...

"Your idol downstairs wants me and Jen to go and live in America with her" Bruce confesses.

At first Amy thinks Bruce is so lucky to be offered such an opportunity. Then it sinks in, as she considers the possibility of losing him. She stops pulling the pyjamas from her bag to look at him.

"Do you want to go?" she asks, holding her breath.

Bruce's doesn't answer straight away and to Amy, it seems to take a lifetime. He looks into her eyes and starts to open his mouth.

"No, I don't think I want to go. I want to stay here with you" he tells her.

Amy leans in to kiss him and give him a cuddle. She hugs him for a couple of minutes before remembering Whitney is downstairs and tells him she needs to lend her something to wear for the night.

"Tell you what. I will pop these down to her and be up in five minutes" she tells him.

Bruce nods and smiles in agreement, watching the sexy blonde and now unofficially his new partner, strip and change into her pyjamas.

"What?" she giggles, knowing he is sitting there watching her get changed.

"Nothing" smirks Bruce, watching her remove her knickers and jump into her cotton pyjama bottoms.

"Okay back in five. Don't go anywhere" she tells him, kissing him on the lips again and running down the stairs.

She enters the living room where Whitney is waiting on the sofa for her.

"I hope these will be okay for you?" Amy says, handing over her favourite silky pink pyjamas.

Whitney takes them from her and tells her they will be fine, capturing Amy's real figure.

"You know, with a figure like yours Amy, you could be a model" Whitney says.

"Really?" responds Amy, sitting down on the sofa to hear more and forgetting Bruce upstairs once again.

Amy watches as the famous figure starts to strip right in front of her. It's not until Whitney gets down to her underwear that she notices Amy just staring at her body, with a glazed look on her face.

"Oh I am sorry" says Whitney, covering her underwear with the clothes she's just taken off.

"I am so used to getting changed in front of people, that I forgot I should have asked if you minded first" she adds, waiting for Amy to respond.

Amy looks a little embarrassed and tells her it's fine.

"I just can't believe the body I've seen on TV so many times is standing right in front of me" gasps Amy.

Whitney drops her clothes on the floor, standing there in her bra and knickers and picks up Amy's favourite pyjamas to put on.

"If you like, I could just stay in my underwear all night" Whitney flirts, watching Amy's eyes fixated on her pink outfit.

"Yeah, I would like that, I mean, no it's fine" says Amy, getting all flustered caught up in her own thoughts.

Whitney quickly puts the pink outfit on, pours them another drink and sits back down with her on the sofa. The girls sit end to end on the sofa and start chatting again, this time in conversation of a more personal and sexual manner.

"So have you and Bruce EVER, you know?" asks Whitney, playing footsie with Amy on the sofa.

Amy tells her the truth and that there has been many occasions where they could have, but didn't.

"What about with another girl?" asks Whitney, keeping the personal and sexual questions coming...

Amy once again doesn't hide behind the truth and tells her she hasn't had a full experience, but has dabbled.

"So you like girls too then?" responds Whitney, with a naughty smile on her face, to which Amy gets a little shy, just nodding her head.

"So come on then, If it was offered to you on a plate, would I be your type?" Whitney asks, starting to tease herself with the idea.

This time Amy doesn't answer and directs the question back to Whitney.

"I don't know" quivers Amy.

"Why, would I be your type?" she asks, wanting the celebrity to answer the tough question first.

Whitney looks at her, smiles and tells her she is stunningly beautiful. Amy blushes and responds with a little giggle.

"Tell you what we should do" says Whitney, with a naughty idea.

"We should hook up, then go upstairs for a threesome with Bruce" she says, not giving Amy a clear sign of whether she's joking or not.

Amy jumps up, remembering she told Bruce she'd be back upstairs in a minute and makes a quick excuse to her flirting idol, telling her she will be back in a minute. Amy runs back upstairs and enters the bedroom where Bruce is still sitting on the bed. She tells him she is sorry and sits down with him on the bed again. He knows she adores Whitney, so tells her it's okay.

"So what are you girls talking about down there?" Bruce asks, trying to sound interested.

Amy wants to tell him, feeling fit to burst.

"I think she is hinting at a threesome with me and you" utters Amy in excitement.

Bruce just shrugs it off and tells her to go and carry on with her chat.

"Did you hear me Bruce? I think Whitney wants to have a threesome right now" she says again.

Bruce jumps off the bed and huffs to Amy's confusion.

"What is it?" she asks, not wanting to upset him.

Bruce explains that whilst his marriage is ending and he's coming to terms with it, he has also spent the last six days feeling unloved and felt most of the time, that Jennifer has been trying to pimp him out.

"I know it's hard to get over, but we will do it together" she responds, walking over to him and claiming to understand his pain.

"Together?" he responds, letting her rub his chest.

"Then what are you talking about having threesomes for then?" he asks, showing her she's no different and that's the reason he's walking away from his marriage.

"Yeah but this is Whitney. We will never get this chance ever again" says Amy, trying to tell him she's nothing like Jennifer and if it wasn't for Whitney, she wouldn't be suggesting it at all.

"I will spend the rest of my life making you happy everyday" she promises, with honesty written all over her face.

"But all I want right now is for Whitney to come up here and we have some naughty fun" she adds, telling him just how horny it would be and how happy it would make her.

"And all I want is to be loved" sighs Bruce, clearly dismissing any chance of a threesome taking place in his bedroom tonight.

Amy knows she isn't going to get what she wants and doesn't want him to think she doesn't understand or support his decision. She tells him it's okay and that if he doesn't' want it, then she doesn't either.

"But what do I tell her then? She will keep hinting all night" she asks, in one final attempt to get him to change his mind.

He tells her to go back downstairs and say he has fallen asleep.

"Spend a few minutes with her and tell her you are going to bed" he adds, with a plan.

Amy agrees and shuns aside her true fantasy to make him happy. She moves towards the bedroom door, then Bruce calls after her...

"If you come to bed in the next five minutes, we will get our relationship started" he tells her, making it clear he will have sex with her for the first time tonight.

Amy smiles as he throws her a duvet to give to Whitney and sprints downstairs into the living room, where Whitney is and follows Bruce's instructions. She tells the superstar that Bruce is asleep and she took ages trying to find a duvet for her upstairs. Whitney believes her and takes the cover from her, wrapping it around herself on the sofa. Without sitting down again, Amy tells her she is tired and is going up to the spare room to get some sleep. Although Whitney is a little disappointed that their bonding and sex talk seems to have fizzled out, she is pretty tired herself and the two girls say goodnight to eachother with a kiss on the cheek. Whitney lies back and closes her eyes as Amy walks over to the light switch and turns it off. She takes another quick look at the sexy superstar, considers what might have been and rushes back upstairs to Bruce.

"Wow that was quick" says Bruce, not expecting her to return that fast as he's getting undressed.

Amy watches with a smile on her face at the door, as the bald headed man of her dreams, slips out of his jeans to reveal the tight package in his shorts and then remove his shirt to reveal his smooth toned chest. She slowly walks over to him, knowing that this is it and starts to feel nervous... He takes her by the waist and starts to nibble on her neck as he places her down on the bed. She starts to moan as he slowly starts to unbutton her top and work his way down with kisses towards her breasts. Just as she starts to relax and prepare herself for him to make contact with her naked breasts, he jumps up, runs across the room and switches off the light. Amy stays on the bed in the dark, allowing her top to fall open as she watches his shadow move back towards her on the bed. He mounts the bed and quickly slides off her bottoms. He parts her legs and moves down between her thighs. Just then she feels his warm wet tongue run up her smoothly shaven pussy lips and onto her clitoris.

"MM-mm" she moans, as he starts to circle on her clit and nibble at it softly with his teeth.

Her pelvis starts to rock as he puts a little more pressure on her swelling spot and she places her hands on his head to help her thrust against his mouth.

"That feels so good" she moans, as he places a single finger inside her wet pussy and starts to finger her, still flicking his tongue.

"Oh my god" she moans, as he starts to speed up and finger her a lot faster and harder.

He wiggles his single finger deep inside her at speed and dribbles his saliva all over her blood filled clitoris to build her oncoming orgasm. Now with the tension building and her legs starting to shake, he tries to lever his head away from her vagina, as he continues to apply more pressure.

"Stop, MM-mm stop, I'm going to cum" she gasps, feeling her orgasm shudder through her body and down towards her pussy.

Bruce stops to her sexual frustration and climbs up the bed to join her face to face.

"Oh my god, that was amazing" she pants, eager to explode.

"We've only just started" he whispers.

He places a hand on her head and pushes her gently towards his shorts. Straight away, she knows where he wants her to go and she shuffles herself down the bed to take up position. Bruce removes his shorts as she reaches out her hand to find it. She misses a few times, then finally has his erect penis in her hand. She lets out another moan of pleasure and moves into suck it for him. Just as she is about to make contact, he stops her and pulls her back up the bed.

"We need a little chat first" he says, to her confusion.

"What do you find hot about Whitney?" he asks, letting her rest her uncontrollable shaking body against his.

"Everything" she pants, trying hard to move back down the bed and carry on.

"Would you lick her pussy?" he asks bluntly in the dark, unaware of her facial expression.

"In a heartbeat" she answers, trying to grab hold of his penis again, as the conversation is now helping her delayed orgasm towards it's peak.

Bruce lets her hold onto his hard penis again and searches for her pussy with his own hand. He runs his fingers between her legs and inserts the same finger that was in her before.

"MM-mm" she groans again, as she feels his finger start to work on her tightening pussy once more.

"And how much do you want me to go and fetch her up here right now?" he whispers in her ear, as he pushes his finger deep inside her dripping pussy.

"So..." she pants stuttering.

"So... Much" she adds, on the verge of exploding onto his finger.

He takes his finger out quickly, making her wait a little longer. Now with nowhere else to turn, Amy can't cope and is desperate for her orgasm in the dark. Bruce makes her wait even longer and rock impatiently, whilst he explains something to her...

Bruce's Lesson In Fantasy, Courteous Of Jennifer

Whilst men and women on a daily basis fight against lust and temptation, what many of them don't realise is, there's no need to fight it.

Fighting yourself over a temptation or someone that you desire sex with, only makes you think about it more. This leads to more thinking about that lustful person than you should and this is worse for you in the long run. Think of it this way... We all know what happens when we are told we can't have something, don't we?

We want it more right?

Then by fighting your temptations, you are doing exactly that aren't you? You are reminding yourself that you can't cheat, can't go to bed with that person and this sometimes is the reason why temptation gets the better of us. It's not because we weren't strong enough, it was because we put that temptation and fantasy up on a pedestal and kept saying no to it...

We should all know what to do with a temptation that looks to be getting the better of us, that's masturbate. Pure and simple, masturbation as millions of us know, can stop us making the ultimate cock-up (Excuse the pun) A better way of dealing with temptation, lust and unfaithful desires is to open up with your partner and be honest. Yes it might sound crazy telling your life long partner that you've had a sexual urge about someone else, but what is the alternative, one of you cheating? Breaking up?

If you can open up, encourage your partner to do the same, neither of you should fear lust or temptation again.

As mentioned once before... Temptation isn't something that may come along or it may not, it's inside all of us, so dealing with it honestly, should be the only way.

Face facts time... If you had an open and honest partner that told you he fancied one of your friends, wouldn't you like to know about it and perhaps enjoy the sexual fantasy together? Or the alternative of him going it alone and reminding himself everyday that he can't have sex with her? Would you rather an honest sex life where it makes you stronger together or a relationship doomed to end, because one of you were tempted or cheated?

Here's something to think about... Has your partner ever admitted to fancying someone real? (Not a celebrity) Being tempted? Having unfaithful or lustful thoughts about someone else? No?

So he really spends twenty-four hours a day blinkered to the real world and away from other female's does he? That's fine if you believe that. Now ask yourself this? Have you admitted to fancying someone real? Told him? Have you been tempted even just a little bit? Have you found yourself looking at another man? Have you thought about what his cock would feel like just once? No? Are you a Nun?

An honest relationship is the only way to stop things from happening that shouldn't. You shouldn't be scared of the women he fancies, if he's been honest and you can enjoy it together. Neither should you be scared to tell him about the bulge or bum you looked at and turned you on the other day. You should only be scared of the imminent break-up if you cannot be honest with each-other.

Amy wraps her arm around him still wanting to have her orgasm but understands from the start of their new relationship, he wants it based around honesty.

"But what I don't understand is, why are you telling me all this? I have already been honest and told you I am tempted by Whitney" she asks him.

Bruce is ready to get started again and explains that although she's been honest, she still isn't using it during sex correctly. He pushes her shoulders back down and this time she latches onto his penis before he has the chance to change his mind again. She takes hold of his throbbing erection and starts to suck on his helmet.

"Okay, now start masturbating whilst you suck it" whispers Bruce, enjoying the blow job.

Amy keeps his stiff cock in her mouth and runs her other hand down between her legs.

"Don't just tickle your pussy. I want to feel you fuck yourself thinking about Whitney" he demands, as she squeezes her mouth closed so it suffocates his erection.

She starts masturbating and fully letting go, nearly forgetting Bruce is even there... She fingers herself hard, rubs her clitoris and even slaps it a few times to make it swell even more. As her tightly closed mouth sucks on his cock and the sounds of her wetness squelching, Bruce pushes her lower down, until her mouth is in line with his scrotum.

"Now start licking" he tells her.

"Show me just how you would lick Whitney's pussy right now" he orders, as her tongue and mind now vision Whitney's vagina.

"Now show me how you would lick her pussy out" Bruce groans, lowering her head some more, until she is level with his bum.

Amy can't see a thing and licks round his anus and the smooth bit, until she fully imagines it to be Whitney. With that she sends her tongue on an exploration of his anus and continues to finger herself, as she imagines the taste of the superstar in her mouth. Now lost in the moment, Bruce positions himself able to reach her pussy again, whilst she still rims his hole. He sends two of his fingers deep inside her soaked vagina, as she comes up for air and to have a moan.

"Are you enjoying licking Whitney's pussy?" asks Bruce, as he sends another finger deep inside her.

"MM-mm yeah" moans Amy, firing her tongue back towards his bum and letting herself go again.

"I can't take it" she groans, as he fingers her to the point of ecstasy.

"I'm going to cum" she screams in delight, as she can't physically use her tongue anymore.

With that she feels an overwhelming tightening inside her pussy and explodes her orgasm all over his fingers.

"MM-mm" she shudders, letting out her final drops.

"Woah no" says Bruce, jumping up from the bed.

"What's happened?" she asks, trying to get her breath back after the big orgasm.

"I didn't say a finger up my bum too" he says...

Amy laughs at him once she knows she may have got a little carried away with Bruce's bum becoming Whitney's vagina and may have slipped a finger up there when she couldn't lick anymore.

"I thought you wanted me to imagine it was her down there?" Amy says laughing.

Amy lets out a sigh, as Bruce sits down next to her.

"Can we have the lights back on now?" she asks, wanting to see him again.

Bruce starts laughing, until she asks him what he finds funny.

"You don't think we've finished do you?" he asks, parting her legs with his body and climbing on top of her.

"That was just your first orgasm during foreplay. You've got at least another four to go" he adds, thrusting his penis without aim straight into her pussy.

"Oh my god" she shudders, feeling his full length inside her ready to cum again.

As the morning light starts to shine through the curtains in the bedroom, Bruce wakes up to find Amy face down on the bed sleeping with one leg in her pyjama bottoms and one leg out. He quietly gets out of bed and makes his way along the hallway to the bathroom to have a shower. Without a sense of guilt, he decides he wants to tell his wife first, before she hears it from anyone else. He enters the bathroom, locks the door and starts dialing her number with his mobile. As soon as she answers, Bruce has second thoughts and starts stuttering down the phone, trying to find something to say. He asks her about the move to America and whether or not she really wants to go but she picks up on his tone quickly and knows he wants to tell her something.

"Did something happen last night with you and Whitney? Or you and Amy?" she asks him bluntly.

Bruce doesn't want to lie, so doesn't respond.

"Okay I take it you did then" says Jennifer down the phone.

"Which one was it then?" she asks, wanting to know the truth with a calm voice.

"Amy" stutters Bruce, as he lets even more guilt build inside him.

Jennifer quickly tells him that it's okay and she knew it's been coming. Bruce snaps...

"Don't throw it all at me" he yells in a defensive tone.

"You've been pushing me towards sleeping with someone else for ages" he adds.

Jennifer doesn't want to rattle him and points out again it's okay. Infact the only thing Jennifer is interested in, is the move to America, so asks him if he's going with them again.

"Do you still want me to come?" he asks a little confused.

Jennifer tells him she does, but only if he wants to.

"Only if you think we've got something worth saving" she says.

"Only if you don't want to be with Amy now" she adds.

He explains he wants to go with her but is struggling because of all the lies, cover-ups and betrayal over the last few days. He tells her that he needs time to think about it but wants to sort everything out before they go anywhere.

"There's no way I am leaving Amy or anybody in danger" he says abruptly.

Jennifer understands and completely agrees. She then reminds him that she will sort it out.

"Yeah well don't you forget, my clock is ticking and I will go to the police if you don't get it sorted" he replies.

Just before he says bye, Amy knocks on the bathroom door. Bruce quickly tells Jennifer that he's got to go, hides his phone and opens the door to Amy.

"I was just about to have a shower" says Bruce, not mentioning the phone call.

"Oh good, maybe I could join you" responds Amy, still in her pyjamas.

Bruce makes an excuse and reminds her Whitney could come upstairs at any time.

"If Jen is going to find out about me and you, then I want it to come from me first" he says, not mentioning he has just told Jennifer.

Amy understands.

"I will behave and be a good girl until no-one is around" she whispers, quickly kissing him on the cheek and leaving him to have his shower.

Bruce closes the door and not for the first time, feels lost, confused and baffled by his feelings...

CHAPTER 19
HEN NIGHT AND A VODKA BOTTLE

After his shower Bruce makes his way downstairs and into the living room. He notices Whitney still fast asleep on the sofa in Amy's pink pyjamas. He notices Amy standing in the kitchen making him breakfast and looks the blonde up and down in her blue and black flowery blouse, short yellow skirt and black leggings. He walks over to her.
 "Feeling better after your shower?" she asks, turning round with a big smile on her face, then playfully suggesting they go back to bed.
Bruce reminds her she needs to behave when others are around and she points at Whitney through in the living room still sleeping.
 "Come on, we could right here against the sink" she says, craving the mind blowing sex she had with him last night.
Bruce plays along but it's not long before she works out something is bothering him. She looks into his eyes and asks him if he has any regrets about sleeping with her.
 "No, not at all" he responds, reassuring her.
 "Why do you?" he asks, knowing she loved every second of it.
She confesses she was really nervous beforehand but it was the best sex she's ever had.
Bruce smile and gives her a quick kiss on the lips.
 "That's why I want to do it again right now" she says, getting frisky again.
 "Without my nerves, the second time is going to be even better" she adds, kissing him back.
She reaches behind him and pops the toast from the toaster, then

asks him the million dollar question...

"When can we tell everyone we are a real couple then?" she asks, fearing another excuse.

He looks into her big eyes and melts.

"You know what, let's go and tell Jen right now and get it out of the way" he suggests.

Amy beams from ear to ear and tells him she wants to get showered first. Bruce lets her go and get ready, then walks through to wake Whitney.

An hour later, Bruce, Whitney and Amy arrive at Karen's house to a big welcome. Dave is a little unsure of how Bruce is going to be with him after taking Tina's virginity, but Bruce greets Dave with a wink and a nod of his head. Bruce tells everyone that he needs a quick word with his wife in private and Jennifer walks him through into the kitchen, where both of them are expecting fireworks from the other, but neither of them seem to be in the mood to fight. Jennifer sits down at the kitchen table but Bruce tells her he wants to speak in the garden. They walk into the garden away from the house, so that no-one can hear what they are saying.

"I think it's time we got everything out in the open once and for all" says Bruce, looking at his wife as though she's a complete stranger.

Jennifer agrees to have the chat and be completely honest with him. He jumps in with his first question, asking her what is going on.

"First you tell me to be with Amy, then you tell me you love me. Then you're trying to get everyone to bed me and now Whitney tells me you will only go to America if I do" he explains to the point of exhaustion.

Jennifer desperately wants to tell him something and he knows by the look on her face, but once again there is no response from her. Bruce begs her again to be honest, asking her to tell him where he stands, but Jennifer feels pressured by his questioning and ends up saying something she knows she is going regret...

"Where do you stand? You want to know where you stand?" she says, with an angry tone.

"I guess you sleeping with our friend answers that for you really, doesn't it?" she adds, stirring things up.

Bruce explodes into a rage.

"Why the fuck can't you be straight with me anymore? Why has everything got to be someone else's fault, when clearly it's yours?" he shouts in anger.

Jennifer looks him in the eye and considers telling him what she has been sitting on for awhile now, but can't.

"I think you'd better leave" she says, warning him that she doesn't want another argument.

"Are you telling me it's over?" he asks, wanting at least one honest answer before he goes.

"Just go please baby" she responds, standing in front of him desperately trying to keep it together.

"Is it over?" he asks again, making it clear he isn't moving until she answers.

"Please don't do this" she responds.

"Is it fucking over or not?" he yells, losing his patience.

He stands waiting for the yo-yo to continue but Jennifer goes silent for a few seconds...

"I guess it is" she responds, walking out of the back gate and out of the garden.

Bruce completely devastated, stands watching as she walks away. He turns to go back inside the house and walks back in to complete silence, as everyone waits for him to speak. He signals to Amy with a nod they are leaving and she understands. Everyone else just watches as Bruce and Amy leave the house together and all of a sudden without Bruce or Jennifer there to keep order, the room erupts in arguments.

"He's done the dirty on her and cheated with that Amy girl hasn't he?" snaps Tina, in Jennifer's defence.

"Oh that's right, it's always the man's fault you bitch" snaps Dave at Tina.

"Don't speak to my sister like that, you dick" snaps Lucy at Dave.

Before long Rose, Dave, Lucy and Whitney are all at each-other's throats. It's not long before Dave finds this the perfect excuse and opportunity to dump Tina now he's taken her virginity. He stands up and puts his jacket on ready to leave.

"Where are you going?" asks Tina, trying to apologise for her attack on Bruce.

"Don't apologise to him little sis. It would have been hardly Jennifer doing the cheating would it?" snaps Lucy, at her little sister.

Dave explains this is all far too much for him to take and declares right in front of them all, that he's leaving and it's over between him and Tina.

"Your'e dumping her after taking her virginity?" asks Rose, now getting involved.

"See I told you, all men are dicks" snaps Lucy, rushing across the room to comfort Tina as she starts to get upset.

Dave doesn't want to listen to the abuse being fired at him anymore and storms out of the door, laughing.

"What's going on?" asks Jennifer, as Dave slams the front door behind him and she walks back in.

"That bastard Dave has just dumped Tina" declares Rose, joining Lucy comforting her on the sofa.

Tina stands up before she bursts out crying and runs out of the room and upstairs to the spare room.

"Let me go" insists Whitney, wanting to help Tina, chasing after her.

"I will come with you, she's my sister" says Lucy, following Whitney out of the room.

A devastated Jennifer already upset by the argument in the garden, can't quite believe what has just happened in the living room. She looks at Rose, the only person left in the room. Rose looks at her, but neither of them can find words to say...

"Fuck this, I need a drink" says Jennifer, as if she's completely given up on everything now.

"Jen" gasps Rose.

"It's only ten in the morning" she tells her, then throwing her hands in the air and telling her, she will have a drink too.

Jennifer tells Rose to grab two glasses and join her in Karen's bedroom, where they can do some serious drinking and get some peace and quiet from all the going's on. Rose grabs the glasses as Jennifer runs into the kitchen to find some alcohol. Two minutes later Jennifer enters Karen's bedroom, smiling and clanking two vodka bottles together.

"Okay let's get hammered" Jennifer suggests, flipping off her shoes and unbuttoning her jeans.

"What are you doing?" asks Rose, standing holding the two glasses beside the door, watching Jennifer let her jeans drop to her ankles.

"I'm going back to bed and drinking" responds Jennifer, as she tosses the bottles on to the bed and takes off her top.

"Joining me? Or do you want to go and help the others?" she asks, standing there in her matching black underwear set, then jumping into the bed and under the duvet.

"Fuck it" mumbles Rose, passing Jennifer the two glasses, taking off her trousers to reveal her white boy shorts and jumping in beside her.

Jennifer hands Rose a glass and a bottle of vodka. Rose starts to open the bottle to pour some into her glass but notices Jennifer doesn't even bother with the glass and drinks straight from her bottle. Rose puts her glass on the bedside cabinet and follows Jennifer's lead.

"That's just what I needed" sighs Rose, as the first mouthful of vodka hits her stomach, burning on the way down.

It's not long before the two girls under the duvet are getting tipsy and enjoying themselves. Just then there's a knock on the bedroom door. Jennifer jumps up and stumbles across to answer it.

"Dam it" says Jennifer, stumbling over her shoe in the middle of the room to Rose's amusement.

Jennifer opens the door to find Tina standing there. Tina asks if she can have a quick word about her feelings and the first break-up she's going through. Although Jennifer wants to help her, she feels she's in no fit state to give her any advice, so tries to come up with another plan for Tina.

Jennifer lets Tina standing in the doorway get a full view of the room and picks up her handbag.

"I want you to take this" Jennifer tells her, handing Tina some cash from her purse.

"Get a taxi across to my house, where Bruce will take care of you until tomorrow" she adds.

"But I thought you and Bruce had broken up?" says Tina, looking confused.

Jennifer puts her finger to Tina's lips and tells her not to ask anymore questions.

"And what's going on in here?" Tina asks, looking at Rose in the bed, as Jennifer again puts a finger to Tina's lips.

"Just go over to my house. Bruce will take care of you" stutters Jennifer, kissing her on the cheek and closing the door.

Jennifer tries to walk back to the bed, unsteady on her feet, as Rose giggles from under the duvet.

"What?" asks Jennifer, trying to focus across the room.

"I love your body, especially your legs" giggles Rose.

"But what's going on with those knobbly knees?" she adds, staring at Jennifer's body.

"Hey" shouts Jennifer.

"You can talk Miss flat butt" she adds, grabbing at the end of the bed and crawling onto it.

Rose takes offence to this comment made by Jennifer and throws back the covers. She kneels on the bed, trying to get a look at herself and her bum in the mirror.

"What's wrong with my butt?" asks Rose, looking at it in the mirror.

"Anyway, what about yours Miss wobbly bum?" she asks, watching Jennifer on all fours crawling up the bed and slapping her butt cheek.

Jennifer stops "Did you just spank me?" she asks.

"I'm surprised you felt it through all those wobbly bits" responds Rose, giggling again.

Jennifer picks up a pillow and hits Rose playfully around the head. As Rose falls backwards onto the bed, Jennifer mounts the back of her legs and starts spanking Rose's butt in return.

"MM-mm harder. Spank me harder" demands Rose, playing around with her.

Jennifer pulls down her tight fitting boy shorts and starts spanking her bare cheeks.

"MM-mm even better" giggles Rose, as it starts to sting a little.

"Is that all you've got you lesbian bitch?" she adds, knowing Jennifer is straight.

"Oh yeah" responds Jennifer giggling.

Then out of the blue, she inserts a single finger into Rose's pussy from behind.

"Who's the lesbian now? With a wet pussy like this?" asks Jennifer, pushing her finger in a little deeper without any fight from Rose.

"Hey Jen, does me thinking this feels nice, make me gay?" giggles Rose, as she pushes back against Jennifer's finger to make it even deeper.

"That depends" giggles Jennifer.

"Do you have an urge to finger me back?" she asks, inserting another finger into her rattling pussy, as she drunkenly laughs some more.

"I don't have an urge no, but what the hell, let's have a go" stutters Rose, trying to turn round to get at Jennifer's knickers, then falling all over the place in the process.

Jennifer removes her fingers from Rose's vagina and lies on her back, so Rose can give it a go... Jennifer helps her by pulling her knickers to the side, showing Rose her first proper look at another woman's vagina and tells her to go for it. Rose holds her hand over Jennifer's pubic area but can't do it, laughing too much. Jennifer takes one of her fingers and helps her guide it inside herself. Rose's finger slowly penetrates Jennifer's warm pussy.

"There you go. How do you feel?" asks Jennifer, with Rose's finger wriggling around inside her.

"It feels no different from sticking my finger up myself" laughs Rose, taking it out again.

Jennifer sits up and tells her it doesn't change her sexuality.

"Until you cum in the company of another girl alone, you will stay straight" stutters Jennifer, readjusting her knickers and covering up

again.
The girls sit around for a few minutes laughing and joking about the experience they have just shared together and then decide together that they should stop drinking before anything else happens. Jennifer jumps off the bed and stumbles towards her clothes to get dressed again. Rose watches her struggle to put her jeans on and decides to get dressed too. Rose's struggles as her head really spins and bending over to put her shoes on, makes her fall over. Jennifer laughs and tells her she will see her downstairs, before picking up the glasses and the two nearly empty bottles of vodka from the bed. Jennifer makes her way downstairs and into the kitchen, where Lucy is making a coffee. Lucy sees the bottles in Jennifer's hand.

"Just what I need too" says Lucy under her breath, as Jennifer places the glasses in the sink.
Lucy picks up one of the vodka bottles, twists the lid and takes a swig as Jennifer turns to see.

"Why is there water in this Vodka bottle?" asks Lucy, picking up the other one.

"And this one isn't?" she adds, taking a drink from the second bottle with vodka in it.
Jennifer knows she's been rumbled and can't act like she's drunk anymore. She quickly tells her it was a lesson for Rose upstairs, knowing Lucy won't question it. Just then Rose staggers through into the kitchen still giggling to herself.

"Have you had a mini party without me?" asks Lucy.

"Yeah just me and my new gal pal Jen" stutters Rose, slumping down at the table to try and stop the floor from moving.

An hour later it's midday and Bruce and Amy are back across London at his house, but haven't really spoken a word since they left Karen's. Amy decides it's time they talked, treading very carefully, knowing that he is upset about something. She cautiously asks him what he and Jennifer spoke about in the garden and Bruce tells her, they were just finalising the breakdown of their marriage.

"That's good news isn't it?" asks Amy, hoping he is pleased too.

"That means we can be together now doesn't it?" she asks, waiting for him to respond.
Bruce kisses her on the cheek, telling her she's right and walks into the kitchen. She doesn't stop him walking out of the room, knowing there's still something wrong, but puts it down to him coming to terms with the big change in his life. She decides to give him his space and sits alone in the living room, when there's a knock at the door. Not

wanting to disturb Bruce, Amy slowly moves towards the door, a little apprehensive about who it is and puts the chain on, opening the door slowly.

"Sorry, it's only me" says Tina on the doorstep.

"Jennifer told me to come over and speak to Bruce about Dave" she adds, waiting for Amy to open the door fully and let her in.

Amy takes the chain off the latch and opens the door. She welcomes Tina in and calls to Bruce, telling him Tina is here. Bruce walks through quite surprised to find Tina standing there and asks her to what do they owe the pleasure. Tina takes no time in telling them that Dave finished with her and that Jennifer sent her over. Although Bruce isn't best pleased with Dave, he struggles with the fact that his wife, who just ended their marriage has sent Tina to him. Bruce tells Amy to fix Tina a drink and he will be back in a minute. He runs upstairs and tries to ring Jennifer to find out what's going on. He spends ten minutes trying to reach her by mobile, but Jennifer isn't picking up his calls. Unsure of what to do next for Tina, he decides to go back downstairs and ask if she knows where Jennifer is.

"Last time I saw her, she was in bed with Rose" claims Tina naively.

"You mean they were sleeping on the bed?" Amy asks, suggesting Tina change her phrasing.

"No, they were in bed" Tina responds.

"Half naked and drinking" she confirms.

The news comes as a shock to Bruce and he sits down to think it through. Amy notices Bruce's reaction and tries to make sense of it for him.

"Maybe that's why she's cool with us" whispers Amy.

"Because she's into girls now" she guesses, trying to comfort him with her words.

"You are not helping Aims" responds Bruce, trying to understand it, knowing his wife or ex-wife would never be a lesbian.

She tells him she is sorry and is only trying to help.

"No, maybe you're right" he says, looking at Amy.

"That would explain the coldness, the secrets and the obsession with Rose wouldn't it?" he adds, making sense of it and agreeing with Amy.

He takes out his mobile again and dials her number for the eighth time, but still gets no answer.

"Hello, I don't mean to interrupt, but Jen told me you would help me" says Tina, standing there whilst Bruce and Amy merge in deep conversation about the situation.

Amy decides to be Tina's shoulder to cry on and takes her into the kitchen, whilst Bruce continues to call Jennifer. Finally she answers her phone and he doesn't know where to start.

"Can you tell me why you've sent Tina and her problems my way?" he asks Jennifer, calmly down the phone.

"I thought you could help, knowing more about Dave than I do" answers Jennifer.

"But why is she here? Couldn't she just ask me over the phone?" he asks her.

"She needs to stay with you tonight anyway, because we are going out on Lucy's hen night" she answers, claiming Tina wouldn't be old enough to get into any clubs or pubs.

"So you've sent her over to my place, so I can babysit, have you?" he asks, getting frustrated with her smart answers.

"No I sent her over to OUR home" she responds, with another direct answer.

Bruce has had enough and comes out with what is really on his mind.

"Oh and here's me thinking you've sent her over here so you can continue your lesbian affair" he snaps abruptly.

Jennifer struggles to understand what he is trying to say, but guesses that Tina told him what she saw in the bedroom. She tries to laugh it off, claiming that Tina must have been mistaken.

"Are you telling me you weren't naked in bed with Rose then?" he asks.

"No, we weren't naked. We still had our underwear on" she answers with another smart comment.

Bruce goes silent, feeling his rage building and doesn't respond. Jennifer asks him if he's finished with yet another inquisitive phone-call, but still no answer, as Bruce bites his tongue trying not to say something abusive... Finally Jennifer feels she's being a little too hard on him and explains it wasn't a lesbian affair and the truth is, she was teaching Rose another lesson.

"Whatever" grunts Bruce, unable to believe a word she says now.

"You have a good night and expect Tina back with you first thing" he says before hanging up on her again.

After a whole afternoon of watching Amy and Tina talk things through and not getting involved himself, evening falls upon the house and Bruce thinks about his wife getting dressed up and heading out on the town, being a single woman now. It does his head in so much that he decides to go to bed and try put the thoughts out of his head. Amy takes her time settling Tina down in the spare room and joins Bruce in bed twenty minutes later. Amy starts getting undressed and can't help but think about sex with her new man again tonight. She looks at him on the bed, as she slowly and seductively gets undressed, knowing he's somewhere else. Instead of leaving her underwear on or changing into pyjamas, she purposely stands in front of him and strips completely naked. Still Bruce doesn't notice, so she switches off the light and hops into bed. After a few minutes of lying in the dark and getting no response from him, her sexual urges for him are getting stronger. She decides to bite the bullet and ask if he wants to fool around.

"It might help take your mind off things" she whispers, reliving last night and the sex they had.

She runs her hand under the duvet towards his penis and is surprised to find him standing to attention. With that he rolls over to face her and starts passionately kissing her, like there's no tomorrow. He works his way down her body with his hand and starts fingering her moist vagina.

"Slow down sexy" she whispers and with that, he realises he's letting his frustrations, emotions and anger control his behaviour.

He slows down and starts to kiss her again, whilst his fingers are still working her pussy.

"MM-mm that's better" she groans, stopping his hand and telling him she will be back in a second.

She jumps off the bed and reaches underneath it, to where she planted some handcuffs earlier. She feels around in the dark in search of them. Picking them up, she quickly mounts his body and pulls his arms up to the bed posts. Without much of a reaction from him, she manages to secure his wrists so that he is restrained.

"I am just popping to the bathroom, don't go anywhere" she whispers, giggling.

"When I come back, I am going to fuck you all night long" she adds, getting off him and feeling her way towards the bedroom door.

Bruce with his erection on show, closes his eyes and waits for her to return. The second he hears her leave the room, his mind starts wandering again, hating the thought of his wife out in town. Another minute later, he hears the door open and close again. He opens his eyes to see Amy's shadow making it's way back towards the bed. He closes his eyes, waiting for her to do what she wants to do.

"Come on then, fuck me like I've never been fucked before" he says, trying to sound enthusiastic as he feels her get on the bed.

She mounts his groin and strokes at his hard penis, before guiding it in between her legs. Ever so slowly she slips her wet pussy inch by inch down his solid shaft.

"MM-mm that feels so big" she groans, as Bruce struggles to get up, knocking himself out of her vagina.

"Tina?" he snaps, realising that wasn't Amy's voice.

"Yeah it's me" she whispers, trying to grab hold of his penis again.

"What the fuck are you doing?" yells Bruce, trying to escape the handcuffs and her hands.

"You said to fuck you like you've never been fucked before" Tina whispers, trying hard to get back onto his rock hard penis again.

"I told Amy to do that, not you" he yells again, telling her to get off of him and out of his bedroom.

Tina gets off the bed in a huff and starts to get upset.

"Jenny said you would let me" she says, as a shiver of hatred runs up his spine listening to the youngster's claim.

"Please Tina, just go" he begs, managing to finally free his wrists from the handcuffs and reach down for his jeans at the side of the bed.

Tina runs out of the room, bumping into Amy her on her way back in.

"What the fuck is going on?" asks a confused and naked Amy, switching on the light.

She watches as Bruce throws a top over his head very flustered and over her shoulder at Tina in her underwear, running into the the spare room, looking really upset. She looks at Bruce for an answer...

"Not now Amy" he snaps, walking past her at the door and telling her to make sure Tina is okay.

He goes downstairs and quickly calls Jennifer, who is out on Lucy's hen night.

"Hello baby, ask me again if I want to come to America with you" he says in a very calm and loving voice.

Jennifer although a little drunk, falls for it and thinks that her husband has made the decision she really wants to hear.

"Are you coming to America with me?" she asks, expecting him to say yes.

"Now ask me, if I love you" he says, with exactly the same manner.

"Do you still love me?" she asks, feeling this is the greatest phone call she's ever received.

Bruce delays his answer for a few seconds and then unloads...

"No, I am not coming to fucking America with you, and right now, I hate your fucking guts" he tells her.

Jennifer is shocked but starts laughing, thinking it's some kind of joke.

"What's wrong now Bruno?" she laughs.

"Now ask me if I've just had a teenager try and have sex with me" he shouts, fuming at her.

Jennifer suddenly realises what has happened and shrugs it off laughing some more.

"I thought you were getting used to fucking other girls now baby?" she says.

"I didn't think it would bother you, having one more notch added to OUR bedpost" she adds.

Bruce can't believe his wife's attitude and is horrified that she is treating him so badly.

"She's sixteen you sick bitch" he snaps down the phone.

"You know what, congratulations. I am beginning to hate you" he adds, before hanging up on her for the third time today.

Bruce falls back into the sofa, unable to face going back upstairs to answer Amy's questions and Tina's unhappiness. He decides to leave them to it and just then, Jennifer calls him back. He sits pondering if he should answer it or not but decides to hear what she's got to say next.

"I deliver all this sex to you on a plate and that's the thanks I get" she snaps down the phone at him, without a hello.

"What the fuck do you want from me?" she asks, frustrated about being hung up on again.

"All I've ever wanted is my wife" he answers, choking up a little, before hearing someone coming down the stairs.

"Bruce, are you still there?" asks Jennifer, waiting for him to speak again.

Bruce freezes with the phone in his hand, worried about who it is standing at the door listening to his conversation.

"Bruce if you want to make our marriage work, say now or we really are over and I will find someone else tonight" demands Jennifer, still waiting at the end of the phone...

CHAPTER 20
EAT ME

Bruce tries his hardest to find out who it is at the living room door, but without turning his head and making it obvious, he sits there guessing... Jennifer gives him one last chance over the phone to make his decision and he feels the clock count down, knowing he must make a decision. He contemplates telling her how he truly feels but risks hurting Amy at the door, if it is Amy standing there. As his mind swings both ways, Jennifer at the other end of the phone makes it for him.

"I am drinking, I am out on the town and I am now single. Goodbye Bruce" she says, hanging up on him this time.

Bruce throws his phone down on the sofa and jumps up to find out who is at the door. He is totally devastated when he finds no-one there and can hear the two girls still talking up in the bedroom. He considers calling Jennifer back but when he picks up his phone, he throws it back down again, clearly not happy about being held to ransom like that. Emotionally unstable he thinks about the damage upstairs and tries to work out what to do for the best. Once again he picks his phone up, but this time to ring Dave to find out what happened between him and Tina earlier. Dave answers his phone straight away, claiming he was just about to call Bruce and before Bruce can ask what happened, Dave tells him he needs to tell him something.

"Is it that you dumped Tina?" Bruce asks.

Dave tells him it's nothing to do with Tina and it's about Tony's whereabouts.

"I'm not interested mate" responds Bruce.

"I am planning to go to the police tomorrow anyway" he adds.

Like a real traitor under Tony's thumb, Dave tells Bruce that it might be too late tomorrow.

"What do you mean too late?" Bruce asks, taking him more seriously now.

Dave explains that he overheard Tony talking to his goons and that they are going after the hen party tonight.

"Who Jen?" asks Bruce, forgetting for a few seconds what a bitch she's been and being the protective husband he likes to be.

"I'm not sure if it's Jen, but I do know they want to hurt someone tonight" Dave tells him.

Bruce tells Dave to meet him on the high-street outside the cafe in about an hour and asks Dave whether he minds backing him up.

"Hey, that's what I am here for" boasts the traitor placating Bruce.

Bruce runs upstairs quickly and pulls Amy out of the room, telling her he needs to pop out.

"Did you tell Tina you wanted to fuck her?" asks Amy, coming out of the room after having a long chat with the teenager.

Bruce tells her he did, but only because he thought it was her. He explains that he hasn't got time to talk now and will explain later. Without Amy getting a chance to ask where he's going, he's gone... Amy walks back into the room to spend some more time with Tina and Bruce makes his way to the other side of London to meet up with Dave.

Bruce is heading to the girls hen night, which is now in full swing. Rose is already hammered, Whitney is managing to get away with her pathetic disguise and Jennifer has managed to forget the phone-call with Bruce and is really enjoying herself. Lucy is letting random guys compliment her veil and learner plates that she's wearing and getting turned on by it all. The girls sit in a lounge bar where it's not too loud, enabling them to still have conversation. Jennifer asks if Lucy still feels ready to get married in only two days time and whether she is looking forward to the rehearsal tomorrow afternoon.

"Yeah it should be fun, if we aren't all suffering with hangovers" Lucy answers.

"Is there any last minute advice you can give her?" asks Whitney, from behind her sunglasses.

"It depends what she feels she still needs to know" responds Jennifer, showing she hasn't drunk that much and is more than capable of helping.

The girls look at Lucy to find out if there is anything else she wants help with before the big day, then with everyone's eyes burning her face, she starts to blush.

"Look she has" says Whitney, watching her face turn purple now.

"And it's something dirty by the look on her face" says Rose.

"Well, there is one thing" Lucy says, sitting there acting innocent.

"How do you get a man to, you know, lick you more?" she asks, blushing again.

Rose and Whitney start getting excited and clapping their hands as Jennifer, a little tipsy gets ready to give them a lesson on oral sex. They share a giggle before Jennifer tells Lucy to stand up. Lucy looks nervous as she stands up, then Jennifer grabs the nearest bloke passing and asks if he could do her a favour.

"This is Lucy" says Jennifer to the guy.

"Can you tell me what she is wearing word for word?" she asks him, watching the man run his eyes all over Lucy, then feel like he's being ambushed.

The man takes another look at Lucy and tells them she's wearing a blouse come skirt thing, some black leggings and long brown boots.

"Good" says Jennifer, congratulating him.

"Now can you tell me what this is?" she asks, pointing down at Lucy's crotch.

Lucy starts to turn purple again, as beads of sweat appear on the man's forehead, unsure if he should have a good look or not. Jennifer reassures him it's fine to look and he has a really quick glimpse.

"Well it's her fanny, isn't it?" he responds, looking confused and unsure of where the question is heading.

"Good" says Jennifer, congratulating him again.

"And if she was really horny, what would her FANNY be saying to you, as a man?" she asks, making him look again.

The man now looks terrified and ponders on the question for a few seconds, as the girls eagerly wait for him to answer.

"I guess it would be saying fuck me" says the man, hoping he doesn't get slapped.

Just then he realises he might know one of the girls and looks over at Whitney.

"Don't I know you from somewhere?" he asks, trying to see past her glasses.

Jennifer quickly tells him they are from out of town, so he couldn't possibly know any of them and before he can put it together, she sends him away with a thank you.

"So what did we learn girls?" Jennifer asks, turning to them.

The three girls don't have an answer.

"It tells us even when we are at our horniest, our FANNY only says sex to him" explains Jennifer.

"Why isn't it saying eat me?" she asks, making her point.

Jennifer's Lesson On Oral Sex
It turns out that even when we look our sexiest and we are feeling at our horniest, the average guy still won't consider going down on us and only assume that we want to have sex. Why?

Well there are two main reasons.
1. Most men fear giving oral sex.
2. We don't put the idea in his head, as much as we should.

Women need to learn that receiving oral sex isn't an impossible mission and with a different attitude, you could get licked everyday...

First thing we need to do is be more direct with it. There's no need to be shy about it, so say it out loud and proud...

"I LOVE RECEIVING ORAL SEX"

If you can't do that, start wearing novelty knickers and T-shirts that say it for you. "Eat Me" "Entry Only For A Tongue" You know the kind of underwear I mean !!

Make your man or men around you know that oral sex is your thing.

Now it's out there, change your attitude a little. Become a little more brutal with the subject. If you sit in front of a man in a short skirt and open your legs, what are you saying to him?

First you are telling him to look at your knickers, then you are telling him you want sex right? Where's the oral sex invitation?

Now drop something on the floor, make him notice your legs open and get him to pick it up. Now whisper something about loving oral sex, whilst he is down there. He's no longer thinking about sex with you, because his tongue will become a magnet to your vagina.

We need to change the way the world see it. If a man stood in front of a woman on her knees, straight away you would think blow job wouldn't you? Why can't that be the same the other way round? Why does a man consider sex first, then a finger, then you playing with it yourself, before he would lick it?

Many of us would guess it's because men don't like doing it or are scared to do it. This isn't true... The very simple reason men put oral sex last on their list is because, it's the hardest thing to do.

Bend you over, whip it out and have sex, two minutes...

Slip his hand inside your knickers, one minute...

Take down your jeans, move you into position, move himself in position and then start licking, far too much work !!

If you want a man to lick you out more, you don't just need to be brutal with the subject, you need to make it as easy as possible for him.

Short skirts, crotchless pants will help you achieve this.

Finally there is a stigma that men don't like doing it or can't do it right. Firstly it's fact... Men do enjoy giving oral sex and as for him getting it wrong from time to time, whose fault is that?

The last thing you need to master is being honest with him. If he isn't doing it right, don't tell him he's rubbish or assume every guy out there will lick like a washing machine, simply point him in the right direction. Instead of saying "What are you doing down there?" Be gentle with him and say something like "If you do it this way, I will explode over your face" Those words should be enough to get him there and keep him there in that same spot you want all the time.

Too many women when they are lucky enough to get oral sex, lie back, close their eyes, may enjoy it a little and may give off a little moan from time to time. What he's doing down there? GUESSING !!

If he does give you oral sex, show him, teach him and for fuck sake, FUCK HIS FACE !!

Let him know you are enjoying it, let him know you are going to explode, ride against his face and soak it. Now without lying there and him having to guess if he got it right or not, he knows he's good and you can expect it much more from now on...

Remember, it's easy for a guy to have a women on her knees in front of him and him utter those words "Suck my cock" These words are fashionable. It might not be so fashionable to say something like "Rim me" or "Tongue fuck my bum" but you saying "Eat me, lick me out" or "Fuck me with your mouth" shouldn't be as hard, so stop making it hard.

Does he lick it as much as we suck it?

Your task is to make him lick it more !!

For Whitney this was her first major lesson from Jennifer and really impressed her. She knew that getting a man to give her oral sex was a hard task, but she never really considered why.

"So all I have to do to get more oral sex is be brutal with it, tell the world I love it and show him what to do?" asks Whitney, taking it all in. Jennifer takes a sip of her drink and looks at the superstar.

"Don't forget to make the most of it, show him you're loving it and explode everywhere" answers Jennifer, making sure Whitney has understood it all.

Just then Rose starts laughing and can't believe what she's just heard.

"What's funny?" asks Whitney.
Rose explains she's never really struggled with getting her men to give her oral sex and she already is pretty brutal with her demands.
"But I can't believe the amount of times I've just been there with my eyes closed and done exactly what you explained" she adds.
Jennifer explains again just how important it is for a girl to show a guy that she loves oral sex.
"It's truly the difference between getting it every now and again and him wanting to give you oral sex on a shopping centre escalator" says Jennifer.
"You haven't?" gasps Lucy.
"I have, many times" answers Jennifer, with a naughty smirk.
The four girls sit talking about the subject of oral sex a little longer, as Jennifer starts to reminisce in her head about the good times she's had with Bruce.

Meanwhile only a mile away from the girls party, Bruce has turned up at the cafe and met Dave. Bruce asks Dave to explain everything he knows again and Dave rattles off that Tony and his gang are planning to gate crash the girls hen party and hurt someone.
"Do we know where they are now?" asks Bruce, gearing himself up for a fight, unaware that Dave is about to walk him into a trap.
Dave tells him he thinks they are in a warehouse behind the lap dancing club, leading off from the same car park. Dave leads Bruce through the alleyway where Bruce made his escape the other day with Tina. They quietly approach the car park, when two goons step out of nowhere blocking their path. Dave and Bruce both stop and it's only a matter of seconds before they realise that another two unpleasant looking goons are coming up behind them. With nowhere to run, the four men from each side start closing in...
"You ready to show me what you are made of Dave?" whispers Bruce, declaring they are going to have to take them on.
"Right here with you" Dave whispers, deciding which goon to take on first.
"Go" Bruce shouts, as he starts to run at the two in front of him. Dave gives chase, as Bruce guides his flying fist directly into a face, trying to clear the way forward. The large goon falls back against the wall and slumps to the ground and Bruce knows if Dave does the same now, they are free. He looks at Dave and is shocked as Dave stops in front of the other very large man.
"Hit him" Bruce calls out, following him.
Bruce is instantly confused when Dave doesn't strike or attempt to hit

the brute. Bruce is grabbed and forced up against the wall. The goon that Bruce just knocked down, gets up and delivers a sharp blow with his fist to Bruce's gut, whilst Dave still stands there.

"Run Dave" Bruce grunts, as he takes another blow.
Within seconds all four of the big goons wrestle Bruce to the ground. He manages to lift his head and is amazed again to find his friend Dave still standing there untouched. With that Tony walks into the alleyway to confront them, as Bruce is lifted to his feet.

"Good work young David" says a smirking Tony, as he pats him on the shoulder and congratulates him for helping catch Bruce.

"Here's the cash I promised you" he adds, pulling out a wad of notes and punching Dave in the ribs.
Dave falls to the floor in pain.

"I thought I was working for you now?" stutters Dave, winded and somewhat shocked by the punch.

"I said I would pay you to catch Bruce, nothing about you working for me or me not kicking your head in" Tony answers laughing.
With Bruce restrained, Tony gives out the orders to his men.

"Take Bruce, put him in the car and don't let him out of your sight" he orders his goons.

"Take young David, give him a good beating, then take his phone, ring the girls and tell them to have Amy ready for me" he adds, enjoying Bruce's reaction to these words.
Bruce tries his best to wriggle free, but is soon overpowered and dragged towards one of the cars in the car park, by two of Tony's men. Dave is taken down the alleyway and out of sight.

"I will send Amy your best wishes, shall I Bruce?" calls Tony, getting in his own car.

As this takes place there are two of Tony's men standing outside Bruce's house and they receive the phone-call they've been waiting for. They make their way round to the back of the house and kick in the back door. Upstairs Amy and Tina in the spare room hear the noise and know something is wrong. Amy orders Tina to hide under the bed, as she picks up a bedside lamp and hides behind the door.

"I can still see you" whispers Amy, telling Tina to move further under the bed.
Tina shuffles back as far as she can go, as Amy stands there waiting to hit out with the lamp held in her hand. They hold their breath waiting for the door to open. They hear crashing and banging as all the doors get kicked open around the house. The bedroom is the last door and the two men argue childishly about who's going to enter the

room first. They decide with a game of rock, paper, scissors and the decision is made. The goon gets ready to enter the bedroom, the other goes to wait in the garden for Tony to turn up. Tony's goon slowly enters the bedroom...

"Get out you sick bastard" screams Amy, lunging at the intruder swinging the lamp, but missing every time.

The huge guy twice the size of Amy disarms her in a matter of seconds and throws her across the room and onto the bed. Tina closes her eyes tightly under the bed, fearing for her life as she hears Amy start begging him to leave her alone. He walks over to the bed and tells her she can have it the easy way or the hard way.

"Karen chose the hard way" he laughs, ripping open her jeans.

Outside Tony's car pulls up and just as his hand touches the handle to open the door, he notices a figure running up the street in his rear view mirror. He takes his hand away from the handle and decides to let the person pass first. The figure comes running past the car and Tony is mortified when he sees Bruce running round to the back of the house.

"Hey you have two choices" says an out of breath Bruce, covered in blood pointing a gun at the huge guy on the doorstep.

"Leave now and walk away or I will shoot you" he adds, shaking at the thought of pulling the trigger.

Lucky for him, the goon doesn't put up a fight and backs away knowing that Bruce is angry and unstable. Bruce follows the brute round to the side of the house, still waving the gun and watches him run away down the street. Bruce stands in the garden to make sure he's gone and is suddenly blinded by car lights, as it speeds off down the road. Bruce starts to get paranoid that whoever was in the car would have seen the gun and call the police, so he throws it into the bushes. As he enters the house, he realises it's far too quiet, then hears a man's voice upstairs. Bruce considers going to get the gun from the bushes, but before he knows it, he is creeping up the stairs...

"I told you to lie still" Bruce hears an angry voice shout.

"Tony will knock on this door shortly and wants you to be ready" the voice yells at helpless Amy.

Bruce knows he has a way in now and plans to knock on the door pretending to be Tony, then attack the goon, getting the girls to safety. He takes a deep breath, ready to knock...

"MM-mm, haven't you got a sexy body?" Bruce hears the voice say.

Bruce explodes into a fit of rage, forgetting to knock on the door and charges at it, using all of his body weight to open it...

CHAPTER 21
TWENTY-FOUR HOURS, TWENTY-FOUR MINUTES

Bruce's in the room and fixates his eyes on the huge brute standing over Amy semi naked on the bed. He runs towards him like a train and before the brute can even turn, Bruce dives at him, knocking him against the wall. Bruce starts to punch and wrestle the huge brute to the floor, but it's only a matter of seconds before the brute regains his footing and towers over Bruce. The brute rams Bruce against the wall by the neck, as blood starts to seep from the cut next to his eye. Bruce feels a tightening around his throat, as the brute applies pressure with his huge hands. He starts to gasp for breath and is dragged by the throat onto the landing. The brute plans to throw him down the stairs, but suddenly Amy gets off the bed, picks her lamp up again and takes a run at the huge goon. She smashes the lamp across the back of his head and watches as he loses his grip on Bruce and topples down the stairs himself. Bruce jumps up and checks Amy is okay, before looking at the man lying at the bottom of the staircase.
   "Where's Tina?" panics Bruce, thinking something has happened to her.
Amy points to the bedroom and Bruce moves to the bed, crouching down to see Tina curled up into a ball under the bed. He reaches out a hand and pulls her out.
   "Wasn't much of a rescue package was I?" smiles Bruce, trying to reassure both girls they are safe now.
Amy tells him although he was about to get his butt kicked, she really appreciates him arriving when he did. Then she remembers that Tony

is due and Bruce decides it's time to ring the police and break his agreement with Jennifer. He pulls his mobile from his pocket and checks the bottom of the stairs.

"Where is he? He's going to jump out from somewhere isn't he?" panics Amy, scaring Tina in the process when she finds the goon gone.

Bruce tells them both to go back inside the bedroom and stay there. He creeps down the stairs, checks the whole house, finding nothing. He then sits in the kitchen, holding a wet cloth to his eye and decides to ring Jennifer to ask her what she would like him to do next. Within seconds of her answering, he realises she is in no fit state to have a conversion, sounding hammered, still out on the hen night.

"I don't want another argument over the phone baby, I love you" she stutters, drunkenly down the phone.

"Jen I really need to tell you something, so get a grip" Bruce orders, needing her to magically sober up.

"Get a grip? Get a grip?" stutters Jennifer.

"The only thing I want to get a grip of is your penis" she adds, to his frustration.

The situation isn't helped any further by Rose, Whitney and Lucy in the background.

"Is that the Bruce you are speaking to?" he hears Rose's voice call out.

"Love you. I love you Bruce" he hears Lucy's drunken voice in the background shout.

Then for some reason, Whitney is handed the phone.

"Hello Mr Wit Brit. Are you making me some toast when I get back?" she giggles, sounding smashed too.

Bruce listens to them all drunkenly mess around for a few minutes, until Jennifer takes the phone again.

"So what were you saying baby? Something about you wanting me to take a hold of your policeman?" giggles Jennifer.

"That's right Jen, policeman" he responds.

"That's who I am about to call regarding your latest mission, Tony" he adds.

With the sound of Tony's name, Jennifer starts listening and tries not to interrupt anymore.

Bruce quickly tells her their back door has been kicked in, he's been beaten up again, Amy has been attacked and it was Dave that set him up.

"So shall I call the police now?" he asks her.

"No you can't, not yet" stutters Jennifer, trying to sound sober now.

"But we aren't safe here. They could come back at any minute"

Bruce says.

Jennifer tells him to get the girls to Karen's house now and not to worry about the back door.

"Me and the girls are leaving the club now, so should be there before you" she says.

Bruce finishes the phone-call and rings a taxi to take them to Karen's. Jennifer has a harder task getting the other girls away from the bar, as they claim there is still a good three hours of drinking left to do. As they step out of the club, Jennifer manages to sober herself up a little in the fresh air, but the other three continue to moan about cutting the night short, weaving along the pavement singing out of tune. Half an hour later Jennifer has successfully staggered and guided the girls to Karen's house, on a journey that would usually only take ten minutes.

"Anyone up for another little drink?" asks Whitney, wanting to continue drinking as they enter the house.

"No" grumps Lucy, claiming she's already getting a hangover.

"So what happened then? Why did we have to come back early?" asks Rose, face down on the big sofa.

Jennifer can't remember the whole conversation she had with Bruce and vaguely tells them about the back door at her house being kicked in and someone getting hurt. Hung-over Lucy starts to panic and asks if Tina is okay. As she asks, they hear a car pull up outside and her question is answered when Tina walks in first, unscathed by the commotion. Red eyed Amy follows next and finally Bruce battered and bruised.

"Fuck me Bruce. What did they do to you?" asks Whitney, the first to be concerned by his face covered in cuts, bruises and dried blood. Jennifer can't bring herself to look at him.

"Hey this is nothing, you should have seen the other guy" Bruce says, joking and trying to smile.

"Amy kicked the crap out of him" he adds, admitting that he didn't do much, apart from get roughed up.

Amy doesn't think Bruce should be putting himself down and points out although he struggled with the big ugly thug, if he didn't come in when he did, something terrible might have happened. With that she relives the moment of fear before Bruce stormed in, breaking down in tears... As Lucy, Rose and Whitney comfort Amy and Tina, Bruce signals Jennifer into the kitchen to talk properly. The broken couple sit at the table in the kitchen and Jennifer feels a deep sense of guilt by everything that's happened. She listens to Bruce tell her the whole story again, how he escaped the back of the car in the car park, how he had to take on two of Tony's men and how he held a gun for the first time in his life.

"I am so sorry baby" she utters, trying not to let the drink make her emotional.

"I gave you forty-eight hours Jen and this is what happens" he says.

"Forget the next twenty-four hours, I am going to the police first thing in the morning" he grunts in pain.

Jennifer sits there with her head spinning and try's not to look at the bruises on his face. She knows he is deadly serious this time.

"Please Bruce, just give me the twenty-four hours" she begs across the table.

"I will give you twenty-four Jen. Twenty-four minutes" he grunts again, claiming she isn't going to change his mind this time.

"I thought you said first thing in the morning?" asks Jennifer.

"I did" responds Bruce.

"Twenty-four minutes is all you've got left before you pass out and then it will be morning" he adds standing up and telling her he doesn't want to talk about it anymore.

He disappears to find somewhere to grab a few hours sleep and leaves Jennifer sitting at the kitchen table.

In the morning, Bruce wakes up after an unsettled sleep at seven o'clock. He sees Tina, Lucy and Rose all snuggled up on the sofa. He then catches a glimpse of his unshaven face in the mirror and takes a closer look at his black eye, cut eyebrow and swollen lip. He goes in search of Jennifer upstairs to tell her it's time... He checks in the spare room first, where Whitney the superstar didn't quite make it to the bed and is drooling face down on the floor.

"Now that is class" mumbles Bruce, joking to himself about the state of the world's sexiest woman.

He opens the door to Karen's room and finds Jennifer has at least managed to make it to the bed. He walks over to the bed and stands watching her sleep for a few minutes. The emotion, the desire, love and the pain is written all over his face, as he brushes her hair away from her face.

"It's time to get up Jen" he whispers, craving the morning smile that he used to get from her.

She grunts something and turns over. Bruce knows he isn't going to get that smile now and tries to wake her a little forcefully by shaking her shoulder.

"We've got to go to the police station" he says, trying to wake her.

"I'm not going" she grumbles.

"If you want to go, then go" she adds, putting a pillow over her

head and going back to sleep.
Bruce stands back from the bed and soon finds himself walking down the street lost deep in his thoughts... He comes to the entrance of the police station and stops outside. He considers what he's going to tell them, what is going to happen after and then the fact he could ruin everything Jennifer is planning, if she is planning anything at all.
He takes a step forwards, then stops again...

"Should I give Jen the twenty-four hours she claims she needs?" he mumbles to himself.

"Who will get hurt in those few hours, if I don't do this now?" he asks himself, still mumbling looking at the main door...

CHAPTER 22
EXPLAINING WITH NO EXPLANATION

Bruce makes his mind up and decides to take matters into his own hands by walking straight in the police station and telling them everything. He places his hand on the door. Just then he hears Jennifer's voice calling after him and turns to see if it really is her.

"Before you go in there, there are a few things I need to tell you first" she explains, trying to stall him.

Bruce isn't sure and doesn't want her to change his mind again. He keeps his hand on the door and just looks at her waiting for her explanation.

"I can't, it's too hard to explain" she says, lowering her head.

Bruce pushes the door handle down, showing her he isn't messing around.

"Okay, okay, I will tell you" she says, rushing towards him.

Bruce lets go of the door and turns to face her again.

"There's no easy way of saying this, so I will just come out with it" she declares.

Bruce waits for her to speak and tell him the secret he knows she's been holding back for so long. She takes a deep breath, looking like she is going to cry.

"Tony is my father" she confesses.

Bruce's jaw hits the pavement as he watches his wife burst into tears, turn and run down the street.

Bruce gives chase immediately but is so confused. She runs towards a small public park, where she sits on a bench with her head in her hands and he runs into the park after her...

"How can he be your father?" asks Bruce, when he reaches the bench.

"I was out drinking with your dad only the other week" he says, sitting down beside her.

Jennifer lifts her head and smiles at him. She says she is sorry but it was the only way to get him away from the police station. Bruce sits there unsure if it is another cruel trick to get him to do what she wants or another new level of low she's just discovered.

"Why say it then?" he asks, looking baffled and truly amazed at how well she can lie to his face these days.

She tells him she is sorry again and then tells him she really is ready to come clean with anything he wants to know.

"No more lies, no more cover-ups. I will answer anything you want honestly" she declares, looking into his eyes.

Although Bruce has given her plenty of opportunities to open up with him over the last couple of days, he sinks, really wanting to give her just one last chance.

"Okay then" he says, prepared to do just that.

"Do you want me to come to America with you and do you still love me?" he asks first, unsure if he can cope with the answer.

Without lies, cover-ups and bullshit as promised, Jennifer tells him the truth...

"Yes of course I love you and I always will" she says.

"And America?" asks Bruce, trying not to choke up.

"Why would I want to go anywhere without the love of my life?" she answers without hesitating, looking a little like the old Jen he once knew.

"What about pushing me together with Amy? How could you do that, if you love me?" he asks quickly, thinking he's about to catch her out if she is lying again.

"I've always known you liked her" she explains.

"It was just easier to distract you with her, whilst I got this plan for Tony sorted" she adds.

Bruce really appreciates his wife's honesty finally, but still can't get his head around it all.

"So you pushed me and Amy together to keep me out of the way?" he asks.

Jennifer looks at him and nods her head.

"So you don't want me to go off and live happily ever after with Amy then?" he asks, looking for the reassurance he needs more than ever now.

"I didn't say that" responds Jennifer, to his confusion once more.

"So you do want me to go off with Amy then?" he asks, feeling his head spin again.

Finally Jennifer puts him out of his misery once and for all. She explains she loves him and wants him to move to America with her, but only if it makes him happy.

"If Amy is where your happiness is, then I want you to stay with her" she tells him, pointing out his happiness is all that matters to her. Bruce feels the lump in his throat double in size, as for the first time in ages, he is starting to understand his wife and her behaviour.

"I need you to do one thing for me without asking any questions" Jennifer says, before he can put anything else to her.

"Give you the twenty-four hours?" Bruce guesses, as she takes both of his hands.

Jennifer shakes her head to say no.

He delivers his next question to her, asking what the plan is for Tony.

"That's it" says Jennifer, as if she knew this question was coming.

"That's what?" asks Bruce, getting confused again.

"Don't ask that question just yet, is what I need you to do for me" she explains, holding his hands tighter and asking him to trust her.

Bruce tries to take in everything she has just said, but still struggles to get his head round it.

"I've been completely honest with you baby, so please trust me" she begs, hoping he will do that for her.

"What have you been honest about Jen?" he asks, as a tear rolls down his cheek.

"You said you love me, want me, but would be happy if I left you for someone else. That's like explaining something and giving no explanation" he tells her, getting tired and very emotional.

A sense of guilt sends a shiver down her spine, realising she's broken her husband and wants to make it right again. She explains again that all she wants is for him to be happy.

"So what if I said America wouldn't make me happy?" he asks sobbing.

"Then I would tell you not to come" she answers.

"Does that mean you would still go?" he asks.

Jennifer doesn't respond with words but he knows by the look in her eye, she is prepared to go without him.

"Please Bruce" she says, before she hurts him even more.

"We will get Lucy's wedding rehearsal out the way this afternoon and I will come straight to the police station with you" she adds, begging him to give her the few more hours that she needs.

Bruce stands up looking emotionally beaten, still with his wounds from last night and tells her he really doesn't care anymore.

"Whatever you want Jen" he mumbles, starting his walk to Karen's

house with his head lowered.
Jennifer watches him stumble off looking completely trashed and reminds herself that she did this to him.

"Bruce" she calls from the bench.

He stops, slowly turns and lifts his head to look at her.

"Yeah, what can I do for you now Jen?" he mumbles, looking really sorry for himself.

She stands up and walks towards him.

"Forget what I want for once, let's do it together" she says, trying to make him smile.

"Do what Jen? I am really tired" he grumbles at her again.

"You want to go and tell the police. Well, we can do it together right now" she explains.

"What about you wanting another twenty-four hours?" he asks, looking worried.

She holds out her hand waiting for him to take it. He lifts his arm and takes hold of her hand as she turns towards the police station.

"Just for a few minutes, let's be the team we used to be" she begs, as they step inside the police station together.

CHAPTER 23
OH BUT I CAN

The couple tell the police everything that they know about Tony, everything from blackmailing their old friend Jane a few weeks ago, to what he's been up to now with kidnapping, rape, guns, gangs and attacks.
The police believe everything the couple say, but have a problem.
 "Did anyone witness Bruce being hit over the head with the bat?" asks the police officer.
 "Well, yeah there were hundreds of people, but no-one actually saw who it was" answers Jennifer.
The police officer stands up and paces around the room.
 "And there were no witnesses to Tina's kidnap, Karen's rape, Dean's attack and so on and so on" says the police officer, explaining that there job is going to be hard, almost impossible.
Bruce stands up and tells Jennifer they are leaving.
 "What's the point telling these clowns anything? We might as well be telling them nothing" Bruce snaps.
 "Excuse me SIR, but we are trying our best here" explains the policeman, with some authority.
 "It's just without any proof" he adds, before Bruce interrupts...
 "Isn't any proof? Isn't any proof? And these cuts on my face are what?" shouts Bruce, getting really frustrated now.
 "You've got someone that's been raped and lost a fucking baby. Another girl attacked and her former boyfriend hospitalised too. You've got a young girl scared out of her fucking mind and me telling you there's a gun in the bushes of my garden. What more proof do

you need?" he adds, before banging his fist on the table and sitting down again.

"You don't understand sir" says the policeman, trying to calm him down.

"You've already said you had the gun, which means we would have to arrest you too" he adds, trying to do his job.

This time the thought of Bruce getting arrested angers his wife and she tries to throw her next statement into the fire too. But once again the policeman tells them, without any proof Tony will walk free.

Bruce has had enough and wants to leave. The couple stand up and the policeman informs them that Tony will be arrested, but they really need him to slip up when they bring him in.

"Then let's hope you are good at your job and make him slip up" Bruce says to the policeman, leaving the room.

The policeman walks them to the entrance and stands by the front desk, as they walk out of the building.

"What was all that about? Another domestic?" asks another policeman behind the desk.

The interviewing policeman turns to him and shakes his head in disbelief.

"Believe it or not but those two want to put Tony inside" he tells the officer behind the desk.

"What Tony, Tony?" responds the desk officer, knowing who the gangster is by his first name.

"Yeah that Tony and without any proof too" he adds, shaking his head again.

The couple are walking back to Karen's to get changed for Lucy's wedding rehearsal in a few hours. They both feel a little upset by the outcome of their visit to the police station and the laws lack of interest in Tony, but are glad they pulled together just like they used to.

Within the time it takes them to slowly walk back to Karen's house, what Bruce and Jennifer don't know is, the police have taken their information seriously. Just as they arrive outside Karen's house, a police car pulls up...

"Oh no, what's this?" gasps Jennifer, hoping nothing else has happened at the house whilst they've been away.

"Red line through the middle, white bits either side. It must be a jam sandwich" says Bruce, looking at the police car.

"Don't be a dick" giggles Jennifer, as she playfully slaps his arm like she used to do, then noticing it's the same officer that interviewed them at the station.

They wait for him to get out of the car.

"Don't say that the police don't listen or do their job" the officer says, looking really pleased with himself.

"It's taken just five minutes to raid Tony's house and arrest him" he adds, smiling at them.

He explains Tony will be interviewed about the allegations made against him and hopefully they can get something to stick. He asks them if they could stay local in-case they need more information. They couple agree and the policeman thanks them for their time and drives away again. Bruce and Jennifer go into the house where everyone is gathered in the living room. Jennifer can't hold it in and quickly boasts to Tina that Tony has been locked up and it's all over. Jennifer expects a little more enthusiasm from the group but they seem to be engrossed in something else.

"What's going on then?" asks Jennifer, looking at Rose sitting holding Lucy's hand.

"The wedding is off" responds Rose, telling her and Bruce that the groom has changed his mind, got cold feet and done a bunk.

"Oh that's terrible. I am so sorry Lucy" says Jennifer, walking over to her.

Lucy gives Jennifer a hug and tells her she's okay.

"So they got the guy that's been causing all these problems then?" asks Lucy, trying to change the subject.

Jennifer tells her they sure have and after a few days, they should be able to relax, walk the streets and return to their normal lives.

"Hold on before any of you rush off" says Jennifer, watching Rose dart into the kitchen.

"There's something I need to tell you all" she adds, as Rose stops. Rose, Bruce, Lucy, Tina, Whitney and Amy listen as Jennifer prepares to speak to the group. Jennifer tells them it's been a tough few weeks for them and she hasn't had much time with everything going on, to teach many lessons.

"Don't worry about it. We got the oral one last night and that was amazing" says Lucy, trying to be supportive and understanding.

"Yeah and we've had some time on our own too" smiles Rose, hoping Jennifer remembers their bonding session in the bedroom.

"And don't forget all the toys you gave me" says Tina, trying to make her feel better too.

Jennifer thanks them all for being so understanding, but tells them there's something else she needs to say... Once again the group hush down and listen with interest.

"There is no easy way to say this, but I am moving over to America with Whitney" the life coach tells them.

None of the group seem to be very surprised, as they've over heard conversations about it during the last few days.

"When are you going?" stutters Amy, knowing she might be leaving her husband Bruce behind.

Jennifer looks to Whitney for an answer.

"We fly out tomorrow evening" Whitney says, to the shock of everyone.

"Are you going too Bruce?" asks Lucy, looking at him.

Bruce still hasn't made his mind up and feels everyone's eyes staring at him.

"I'm not sure yet, I have a few things I have to work out first" he says, before walking into the hall to get away from the question.

Bruce walks into the hall and out of the door, so Jennifer follows him.

"Bruce hold on" she calls, knowing they need to talk again.

Bruce continues to walk up the street, so Jennifer catches up with him and tries to stop him.

"Remember what the police said Bruce? We've got to stay close" she says.

He stops and looks at her.

"I don't know what I am doing" he says, feeling his world is crashing down around him.

"I don't know if I should come, stay or even if you want me over there with you" he says, getting confused and emotional.

Jennifer doesn't speak and just gives him a hug.

Just then a car pulls up and both of them jump back as it nearly mounts the pavement.

"Hello you two" says one of Tony's goons, behind the steering wheel.

"I thought you would be long gone, now that Tony has been arrested" says Bruce, angry that the big overgrown baboon has interrupted their conversation.

"You don't think Tony will go down on his own do you? No, he will take all of his baboons with him" he adds, trying to laugh and wind him up.

"Tony isn't going to prison though is he?" says the goon, getting out of the car.

"See I've already spoken to him and the police have no proof" he adds laughing.

"How could you have spoken to him? He's in a police cell" asks Jennifer, being clever.

"I'm not just one of his soldiers, I am his solicitor" responds the simple sounding goon.

"Ah, isn't that nice, jumbo here has brains too" Bruce laughs, still trying to wind him up.

Tony's goon tells them he has a message from Tony. He explains that Tony will be released in twelve hours, when the pigs can't find anything to charge him with and he doesn't want to see any of Jennifer's group living again.

"What's he going to do, kill us all?" asks Jennifer, at the feeble threat.

"Yeah, that's exactly what he will do" answers the goon.

"You have twelve hours to get disappeared" he demands, getting back into his car.

Bruce and Jennifer try and stand their ground, but realise that the big ugly baboon isn't joking.

"Oh and by the way" he says, undoing his window.

"Tony said Karen was really good" he adds laughing.

Bruce goes to lunge at him through the window but Jennifer holds him back.

"Come on Bruce, don't let your wife hold you down" laughs the goon, trying to provoke him.

"I've still got my baseball bat in the car, you know... The one that caved your head" he adds laughing some more.

Bruce sees red and not even Jennifer can hold him back this time. He pulls the huge man right through the car window and starts kicking him in the head.

"You want a piece of me, then you've got it" shouts Bruce, booting him as hard as he can.

Jennifer calls for Bruce to stop but he can't hear her. She knows it's more than a fight going through his head right now and with all of the emotions inside, he could kill him. Bruce kicks him into a beaten up daze and crouches down to grab him by the neck. He throws back his fist ready to swing his final punch...

"Don't do it baby" begs Jennifer, trying to grab hold of him.

"He's not worth killing" she adds, as the others come out of the house hearing the commotion.

Bruce holds the half dead goon against his car and turns to his wife.

"Don't you understand Jen? We don't have any proof" says Bruce, desperate to hit him again.

"This is just one less baboon I am going to have to fight tomorrow" he says, turning back to hit him.

Bruce holds his fist up again and musters every last bit of anger and energy.

"Bruce, I do have the proof" screams Jennifer.

Bruce lowers his fist and really slowly and confused, looks back at his wife.

"What? No you don't" he utters.
"Oh, but I do" she declares...

CHAPTER 24
HERE COMES THE PRIDE

Bruce lets go of the goons neck and helps him to his feet. He opens his car door and pushes him in, telling him to get lost. The goon still dazed by the beating, starts his engine and speeds off down the road. Bruce watches as the car disappears out of sight.

"What do you mean you have proof?" Bruce asks Jennifer, as the group walk over to join them.
Jennifer doesn't want to say anything yet and simply tells Tina to lock all the doors in the house.

"Why, where are we going?" asks Lucy, looking as confused as Bruce does.

"Follow me" says Jennifer, leading them all back down the street.
Rose, Lucy, Amy, Tina, Whitney and Bruce all follow Jennifer down the street and five minutes later they arrive outside the police station once again.

"Why are we back here?" asks Bruce, as the whole group look baffled.

"Inside this police station is a madman who wants to hurt us all" declares Jennifer.

"If we all pull together right now, he will never get out again" she adds, walking over to Rose and standing in front of her.

"I'm with you, what do you need?" asks Rose.
Jennifer looks at them all with anticipation in their eyes.

"What is the madman's name Rose?" asks Jennifer.

"I don't know, you've never said" answers Rose, very sure of her answer.

Bruce knows what's coming next and moves to stand beside his wife.

"The madman inside that raped Karen, tried to kill Bruce and kidnapped Tina is called Tony" Jennifer tells her.

The world comes crashing down around Rose's ears as she begins to spin the fear racing through her body and the floor beneath her starts to wobble.

"You mean my dad Tony?" stutters Rose, looking petrified.

"I mean your dad Tony" confirms Jennifer, with a sorry looking smile on her face.

Suddenly Rose goes crazy and tells them they are all mad.

"There's no way I am going in there and grassing him up" she shouts hysterically.

"You have to do it Rose or we are all in trouble" says Bruce, getting involved.

"Come on Rose, this is the man that planned to take my sister" says her best friend Lucy.

"I don't care, I can't do it, he will kill me" shouts Rose.

"Why didn't you tell me, it was my dad before?" she asks Jennifer.

Jennifer explains she only found out outside the hospital a few days ago.

"Does he know I am friends with you?" Rose asks, getting really worried now.

"He knows more than that" responds Jennifer, pulling a note from her jacket pocket.

Jennifer hands Rose the note and tells her to read it. As Rose reads the note, she breaks down as Jennifer explains what it says to the others.

"Rose had an affair with her father's girlfriend ages ago" she says.

"He doesn't just know about Rose's connection with us, but he knows about the affair too" she adds.

"But I thought you were straight?" gasps Lucy, wanting to be the only true bi-sexual in the group.

"He's going to kill me" stutters Rose, dropping the note to the floor and trembling.

Jennifer explains to Lucy that Rose is straight, but was seduced when she was drunk.

"That's why I had to check if you were straight or bi-sexual for myself the other day. To find out if it was your fault or your father's girlfriend's" explains Jennifer.

"He's going to kill me" stutters Rose.

Jennifer grabs her by the arm to get her attention.

"You aren't bi-sexual Rose. It wasn't your fault" Jennifer tells her.

"But your dad IS blaming you" she adds to Rose's horror.

They give her a few minutes to get her head round it and then Jennifer explains that Rose knows exactly what her father is capable of and what he has been doing to the group.

"There's no other proof like this?" says Jennifer, telling her what she needs to do.

Rose nods her head and wipes away her tears. She looks at Jennifer asking if she will go in with her. Jennifer holds out her hand, smiles and leads Rose into the police station. Everyone has a million questions for Jennifer, but all of them think about how brave Rose is and what she is doing...

Jennifer walks Rose into the police station and is greeted by the same officer that has been questioning Tony and getting nowhere.

"We've been unable to get him to admit anything yet and we raided his home to find no sign of guns or cash" he tells Jennifer.

"Maybe you've got your wires crossed and we have to face facts that we just can't get anything on him" he adds, telling her there's not much else they can do.

"Yes he does have guns and I know where he hides them" says Rose.

Two hours later and after Rose has given the police more than enough to send her father to prison for a very long time. They arrive back at the house where a slightly shaken but relieved Rose gets the biggest heroes welcome of all. Whitney, Lucy, Tina and Amy make a huge fuss of her, telling her she's done a very brave thing.

Bruce and Jennifer go up to Karen's bedroom to piece everything together.

"Looks like you did it again Jen, you really got there in the end" says Bruce, disappointed in himself for doubting his wife's intentions all along.

"Don't feel bad baby, I've been a real bitch to you throughout all of this and you still stuck by me" she tells him.

"There's just one thing I don't understand" he says.

"Why couldn't you just tell me?" he asks, looking at her expecting nothing but honesty now.

She explains for his ears only, that she knew Tony would come back after the lap dancing club and went after Lucy, knowing she was his daughter's best friend.

"So you set it all up from the very start?" asks Bruce.

Jennifer nods her head and isn't happy about the things that have happened to get her this outcome.

"But you could have ended it sooner. Then Karen wouldn't have

lost her baby" he says, trying to get to grips with it all himself.
Jennifer reminds him how hard it was when they first met Rose and what a bitch she was... She then explains that Karen knew about it all along, but wishes some of the things didn't turn out the way they did. Bruce sits down on the bed, considering just how hard he's been on her, knowing now that she has been trying to save everyone.

"So you did all this to get rid of Tony?" he asks, looking at her.
Jennifer explains if she didn't, plenty more damage would have been done, but she didn't just do it just for them, she did it for Rose too.

"So you risked our marriage to help other people?" he asks, declaring he should have seen it himself.

"Don't be too hard on yourself. I've been a real bitch to you" she admits again.

"Hopefully now you understand I didn't mean it and had to be this way?" she add, getting a little upset.
He takes her face in his hands before she can cry and kisses her on the lips. For the first time in ages the couple share a loving kiss, before he pulls away and looks into her eyes.

"So what about us now?" he asks.
Before he can finish his sentence or wait for an answer, she kisses him back and they share an intimate moment falling back onto the bed. Just as they come up for air and look at each-other again, it sparks a fire of passion and within seconds they are kissing and ripping each-others clothes off... With her jeans around her ankles and his hard penis poking out the top of his, he rolls on top of her, pulls her knickers out of the way and penetrates her vagina without any foreplay needed... Within seconds she is in ecstasy and moaning as she rocks against him from underneath and he thrusts harder and harder... The emotions, the passion and the rage that have built up, all surface at once and she can feel his fat penis throb deep inside her tightening vagina. She knows he's about to explode and she can feel her orgasm reach it's peak too.

"Stop" she moans, as he lifts his sweaty head to look at her.
Without saying a word he knows she wants to have eye contact as they cum together and he starts to thrusts hard and fast again. She watches as the pain, struggle and fire burns across the lenses of his eyes. He watches as she moans in relief, with sorrow and love written all over her face...

Downstairs the group sit in the living room talking about what Rose told the police. They raise their voices trying to drown out the noise of the bedsprings through the ceiling. As they all have a laugh, no-one seems to consider poor Amy's feelings, as she tries like the rest of them to smile through the pounding above her head as her heart breaks.

Back upstairs the couple collapse together on the bed completely drained.
"Now that was the best sex of my life" boasts Jennifer, trying to get her breath back.
"Was it?" asks Bruce, panting like he's just ran the London marathon.
She turns to him, looks him in the eye and smiles with a nod. Then the smile disappears, as she turns away to lie on her pillow...
"What's wrong?" he asks, watching her face full of joy one second and drop the next.
She turns back to him with a tear in her eye.
"Was that the best make-up sex of my life? Or was it the best break-up sex?" she asks him.
"Make-up sex, of course" Bruce answers, to stop her from worrying.
"Was it?" she sniffles, turning away again and knowing something isn't quite right...

CHAPTER 25
A PINK INVITATION

Without saying a word, Bruce gets out of the bed, straightens his clothes and pretends Jennifer didn't just make that comment. He leaves her on the bed eager to tell everyone they are free to go back to their own homes and vacate Karen's house, so he can lock it up for her. As he walks in to the living room, he is stunned to be welcomed in by a loud cheer, as everyone is happy that the married couple have sorted their differences out.
"Wow I wish I had a husband like you, that sounded amazing" giggles Lucy.
Bruce can't hide his embarrassment and starts to laugh with them, as Jennifer walks into the same reception. Just then Bruce realises that Amy is sitting in the room and when he looks over at her, she gives him a heartbroken smile telling him she is happy for him. With that Jennifer tells them what Bruce was going to say and Amy wastes no time in making her exit. She stands up, gives everyone a quick hug, leaving Bruce until last. She walks over to him and wraps her arms around him uncomfortably.
"I am really pleased for you both" she whispers in his ear, still looking heartbroken.
Bruce asks if he can walk her home but she declines, saying she hasn't been home since Dean left and has a lot to do. Amy says one final goodbye to everyone and leaves the house. Soon enough Tina, Lucy and Rose are ready to leave too.
"What about me? Should I book into a hotel then?" asks superstar

Whitney.

Jennifer asks her to stay with Lucy and Rose for the night and she will see her tomorrow when they leave for the airport. Soon it's just Bruce and Jennifer alone in Karen's house. Bruce gets to work straight away on tidying the kitchen and Jennifer hoovers the front room and straightens the cushions on the sofa. Without speaking a word to each-other for the next hour, they both tidy the entire house. As evening falls, Jennifer starts to get hungry and they meet back in the living room with all the tidying complete.

"I think we need to talk" says Jennifer, suggesting they go and get a bite to eat before going to their own home.

"No let's do it right here" responds Bruce, not prepared to do anything more for her, if there's a chance she is going to end their marriage.

Jennifer sits down on the sofa and asks Bruce to sit with her. He prepares himself for the heartbreak now coming his way and instead of sitting with her, he takes a seat on the coffee table in front of her.

"I asked before, if it was make-up or break-up sex" declares Jennifer, starting the conversation.

"I asked because I am still going to America with Whitney tomorrow and you haven't given me your answer yet" she says, looking into his eyes.

Bruce somewhat relieved that she isn't ending it, doesn't know what to say and just sits there...

"Did you hear me Bruce? I said I am still going and want you to decide" she asks again.

He wants to say he is going with her, now he fully understands everything, but something stops him from giving her the answer she is waiting for. He considers his love for his wife sitting in front of him and then he considers the fact he's slept with someone else now and that girl has just had her heart broken.

"It's Amy, isn't it?" says Jennifer, trying to figure out the silence.

"No" claims Bruce, hiding the truth from her now.

Jennifer kneels down on the floor in front of him and takes his hand.

"I know you are very fond of Amy and I don't blame you" she says.

"I think it's gone a little further than that over the last few days" he responds, pointing out she is the first girl he's ever been unfaithful with.

"It's not a question of being unfaithful baby, because I knew you were doing it" says Jennifer.

"It's a case of whether it's out of your system now or you want it again" she adds, waiting again for him to tell her he's going to America.

Bruce stands up and tells her he will make a decision in the morning and that all he wants to do, is go home and fix the kitchen door. Jennifer agrees to give him a little extra time and kindly reminds him that they have to leave for the airport tomorrow morning for their flight at four. The couple secure Karen's house and make their way home.

A few hours later Jennifer has tidied her own house and Bruce has managed to board up the kitchen door. Jennifer tells him she is going to have a bath and get an early night for her big day tomorrow.
"Aren't you going to pack?" asks Bruce, ready to go to bed too but only to stop his spinning head from doing anymore cartwheels.
Jennifer tells him she will do all her packing in the morning, after he has made his decision. Jennifer runs her bath upstairs as Bruce sits on the sofa in the living room, trying to make a decision before his morning deadline arrives... He sits tossing the idea backwards and forwards, but can't get Amy's heartbroken face out of his head. He knows he still loves his wife but he doesn't want Amy to hurt for the sake of his marriage. Just then Jennifer calls down from the bathroom and tells him there are no towels. Bruce picks himself off the sofa, still deep in thought and wanders a clean towel up to the bathroom. He walks in and places it down on the side.
"Bruce" she calls, before he leaves the room.
"Come in with me" she adds, with a loving smile on her face, letting her eyes do the talking.
Bruce tells her he isn't in the mood for a bath, but she keeps asking him.
"Please baby" she begs.
"No talk of tomorrow. But if this is our last night together, let's go out smiling" she adds.
He looks at her in the bathtub, feeling he can't say no. She watches as he slowly gets undressed and grudgingly takes off his top as her eyes light up. He slides out of his shorts and she tries not to make eye contact with his penis, just in-case it unsettles any unwanted sexual urges. He steps into the tub and sits himself down at the other end. She has to move her legs a little to make room for him, but soon enough they sit facing each-other in the bath. She looks at him, waiting for him to look at her, but he doesn't. Instead he lies back and closes his eyes... What she had planned for the bath hasn't worked and soon enough, they are both washed and are ready to get out again. Bruce steps out first and walks straight into their bedroom. As he walks into the bedroom, the smell of Amy's sweet perfume is still lingering. He tries to ignore it as he walks over to get on the bed.

Again visions of him and Amy having sex right there come flooding back and he finds it hard to escape the thoughts of the other girl in his life. Jennifer walks in only in a towel and over to the wardrobe to find some underwear. She notices Amy's overnight bag on the floor.

"Is this Amy's bag?" she asks.

Bruce looks over, nods his head and once again, his head is filled with thoughts of Amy.

Jennifer unzips the bag to find out if there's anything in it that Amy might need, then turns to Bruce sitting on the bed naked.

"Did you fuck her in my bed?" she asks, standing there letting her towel drop to the floor.

He looks at his wife standing there, unsure if he should tell her or not. Jennifer pulls a clean pair of Amy's pink knickers from her bag and starts to put them on.

"What are you doing?" Bruce asks sighing, really not in the mood.

She pulls them up and walks across to the bed.

"Did you fuck her on my bed?" she asks again, watching him uncomfortably cover up his penis with the duvet, then look at his wife in Amy's knickers.

Once again he doesn't answer, as he watches her climb onto the bed and kneel in front of him.

"Was she wearing these knickers when you fucked her?" she asks, starting to get horny, watching him try to hide his stirring cock.

Again Bruce sits in silence as he takes a quick glimpse at Amy's knickers on his wife and pictures them on Amy.

"Please, just tell me you fucked her right here, so I can cum in her knickers too" Jennifer demands, making him aware of her naughty thoughts.

Bruce doesn't have to say a word as his face tells her all she needs to know. She whips the duvet away from his groin to find him as hard as wood.

"Just show me how you fingered her" she demands, putting a pillow over her face, giving him an invitation to Amy's pink knickers right there in front of him.

Bruce doesn't move but he can't help prevent his penis from starting to throb for the second time today.

"Come on, her knickers, her pussy, show me" demands Jennifer, from under the pillow.

He leans forward, slowly moves the knickers to the side and starts to imagine Amy's vagina again, as he looks at his wife's neatly trimmed pussy. He moves a single finger slowly towards her lips, getting the urge to fuck her when he feels just how soaked she is getting.

"MM-mm, did you like fingering her tight pussy baby?" asks

Jennifer, rocking against his finger for a few seconds.

"Now tell me you licked her" she adds, feeling him finger her harder.

He carries on fingering her, then she stops him, demanding he show her how he licked Amy's pussy.

He moves himself into position and lowers his head. He pulls the knickers out of the way and drives his tongue straight in between her lips in search of her clitoris. He makes contact with her swollen bud and it sends her on her journey towards an orgasm.

"Did you stick your tongue right up her pussy baby? Did you nibble on her clit?" asks Jennifer, thrusting hard against his tongue, mouth and chin as she gears up to explode.

"Did she cum all over your face? What did she taste like?" she asks, screaming in delight as he rams his tongue inside her and starts lapping up her juices.

She lets him continue face fucking her for a few more minutes before holding back her orgasm and declaring she wants him to fuck her.

"Show me exactly how you fucked her baby" she pants in delight.

"Where did you cum?" she asks, eagerly awaiting his cock.

Bruce gets up, Jennifer lies there for a few seconds thinking he is moving into position, but then hears the belt on his jeans and realises he is getting dressed.

"What are you doing?" pants Jennifer, sitting up and tossing the pillow out of the way.

"I can't do this" says Bruce, putting on his shoes and telling her he's going for a walk.

Jennifer rubs at her gushing pussy, claiming that she really needs to cum, but not even the sight of her masturbating is working now.

"I need some space to think Jen" he tells her.

"I will be back in the morning to give you an answer" he says.

Jennifer knows she isn't going to be able to stop him and understands he needs the space he is requesting. Unable to do anything about her palpitating orgasm now, she decides to let him go, reminding him he needs to be home by eight in the morning or she will have to leave without him.

"Do something for me please baby" she asks him.

"No, I ain't going to let you have an orgasm first" he says, smiling at her.

"If you decide you don't want to come with me, don't come back to say goodbye" she tells him.

She explains it would be too hard to say goodbye.

"Be back by eight if you are coming, if not, be happy" she says kissing him, realising that it could be for the last time...

CHAPTER 26
DAM

Bruce has been out walking the streets all night long, in search of answers only he can give himself. He doesn't notice the dark sky starting to get light or the early birds around London starting to commute to work. Unaware of the time, he knows he's running out of it to return home.

Back at the house Jennifer has been up since six o'clock packing her two suitcases for her big move. Although very excited about her American journey, she finds herself checking the clock on the wall every minute, hoping Bruce will return soon. With only half an hour to go before the eight o'clock deadline she set him, she starts to consider he won't turn up and starts to put her backup plan into action.

Out on the streets Bruce has finally come to a decision and works out he can't possibly live without his wife. With a new outlook and sense of well being, even though he's been walking all night, he takes his first glance at his watch.
    "Dam" he mumbles in a panic, as his watch reads **seven forty-five**.
He knows he is well over fifteen minutes away from home, so decides to lunge at his mobile and ring Jennifer. He calls and calls her but unaware to him, she's putting her backup plan into action and that

means ditching her phone. Now with not enough time to get home before his wife sets off on her journey to the airport, he decides there is nothing for it and he must get to the airport before the check-in at four. Bruce quickly weighs up his options and plans out his day as fast as he can, whilst heading down the road. First he wants to go and tell Amy he's made a decision, then he needs to pack before heading to the airport and catching up with Jennifer and Whitney. He stands in the middle of the high-street and tries to wave a cab down to take him to Amy's house first...

"Dam" he mumbles again, as the taxi driver ignores him and doesn't stop.

He decides to set off on foot and try and hail a taxi again as he makes his way across London. Twenty minutes into his journey on foot he manages to hail the required taxi and jumps in, looking down at his watch again. His watch now reads **twenty past eight**.

He sits in the back of the taxi thinking what to say to Amy and the fact his wife now thinks he's not coming. He struggles to come up with anything, as the two subjects conflict in his head.

"Dam" he mumbles for a third time in half an hour, realising he should have gone home first and packed, then gone to Amy's house.

He arrives at Amy's house and looks at his watch before getting out of the taxi and paying the driver. His watch now reads **twenty past nine** as the driver apologises for the bad traffic. He gets out of the taxi to knock on Amy's front door. He gives it a knock and waits for her to answer.

"Dam" he mumbles yet again, remembering he doesn't know what he's saying to her yet.

He disappears around the corner and watches as the blonde answers the door, looks around and goes back inside. He walks up and down the next street a few times, thinking about the best way to deliver the news and then thinks he has it... He returns to her front door as his watch tells him it's **ten to ten**. He waits for the door to open it again and is surprised to see Karen standing there, when it does open.

"Karen" he gasps, really pleased to see her.

"Hey stud" she responds, giving him a hug on the doorstep and inviting him in.

Bruce follows Karen into Amy's house and asks where she is.

"She's in the bedroom" Karen answers, asking him to go and see her.

Bruce walks towards the bedroom door and gets that same sweet smell, he had at home in his bedroom last night. Karen tells him she will make him a coffee, so he thanks her and places his hand on the doorknob.

Meanwhile across the City in Bruce's part of town, Jennifer is wheeling her two suitcases, as she plans her goodbye visit to Rose, Lucy and Tina and of course, to meet up with her new friend, companion and employee Whitney.

Bruce enters the bedroom and is blown away to find Amy packing her bags.
"Aims, what are you doing?" he asks, as though the vision is not clear enough.
Amy turns and smiles at him, claiming she didn't hear him come in.
"I am packing" she tells him.
"I see that, but where are you going?" he asks, walking over to the bed to join her.
She finishes folding a top and places it in the bag, then looks at him.
"I am coming to America with you" she tells him, knocking him sideways with shock.
"Didn't you get my text?" she asks, picking up another top from her bed.
Bruce doesn't know what to say and pulls his mobile from his pocket, claiming he didn't get the message. She starts to giggle at him pressing buttons on his phone.
"What?" he asks.
"I guess that's what you came here to tell me. That you are going to America" she says, smiling at him with that same heartbroken look in her eye.
He doesn't quite know how to answer it and really wanted to tell her himself.
"Who told you?" he asks, looking upset.
"No-one" she answers.
"I just guessed this is the way it would turn out" she says, putting another top in her bag.
Bruce doesn't know how to make it right and realises now that there was never going to be a happy ending to this conversation, no matter how much he desperately wanted one. Before he attempts to open his mouth and tell her how special she is to him, she stops him, telling him he doesn't have to say anything else and that she knows. With that the couple embrace as though they both understand, it will probably be for the last time.
"My feelings for you were always true" he says, holding her tightly

as she starts to cry.

"I told you, I know" she says pulling away.

Just then Karen enters the room without knocking, carrying Bruce's coffee cup.

"Oh sorry" says Karen.

"Having a quickie for old time sake, are we?" she asks, back to her usual self in her dirty mind.

"Just saying goodbye" whimpers Amy, wiping her eyes dry and laughing at Karen's sexual comment.

"Oh that's a shame. I thought we could have a threesome before we all leave" Karen responds, pinching his bum.

Although Karen is serious, she knows the comment will make them both smile and it does... Just then Bruce realises Amy is still packing and he doesn't know where she is going.

"Me and Aims are heading over to Spain to hook up with Michelle" Karen declares.

"When are you coming back?" Bruce asks, like it matters to him, knowing he will be half way round the world himself.

"We aren't" Amy tells him, with a sad look again.

"Michelle is settled over there now and has hooked us up with an apartment next door to her" Karen explains.

"Just think all the girls back together as neighbours" she adds, getting excited.

Bruce turns to Amy and looks her in the eye.

"Are you sure this is what you want?" he asks her.

"Course she's sure" answers Karen, as the two of them remain fixated in each-others eyes.

"I mean... Are you sure Spain knows what's coming?" Bruce asks, claiming that the three of them back together spells nothing but trouble for Spain.

"Any time you want a holiday or a break, you know where to come" Amy says, wrapping her arms around him.

"Or if you ever change your mind about us" she whispers.

Before Amy can get upset, Karen makes her laugh again by jumping up into his arms and knocking him back onto the bed.

"Hot" Bruce shouts, giving Karen the wrong idea as she tries to pull open his top.

"I know I am hot, lets have that fucking threesome right now" Karen giggling, trying to grab at his bulge.

"I think he was talking about the coffee you've just tipped all over his trousers" explains Amy, noticing the wet patch on his trousers and the empty cup on the bed.

Karen lets him get up and calms herself down. Finally it's time for the two girls to say goodbye to Bruce once and for all.

"See you around baby" Bruce whispers to Amy, giving her a hug.

"Bye Bruce" Amy whispers, fighting back her tears, managing to hold it together.

"Come on, my turn, my turn" Karen shouts, jumping up and down on the spot.

Bruce lets go of Amy for the last time and turns to Karen.

"You look after her for me Karen. Love you" whispers Bruce, giving her a hug too.

Suddenly Karen bursts into tears and whimpers like a baby.

"You look after yourself too Bruno" she stutters, as tears stream down her face.

Bruce doesn't hang about, letting Amy take hold of Karen and leaves the room without looking back. He closes the door, takes a deep breath of Amy's perfume and leaves at **eleven fifteen**. Bruce looks up and down the street, knowing now that time isn't on his side and it just being his luck, there isn't a taxi in sight...

"I knew I should have gone home and packed first you dick" he says to himself, checking his watch for the time again and noticing that it is only two minutes since the last time he looked.

Finally he finds a taxi parked round the corner and jumps in...

Over at Lucy's, Jennifer is saying her final goodbye's to the three girls she's leaving behind. First she sits with Tina in one of the bedrooms and explains she is a very special girl.

"Yeah but I didn't exactly wait until I was ready to lose my virginity did I?" says Tina.

Jennifer tells her she was ready to have sex anyway and that the toys were just to enhance her first experience with a boy. She tells her to keep using the toys and when Whitney and her return to the UK, she wants to see a sexual deviant. Tina gives Jennifer a hug goodbye and is quickly ushered out of the way by big sister Lucy.

"Ah Lucy, by far one of the best students I've EVER taught" says Jennifer, welcoming her into the room.

Although Lucy knows that Jennifer is leaving, she isn't that upset knowing every time Whitney returns to the UK, Jennifer will be with her.

"You just remember" says Jennifer, giving her a hug and telling her that she's beautiful.

"You should never stop asking questions or learning" she adds, kissing her on the cheek.

Lucy backs away from her.

"Okay then, here's a question for you" says Lucy.

"I should be sad that you're leaving, so why is it I am really horny right now?" she asks, claiming even Jennifer being nice to her makes her wet.

Jennifer gives her another quick hug and tells her to keep working on her self-control issues.

Finally Rose walks into the room.

"I am surprised you want to say goodbye to me" says Rose, after all the trouble she, her father and her ex has caused.

Jennifer tells her she is such a beautiful person inside and that she needs to show that off more than she does.

"I know you've lost a boyfriend and a father, but look what you've gained" says Jennifer, smiling at her and wrapping her arms around her.

"You are now free from fear, pain and can only live in happiness from now on" she adds, whispering in her ear.

Rose tells her she does already feel a great weight has been lifted off her shoulders and thanks her again for everything she's done.

"You are very welcome" says Jennifer, leaving the room.

"And remember Rose. You are the only girl in the world that has touched me down below" she adds, giving her a wink, walking out.

Bruce checks his watch pulling up outside his house and knows he's got to be quick packing his bags, in order to get to Heathrow on time. It's **quarter to one** and he needs to check-in at four.

"Dam" he mumbles, getting out of the taxi and noticing he hasn't got his door key.

He stands there and rings Amy quickly to ask if he left them at her house. Amy confirms he must have dropped them when Karen jumped on him and asks what she should do with them now.

Bruce just tells her to stick them in a drawer, telling her he doesn't need them anymore.

"Bruce" calls Amy down the phone, before he hangs up.

"We are leaving to head to Gatwick now, so remember, I am always at the end of the phone if you need me" she adds, wishing him good luck and saying goodbye again.

Bruce stands looking at his front door, as the watch on his wrist reads **ten to one**. Just then he remembers about the kitchen door and the fact it's only boarded up from the inside. He runs to the back of the house and tries to find something to loosen the wooden boards off with. He can't find a thing and starts pushing it with his shoulder.

"Dam my handy work" he mumbles, throwing his full force at the wooden barricade, but getting nowhere fast...

Soon enough he manages to loosen a few boards and after sweating profusely, he manages to squeeze through a tiny gap in the door and into the kitchen. He looks up at the clock on the wall and can't believe it's taken him nearly half an hour to break into his own house. It now reads, **twenty past one**. Just as he thinks he's got enough time to race upstairs, grab some things and head to the airport, there's a note from Jennifer on the table. The note tells him she doesn't believe he isn't coming and knowing him he's running late. It also tells him that she will be at Lucy and Rose's first to say goodbye and she will wait for him there. It tells him to bring her wedding ring and that if anything should go wrong, she will be waiting at the departure gate with his boarding ticket at four.

"Dam you wedding ring" he mumbles, picking up his wife's gold ring from the table, knowing he needs to put it back on her finger.

"Dam you drama school" he mumbles, realising his time has been cut even shorter now.

"And Dam you smelly armpits" he shouts, also realising that breaking into his house, means he really needs a shower.

He runs upstairs, throws a rucksack on the bed and starts to drag everything out from the wardrobe. He still smells Amy's sweet perfume merged with his wife's smell too, but it's soon overpowered by his own pits. He starts frantically trying to multitask, pack whilst getting undressed to shower and funny enough, takes him longer than it would have if he was doing one after the other.

He runs into the bathroom and drops his boxer shorts to the floor. He switches the water on and jumps into shower.

"Dam you shower gel" he yells, noticing that Jennifer has emptied the bathroom, taking everything with her.

He jumps out of the shower dripping wet and runs downstairs completely naked, into the kitchen, slipping on the laminated floor and slides towards the sink where a bottle of washing up liquid falls on his head.

"Dam you laminate" he grunts in pain, as he tries to catch his breath looking at the clock again.

"Dam you time" he yells, getting up noticing another twenty minutes have past and then running back up to the bathroom with the washing up liquid.

Without any shower gel or soap in the house, he quickly washes his pits with the lemon washing up liquid. Three minutes later he is out and back in the bedroom getting dressed.

"Dam you rucksack" he shouts, realising he's already stuffed everything into his bag and now needs to empty it again to find something to wear.

Finally at **five minutes before two o'clock** he is ready to leave. He makes sure he's got everything, double checks his passport and that Jennifer's wedding ring is in his pocket as he leaves the house.

He races back down towards the high-street and heads straight for the drama school, where Jennifer told him to meet her. It crosses his mind to go straight to the airport, but as the school is only five minutes up the road, it wouldn't make a dent in his already late schedule too much. He arrives at the school out of breath and can smell the washing up liquid doing it's job, as the sweat pours down his face. He races through the school and up to Lucy and Rose's room.

"What are you doing here?" asks Lucy, opening the door looking surprised.

"Is Jen...? Is Jen...?" he pants heavily.

"Is Jen... still here?" he asks, managing to finish his sentence.

Lucy tells him she left over an hour ago in a taxi to go and say goodbye to Amy and then to the airport. Bruce checks his watch again and realising it's coming up to **twenty past two**, doesn't even say hello or goodbye to Lucy standing at the door. He races off the school grounds and reaches into his pocket for his mobile.

"Dam you kitchen table" he pants, realising he has left his mobile on the kitchen table after double checking everything and getting it wrong.

Now without time to run back to the house, he starts to fear the clock counting down on him. With his legs already tired and the fact he's been up all night, everything starts to take it's toll and he starts to fear missing the flight all together. He races down the road and back to the high-street in hope there is a taxi there when he really needs it. He feels his legs tire even more when he realises that he's running, but he isn't going anywhere fast... Finally at **half past two** his fortunes start to turn and his wish comes true, as there sitting at the end of the road is a black cab...

He races over to it with a new lease of life and jumps in.

"Heathrow airport as quick as you can please mate" he gasps, sitting back to catch his breath as the Caribbean driver nods his head and takes off at speed for him.

As if it were fate, the cab manages to miss every red traffic light and get a clear run towards the airport. Bruce bounces up and down on his seat and instead of watching the cab metre, he watches his watch on his wrist as the time swiftly passes **three o'clock**. Knowing that he has an hour to go and the road signs start showing the directions to the airport, he knows he can still make it... He sits there gearing up for his final sprint through the airport, as the cab driver opens his window.

"What time is your flight?" he calls back to Bruce, in his Caribbean accent.

Bruce tells him he needs to check-in, within the next hour.

"Oh dear" says the driver, to Bruce's confusion.

They turn the next corner and Bruce realises why...

The cab and Bruce sit at the back of a traffic queue that goes on for at least two miles. He sits there nervously watching the second hand on his watch, as the cab seems to move slower than a snail. Bruce waits impatiently until his watch hits the **twenty past three** mark and he tells the driver he will run the rest of the way.

"If you go through that street over there, you should make it in ten minutes on foot" says the cab driver, trying to be helpful.

"Okay sir, that will be twenty-five pounds please" says the cab driver, ready to release the lock to open the back door.

"Dam you wallet" Bruce mumbles, pulling it out to find only a tenner inside.

He offers the driver the tenner, telling him it's all he's got and the driver looks back at him in the rear view mirror.

"I guess you will miss your flight then" says the driver, refusing to let him out.

Bruce begs the driver to open the door and tells him it's a matter of life and death.

"It's a matter of life or death that you catch an aircraft?" questions the driver.

Bruce tells him it's life and death for his marriage, pulling out the ring to try and prove his story to the driver.

"If I don't get on that plane and put this ring back on my wife's finger, it's over" Bruce tells him.

"Oh, nice ring sir. That would pay your extra fifteen pounds for sure" says the driver, as his eyes light up.

"I can't do that" says Bruce, not giving the idea a second thought.

"Well you won't be needing it, if you don't catch your plane, will you?" says the driver, making sense and trying to hustle him.

Bruce realising the driver can be bought, offers him his gold watch. The driver looks at it and takes his time answering...

"Well?" Bruce says, desperate to get out and dash to the airport, as the cab slowly starts to pass the road Bruce needs to run up.

"Watch and ten pounds, that's my final offer" says the driver, taking full advantage of the situation.

"This watch is worth ninety quid" claims Bruce, as he slides it off

his wrist and hands it to the driver.
The driver takes pleasure in ripping him off...
With the door open Bruce jumps out and looks down to see how long he has left. Realising he hasn't got a watch anymore, he bangs on the cab window and asks the driver to tell him the time before he sets off.

"Sorry sir, I don't wear a watch" says the driver, smiling at him.
Now with no concept of time, Bruce makes a mad dash down the road towards the airport. Although out of breath and completely drained, he starts to fear he will miss the flight again and he doesn't dare stop running... Finally with the airport entrance in sight and a big clock telling him it's **quarter to four**, Bruce runs like he's never ran before... He thinks about losing his wife for good and that horrid image gets him to the doors without stopping. It's **ten minutes to four o'clock** and the check-in desk is about to close. Bruce comes face to face with another problem and he stops, taking a look around at the busy airport, realising he doesn't have a clue which desk he needs to check-in at.
He approaches an Indian guy in a uniform.

"Do you work here?" asks Bruce, clutching his rucksack knowing he's so close.

"Yes" the Indian bloke replies, smiling at him.

"Where are the check-in gates for America?" Bruce asks, ready to sprint again.

"You will be wanting the international departures sir" answers the guy in the uniform.
Bruce starts to lose patience with him standing there and his airport fixed smile.

"Where is the international departures then?" asks Bruce, trying to hurry him along.

"Yes, that is the gate you will be wanting sir" says the guy, trying his best to speak English.

"Where is it?" yells Bruce, trying to not lose his cool.
The Indian bloke in the uniform jumps in fear, telling him he doesn't know where it is.

"I thought you worked here?" asks Bruce, getting angry with him.

"Yes I work here, in the gents toilet" the nervous Indian responds.
Just as Bruce goes to walk away to ask someone else, another person notices the tension between the two men and approaches them.

"Can I be of some assistance sir?" asks a second Indian man.

"Do you work here in the airport and not in the toilets?" Bruce asks, not wanting to go through it all again.

"Yes I work here" answers the man, speaking little English.

"What is wrong with you people, where are the customer service team?" Bruce asks, knowing he's wasting far too much time.

"You must be a fairy" says the first Indian man, still standing there.

"Do what pal?" asks Bruce, knowing he hasn't got time for a fight, but will come back and knock him out, if he misses his flight.

"I said you must smell like a fairy" the Indian man says again.

"Washing up liquid, yes?" he adds, smiling and finding it slightly amusing that Bruce smells this way.

Bruce decides to ditch the two unqualified helpers and find the check-in gate himself. He runs over to the big airport board and searches for the gate he needs.

"Can I help you sir?" says a third man, walking up beside him speaking full English this time.

"No, you're okay thanks mate. Tweedledum and Tweedledee over there have already made me late" he snaps, looking at the big clock to see he has only minutes left.

"I can help you sir" insists the man, as Bruce turns to him.

He quickly asks where the American departure gate is and tells him that he is flying to L.A.

"Oh dear sir" says the man.

"Don't oh dear sir me, I've had one of those today already from a Caribbean taxi driver" Bruce snaps.

The man turns Bruce around by the shoulders and tells him with a smile, that he is already there...

"You see that line? That's you" the man says.

Bruce looks over at the line and is amazed to see Whitney and Jennifer standing in the distance. He turns and kisses the guy on the cheek, claiming he's saved his life.

"And you've made a gay man very happy sir" says the man, accepting the kiss and blushing a little.

Bruce sprints towards the gate, where in the distance he can just make out Jennifer and Whitney.

"Don't give up on me baby" Bruce mumbles, trying to catch his breath.

He stops as only thirty feet away, watches Jennifer hand Whitney his boarding pass, looking like she is giving up and walking through the gate...

"JENNY" he shouts at the top of his voice, but she cannot hear him over the airport noise.

"WHITNEY" he calls even louder, hoping she will hear him instead.

Jennifer continues to walk through the gate, out of sight and then a break through...Whitney looks up and notices Bruce standing there... Bruce races towards the gate once more, thinking that the superstar has saved the day, then he stops dead...

He watches as the diva rips his boarding pass into tiny pieces and smiles at him. Bruce feels his heart sink, as he watches Whitney disappear after Jennifer...

"Dam"

COMING NEXT...

THROUGH JENNIFER'S EYES 3 (HEARTBREAK)

Although the past two weeks haven't entirely gone to plan for Jennifer, the new girls or her lessons, everyone seems to be happier in the end.
Everyone but Bruce that is, as he sits at the airport alone, watching his wife take to the skies, leaving him behind in London.
Now Jennifer must face a new life in Hollywood without him, teaching the rich and famous her gift.
Will she believe Bruce when he tells her Whitney tore up his ticket?
Will she be able to teach the superstar in her own country?
Will Bruce ever find her without a mobile number or address?
New paths and laughs await the couple – but will it be together or apart?

ABOUT THE AUTHOR

This is the second book in the Jennifer series written by J G Perrin and the author promises to lighten it up in number three, with a comedy called Heartbreak.

OTHER J G PERRIN BOOKS
Through Jennifer's Eyes (Self Help) [ISBN 978-1482345810]
Through Jennifer's Eyes – Blackmail (Novel) [ISBN 978-1482390452]

For more on the author or a look at the next release, visit:
www.jgperrin.co.uk

Printed in Great Britain
by Amazon.co.uk, Ltd.,
Marston Gate.